MARILLA

Marilla

Meredith Bean McMath

Servant Publications
Ann Arbor, Michigan

Vine Books is an imprint of Servant Publications especially
designed to serve evangelical Christians.

Published by Servant Publications
P.O. Box 8617
Ann Arbor, Michigan 48107

Cover illustration by David Hile
Cover design by Diane Bareis

96 97 98 99 00 10 9 8 7 6 5 4 3 2 1

Printed in the United States of America
ISBN 0-89283-896-5

Other titles in the Celebrating the American Woman series:
Theodosia
Annabelle

Library of Congress Cataloging-In-Publication Data

McMath, Meredith Bean
   Marilla / Meredith Bean McMath.
      p.   cm. — (Celebrating the American woman : bk. 3)
    ISBN 0-89283-896-5
    1. Frontier and pioneer life—West (U.S.)—Fiction. 2. Women pio-
neers—West (U.S.)—Fiction. I. Title. II. Series : McMath, Meredith
Bean, 1957- Celebrating the American woman ; bk. 3
PS3563.C3863M37   1996
813'.54—dc20   95-42205
                                                 CIP

Dedication

In memory of my grandmother, Virginia (Hattie Mae) Hay,
a woman of courage and independence.

Acknowledgments

Special thanks to Wanda Munsey Juraschek for her editing skills, historic resources, and encouragement, and to Liz Nottess for her knowledge of Colorado's land as well as its heart. Thanks to Anita Barrett for her well-timed support. Appreciation to Donna Miner for the inspiration found in the pages of her photographic history of Colorado. Grateful thanks to Beth Feia, Heidi Hess, and Gloria Kempton for being the best editors a writer could hope for. To my family for believing in books.

And to Chuck, my tall, witty, redheaded husband: this one is yours.

Preface

"If I were asked to what the singular prosperity and growing strength of Americans ought to be attributed, I should reply: 'To the superiority of their women.'" Alexis de Tocqueville made this unique observation after visiting America in the early 1830s.

The books in this Celebrating the American Woman series were written because I wanted so much to tell someone why de Tocqueville was right. I wanted to bring to life the Christian American woman's unique ability to blend a spirit of independence with a willingness to compromise, the love of justice with the love of mercy, an iron strength with a profound softness. But I also wanted to tell someone what de Tocqueville couldn't have known back then: how sisters (and brothers) in Christ have had influences on one another that extend well past their lifetimes. I wanted to show how God uses a sometimes tenuous but very long line of persons to bring about life-giving change to us as individuals. And so the lives of the characters in my books intertwine to influence one another—sometimes years later and sometimes in an entirely new generation, now and then knowingly but more often unwittingly—just as they do in real life.

The verses and quotations at the beginnings of the chapters are little pearls of thought and rhyme that set the tone for the words that flow. Like the nursery rhymes that take on new meaning when we read them again to our children, American women's history can be read a hundred times, but if reread in a new context it might be brought to shimmering life before our eyes.

Meredith Bean McMath

ONE

Those who smile rather than rage
are always the stronger.

Old Saying

*D*elivery, I tell myself as I lie here in bed listening to the slow rumble of horses' hooves and wagon wheels outside my window.

With heavy lids half open, my eyes lazily follow the crack in the ceiling above me, meandering down to where the ceiling meets the wall. Staring at the yellowed and peeling edge of the old rose wallpaper—just where the brown paste causes the paper to curl its lip away from the yellowed ceiling—I think to myself that from the bottom of my heart I wish I were anywhere but here. And I could be out of here, if only...

Suddenly, I jerk upright.

A cold fear grips me as I remember what I've done. With eyes wide open I look toward the vanity. *Right there* in the drawer lies the ledger book I stole from MacDonald's desk in the middle of the night... just last night.

My mind reels as I go back over it all and then I shut my eyes. *It's all right, Marilla; it'll be all right. No one saw me enter his office. No one saw me. No one heard me. I came back up here to my room... wanted to wait until the streets got quieter before I took the ledger to the sheriff. And then? Then I must have fallen asleep!*

But don't panic now! I tell myself.

What time is it, anyway? My eyes fly open and come to rest on the little clock by my bed.

Five minutes to six. All right, then. I haven't overslept and there's thirty-five minutes yet. Just enough time to get over to the jail and back before morning duties.

11

I shake my head in disgust to think I had fallen asleep at all, but it will be all right soon. Everything will be set right. I'm going to make it right!

Think of the task at hand, Marilla. Have to be back before Lillian comes downstairs.

I jump up and begin to change clothes. While I nervously fumble with the worn little buttons of my yellow calico, the clock chimes six times, and with each tinny ring the fear strikes at me as if I were the hollow bell.

"But if I'm successful, I'll be free... from MacDonald, his hotel, his town," I tell myself. "It'll all be worth it, then."

I grab my winter cloak from the peg, throw it on the bed, and stare at it as I think it all through again: *Sheriff Potter's a good man—a friend to my parents—so I'm not risking my life to do this, am I? But what if Liam MacDonald finds out somehow? Perhaps Potter would let me stay at the jail until it's over. Maybe this is just a bad dream. Yes, that's it. I dreamt I took the ledger.*

I walk to the vanity and slowly open the drawer. No. There it is. No dream. And if I don't take it to Potter this minute, MacDonald will come looking for it.

Well, I could throw it away now. I could burn it in my stove here. I look up, blink once, then twice. Shake my head. No. I've waited too long for this day. It's gone too far.

I snatch the ledger from the drawer, then pause once more. Perhaps if I go downstairs and return it right now...

No! I have to do this. For myself, for my parents, for the love they had for me. My life isn't worth anything right now, anyway.

All right, then, it's worth the risk, so just quit thinking about it! I couldn't get the ledger back unnoticed now, anyway, and I don't want to think what MacDonald would do if he saw me come back with it.

I hurry to button my old brown boots and then pull at my pale hair with shaking hands as I try to draw it back into a knot. I throw on my cloak and peek out the door to look along the hall. Empty.

I step out and across the hall and fairly run down the back

stairs. Opening the back door as quietly as I can, I look to see no one on the street. My heart is pounding again. The hotel livery is quiet. The storeroom is empty. Good.

But I stand there another moment.

Suddenly I'm struck by how bleak this back street looks in the cold morning—the mud mixing with the fresh snow in dirty ruts along the road, the gray row of ramshackle outbuildings—or maybe bleak is simply how I feel.

The town of Independence in Colorado Territory lies across a gap high up in the Rockies, and the snowcapped mountains stand to either side of town like frozen sentries. I know those mountains are tall, but from this high up, they look like mere foothills.

Everything seems cut down to nothing up here, unless... unless you stand up for yourself.

That's what I'm doing. Standing up. *Relax, Marilla, you can do this.*

A breeze nips my nose and I sniff at the cool morning air and catch the musty scent of mud and hay and horse. Carefully, I step out and down the short steps and make my way past a few outbuildings. The gritty mush under my boots is like sandy molasses.

Now I turn in toward the main street, Liberty Avenue. Ha! *Liberty*, my eye! At the crossroads I look back toward the hotel to see the delivery cart is gone. Good.

But now I look again. A few people are standing or moving at either end of the road, and so I have to wait. Liberty Avenue does not look a whole lot better than the back street. Such a grand name for a muddy rut lined with squared-up timber. No one has bothered to make their buildings look permanent. Wouldn't that be foolish? No telling when the gold will run out.

So here the buildings stand—plain, unpainted, crammed together, never quite straight, and fronted with sign after outrageous sign hawking every kind of service and product, promising everything but delivery of the goods. I suppose, all in all, I prefer the bleakness of the back street better.

Another chilly wind whips at me. It tugs at my cloak fringe and hurls the little black tassels into the air. Then I hear the loose clapboards rattle and the shop signs creak as the gust scurries its way along the road. Shivering, I look down the muddy rut again and pull my cloak tighter about me.

"You know it's not the cold making you shake so, Marilla," I whisper to myself.

Finally, it's time to go. Trudging across the road, I notice everything around me is so deathly quiet I can hear my own squishing footsteps. Too little noise.

From sunrise to deep in the night, the streets of Independence are usually filled with miners, supply wagons, gamblers, con artists, gunmen, and various "soiled doves"—dog fights and men's fights, buckboards and rolling drunks—but by daybreak everyone has usually found a place to go. I shake my head. In the few months I've been here, this curious population has swelled by hundreds because of prosperous mining. And the greed of these people begets violence in forms I could never have imagined if I didn't live to see it every day.

Along with the noise of the street, there's the incessant sound of hammer and chisel as some kind of building goes up somewhere along the road. Irritably, I think, *And what Liam MacDonald doesn't own before it's built, he finds a way to own after it's up. Owns most of the people, too.* I grip the ledger beneath my cloak more tightly, *But not Marilla Hay. No, sir. Not anymore!*

I turn to look at the front of the Independence Hotel back across the street to make certain no one is up and around. What a sorry sight the place makes in the morning light: the porch sags in the middle like wet wash on a clothes line. A nervous shiver passes through me as I see someone walk up the hotel steps and head through the doors. I feel as though Liam MacDonald is watching me from there, even now. Yet a little hope wells up in me once more as the thought occurs I might be free of him soon.

I turn quickly and come round to the back of the jail where I begin tapping earnestly at the door.

"Sheriff Potter!" My throat is so dry I can hardly make a sound; the air so cold my breath lingers in little puffs before my face. I imagine for one horrible moment that time is standing still, the sun will never reach over those mountains, and Sheriff Potter will never appear at the door. "Sheriff Potter, please come. Are you there?" I whisper.

Potter's large face looms at the window so suddenly I step back and almost slip in the mud. I see him mouth the words "Miss Hay?" with a curious look.

He opens the door, and I sweep in. *I am safe.*

"What can I do for you this morning? Mighty early...!"

"My business is very urgent, very..." I am shaking.

"Catch your breath, Miss Hay, and please take a seat."

I sit down on the nearest bench and try to compose myself. Glancing around the bare room I see, gratefully, that no else is here. All right, then, I can breathe now. I will put all my cards on the table from here on out, and I can do this only because I know this man. I look up at him. He is pulling on the white of his beard, and his friendly gray eyes are looking patiently down on me from under those bushy white brows. It occurs to me he looks something like Saint Nicholas... with the build of a lumberjack.

I let out a deep sigh, and his face creases into a broad smile. "And what is your *urgent business* this morning, Miss Marilla?" He shifts his great belly over his belt as he walks toward me, and the old strip of leather squeaks uncomfortably with the weight.

At the noise I squirm a bit on the bench, but his gentle voice makes me smile self-consciously. *Oh, of course I can trust him.* "Sheriff, I have a ledger here." I draw out the book from my cloak. "It belongs to..." I drop my voice. "It belongs to a gentleman who I believe takes money from the Clark gang for certain... services provided. It has names and amounts listed and the man seems to have partners in the... venture."

"Really?" He walks around to his desk and draws in his breath with a whistle. "Clark gang, eh? If what you say is true, you have a real find, Miss Hay. You know we've been unsuccessful in nabbing those fellows, and the Denver boys are hog-tied. You think this ledger could lead us to them?"

I nod vigorously. "The Clark gang even stays at the hotel

sometimes under assumed names, sir. It's all here."

"They stay at the hotel?" His eyes go round in his head. "Miss Hay, don't you think I'd know if the boys were in town?"

I gulp. "I don't say such things lightly. I've seen... I know the Clarks. They've stayed at the hotel at least twice since I've been here, and they're real bold about who they are, sir, but I've been too scared to say anything before..." I turn bright red as I hold up the ledger. "But now I have proof! The evidence is all here, sir, and..."

"And just who exactly does this belong to?"

"Liam MacDonald."

"SHHHhheeeww, MacDonald?" Sheriff Potter looks doubtful again.

"It's all here, sir. I got it right from his desk, and it's in his handwriting." I open the old book to show him some of the ledger entries. "The list of names here are in some kind of code, but I was thinking the bank could match the figures with deposits and names..."

Just then he begins cracking his knuckles slowly, thoughtfully, as he stands behind me. He finally says, "Well, not everybody puts their money in the bank."

I look up at him and he is smiling and scratching his face with the hand that has only three fingers; I try not to stare. "Oh yes, but I know MacDonald does; I make deposits for him all the time."

He walks around his desk, thinking and looking up and down as he weighs the situation. "This is a serious accusation, as you know. It'd bring a man to hang, and he's... well, he's your employer, Miss Hay. Been good to you after your parents died. You want that for MacDonald?"

"It's not a matter of want." I pinch my lips shut as I think, *Although my mind wanders that direction often enough.*

"Well, the ledger's got to be enough proof on its own to convict a man." He scratches his face with his three-fingered left hand as he thinks. I remember staring at that hand so often when I was a child, but I've learned some manners since. Then, ever so slowly he says, "And no one has any pictures of these fellows. The descriptions are so useless I haven't even posted 'em. Lots o' men like to claim they're desperados, Miss Hay. Gives 'em an edge at the Faro table. How do you know the fellows at the hotel are really the Clark gang?"

Ho! I think, *Every one of us who works at the hotel knows exactly who they are, but they're afraid to speak up.* But that's no answer to his question. I stare at my hands for a while and finally say aloud what I'm thinking. "They use their own names when they're at the hotel, Sheriff, except for the registration desk. They don't even try to hide who they are, and I thought if you caught them at the hotel with bank monies..."

"Let's not get ahead of ourselves," he replies rather sharply.

I'm growing impatient. "I have no doubt the ledger will convict Mr. MacDonald, sir, and you could then make him serve you to catch the gang. All you have to do is catch them with their satchels full of bank monies, and they're always full." He continues to stare at me as I add for emphasis, "I'd bet my life on it."

"You may have to, Miss Hay," he says sadly. "If Liam is who you say he is, you may have to."

That much I already knew, but hearing it from him makes it real, gives it teeth, and a chill crawls slowly up my spine. But I've made my decision, haven't I? He will check the truth of my story, and it will convict MacDonald and the Clark gang. It will. Truth will win out.

But as I place the ledger carefully on his desk, he takes my right hand firmly in his two warm ones, and I cast a glance at his fatherly grip over mine. I remember how the war caused him to lose the two fingers on one hand. Like most who fought in the War Between the States, he decided he was willing to lose his life back then—though he hoped he wouldn't have to—just the decision I've come to today, and the thought gives me courage.

"It'll take some time to look this over," he says with concern. "I'll take action as soon as I can, but you know, he may miss his ledger before then. You want to stay here?"

"Thank you, no," I say, and at that he pats and releases my

hand with a faint smile. "I wouldn't want Mr. MacDonald to get suspicious," I add.

He smiles. "Brave girl."

I blush as I walk to the door, thinking, *You are the brave one, Sheriff Potter. I don't feel brave at all. Right now I feel scared, real scared.* But right then a question occurs to me and I turn back to Potter. "Sheriff, I've been wanting to ask you, has the... has the Good Gentleman ever contacted you? Does he work for you?"

His brows pull together at the question and his smile fades. "No, Miss Hay. Perhaps he knows I don't take kindly to vigilantes."

"Yes, sir." I hesitate a second and then walk back to him, rise on to my boot toes, and kiss him on the cheek. "Thank you again, sir."

I move back across the road toward the hotel, but my mind is not at peace. Now I am forced to play a waiting game. I go over the interview in my mind again and again as I make it up the back road. *He will help, he will help!* I try to feel hope, but I feel ill at ease. I think again of Potter telling me I am brave, and the idea seems ridiculous to me. If I were brave, would I be so afraid? If MacDonald finds out about this, I'll have to get out of here as fast as my feet will carry me and I will, too. No, I'm not "brave," whatever the word may mean to other people.

Inside the door, I remove my muddy shoes, put my cloak over my arm, and lightly run upstairs. Breathing more deeply only when I am inside my room, I finally catch my breath, pull on my work apron and rub my face with the apron's edge. I have to take the evidence of a chill from my nose and cheeks.

Passing down the back hall, I'm hoping no one is around. To the left is the empty dining room. Straight ahead is the bar room. Though there's always someone in there, I don't have to go that far right now. Halfway down the hall I turn right and come down the three steps of the dog trot to find myself in the hotel's large kitchen.

The cook, Mrs. Philipus Reed, is already busy with breakfast, her wide back hiding almost half the cookstove. Her slender helper, Emma Johns, is cutting meat on the butcher block. Emma looks up quickly and nods and I nod back as I pick up a slice of ham and a biscuit from the block.

Swallowing the ham and biscuit quickly, I now feel at least half ready to face a day's work. Back up the steps and down the hall, I pass through the reception desk area to the lobby. Then I sit myself down on the settee and wait for Lillian, my supervisor. Plucking nervously at my skirt for a moment, I force my chin up. *I will get through this day. Even if it kills me.*

Soon enough I'm drawn to concentrate on the lobby instead of my fears. Obviously built to be grand, these lobby walls—a deep royal blue—are set with wood trim expertly carved and gilded. A muted blue carpet fills the expansive floor with an old gold and burgundy pattern. Six large Corinthian columns are set in pairs down the length of the long room. I'll grant it would make a nice view if the place were well cared for.

The columns were originally painted to look like marble, as was the lobby desk in the middle of the room, but now the plaster is cracked and chipped beneath the paint. In fact, the walls themselves are peeling and the carpet is thickly stained from muddy boots, sloshed drinks, and heaven knows what else.

The lobby entrance to the dining room is set with a large, graceful arc, well carved and trimmed with gold, but the carving has been notched and the wood shows through the paint. I remember one night being rudely awakened by some guests in the bar playing a noisy game of knife-throwing: the target was the upper carving on the arc, and so the proud shield of the original owner's coat of arms now hung hacked to pieces. *I suppose wooden shields fell out of battle fashion very quickly,* I smile to myself. A similar arch over the reception desk has fared better; you can even make out the emblems on the shield, but it's still a sorry sight.

I like this room much better in the evening when the etched glass balls of the brass chandeliers cast their soft light, making the little gilded stars on the ceiling shine. Some nights I wish everyone would leave so that I could take a book and sit and read under those stars, but I've never once had the chance... or the time, for that matter.

This room and the whole of the hotel depress me in daylight.

Now I turn and pick up the tattered remnants of last week's *Rocky Mountain News* and bury myself in the pages. People wander in and out of the dining room door to and from the bar behind it as another day in a mining town begins.

All too soon Lillian Wirsching, the hotel matron, arrives and I reluctantly stand before her, ready for the assignment of duties. She is only a bit older than I, yet her brown hair is already streaked with dull gray strands. She's a tall, thin woman with a heart-shaped face, but her complexion is always such an unhealthy shade that I half expect her to keel over some afternoon. Instead I have found she's made of iron. Her gray eyes look into mine this morning, and she takes me by surprise when she pulls my chin up with her small, cold fingers. "What's wrong?" she asks. "You look chilled."

"I am feeling a might poorly, Miss Wirsching, but I can do my duties." But I am thinking, *Will nothing get past this woman?!* I look up at her, shift my eyes, and then hold her gaze for yet another moment. I cannot trust her. She manages the rooms when the gang comes here to stay; she's MacDonald's trusted worker and keeps things running smoothly for him. I look away and cough a little.

"Well of course you'll do your duties," she says. "And don't be coughing on the guests, and don't touch the bed linens after you sneeze."

Her compassion is touching. But thankfully she finally sends me on my rounds, and I go to work with a passion, trying to release all my worries in a flurry of activity. Change the water in the basins, change the linens, dust, help the laundress, help Mrs. Reed in the kitchen, sweep the lobby; I lose myself in the day's effort. MacDonald may be a scoundrel in every other way, but the truth is he runs a fair hotel for Colorado Territory; not one place in a hundred miles would bother with new towels every day. I suppose if I liked what I did, I could even be proud of the work, but I hate it. I hate it with a passion equal to my effort.

Late in the afternoon, as I scoop the ashes out of the wood stove in the last room of my rounds, I hear the rattle of Lillian's chatelaine of keys coming down the hall.

Soon she pokes her head in the door. "MacDonald wants to see you. Get along down there quick!"

I set the tin scoop down shakily in the bucket, stand and face her. "Yes, ma'am." Two short words and yet my voice has cracked.

She gives me a strange look, and I step past her to go downstairs, but as I brush by her at the door she grabs my arm in a lock. "Marilla…"

I turn to her, and she looks altogether a different person. "Yes?" I ask warily.

Her face has softened, and she whispers, "Watch yourself." But as she speaks the last word, her mouth draws taut once more.

I look down. "Yes, ma'am." Her words have only served to heighten my fear.

I cross the hall, run uncertainly down the back stairs, and trip on the last step. Then I turn to my left and hold my breath as I face MacDonald's door. I could run right now. I could, but it seems ridiculous. MacDonald wouldn't hurt me. He wouldn't. At least he hasn't before now. It occurs to me to pray for protection a stray second before I knock on his door. But I don't. I haven't asked God for anything since the day my parents were buried.

"Come!" a gruff voice calls out.

I enter as calmly as I can on legs that will not stop shaking and I stand before his desk but with my head down. *There is every chance he doesn't know,* I tell myself. So I determine to look him in the eye, until I catch a glimpse of the green ledger lying before him on his desk.

I want to run through the door, but I stand like a squirrel too frightened to bolt. My stomach churns.

With large, yellowy eyes MacDonald stares at me. Grinning all the while, he holds his suspenders out with his dirty, fat fingers, then suddenly snaps the bands with glee. The smile on his fleshy, wrinkled face makes me ill. I look away. *I will not cry, I will not cry,* I tell myself, and I begin staring at the hide of a large mountain lion on the wall.

"Marilla, *dear* li'l Marilla," he says gloating. "'Spose I'll have to keep this in the safe from now on." He leans comfortably back in his chair. "Look at me, Marilla," he says firmly.

I turn to him with eyes wide open. My shoulders are shaking with the fright, and I can't even think how to calm myself.

"Now, Marilla, haven't I tried to be your friend? Since your parents' passing, I've agreed to provide you with food and shelter and some honest work... and that ain't been easy to find for a woman in this town." He snorts, then he stands up, smooths back a greasy strand of gray hair from his forehead, and comes around from behind the desk. My back stiffens. "But you shoulda knowed," he says, tapping the ledger, "this kind of thing can't hurt me. I own this town. You hear me, girl?" He whispers, "I says you shoulda knowed that." He remains quiet for a few moments, and again I keep my head down while I look away. Suddenly, the ledger flies off the desk and hits the wall with a whump that makes me jump out of my skin.

"Stupid! You're a plain stupid girl. How do you think we could keep the boys in business if we didn't have Potter?" Then he says with a grunt, "And you shoulda thought more for yourself. This'll put you in jail quick as any of us. Girl, you're stupid. Bet you hadn't even thought of that, had you?" And he laughs that high-pitched laugh that always brings to mind a little runt pig we used to have at the farm.

But his words have made the hairs on my neck rise. I was afraid he'd done something like that. He's written my name in the ledger, too, as an "investor" in the Clark gang.

I am feeling the despair he intends me to feel, and my spirit gives up hope. I try to sound humble as I say, "Yes, Mr. MacDonald. It's obvious you own this town. I should have known better." I hold back my tears and swallow hard.

"You work here, you work for me," he says with contempt. "When I'm ready to let you go, you'll go and not before. I own you, gal, by rights. What I done for you deserves some kindness I think. Yes, it does. Now, get out o' my sight 'afore I've a mind to smack you for this bit o' insolence."

"Yes, Mr. MacDonald." And I move to get out as fast as I can.

But as I touch the doorknob, he yells, "MARILLA!"

I wheel around. "YES... sir."

He smiles smugly. "You got to pay me back for this. Yea. I'm gonna give you a chance to show your appreciation." My spine goes rigid once more as I think what he might mean. He smiles slowly. "You're gonna make a delivery for me." I let go of a small breath of relief. "I can't spare anyone else right now, so you'll do it. Take this bundle to this address in Denver." He pulls a thick leather envelope from his drawer and shoves it toward me over the top of the desk. On top lies a smudged slip of paper.

I read the address written there. "Denver?"

"Says Denver on there, don't it? I'll give you a week."

"Yes, sir."

Sick to my stomach I rush out of his office, and I pass Lillian standing near the door—the prying witch. I turn and fly up the stairs, across the landing, open my door with a whoosh of air, and then slam it shut behind me, falling against it.

So, I've been played for a fool.

The sheriff is in with MacDonald. *In with MacDonald.* Isn't everyone? Perhaps Potter is "Mr. X" or "Mr. Y" in that ledger, and I, "Miss X." Oh, what a fool! My face feels hot when I think of kissing Potter on the cheek and thanking him. MacDonald is right. How stupid can I be?

I feel the leather envelope in my hand and suddenly throw it from me as if it were a copperhead. It lands on the bed.

Of course the Good Gentleman doesn't work with the sheriff. He knows, of course, and I'm an utter fool, and with that thought I fall onto my bed and bury my head in the pillow.

Denver? Why would MacDonald trust me after what I just did? I don't understand.

But maybe I should look in the envelope. Yes. Should I? What harm could it do?

I pull myself up on one elbow and stare at the grimy envelope lying there. Rather gingerly, I untie the string and unfold the leather to see a stack of dollars. When I read $100 on the corner, I draw back my hand.

But then I slowly reach out and touch the flap again. Just how much is here, anyway? Looking inside, I begin to count. One hundred, two hundred, three hundred,... one thousand dollars!" *As much as I gave MacDonald from the sale of the farm!* Money he stole from me. *My* money.

I bind it back up quickly, lay it on the bed and stare at it once more. Why would he give it to me to take? It doesn't make any sense.

Finally it comes to me: I'm the only one he can trust—any other of his men might take it and run. Lillian's "trustworthy," but he can't spare her like he can me. He's not afraid of me. He knows I'll deliver it. I'm sure he wouldn't believe I'd even look inside the thing.

Well, he was almost right.

I'll deliver his money—it will give me time away from here. I moan as I go back over the day again in my mind.

Just then I jump as I hear a knock on the door and, without waiting for me to open it, the door swings open.

Lillian.

She stares at me for a moment, and I stare back at her in surprise. Her eyes dart toward the bundle and back to my face. "The envelope. You want me to take the envelope for you?"

My brows knit together as I study her face, and I prop myself up on one elbow in bed. "You want to go to Denver?"

"Yes. I'll take it and be gone before Liam can complain about the switch." She says lightly, "After all, I'm his usual choice," but the lightness in her words dies out as she looks to me for an answer.

When I hesitate, she sets her mouth and steps forward to take the envelope from me, but I snatch it back from her grasp. Why would she want to take it for me? She knows everything about MacDonald, and for some odd reason she wants to do this for me? She must know it's money. She wants the cash… and then MacDonald will blame the loss on me.

"He asked me to go. I'll go," I say steadily.

Her hand drops to her side and her eyes flash with anger. "You don't know what you're doing, Marilla. Do you know what's in that envelope?"

Ah, yes, I must have guessed correctly. "Yes, yes, I do, and I also know exactly what I'm doing, but more importantly I think I know what *you're doing*, Lillian. So don't even try to take this from me."

Drawing her mouth to a grimace she says, "What?" But I stare her down. She lets out an exasperated gasp. "Fine, have it your way, then. There's enough rope in this town for the both of us, I'm sure." And she backs out of the room, slamming the door behind her.

I shake my head and smile. Enough rope? Whatever does she mean? Does she mean enough money? She's always putting me on edge, trying to catch me off balance. But ha! Today I won the contest. I think I'm beginning to know how to play the game.

I stare at the red-and-white striped ticking of my pillow and wonder how in heaven I came to be here, anyway. It's as unlike my growing-up years as day is from night. I shake my head at the thought: it all started with Mr. Edward Prue. My parents, like any homesteaders, welcomed Mr. Prue to our cabin as he was traveling through. He fell sick the night he came and died within two days.

I rub my eyes with my palms as I think back on it again. They contracted Prue's fever. September of '75, wasn't it? It seems like years ago. Father died, then Mother a few days later. On her deathbed, she said they had provided for me, but she had the fever bad, and she could only tell me a few things: that Father had an agreement with Liam MacDonald, and that I would be well cared for. After she died I took a few days to get their things in order. Mr. Shaw, our only neighbor, helped me with the burial. The grief and shock were terrible. I blamed God for my loss and vowed to make it on my own from there on out, not understanding how much it takes to stand alone—how bitter I would become.

I searched the cabin top to bottom for some sign of a document from Mr. MacDonald, but I never found a thing. So I arranged for Mr. Shaw to take care of the farm for a day while I made the short trip from our farm to the city of Independence to visit Liam MacDonald to ask him about the arrangement Father had made.

I slam my fists into the pillow as I remember it. I was only going to be gone a day.

Ever since I was a girl, MacDonald had been in business with Father to purchase the produce from our farm. The Independence Hotel was a good client. MacDonald ran a high-class hotel, Father always said. He never, ever spoke ill of him. Of course, Father never spoke poorly of anyone.

Now and then Father would complain that he had to drop his prices to compete with other farmers. He never told me anything about business. Nothing—thought it was too much for a woman to understand, so I came to MacDonald with the trusting innocence of a woman who'd only known honest people, with a father who'd done business with what he always supposed were honest people. I was innocent and ignorant, a country girl in the worst sense.

When I first came into MacDonald's office, I remember being awed by it. First there was the temple to chaos on his desk that I took to mean he was a serious businessman. Newspapers and documents were piled up across the large surface. There was even a bear trap, too—rusted while set open, at least it looked well rusted. Then my eyes drifted to the walls where dozens of animal hides were nailed—hides of every animal imaginable laid like wallpaper. While my eyes scanned the furs, I told MacDonald all my mother had told me, and that I'd like to see and discuss the document my parents had signed with him.

When I finally concentrated on Mr. MacDonald some, I was surprised to see how little he cared for his personal appearance. After all, this was a fairly nice hotel. I expected... well, some sort of gentleman, I suppose. But I immediately made allowances for him, in that most folks in town didn't give a fig how they looked.

But Mr. MacDonald's behavior, as I recall, was just as I expected. He was polite and listened to my story with great interest, and when I was done he grew quiet.

I waited patiently for a reply but I finally had to say, "Mr. MacDonald... the agreement?"

Another pause ensued.

"Miss Hay," he finally began, curling and uncurling his fingers on his desk. "Your father showed great foresight. He knew you couldn't handle his homestead alone."

That stung me.

"Your parents were so worried for your welfare, in fact, they came to me to ask me to be your... guardian—give you some honest work and a roof over your head."

I let the information sink in, and then I realized he'd said *gardeen* like he'd never heard it said before. "Guardian?" I asked in a squeaky voice, wondering if by chance I'd misunderstood. But he nodded and then watched for my reaction.

"The money from the sale of your farm will be used to seal this here agreement," he continued, "and, in good faith, I promise to supply all your needs for as long as you'd like to stay here, and of course, put your father's money in a trust for you. Should you ever decide to leave, I'll give you back the proceeds."

Sell the farm? No. That shocked me so, my mouth had dropped open. It seemed strange that my father would ever commit to such a thing, and yet they *had* been concerned I couldn't tend the farm alone. I sputtered, "Mr.... Mr. MacDonald, m-may I see this agreement?"

He sat back as though he'd just won his case. "Well, honestly, I got to tell you they died 'afore we could write anything up, but I'm willin' to let the agreement stand as spoken, as a gentleman and in defilement to your parents' wishes." He was as cool as ice in his delivery, although I knew he probably meant to say "deference." Poor grammar was really no reason to distrust a man.

"Oh."

"Miss Hay, are you disapproving your parents' choice for you?" His jowls bounced as he said the words. "Have they brought up a gal who's strong-headed and willful?" How he could twist the knife.

"No, no, of course I want to respect their wishes," I replied starkly. "It's just... it's just that I was hoping to handle the farm by myself."

Mr. MacDonald had shaken his head and smiled. "I understand a *young* gal might have such a hope." He was oh, so patronizing. His tone said, *I understand a very young woman would think she could, but she ought to know that she can't.*

As I think back on the conversation, my naivete appalls me. I knew nothing of the world and nothing of business. The only "snakes in the grass" I dealt with were the ones I could kill with the sweep of a hoe. I had no idea how to take care of myself in this other world—all I knew was how to work a farm, and it was all I ever thought I'd need to know.

So what could I do? I hadn't really thought about how to run a business, and I didn't have a lot of confidence. My father had trusted Liam MacDonald, and Liam thought it was foolish for me to farm. Everyone would think so.

Besides, I had no money to hire help. I didn't know how to keep books or make estimates. And who would buy produce from a young woman? If I tried and failed, I'd lose the place anyway.

As I thought on it, he suddenly said, "You'd be doing the right thing, Marilla—the right and proper thing." He looked down then and said with some feeling, "I would promise to do my best for you, surely I would." He said it so kindly and sincerely to a young girl who had just lost her parents and felt there was nowhere else to turn, I couldn't help but melt a little inside. I so desperately wished to believe someone would take care of me the way my parents had.

"Now, please come and work for me. I could really use your help; we need a smart girl around here." He looked at me expectantly.

I smiled as his words broke down the last of my defenses. I could work for MacDonald awhile, and if it didn't work out, I could probably even buy the homestead back or something.... At least I'd start out doing what my parents wanted. And I could learn more about farming in the meantime, maybe subscribe to the *Rocky Mountain News*–prepare myself for the task, if I still wanted to.

So I made a decision. And now I know I was building a little jail cell around me with one reason and another and another, and I have lived within its bars for these six months. My name in the ledger adds a new padlock to my cell door.

I agreed to sell the homestead, give the money to MacDonald, and come to work for him at the Independence Hotel. I had been neatly talked out of owning everything I had ever cared for.

MacDonald had said we could arrange things right away, that he already knew a man looking for just such a property. He asked me to walk over to the land office with him right then and I numbly agreed. As we turned to leave his office, I noticed, with a shock, that the pelt of a common house cat was mounted over the door frame! I went a little pale as I looked back at him.

He chuckled. "A little joke." But I trembled a bit as I walked under and through. *Was I about to provide him with another hide for his collection?* I let the thought pass.

The sight of those pelts should have warned me, for in a few short days, I had come to realize just what sort of person MacDonald really was. Within a week I was asking for my money and preparing to leave; I wanted to try to buy the farm back, somehow.

What an idiot I'd been. When I asked him for the funds, he just laughed and mumbled something about how it wouldn't be right to give money to such a young, irresponsible girl. He was happy as a pig in mud, and I walked out of his office a little wiser and a whole lot poorer.

Just outside his door I remember an incredible rage welled up in me. I wanted to see *his* hide up on the wall. Then I had to laugh at that ugly thought. That calmed me down and I gathered my thoughts and weighed my options.

I shook my head as I realized sadly, *Well, I could always marry a miner!*

Three lonely fellows had already asked me to marry them in that first week: the first one right in the hotel lobby and the next two on the street. The first time, I was so shocked I couldn't reply. He seemed so earnest, and right then and there started telling me everything about himself, taking my silence for encouragement, I suppose. Then his friends pulled him away. I was still just standing and staring at him as they brought him around by shoving him toward the bar.

Most of the miners are quite serious about marriage—firmly dedicated to the idea during the seconds it takes to ask a woman—but marriage to a miner has got to be the most wretched life I can imagine. The miners get a hunted look in their eye after they've been at it for a while. Their only conversation becomes where to find the gold, who has the gold, who lost the gold, and how to get it again. If they get their gold, someone steals it from them at the boarding house, or they lose it gambling, or to a saloon girl. If they do manage to send it out of town, it gets stolen off the stagecoach. It's all a gamble and a nasty hard life while it lasts, from what I've seen. No, I didn't want any part of that.

I could hire myself out as a cook or washerwoman, but that work isn't any different from what I do now. At least, for the moment, MacDonald takes care of me. And if there is a way to let the law get at him, I should stick around to see it happen. Lastly, there was this flicker of hope that somehow I'd get the homestead back if I stayed.

So in this restless and bitter state of mind, the first month passed, then another, and another. Six months. And oh, how I nurse this little flame of hate; it keeps me going each day, this incredibly strong desire for revenge that permeates my thinking day and night. It's been six months since my parents died, but it may as well be six years, or sixty, for today I've had all the hope kicked out of me.

As I stare into my pillow, I suddenly wish the Good Gentleman would just up and kill him. I raise my head. Do I really want that? No. I think of Potter. I have no faith in this legal system, that's certain, but I don't really want to see the territory run by vigilante committees, do I?

This fellow (the folks who whisper these stories have nicknamed him "the Good Gentleman") has begun to corner MacDonald's partners, one by one. He has done this to three so far: found them alone and approached them, disguised somehow, to tell them they had better lay off or else. Two of the men took his warning and have left town already. I don't know why everyone calls him the Good Gentleman. Perhaps it's because he doesn't kill his victims.

I overheard a man in the dry goods store telling about some fellow sending all his gold dust money to his grandmother back east: "Well, he's a good fellow, for all that, but a good gentleman (he raises his voice for emphasis), a *Good Gentleman* would have done it on the sly!" And he smiles wide and everyone around him chuckles.

"Good Gentleman, indeed," I say to myself, "he'll be dead soon, I'm sure. What good can one man do in this town? And what good can I do? Now MacDonald has me running errands like I'm one of the gang."

I roll up and sit on the edge of my bed and steady myself, then grasp the blanket with angry fists and pull hard to vent my fury. I look at the vanity bureau to the left of the door and stare at my mother's ivory-handled hair brush, powder puff, and comb. I release my grip as I think the mildly pleasant thought, *I will be in Denver soon.* I stand up, cross over to the vanity, and sit down on the little stool.

I pull my hair into another knot and slowly turn my face from side to side. Mother used to say I grew apples on my cheeks—not anymore. I look so pale. Is this face truly mine? I've never been so thin. MacDonald's men never bother me anymore, and I don't wonder, for I look like a bundle of dry straw. Well, there's a blessing to be found in everything, I suppose.

Clucking my tongue I stare at my face in the mirror once more. This place is kicking the life out of me; next, my fair hair will turn to snow before its time. Like Lillian. My hazel eyes, the ones my mother blessed me with, look more tired than Mother's ever did, even after planting season. And I always feel tired.

Shifting my eyes to the wall, I examine the faded rose print there. It always reminds me of my mother's rose hip perfume bottle, and at that, I smile—her perfume bottle was the one extravagance she kept on her table in our homesteading cabin. Lawsy-day, lawsy-day—that things should come to such a turn for me. Oh, I miss my parents with all my heart. The rigors of farm life were nothing compared to this dreary existence.

Reaching under my bed I pull out the bag I will pack for the trip. I stand and slowly begin to gather some things. No, I'm too weary to pack. Falling across my bed I cry a bit as I think back over the day, and soon a restless sleep overtakes my tears.

TWO

Warning! Foot-pads, thieves, and dance-house loungers must get out of Lake City and stay—otherwise hang.... By order of THE VIGILANTES."

"Eviction notice" posted in Lake City, Colorado, in the 1880s

The dream is beautiful and I hold to the vision for as long as I can: I'm surrounded by tall gray mountains ringed with emerald trees and topped with sugar snow as I sit beside a river that gurgles and jumps along deep, wide, fertile fields of grass and grain. Just above my head I can hear my parents' loving chatter as they unburden the limbs of heavy fruit trees. And I'm playing there beneath their pleasant voices in the cool shade.

But the dream's hold begins to loosen, and the real world forces my eyes open with its tinny, rumbling noises. As I come fully awake, I remember that I am just as fully alone. Turning my face into the pillow with a little groan, I toss my head from cheek to cheek to shake off the melancholy of this morning ritual and somehow try to accept my situation.

Now I rub my eyes, rise and begin to pack my things with gathering speed. I want to be on the coach before Mr. MacDonald changes his mind about sending me to Denver. It's only six in the morning. I shed my calico wrapper and put on my old black traveling dress. As I peer into the mirror, I notice the old black crepe is frayed around the collar. And my eyes are puffed from last night's tears. For all the world I look like a mourning widow.

With disgust I bend over the washbowl, take two handfuls of the freezing liquid, and slap my face down into it. I rub my hands vigorously on a towel to try to warm them, for there is no time to light the stove before I leave. I'll go down to the coach early. I want no chance of missing my conveyance to Denver. *Denver.*

A week in the broad streets of Denver! They call it the "Queen City of the Plains" nowadays, but it is really plain old Cherry Creek. I went there twice with Father: once a few years ago, and once when I was a little girl.

The first time was in '64, wasn't it? Yes, I had just turned ten and felt very grown up to have two digits to my age. I remember coming into town and thinking, *I am all grown up, and so I am visiting the big city just as a big girl should.* But as our carriage turned into a wide lane, I felt Father's hand come over my eyes and it startled me. He said a fellow had just been hanged there and left dangling from a pole and that I should not see it, but I pulled my face to the side and told him I was grown up enough to see.

And I looked.

Then I got sick.

When my stomach was empty, I felt better, but my mind was still ill at ease. I wanted to understand what I'd seen, and so I began to pester Father about the hanging. He told me a Committee of Vigilance had strung the man up there. The fellow may well have deserved it, but it was so brutal it seemed inhuman to me. So brutal, in fact, the memory of it still makes me queasy.

Father hated the whole thing, said it was good it didn't happen too often, but it happens more and more these days. He used to say God loves justice, not revenge—that law needed to prevail out here. Unfortunately, the marshals aren't much better than vigilantes, from what I've heard. While Judge Storey and others of his ilk have had charge of the marshals, their reputations have rivaled those of thieves! I've heard people say they'd rather board a criminal in their home than take in a marshal. I'm almost glad my parents aren't around to see these things.

"I'm growing as bitter as Lillian Wirsching," I say aloud with all due solemnity.

"Oh, Lord, don't let me become like Lillian," I say loudly. And then I pause. Was that a statement or a prayer? Have I suddenly, out of some childish habit, called on God? The God that let my parents die? The God that let me sell my property and come and work for MacDonald? I press my lips together. "No, if he's there, he certainly isn't listenin' to Marilla Hay," I whisper. "That, or he hates me somehow, that's for certain." I gaze around the room and press my lips together before smiling grimly. "No, I won't become like Lillian. She'd never turn MacDonald in—she'd never even try." Pride and bitterness well up in me as I angrily stuff another item in the travel bag.

"I just need a new plan, that's all."

Oh, for a plan like Mary has—a plan that could give me comfort! Tough Mary Baylor. Her blue eyes remind me of diamonds set in her strong, wide face. So unlike me in so many ways and yet my friend. Her thick and shiny black hair—the opposite of mine in color as well as form. Her wit is sharp and her sense of survival unswerving, whereas I doubt my wit could inflict so much as a flesh wound on the deserving, and as for my sense of survival— well, if I have one at all, it is more than likely a half-wit.

At times I wish I *were* Mary. Even though I've often felt the sword of her remarks, she's the most straightforward woman I know, and I like her well for that. Very well. Why she has befriended me I have no earthly idea, other than to believe I must amuse her some. *Mother and Father, do you mind if my only girlfriend is from the lineup?* I smile at the thought. She's in charge of the hotel bar, a formidable task and one she handles with great finesse. Somehow I am able to put the rest of her life out of my mind.

After a couple months in town, Mary and I started having dinner at the same time in the hotel kitchen and we'd talk a bit. Before long, we began to trust each other. I remember the night I told her how MacDonald tricked me and how she laughed long and hard at that.

"Well, I know better now," I told her.

"You should have shot him right then, honey. Everybody knows you're an innocent; you could have gotten off easy. Self-defense."

I blushed. "If I'm so innocent, Mary, how is it that I'd thought of that already?" And we laughed together.

Mary winked. "You ought to get yourself a plan," she said quietly.

I nodded and went silent for a while.

Suddenly, she let out, "I've got plans for myself. I always do." Then she told me how she breaks into the rooms of the Clark gang when they stay at the hotel and takes some of their stolen monies. "They don't need it all. That's obvious or they'd have missed it by now—and someday I'll be able to walk out of here and buy my own place."

In telling me, she was putting complete trust in me. "I know you will, Mary. If anyone can, you can. But however do you break into the rooms? Doesn't Lillian always have the keys?"

She smiled. "I know how to pick a lock," she said coyly.

"Oh, will you teach me?" And so she did. And I began to slip in and out of MacDonald's office and desk like an old hand. So, as a graduation exercise, you might say, I had taken MacDonald's ledger—the ledger that I thought would solve all my problems.

I have a lot to learn yet.

Perhaps if I can figure out who the Good Gentleman is, he could help me. The thought picks me up a bit and I wonder who it could be. If it's anyone from in town, I bet I could figure it out. Who are the fellows I know with backbone enough to manage it?

There's the blacksmith's assistant, Peter Sams. Strong and simple, with a dark look about him. Hmm, too simple. He can follow orders, but without some assistance he has a tendency to sit and stare at the fire.

Then there's Alonzo Hughes at the dry goods store. Alonzo has a gentle look about him. In fact, he reminds me of a deer. Tall and thin, red hair and large green eyes. He seems nervous whenever men talk about the Good Gentleman. Come to think of it, he reminds me of a frightened deer, but then there's rumor that the dry goods owner is one of MacDonald's partners.

Alonzo does me a good turn by letting my bill run high at

times, but isn't he accident prone? I laugh as I remember the last time I was in the store: how he set off a row of things falling with his nervousness. He was telling me not to worry on my bill and waving his hand for dramatic emphasis when his flailing elbow nudged a row of brooms, which fell and knocked the scales over, which scattered a dozen jars of Mrs. Weldon's jam across the counter, which caused several to roll off and hit the floor, which spattered the contents with a nasty ker-splash all over the straw hats and flour sacks at the foot of the counter.

With undue haste, Alonzo had jumped in to save the brooms, fell short of his mark, and stood there—his thin form dangling among the sticks like a poor man's scarecrow.

My eyes had tears in them and I pursed my lips to keep from laughing as I looked away. Of course it broke up all the men standing around him. Was Alonzo putting on an act? If so, it was a rather expensive one.

Of course, there's the bank teller, Jonathan Jones, the one who bought my parents' homestead... and everything in it. The things I brought with me to town the day I had my first talk with MacDonald are all that I have from the cabin, and it didn't take long to figure out I'd made a horrible mistake. I'd cut myself off from the very things I loved—treasured things that held the memory of my parents. If I had it to do over, at the least I would have taken one of Mother's quilts and one of Father's carvings. I've grieved the loss of my parents and then grieved again the loss of all their belongings.

And Jones has never once offered me any of my parents' goods, not even for purchase. For that I dislike him immensely.

But he is the one who got a new puppy for Melissa Pruett when we found her dog shot dead. That was a nice thing he did. I saw him bring the puppy around to their porch. He knocked on the door and ran around the side of the grainery before Mrs. Pruett came to the door. She shouted for Melissa, saying the Lord had heard her prayers. Here was the very doggy she'd asked him for! I couldn't let that go and mentioned it to him the next time I visited the bank.

"I saw what you did for Melissa Pruett, Mr. Jones. What a kind thing it was."

A redhead with a pale complexion, he appeared to blush. "Mother says a good woman knows how to keep a secret," he said in his rather feminine voice.

Well, he is a mama's boy, isn't he? Besides, he must be in with MacDonald. MacDonald had him as the man to sell the property to, and in the twinkling of an eye he bought it up.

But now I've hit upon the man: Jacob Stone! He's built like a lumberjack. He has an honest face and a quick tongue, the man to do any odd jobs in town, and he's an excellent carpenter. He's always had a kind way toward me. Then again, I've heard him make horrid jokes about the Good Gentleman. Well, I suppose a fellow who wanted to remain anonymous would have to say things like that, wouldn't he?

Maybe I could talk to him and hint about it, and well... maybe, but first there's Denver.

With the packing done, I look around my room once more, walk over to the pegs, pull my cloak down, and throw it over my arm. I pick up my satchel and realize I've got to check the embers in the stove from the night before to make sure they're dead.

I step to the little wood stove and open the grate to poke around and observe the ashes. As I'm stirring I look at the clock and realize the coach to Denver leaves at 7:00. And it's only 6:15. "I could go and have a talk with Jacob right now," I say boldly, but then a cold fear grips the pit of my stomach. *What if I'm wrong? And what if word gets back to MacDonald again?* Yesterday's events have brought about their proper influence, and I quickly force my thoughts on to a different track. "I suppose I could just read up here for a little while," I say softly, feeling utterly disgusted with myself.

But then the sounds rising from the stove flue catch my attention and I jerk my ear toward the stove. The stove flue always amplifies the sounds coming from Mr. MacDonald's office below. His stovepipe connects with mine and they ramble up to the roof. As a consequence, my little stove often "talks" to me. If I bend my ear toward the grate, I can hear more than a little of MacDonald's conversations at times. More often than not, I don't want to hear his voice any more than I have to in a day.

A gruff voice is telling MacDonald something now. He is telling him to do, what? To *shut up and listen!* No one I know speaks to Mr. MacDonald like that!

Now my ear bends all the way to the grate to hear better.

The voices are low again. Then I hear Liam MacDonald's voice, but it's high and quivering. Why, he actually sounds, yes... frightened! "I've got my boys outside," he whispers.

"Not another word outta you," and then more low noises.

This has to be he! This has to be the Good Gentleman! It is MacDonald's own judgment day. Oh, what a treat. I clap my hands for joy and plop right down on the floor to listen more. But still I can't hear well enough. I have to get lower, bother it. I shove my bag and cloak aside, and now my skirts are all bunched up under me and I struggle to push them behind me. Finally I'm able to lie down and put my ear all the way to the floor.

There now! Now I can hear *everything*.

"Face down, FACE DOWN. Cooperate, now, Mr. Mac-Donald. Rest easy, it'll be a while 'afore anyone comes for you." This man's voice sounds like a rasp on hard wood, and it's no voice I recognize.

Then all is quiet.

Now Liam's grunting. The man must be tying him up. Oh, this is delightful! Muffled words. More grunts.

Paper is rustling and things are falling to the floor... as if the fellow is looking for something? I'll lay bets he's looking for Mr. MacDonald's safe! Of course!

But he keeps it hidden behind a trick bookshelf. The fellow's mumbling, still shoving things around. And, aw no, *no!* He's leaving! He didn't find the safe! Oh, now, that's too bad.

I close my eyes in consternation, my ear still to the floor, and a brilliant idea pops into mind. I will let the fellow get away, then I will knock on MacDonald's door, release him from his ropes, and demand my money! He is cowed. This is the perfect time. And...

yes! Then I'll hint at an alliance with the Good Gentleman to *really* put fear into him.

Fear.

As I open my eyes and stare across the floor, my own fears take hold once more as I wonder if it would be safe to try. But then my own doorknob turns and the hackles rise along the back of my neck.

With my eyes wide and still level to the floorboards, I watch as my door creaks open. This is not Lillian. This is not Liam. I am frozen in place.

The bed is between me and the door, and so I stay where I am. The door shuts noiselessly, the bolt is quietly slid in place, and a pair of large, long moccasins tread across the floor.

The noiseless feet head for the window, and soon he comes into my view (such as it is, over my shoulder from the floor): a tall fellow in a long coat and a dark, round-brimmed hat with his back to me stoops down to peer out the front panes. He has stringy black hair that falls around his shoulders. An Indian! Now my heart is pounding. This must be the Good Gentleman!

But he'll see me when he turns to leave.

Well, then, I can tell him about my situation and he can help me! All right, it's now or never, I think hastily, but even as I part my lips to speak, the paralyzing fear rises up in me and strangles the inclination.

I've been made a fool of so very recently by my heartfelt confessions, and my last little mistake in judgment nearly cost me my life. I realize I know absolutely nothing about this fellow—not his motives, nor his state of mind—nothing. Just rumor and fluff. There is no one I can trust.

Even before I've thought more on the matter, my legs have begun to slip under the bed. I'd already pushed my satchel and cloak there. I inch my head toward safety as I watch him move back and forth at the window. He has a blue bandanna tied around his face, and his hat is pulled low on his brow. Hastily I decide this is as much of the Good Gentleman as I ever want to see. I close my eyes.

I am thinking it is a cowardly thing I'm doing, but life... even such as my life is now... has suddenly become very precious to me, and I'd certainly like to live long enough so that I might have the chance to learn to be more brave.

But I catch my breath because he turns on his heels toward the door before I'm completely under.

He sees me, and now he jumps back as if he were snake bit, saying, "UNG!" His sudden movement causes me to throw my head up and bang it soundly on the under-frame of my bed.

"Ow... ow... *ow*!" I grab at my head.

"Get out from there," he says gruffly.

"Ow... ow..." I grit my teeth and work my way slowly out. "Don't shoot me. Don't shoot... Ow... ow... *ow*."

I begin to raise my head to look at him as I sit up, and he tells me, "Stand up!" but his voice cracks funny on the word "up" just as he sees my face.

A chill travels up my spine. He knows me. This man knows me.

Well, if he knows me, it's all right, I think with some hope. Still rubbing my head, I begin to smile where I sit, but then I pinch my eyes shut again because of the pain.

The hope of some sort of sympathy is wrenched from me as his hand comes around my left shoulder like a vice and yanks me up.

In another moment I am "face-to-face" with him, so to speak. "Ow. Stop that!" I protest in a whisper. "Can't you see I've pounded my head?"

He hesitates.

I pinch my eyes shut once more and raise my hands in defense. "Let me go. My head hurts, you clod. I don't care if you are the Good Gentleman!" His hand begins to release its grasp on my arm. How dare he treat me as if *I* were spying on *him*! He came into *my* room!

In the same instant the thought forms in my mind, I do not hesitate to perform the task: out of pure and angry instinct, I open my eyes and use both hands to yank down on his bandanna.

I catch my breath to find a thick red mustache under there. Suddenly I realize that I'm staring into the green eyes of Jonathan Jones, the puppy-loving bank teller, standing before me. At least... this man looks like Jones, but with long black hair? And a raspy voice?

Oh. Oh, no!

Ah, now I see it.... The black hair is attached to his hat. It's a costume hat! I want so very badly to laugh, but I'm afraid of him, too. "Mr. Jones?" I'm working hard to keep the gurgle from my throat. "*You're* the Good Gentleman?" I pull the back of my hand to my mouth.

"Well, of course not, Miss Hay," he says with the whiny voice of the bank teller.

I am no longer afraid. "Oh, please." I giggle. "You don't need to keep pretending. I mean no offense. It's just... you can trust me, and..." With all the strength I can muster, I stifle my laugh and pull my hands behind my back. He pushes me from him and narrows his eyes.

In a whisper-cool voice—not at all the voice I heard below— he says, "You may be callin' the cards right now, Miss Hay, but I'm tellin' you this game is by no means over." And with that he draws his gun.

"What ever do you mean? Oh n-no," I stammer, "you don't understand." I am feeling more than a little queasy; now might be a good time to explain myself. "Mr. Jones, you don't need to point that thing at me." I try to gain a little composure by staring at my shoes as I speak. "Mr. Jones, *really.*" I swallow and brush back a hair from my forehead with my free hand. I am suddenly, excruciatingly self-conscious, and I'm not at all sure I should bother him with my troubles, but I venture, "I'm *with* you. I'm actually glad to know you... who you are, and I can see you've been, well, your voice and manner are so different... you've been acting a part to frighten MacDonald and..."

"Keep it down!" he says.

"Mr. Jones," I whisper, "I can *help* you. You once told me a good woman knows how to keep a secret. Well, *I'm* a good woman."

"Oh, really?" he says rather snidely as he backs up to the door and cocks his ear toward it.

I blush as I think of a way to prove myself. "Well, I *haven't* screamed for help, have I?" I blurt out. *Haven't screamed? Heavens, no! My words are coming out in little squeaks to keep myself from laughing!*

"Shh," he says sharply. He looks down to the floor, then nods his head. He looks at me again. "That you fear bodily harm shows you've got a spark of brains in you, but don't go mistakin' me for a fool. I know who pays your way, and I'll put you out if you cause me any trouble, so you... you better not think about calling out right now." He's watching my eyes intently.

"Well, of *course* not," I say with exasperation. "Why do you think I've been whispering all this time?"

No response. By heavens, perhaps he's mad. It occurs to me I don't know which is the act—the timid bank teller or the gentleman vigilante. My heart sinks. And how exactly does one reason with a madman? I gulp and give it my best as a desperate thought occurs to me. "I don't believe you'd hurt me," I whisper with a tentative smile. He just looks at me and raises his eyebrows. "I... I saw you get that new puppy for Melissa, remember?"

He grunts and says under his breath, "Her mama watched me kill the other." He adds with a stiff smile, "Yeah. The dog got in my way."

I stare and gulp and I can feel my cheeks flush. His right eyelid begins to twitch. If this is an act, the detail is impressive.

But my brows furrow and I muster courage to ask, "Then why didn't you just go on and kill MacDonald just now?"

His mouth falls open and he looks at me. Stares at me. He cocks his head toward the floor and then glances at the spot where I was about to slip under the bed. "You heard?"

"Yes."

Uh-oh.

"And you didn't run get help for him. Why?"

This is good. *This is good.* "Same reason I'm whispering... 'cause I want Liam to get what he deserves. In fact, you didn't go quite far enough to suit me, but I told you… you can trust me."

It was just a twitch in his mustache, but I thought for a second he was actually going to smile. "And you're not planning to yell now?"

I shake my head back and forth in a vigorous *no*. "I keep telling you…"

"And if I leave now, you'll stay quiet?"

I give a quick nod. *"Absolutely."*

His shoulders slump forward. "Lord, help me." He looks away as if deciding something. He steps back then, still holding his gun on me. For one moment he looks as though he's going to simply leave. But then he steps toward me again.

Then he backs up three steps. The dancing vigilante.

Now he actually turns a full circle on one heel in the middle of the room, but, sure enough, he pulls the blasted gun back around on me again. At this point, I don't know whether to laugh or cry.

Like a long-tail cat in a room full of rocking chairs, he takes himself around the room, but now suddenly he sets his jaw and turns his head toward the door again. "No. It's no good. You'll have to come with me."

What!? My head is reeling as I try to take this in. "No, NO! I don't need to *go* with you. What you're doing…"

"Naw, I made a mistake comin' in here, and now I've got to fix things," he says.

Quick to think of a way out of this, I say the next thing that comes to mind: "But, Mr. Jones, I was already *leaving* town on this morning's coach. Do you see?" I point to the bed. There's nothing there.

One brow rises.

"No, I mean under. Under here is my bag and my cloak." I scramble down and reach under the bed. I hear him cock the trigger as I go, but it's too late to hesitate. Pulling out the bag and cloak with my right hand, I stand up and shake them at him nervously. "See? I'll leave town right now, and I won't ever come back, if that's what you want. I won't. Just let me explain…"

"Look," he says with a sudden calm, "I'm not takin' you but just down the stairs. Bring your things. You'll still catch your coach."

But his eyes are a little too bright. His voice a little too snappy.

"Oh," I say carefully. "And *why* do you need me to go down with you?"

He places his gun back in his holster and motions me toward the door. "This ain't the place to talk. Down there you can tell me all about how you can help me...."

His change in behavior makes no sense at all and neither does his reasoning, but I've no time to think it out, for suddenly I hear McDonald's man knocking on his office door below us. Jones sucks in his breath and hesitates. "We'll stay put 'til they go out looking," he whispers as he raises a finger to his lips. I notice it is shaking.

I nod to show my heartfelt willingness to cooperate even as I hiss, "But they'll come looking up here." Now a brilliant thought occurs to me. "Why don't you go out the window! Onto the porch roof! Go! You can go down the porch... the thing... the porch... thing-thing." My left hand is vigorously trying to describe a porch *post*, but the word has utterly gone from my mind.

He looks at me severely. "Not unless you're good at climbing in skirts," he says steadily.

We can hear the bustle downstairs. MacDonald is yelling for his men now. I close my eyes and pray he doesn't send anyone up the stairs. Silently my lips form the words, "Oh, please, Lord, oh, please..."

Too late.

I can hear Stubs making his way up the stairs. It's not hard to hear a man coming when he weighs near twenty stone and stands as tall as an angry grizzly.

I know Stubs will wake Lillian and they'll go from room to room, but my thoughts are interrupted by a sudden pounding on my door.

Jones scrambles back away from the door, and I'm thinking

how in a few seconds I might be standing between them as a two-sided target.

The door is shaking from the pounding of Stubs' fist and demanding an answer. Now Stubs rattles the knob so hard I'm afraid he'll yank it off.

Jones nods to me and mouths the word, "Talk."

I turn back to look at the door and muster my strength. "What? Who's there?" My voice sounds frightened, and why on earth shouldn't it?

"It's Stubs. You got a man in there, Marillie? Open this door or I'll bust it in."

I pull my hand to my neck and look back to Jones, and he mouths the word, "Answer."

But as I face the shaking door again with not a clue as to how to answer Stubs, I hear Lillian Wirsching calling sharply from down the hall, "Stubs? STUBS! Just what do you think you're doing?"

I stare at Jones with widening eyes as we both listen.

"MacDonald told me to come check the rooms. He's lookin' for a man in a blue long coat, black hat, and skerf up his face what come and tried to rob..."

"Any excuse to go in on a girl!" says Lillian as she's walking toward my door. *"Get away* from there. What would that *child idiot* know about it?" I gulp at the insult, but Jones just keeps on staring at me, as tense as a cat on ice. Lillian continues, "And you're waking everybody up, you fool. You should know to come to me first. I'd know if anybody come up here, wouldn't I? An' I ain't heard nobody open no doors. You tell Liam that, you ox. Mr. Taylor's right nex' door, and he said he'd shoot the man that woke him before noon! Get on down the stairs now—*pounding like a blacksmith at this hour*—you just go right back down and look there, d'you hear?"

"Well," Stubs says weakly, "I was just gonna go round... and she won't open her door." I hear him step away. Only Lillian Wirsching could climb into the boxing ring with a bear and win.

"Marilla?" Lillian says sharply.

"Yes, ma'am?" I say, hoping my frightened voice won't give me away. I blink back the tears.

"Have you heard anyone come up here?"

"No, ma'am." No, I most certainly did not hear him come up.

"There. Neither did I. That girl's too stupid to lie. Go tell MacDonald that. Better yet, I'll go tell him myself." A moment passes. "Well, come on!" she says brusquely.

A gush of relief overwhelms me as I hear them going down the main stairs, and I can't believe my ears. I smile wanly at Jones, but he only stares at me with those green eyes. He passes me to walk up to the door to listen again, and I look him over as he stands there, bent and still with concentration.

And I think to myself, *Surely, this can't be happening.*

I close my eyes and a vision comes to mind. I don't know if it's because my knees are shaking or because of the shock, but the thought of being abducted by the timid teller, Jonathan Jones, has suddenly made me want to burst out laughing again. Opening my eyes to see the reality only makes it worse: there stands the Good Gentleman, a costume hat fringed in thick black hair, his own thick red mustache for contrast, and a bandanna that has risen back up to cover his chin and now rises and falls with each breath. It's really all too much.

I can hear Lillian down in the lobby, now, still fussing at Stubs. I gasp as Jones reaches out and grabs my wrist.

As I hear Lillian and Stubs going out the front—with Jones listening intently—his grip on my wrist slowly tightens until tears sting my eyes. "It hurts!"

He turns and looks at me wild-eyed for a moment, but his grip eases up a bit. "Get those," he says, looking to the bed. I have the barest second to bundle my cloak and bag up under my right arm as we head out the door. All the way down the stairs I'm trying to keep hold of my things as he pulls me along behind him. He nods and we move straight across the hall to the back stairs. We can hear MacDonald out on Main Street with the others as we inch down one step at a time.

It will be a miracle if we can get out of here. And how will he drag a woman with him all the way out of town? *Ah, but he's a man with no sense, remember, Marilla?* For one short moment I wonder if I shouldn't yell out. After all, if MacDonald thinks I'm going with Jones because I want to, he'll kill us both. But then, it doesn't matter if I scream. The second MacDonald sees him, he'll be more than happy to kill the both of us.

And so, rather than think any more about the way in which I'm going to die, I stare at my wrist and concentrate my efforts on wishing he'd loosen his ironclad grip.

There is a moment at the bottom of the stairs when he turns to look at me and presses his lips together as if he is thinking on releasing me. But in another second he turns and we reach the back door. Somehow I know my fate is sealed. Jones looks out and waits a moment, then shuts the door quickly as one of MacDonald's men rides by. He opens it again slowly and pulls me out the back door with him. He practically picks me up to make a rush to the other side of the road to the livery, and once we are inside the great doors he pushes me toward a flatbed wagon. Two horses are waiting before it. "Get in," he says. "Lie down. Keep quiet."

"But I don't have to go! I can help you," I plead in a hoarse whisper.

"No time. Get in."

"There's time to leave me!" But when he steps toward me, ready to pick me up and place me in, I scramble up into the back of the wagon.

I've the vague feeling I've done this before. As I look around I realize this is my parents' farm cart. *I'm being abducted in my parents' own farm cart!* But then I think rather dramatically that this is where I might die. I shut my eyes to hold back my tears as he jumps up behind me and quickly makes a place for me in the middle. I lie down on my stomach with my arm under my head and try not to whimper.

He throws a rough blanket over me, then his coat and hairy hat. He's taken my satchel. The smell of the old blanket is putrid, and I'm already having trouble getting a full breath. Though I'm growing more and more terrified, the only way I can tolerate the situation is knowing I can explain it all to him in a calmer moment. Yes... a calmer moment. Perhaps when he's ready to kill me outside of town—right before he shoots me. There I'll begin my story, and he'll have to believe me because I am honest, and I have done nothing deserving this kind of death. He'll see the truth in my eyes. And there will be a spark of kindness in him that will keep him from pulling the trigger, or strangling me, or stringing me up... or... I just have to believe there's a spark of decency in him somewhere. My brows pull together as they rest on my arm, and I have choked myself to silence on my own thoughts.

Ever so quickly, he moves some barrels around my legs and puts two half-full sacks of seed on my backside and more along my sides. "You're showing good sense so far," he whispers. "Just stay quiet, cooperate, and you'll do fine. Make any noise, and I'll see you regret it."

He snaps the reins and the cart begins to turn about and move out of the livery. I can tell we are riding along the back street and heading north out of town. This is insane! Any second Mac-Donald's men will jump him and fill him with lead. I hold my breath to keep from screaming.

Half a minute passes, then a full minute. A few men are yelling and running here and there, but—unbelievably!—they pass us. Clearly they are completely ignoring Jones and his wagon. Is it possible he is getting away with this?!

But then I realize that to anyone who sees him, this old cart represents shy little Jones, the would-be farmer, come in on a Saturday for store items. *If you're gonna lie, lie bold,* as the saying goes. So I suppose if you're going to escape, it's best to just move right through your pursuers.

Perhaps he's not so crazy after all.

We trundle along quietly; he turns the horses left, then right, and now I know we've reached the western edge of town. No one stops him; no one even hails him. The usual noise of Liberty Avenue finally trails away from us as we jolt along. Soon I know we must have passed the huge rock half a mile from town, for the noises have disappeared altogether and we are heading down into the valley toward my parents' homestead. Will I die before I see it once more?

Despite these thoughts, I have a chance to think back on the frightened voice of Liam MacDonald, and I take pleasure in the sweet revenge of it.

On the other hand, the ride in the old flatbed is giving me bruises, and the pains jolt me back to the present. That... and the rumbling behind us.

Rumbling?

Horses! My heart skips a beat. The riders are shouting to Jones and coming up behind us fast. *Please*, no. He's slowing the cart down and as he does, he whispers nervously, "Quiet. If I die, you're goin' with me."

As opposed to when you'll have me die all by myself, I think dolefully. *There's a fine choice.*

The wagon has rolled to a halt and the men suddenly ride up beside us. I recognize the voices, all McDonald's men, and I hold my breath. "Jones, what you doin'?" says Stubs.

"Goin' home." Jones replies in the squeaking and now shaking voice of the quiet teller. The voice change surprises me. I bite my fist, and now my whole body is shaking.

"You see anybody out here?"

"Who's out here?" Jones says in an even more trembling voice.

Oh, he's good, very good.

"What's in yer cart?" one asks thickly—sounds like Iverson—and I feel the sacks around me being poked by what I presume to be a rifle. *I can't breathe.* Pinching my eyes shut, I do what occurs to me to do: I pray, pray hard, and don't stop to wonder why.

Jones says quickly, "I got four hundred pound a' seed for the chickens, and one pound brown sugar, and forty pound of flour."

One of the men spits. "Yea, I saw you. Needed four boys to help you load it all, din't you?" He laughs.

Another says, "This here is a red herring, boys. Liam said feller was big as a grizzly. Come on."

But another continues to press Jones. "Yea, he was lookin' for a *man*. That's right. You just the little farmer, ain't ye?" They laugh and laugh at that, but at least they've stopped poking the sacks.

Jones says in a whine, "One day, I'll surprise you all. One day I'll be big aroun' here—big as yer fine Mr. MacDonald. I'll own lots and *lots* of land. You'll see."

I think they're going to fall off their horses laughing, but he starts up the cart as they howl.

Then one of them—Iverson?—yells, "HOLD!" and my flesh begins to crawl once more.

"Just remembered..." Breathe—breathe—and hold again. "Stand up, Jones."

"Stand?" he whines.

Iverson's pistol cocks. I hear it so loud I could have been the one holding it.

"Yeah... *I says stand.*"

The cart sways. Jones has stood.

Another seemingly forty-year second goes by and then Iverson spits. "Toss me that sack of sugar," he says. "I think I'll have Bessie make me a pie tonight." And they laugh.

Jones removes one of the sacks from my back and I hear his strained effort as he tosses it.

"He missed!" "Th'ows like a girl!" "Come'n get it, you fool. Put it back here." The men laugh and laugh.

The cart sways again and comes still as he jumps down.

"*Sod buster,*" says Iverson with a chuckle. "Let me show you how *I* cut a row, farmer." I hear a cracking thunk and "Unh," all in one second, and I know that Iverson has kicked him in the head. The men are laughing again.

Not too oddly, I find I am glad to hear it.

I hear them turn the horses back to town and Jones slowly groans as he pulls himself from the road and walks back to the wagon. Another groan, the wagon sways, and he is up into his seat. *I will not ask this madman if he's all right. I will not ask him if he is hurt. I will not offer to help.* But I do let the air out of my lungs with relief, only then realizing I'd held my breath all this time.

Perhaps he is hurting too bad to kill me? I hope his head hurts real bad.

As we move on down the road, I try to figure this man out by thinking back on what he's told me so far. More painful than the ride in this flatbed is the memory of the words: *MacDonald pays my way.* It's true. To anyone on the outside, I have seemed to be "obedient" to MacDonald. But I've really been biding my time, holding out for the exact moment when I could get back at him, and now, with my fine act, the whole town thinks I'm just one of his own. And I'm going to die as if I were a common criminal— as if I were one of MacDonald's! The pang of indignation makes me suddenly want to scream, but I hold it in, for I'm afraid of his anger. Afraid of *him.*

And then it comes to me—the only real chance to get away from him is right now.

Slowly I shift the rest of the sacks off my back and make my way toward the back of the cart. Soon my feet have reached the edge.

And we trundle on.

I peek up from the blanket to see the opening in a forest dead ahead. *I'll slip off there,* I think, but while I wait I grow more and more terrified.

Finally, the wagon reaches the edge of the forest where the trees come right up to both sides of the road. If only I can manage to slip off the back quietly, I can then sneak into the woods. I pull at my cloak and begin my descent.

As luck would have it, I slip off easily, right into the road. I've bruised my knees a bit, but my cloak broke my shoulder's fall, thank heaven.

But so as not to spoil me with the feeling of triumph for more than one second, Jones chooses the next moment to cry, "Whooaa" and pull his horses to rest.

A chill rides up my spine.

But I lie still.

While staring at the mud before my eyes, I hear him say, "Miss Hay? You can... Miss Hay? MISS HAY? *Tarnation*, woman. Of all the stupid tricks to pull." He scrambles down from the cart and comes around to the back.

I keep my face toward the mud.

All goes silent again as he walks back and stands over me.

"Miss Hay?" he says quietly.

"Yes."

"Would you mind standing?"

"Yes. I would."

"Have you hurt yourself?"

"Not that I know of."

Here he snorts.

I have had enough. Caught twice in two days, pushed around by men who either don't know to speak the truth or don't know the truth when it's spoken, I am sick to death of it all. I have gone numb.

And so without emotion, I say, mainly to the dirt before me, "Mr. Jones, if you're going to kill me, I'd just as soon take it now." Well, this is not the endearing, passionate speech requesting mercy I had planned to give him. This is not the way to win my freedom. In fact, I realize with a lump in my throat, this particular path in the conversation *is not even going to keep me alive*. Yet I could hardly have kept myself from saying the words, I am so bone-tired of this game.

"Kill you?" he says with a great laugh. "Me? Kill you? What in blame... Are you crazy?"

I turn my head slightly. "Are *you*?"

"NO! *No!* I'm *irritated* as the blue blazes right now, but not quite enough to kill a defenseless woman who hasn't a brain to.... Get up now! Get up!"

I stand. As timidly as I can, I ask, "Then what's going to happen to me now?"

His head sweeps down to a view of his boots and then he kicks at a chunk of mud. "Don't know, but we'll figure something out," he says without looking me in the eye.

We? Then there is a committee of vigilance. *He's* not going to kill me: *they're* going to kill me, and my stomach lurches at the thought.

Would they hang a woman? Would they hang one of MacDonald's people just to send him a message? It's been done before. If he's trying to scare me, it's working. "I want to kn-know..." I'm trying to hold back a gush of tears. "I want to know *now* if you all are g-going to hang me." I have never stuttered before in my life, but now seems as good a time as any to begin.

He looks up suddenly. "Hang you?" He sniffs and chuckles. "No, I don't think they'll *hang* you, woman. But that'll be up to the Denver court."

Denver? The law? I'm totally confused and I shake my head furiously and wipe yet another tear from my eye. "Mr. Jones, I don't know what you mean, but surely it's time you let me explain myself. Surely, you'll hear me out, and..."

"No," he says flatly. "No, I don't think so. Now please get back in. *Get back,*" he says sharply, and then more softly, "if you would be so *kind.*"

I climb back up in a fit of complete exasperation. I watch him in cold anger as he walks around the cart and pulls himself up into the seat.

This is all so pathetic. I could have helped him... them. I could have stayed in town and been eyes and ears for him. I... well, I could have gotten back at MacDonald, but now it's all so muddled. But he wouldn't have taken my help anyway, for he's touched. He's touched! You'd have to be mad to try to be the Good Gentleman. Ridiculous. Good Gentleman, indeed. He's just like any other common... *He's just like MacDonald.*

But as we begin the ride again, I see we are heading to my parents' cabin—his cabin now, and I realize I haven't seen the place since the day I went to Independence. I've traveled this road with MacDonald's horse and wagon several times, but I've never been able to bring myself all the way to the homestead. The pain always got too strong, became a little too real. But I don't feel that way today. Despite all the circumstances, a feeling of sweet anticipation comes over me.

The road that leads up to it is a pleasant view, both to my eye and to my mind. The sight of the cabin from a distance makes me draw a deep breath.

Soon we pull up to the front of the cabin. Eager to see my parents' house, I clamber to the back and reach the end of the cart, but Jones suddenly yells, "Stay put!"

I halt, my foot hanging off the back end of the cart. He comes around to the back and he's carrying something. He swings it up and there is my bag.

"My bag!" I say without thinking, but he's unbuckling the clasp. "What do you think you're doing?" I say indignantly.

"Quiet," he says. "I'm just makin' sure…" He's busy with the latch and takes his time finishing his words. "…you forgot something."

"You're *making sure* I *forgot* something?" I say derisively. He speaks like a madman. Well, all he's going to find are my personal things, and it's infuriating. I fold my arms. But slowly it dawns on me: he's looking for a weapon.

"I don't have a gun!" I sputter, incredulous at the idea.

He stops to look at me and grin. "Don't have one *on* you, that's for sure."

"And how is it you come to be so certain of that?" I snap.

He shakes his head once and laughs. "Well, I figure I would have seen it by now." He goes back to digging in my satchel. He pulls something out I don't recognize. "Ho, ho. And what's this?" The blood drains from my face as I realize he is looking at MacDonald's packet of money. I'd forgotten about the money.

"That's Mr. MacDonald's," I say quickly.

"Well, I figured that much," he says smugly.

"I'm supposed to take it to Denver…"

"I don't think it's going to arrive," he replies.

"You're nothing but a common thief!" I say boldly.

He takes the insult lightly, laughing and shaking his head. For the first time I notice his forehead—a red gash in the middle of a heel-wide welt. He must have been kicked very hard. And if he could let Iverson kick him in the head that hard without fighting back, he is most assuredly a very determined sort of person. Completely crazy and utterly determined.

Gulping hard, I try again: "I'm sorry. I didn't mean... I know you're some sort of vigilante and that you want to get back at MacDonald, and I... You should know I can help you."

"But meanwhile you'll just carry some monies to Denver for Liam MacDonald. Understood."

Not understood! Not understood at all. "It's not like that!"

"Not like what, Miss Hay?" he says tiredly.

I cannot answer.

"You know how much money is here?"

I blush and nod. "But I'm not... I'm not just one of Mac-Donald's men. I don't work for him...."

He laughs again. "Well, you're half right." He holds out his hand to escort me from the cart. I try to jump down on my own instead, but he grabs me by the wrist and pulls me rather roughly down out of the flatbed. I yank my arm from his hold the second I touch earth and kick up a small cloud of dust as I scramble back from him. He holds up his hand as if he's touched some horrible thing. The feeling is mutual, and we glare at each other.

"Transfer of stolen monies is a serious business, Miss Hay," he says coldly.

I grip my cloak to my person and stammer, "How can you say... well, *I* didn't know it was stolen! How do *you* know it was stolen!?"

He leisurely pulls his hand to the handle of his gun. "Boy, you play the innocent bigger, better, and longer than anybody I've ever seen! But don't fool yourself." He draws his face toward mine with a look of smug satisfaction. "I've seen harder women than you get up on the witness stand and crack. They all think they won't... but they *all do*, Miss Hay." He steps back and grunts. "Aw, please, don't give me those fish eyes. You should try and be more original!" Ever so slowly I begin to strangle the hood of my cloak with my hands. "We'll be taking you to Denver soon enough, and then the proper authorities will handle your, uh, *claims*." And with that, he tosses my bag toward the cabin. "Take yourself in there for now. Should be more than a little familiar to you," he says with a neat little sneer.

"I will *not* cooperate with this!" I reply with venom. "You haven't heard me out. And you've NO RIGHT to accuse me!" I stamp my foot, but as I do I catch the look in his eye.

He stares me down and I feel all the fight go out of me as he says, "Listen, *Miss* Hay, I *do* got a right. More than you know. But I ain't your judge and jury, so you can just save your explanations for Denver." He looks back down at the leather money envelope, flips it in his hand, and says casually, "You're gonna need 'em."

Very quietly now, and full of fear, I say, "Why won't you listen to me? You can trust me, and you don't even know it." He laughs at that, and so I ask, "Would you know the truth if you heard it? Have you ever thought to trust someone, Mr. Jones?"

He smiles suddenly. "Yes indeed, Miss Hay, I have. I know the truth, and I put my trust in the Lord God." He smiles lightly and tosses his head. "Oh, and I trust my neighbor, too." He turns and crosses the east yard to the cabin not five hundred feet from my parents' home. My arms drop to my sides in amazement.

So *that's* his partner—or one of them: the reclusive Mr. Shaw.

Matthias Shaw came here a little more than a year ago, as I recall, and my folks and I hardly ever saw him the first few months. When we did, he would only speak to my father, never to my mother or me, not so much as a tip-your-hat-and-how-do-you-do. Here we were, out here together in the virtual wilderness, with Independence before the gold rush no more than a fly speck on the wall and twice as useless (as my father used to put it), but Shaw was not the least bit interested in his neighbors.

With chagrin my father watched Shaw struggle to build his cabin all by himself. When he got to laying the logs above his head, the man cursed and cursed, and when one rolled down on him one afternoon and almost severed his thoughts from his actions, he finally brought himself to cross the fields to get my father. But that was the only time he asked anything from us. Mama and I used to put some things from our garden at his door now and then. He never even said thank you.

Father used to call him something from the Bible... What was it? Ah, yes, a "bitter root."

He did his duties at my parents' gravesite in typical silence and only nodded in reply when I asked him to look after the milking and the hens the day I left for Independence. A cold sort. But look here, apparently Shaw is neighborly with this madman.

I watch as Shaw comes out of his cabin and they begin to talk. Jones points toward me, and Shaw looks around him to see. Built tall and wide, Shaw is probably the same height as Jones, but a good ten years older. He has a long dark beard and mustache, and thick eyebrows that appear to be attached to the upper edge of his tinted eyeglasses. He hardly ever gives expression to his face, although at the moment he's making a face the likes of which I've never seen as he stares this way. I can see the gray streak in his beard from here, and his jaw is hanging wide in the middle of it. Now he is shaking his head and clearly he has begun to yell.

Shaw starts to pass Jones toward me, but Jones holds him back. Jones is gesticulating again and Shaw is yelling again. Jones whacks his hand on Shaw's door and now both of them suddenly bow their heads.

I stared and stared at that streak in Shaw's beard the day we buried my parents on the mountain not so long ago. I didn't want to look at the mounds of rock rising at his feet, nor at the grave of my brother between them.

Now Shaw rubs his forehead hard and Jones slaps his hat on one knee in frustration and begins to pace back and forth in front of Shaw. Good. I must be giving them both a terrible headache. I only wish I could hear what they were saying.

I cross my arms and turn my head and drink in the sight of the homestead, my parents' homestead—once my home.

THREE

Some it pays, and others not,
So it is the world around;
Many would not make a cent,
Were it heaped upon the ground.

Old Saying

G lory. It's just as I thought it would look after this impossibly warm weather. I cannot help but smile. This spring has done its best to make up for one of the most spiteful winters this territory has ever known. But the bitterness of this reunion stings my throat and brings tears to my eyes, for this is far from the triumphant return I had planned.

Blinking back the tears I look over the place with loving eyes: the home my father built is framed with the low rounded branches of crab apple and cherry trees that hug its sides and back with limbs just now beginning to bud. Mother insisted on at least a dozen fruit trees. The pale gray logs of the home glow soft in the morning sun. Two narrow, long glass windows on either side give cheerful eyes to the place, and a good thick door is set between them like a dark nose in the middle. Half the roof's shingles have curled with age and wind. The place looks like a little fellow who just woke up from naptime, and I smile at the thought.

With the help of friends, my parents laid this place in the wilderness, and their charming personalities are still clear to see— at least to me. Flower beds spread out from both sides of the front door—oh, but the bulbs need separating. Father designed the house a little differently than any he had ever seen, putting his touches on the woodwork inside and out, from the carved supports under the eaves to the chiseled panels on the hutch inside. A whitewashed frame barn as large as the house but taller sits to the home's left. The chicken coop and pig pen are behind that, if Jones has kept them. To the right of the cabin, hidden by the trees, a smokehouse and a privy.

But what really fills my eyes with delight is the western view behind the house: the blue green of the spruce and the clear green of the aspen and the majestic mountain rising up behind them, capped with a bright white peak on the dark gray slopes. Then there unfolds the impossible blue expanse of the sky above, and I am filled with awe. My dream comes back to me full force. But this is real. The air here is certainly more real than the stuff I breathe in town, the ground more solid. The various hues are brighter and more vibrant. All that is living here grows with purpose or it will not grow at all. All that is solid rock remains solid rock.

The peaks have a beauty and splendor dressed in snow, laid out white and pure and clean. There is no mud, no noise, no Independence Hotel! Only nature working up to the unfurling of the aspens and the mountain flowers.

"Oh, it is good to be back here," I whisper. "Lord, if this is Your doing then I... I thank You. It's an odd way to bring me back for a visit, and that's for certain, and I'm not complaining about the view, but..."

I look over at Jones and Shaw. I thought I was frightened when I dealt with MacDonald, but at least I've known how he works things. This unknown is certainly the more terrible feeling.

I slowly walk toward the cabin and grab up my bag as I go. "Lord... if You're listening, I'm asking You to show me the way out of this." But why should he hear me?

I walk to the house in quiet thought and grab the leather latch on the door and push. I've done that a thousand times, but this time the old squeak brings a sting of tears to my eyes.

Carefully I step inside to look around the old room. I wipe my eyelids with the back of my hand and let my vision adjust to the soft light, the morning sunlight warming the whitewashed walls. Jones hasn't changed much about the place, and I'm glad for that. Two brightly colored Indian blankets hang in the far right corner around the bed. The kitchen is off to the left corner near the door, with the old worn table my father made plunked next to the cupboards. Mother displayed every brightly patterned plate she could find on the hutch next to the fireplace—Jones has left them all in place. It's still cheerful. In a way, they're... they're still here.

Under my breath, I say, "Hello, Mama, 'lo, Father. *I'm home.*" The lonely sound of it makes me laugh and tear up again at the same time.

Ain't enough cheerful in the world, Marilla. Your father and I have little enough time in the day, so you just keep on making up a little batch for us now and then, all right?

My mother's words come back to me now and then, bringing a fleeting moment of warmth. "A batch of cheerful. Yes, Mama." I turn to look at the spinning wheel as if she would be sitting there. Mother's huge wheel stands quietly on the right, untouched and unused.

Empty.

I walk to it and touch it, then hold the thin rim in my hand and pull down on it to make it whirl as I did when I was a child. It spins as though it will spin forever. Jones has kept it oiled. That's good. As I watch the fine broad wheel spin smoothly and silently in a graceful balance, I stare hard into the spokes and think, *Wouldn't it be nice if life could run along just as effortlessly as this?*

I brush the tears from my eyes and turn to look at the fireplace. The chairs are sitting all about like in the old days. I let out a gurgle of a laugh. Well, if I don't laugh I'll come to tears again, for certain. So many chairs Father made—he thought it was true hospitality to have a chair for everyone, and you never knew how many folks would drop in for a visit. Happy days, those were.

The sight of the place, the smell of it, makes me feel tremendously glad to be here. I move silently to the back of the cabin to take in my favorite view in all the world. There I open the latch to the casement window. I push it out slowly and breathe in the sight: the lush backyard my father cleared of trees, but dotted with fruit trees Mother planted and all of us pruned and picked. They've grown so much since planting ten years ago! Behind them lies a flat field, the rippling stream running alongside the log spring house, two rolling fields, and then my eyes float up the steepest mountain there. On the summit stands a cross placed in honor of my brother's grave. Only now my parents lie there, too. The wind in the clouds drags deep gray shadows across the rocky ridge, and I breathe deeply once more, taking it all in, and then let out a long sigh.

I will not cry.

The door gives its familiar squeak, which sends prickles up my spine. In walks Jones. I turn and stare out the back window as I hear him walk straight to the cupboard and open one of its doors.

"Well, you ain't going to Denver today," he says coolly.

I gulp. "I'm not?"

"No. You're gonna have to take care of this place for a bit." He is obviously waiting for my reaction, but I'm too stunned to reply. Without my asking, he adds, "Never mind why you ain't going, yet, but you can just believe it ain't 'cause we're wanting your company."

"This place..." he calls it. My father *built* this place. *My father,* not him. That he can open a door in the cupboard my father made as if it were his own is more than painful. It is humiliating, for I'm the one—the very one—who allowed it to happen.

I turn to glare at this intruder and see that he is putting salve on his forehead. The skin around it is already turning blue, and the scrape has a bright red gash in its center. He stops what he's doing to look at me.

Something in his eyes makes me gulp as an uncomfortable subject comes to mind. "This is my parents' house...." I say carefully.

"Was." He dabs his forehead again.

I wince. "But, still, you know it's unseemly for me to be here. If... if you're really on the side of law, you must know it isn't right for me..."

He points with the pot of salve in his hand toward the corner of the room. "You sleep there," he says with not a little irritation. "I'll be sleeping in the barn."

"But, really, Mr. Jones, it's not proper."

I jump as he slams the pot on the cupboard. "Look, you're not a *house guest* here, Miss Hay." On goes the pot's lid with a thunk. "You can just hang up that little Sorry Sue act. It just doesn't wash with me. *Us.*" With another slam, the pot finds the upper shelf. "And I don't want to hear any more, 'cause it won't work. *Unseemly?* I doubt you even know the meaning of the word, but you've got nothing to worry about on my account. Believe me! So help me, if I could send you somewhere else tonight I would…" Here he stops and draws in his breath.

"Look, while you stay here, and for as long as you cooperate, I promise you won't come to any harm." He grows calm. "But I have an arrangement with Mr. Shaw. He is a fine shot—a very fine shot—and he is to shoot you if you pass my fence line in any direction. Do you understand me?"

His eyes and voice are void of feeling. I murmur, "Yes, I understand you, but you needn't threaten…"

"Well, yes I do… I have and I will, whenever I have to," he says uncomfortably. He pulls at his nose and stares at his shoes, but then his head shoots back up. "Can you cook?"

"Yes, but I…"

"Good. I'll be at Shaw's. Make a supper for three, to be ready at six o'clock." With that he begins to walk out.

"I said I *could* cook, Mr. Jones, I didn't say I wou…" I stop as I watch him reach up and pluck my father's rifle from its peg above the door. Oh, how I wish I'd thought of it.

As he pulls it down, he turns slowly back to me and takes in my venomous look. "See?" he says with a triumphant smile. "You don't have anything better to do around here than cook now, do you?"

I go pale and nod.

He smiles again and holds the rifle out toward me. "Wasn't loaded anyway." I blush with anger as he rests my father's rifle in his arms. "Miss Hay, need I mention you're not to entertain?"

He pulls the leather door handle back inside toward the latch. "Keep it in 'less you have to go outdoors, and I wouldn't stay out long. Shaw'll be watchin'.."

Well, he's learned a little of homesteading, I think dryly. The leather handle pushed through to the outside of the door means "Come in and rest" to wandering strangers—the silent note of welcome that brought sad Mr. Prue to my parents' door.

Jones slams the door, causing the wooden lever to fall into place behind him. "Well, at least I can keep you out!" I hope I've said it loud enough for him to hear. I shake my head and pull my hands to my face in utter frustration. Jones can look and sound as mean as Liam MacDonald at times. Still, if he were such a ruthless sort, wouldn't he be hurting MacDonald and his partners instead of just threatening them? Wouldn't he have hurt me when he had the chance? I let go a long breath, clasp my hands together, and try to take the situation in.

I don't know anything, it seems. Could a person kill a man—or a woman, for that matter—as easily as he would a dog? He said Shaw would shoot me, and he certainly looked as if he meant it. And Shaw would—of that I'm certain. He would, but I don't really think Jones could. Then again, I once thought MacDonald was a fairly nice man with a mild dislike for house cats.

Ah, but never mind all that. I'm here, with the good and the bad of it, and the truth will win out, I fervently hope. But right now it looks as though I will have to cook for them, and so I move to find the fixings for a meal.

"At least I am home!" I say out loud. I am not taking care of just *anyone's* cabin. This is still *my* cabin, or at least my *parents'* cabin, in many ways. So. I will not mope about. And so what if the man is crazy? If he is crazy, I'll… well, it'll come to me at the time, but in the meanwhile… it's just so good to be here.

In the corner cupboards I find everything pretty much where it was, and so I spend the day looking things over and doing a lot of cleaning. All my childhood memories come back in loving detail as I work about the house. I pretend to be cooking for my mother and father, and so the task pleases me. I decide to release the frustrations of six months stuck in a mud-filled, noise-sated curse of a mining town on this, the home my father built, and I reassure myself that I have no reason to fear the neighbor or Mr. Jones. I don't want to go back to Independence. And these two will send me to Denver soon, and surely someone in Denver will hear me out.

And I don't care if I'm here long enough for MacDonald to send Potter after me. I don't care about anything anymore, except this little house.

When Shaw and Jones come back later, I place a fine supper before them, as good as I can manage for not being in a kitchen to cook for six months.

They bow their heads to pray, and I bow my head with them but stay standing at the cabinet. When they give "Amen," I turn back to cleaning up, but I hear, "Miss Hay?"

"Yes?"

"You'll join us," says Jones.

I can't tell if it is a command or an invitation, but I gather a bowl and spoon and sit.

Then a most interesting thing happens. I notice they only eat what I've already tasted. They're afraid I might try to poison them! Oh, this is too funny.

"Gentlemen," I can't quite hold back a laugh, "you needn't be afraid of me."

They eye me suspiciously. "Nevertheless, you just sit with us at meals," Jones says finally.

"Oh yes," I say, "I'll just think of myself as an honored guest." I toss my head back with a laugh.

The men shift uncomfortably in their chairs and glance at each other, and the meal continues in a dead silence.

After dinner, I clear the table as Jones tells Shaw about his day. He fills him in on how we made it out of town, and then he begins to whisper, but I know he's talking about how Lillian talked Stubs out of breaking down the door. They both laugh after it. *Now he laughs,* I think with consternation.

But now, quite loud enough for me to hear, Jones says when

he got to the bank later in the morning he found that someone had broken in and busted up the place. "MacDonald, of course," he says to Shaw. "All the bank records were taken."

I shrink away from the table at his words.

He turns his head slowly to me. "And rumor has it that Miss Hay gave MacDonald the idea," he says in a grating voice. "That right, Miss Hay?"

I catch his look. Confound it, I *did* give MacDonald the idea. I blush to my roots and step back another step, only to have the spoon clatter to the floor from the bowl I've let fall to my side.

Obviously satisfied, Mr. Jones sits back in his chair and crosses his arms. "Lillian called her a child-idiot, but I'm betting this little gal is at least too smart for her own good."

I stoop and pick up the spoon and come up slowly, not knowing quite how to explain but knowing I need to. Something in me wants to throw the bowl at the wall.

Shaw just shakes his head. "Don't know what you're gonna do with her, Jones. She's sly—slippery-slidey as a skinny eel—and she's gonna give you trouble."

That does it. The war of words has finally pierced my thin armor. I grow livid with anger, throw the bowl and spoon into the dry sink, and turn on them. "Mr. Shaw! I am *not* sly! *You* knew my mother and father, so you should be better expected to give me the benefit of the doubt! And, Mr. Jones, I didn't tell Liam to do that, and I *wish* you two would let me explain myself!"

"Listen to her!" Shaw says with disgust. "Next you'll be telling us you don't work for him." And with that he gets up, says goodnight to Jones, and slams the door behind him as he leaves.

Jones rests his elbow on the table and rubs his chin awhile.

"Mr. Jones," I say meekly, "*please* let me explain."

"I don't want to hear it, Miss Hay. No point. Until we get MacDonald, you'll have to stay here. If you're innocent, the law will see to it you're exonerated, and I presume you won't mind some honest work in the meanwhile." I shiver at the word "honest," as if what I've been doing at the hotel… "But if you ain't, I guess the only incentive I can give you to stay around is Shaw's Whitworth rifle, and that's about all I've got to say." He stands up and stretches. "By the way, I'm a light sleeper, Miss Hay. I wouldn't head for town in the dark. If I come looking for you... you'll wish Shaw had got to you first." He's watching my eyes to make sure his words have had an effect. He makes me so nervous I want to laugh out loud, but I gulp it down, stare back at him, and nod instead. "All right, then. Good-night, Miss Hay."

I roll my eyes and look away with my arms crossed. "And good-night to you, *Good Gentleman* Jones." But I keep my face turned from his. *Oh, and what a good gentleman he is. And he dares speak of the law. The law? As if I didn't see the law twisted and misused every day!*

But realizing I'll be here in the morning suddenly brings a thought to mind. He's already to the door, so I quickly ask, "Mr. Jones, do you still have Millie?"

"Millie?" His brows come together.

"Our cow," I say, feeling slightly foolish.

He snorts and nods. *"My* cow."

I blush. "May I milk her for you?" Odd but true. It's one of the things I always liked to do in the morning.

"May you mil... *May* you milk a cow?"

I thought it was a simple question, but he makes it sound as though I've announced Queen Victoria for tea. He finally nods an uncertain yes, gives an odd grunt, and the door slams shut behind him.

As I make the bed ready, I think over the day and finally come to mull over his words once more. Is he really a vigilante? No. He couldn't be. He said he'd be taking me to Denver authorities. On what charges? He doesn't have the ledger. Now there aren't even any bank records! But maybe all he needs for proof of guilt is that I work for MacDonald, that I sold my farm out from under me and chose to work for him. Or maybe it is enough that I have a thousand of MacDonald's dollars.... My heart sinks. I go over all the conversations in my mind. Nothing is clear. Maybe Jones is insane. Maybe I should just go to bed and stop giving myself a headache. I don't want to pray, either. I'm too angry to pray. Angry at God for putting me here.

I layer the bed with Mama's quilts. My parents' side table sits to the bed's right. Peeking in the drawer, I find to my surprise that many of their things are still there: combs, Father's dented shaving cup and fine bristle brush, Mama's satin ribbons, and tucked in the back, the beautiful little cranberry glass bottle of rose hip perfume! It has a wide base and a delicate neck, stoppered with a delicate silver filigreed cap. I hold it up to the candle and stare at the color in the glass. The fragrant scent comes to me, and for a moment I can hear the rustle of her skirts beside me. I won't cry. I won't let myself cry every time I think of them while I'm here. They wouldn't want that, I tell myself, and so I hold back the tears. Of course they would want me to pray, but....

I lovingly lay their things back on the table, touching each of them again and remembering. At least I am home.

But later, as I snuggle down under the numerous quilts, I recall Jones' words about the bank records and my eyes fly open as it comes to me. *Of course!* I groan. He's the bank teller! *That's* how he's become the Good Gentleman. He can see the amounts people have given and taken from MacDonald. And that's how he knows about me, I realize to my sorrow. Or at least he thinks he knows about me. He could see I gave MacDonald the money from this farm.

And MacDonald put me in the blasted book, too. I should be glad he couldn't find the safe.

So what will Denver do with me? Jail? I don't know. Today, the only thing I am certain of is that I don't know anything about anything. And I can't even bring myself to go on thinking about it. My thoughts sway with anger toward Jonathan Jones. The man won't even hear me out. He must be mad. Acting like a mealy little man in a teller booth and then coming out from behind the bars with guns blazing, wearing a costume hat. This is a nightmare.

How long will it take MacDonald to figure out it's someone at the bank? It will surely take a while to figure on Jones; everyone is convinced he's spineless. Folks at the hotel think he's a teller because he has no muscle, and that he lives on the farm because he doesn't like people. He bought my parents' place right when he came to Independence and he's never socialized with anyone.

I do not sleep well this night. It isn't the occasional flea, or even the lack of town noise. It's that I can't forget the leather parcel of money. What will happen if I don't come back in seven days? Will MacDonald think I took it and try to find me? Surely I'll be in Denver before it matters. What I really have to worry about is Denver.

And so as I wake up bleary-eyed the next morning and begin to scratch my legs, I feel even more confused about my fate. But when I have to keep scratching my legs, I at least determine that if I'm to stay here another night I will replace the bed's ticking to keep down the fleas.

I also determine, with all the optimism I can muster, to get to know Jones the madman better and somehow find a chance to explain myself. The way I've dealt with my sorrow at the hotel is to work until I can't think and then go and have my little talks with Mary now and then.

I miss not having Mary to talk to, but I suppose there's lots of opportunity for work. I'll just go ahead and change the ticking. As I pull the straw mattress off the rope bed I hear a knock at the door.

"May I come in?" It's Jones.

"By all means." I turn from my task and walk to the door.

As I open the latch, Jones enters and asks about breakfast. He explains their routine, but adds, "It's Sunday, so we can each get our own meal."

"Oh, Sunday." At the hotel I worked every day of the week, and I'd almost forgotten there was such a thing as "keeping Sabbath." My thoughts go back to the various chores Mama and I did all the days of the week until... Sunday.

"Yes, no one works today." But he is staring at the mattress on the floor.

"Ticking. Fleas."

"I haven't used that bed in a while, actually. I sleep on the floor to keep the fleas off."

"Well, if you send me to Denver today I won't have anything to worry about tonight, will I?" It is half statement, half question.

"You just don't worry about when you're going to Denver," he says firmly.

"Well, right," I say in frustration. "Then I'll just replace the ticking and be done with it." I turn and reach down for the bedding.

Sabbath. I haven't thought of it in so long! *Monday: washing day, Tuesday: ironing, Wednesday: oh, yes... baking, Thursday?* I pull the mattress up. *Plus the sewing and mending. That left Friday and Saturday for cleaning the house.* These daily chores made up the clockwork of my life until only a little while ago. Seems forever ago.

Jones walks around me and lifts the other end of the mattress. I want to protest but I hold my tongue. He and I walk the mattress to the barn so I can get new straw, and when I offer a quick thank you, he releases the mattress and brushes off his hands like he's brushing me off as well. He leaves and I think, *Good riddance.*

When I'm done restuffing the ticking, I walk around the barn and check on the animals. Satisfied as to their treatment, I go and get a pail with which to milk Millie.

"Coming to milk you, Millie," I say quietly as I plod to the back of the barn. *Jones didn't even know Millie's name.* Funny to have a family history disappear just like that... all the things my father built and my mother made: They're well cared for by him now, but they don't carry my parents' name anymore. In a snap, the legacy disappears. As I brush Millie's side with my hand and pull up the milking stool, I think, *No, that's not quite true, for I suppose I carry their full mark on me. In fact, I am their mark. Would they be pleased with me now?*

Leaning my head against Millie's side, I admit to myself they would not. I was always a stubborn child. They gave people the benefit of the doubt. And, while I can't quite put myself in Jones' shoes, I know my parents would expect better from me under the circumstances.

I settle down and milk Millie; the familiar pull and squeeze and the smell of the hay and the swish of her tail take me back to my girlhood. *What is it makes me love to milk?* I wonder. Well, I suppose it was the first chore I could do around here that brought a sense of accomplishment. A little girl getting a whole bucket of milk from a cow—now that was something to smile at! Why, I could live on milk alone for quite a while. I know how to take care of myself! Right then and there I decided I wanted to be a farmer—one of the most frustrating, back-breaking, and absolutely satisfying avenues a person can travel in this life. I sigh to realize those dreams will never be. Even if Denver lets me off, even if I convince Jones, I will never have the opportunity, as I did six months ago, to say, "I own my own farm and am beholden to none."

When I have a full bucket, I stand and pat Millie's flank and then suddenly fall to hugging her around the neck. "Millie, I wish you were mine again. I'm sorry... I am so sorry I let you go." I sob into her warm fur, but then I have to gulp a laugh as Millie gives me a wide-eyed and troubled sidelong glance. "All right. No apologies, then," I say and pet her nose a moment more. Soon she tries to make a snack of my fingers, and I have to laugh again and wipe my eyes.

Walking the bucket back to the doors of the barn, I happen to glance at the ladder to the loft. I stop and stare upward. How shall I convince this man? I smile and set the pail down. I shall show him I'm a good woman by doing nice things for him like fixing his bedding.

I climb up into the loft and find his things: he has already made his bed, and this forces me to smile. The man makes his bed, for heaven's sake! There's more of the bank teller in him than he lets on. But his bed is made of straw, too, and so I could make it nicer by refilling it. My eyes wander to the left of the blankets: in a well-cleared spot, he has a lamp, a large black book that must be a Bible, and a mantel clock. A mantel clock? Oh, to wake him up! After all, he is a clerk. I laugh a little, and then I see a large trunk over in the corner. For a few tantalizing moments I'm tempted to go over and open the lid, but then I remember his flashes of anger, think better of it, and set about to make new bedding for him instead.

I return to the house with the bucket of milk, half hoping to find Jones so he'll help me pull my mattress back from the barn, but he's nowhere to be seen. I give up and go back to the barn, pull the mattress onto my back and drag it to the cabin, feeling ever so much like an ant hauling a flapjack. I packed in way too much straw.

In an hour or so, Jones knocks loudly on the door, and I ask him to please enter. As the door opens I smile at him, ready to show him the humility and earnest good works I've been thinking on for the last hour, but I see in his face a look of utter consternation.

"*Don't* go to the loft," he says in measured calm through gritted teeth. "*Don't* touch anything up there. *Don't* so much as put yer little *foot* on the ladder. Do you *understand* me?"

"I'm sorry," I gulp. "I was just trying to take care of the fleas... in your mattress...." So much for doing a good turn.

He lets out a little sigh, which sounds not unlike a hiss, shakes his head sharply once, and walks out.

"May they eat you alive!" I mutter. *Oh, Lord, this isn't going to be easy.*

Over dinner, I find I am again trying to piece the man together. He is ruddy and tired looking, a bit older than me. He's good looking, although not in any classic sense. He has a long, squarish face—maybe too long—and a thick mustache that falls to either side of his mouth. On Jonathan Jones, the bank teller, the mustache looks like an affectation, but on Jones the Good Gentleman it's almost pleasant. He has large green and very expressive eyes— a little too expressive, perhaps—and thick, wavy red hair. Mary warned me to stay away from redheads. They were trouble, she said, shiftless and maltempered. I'd never put much stock in such notions... until now.

After the plates are cleared, Shaw and Jones walk out together. I take the bucket of wash water out the back door and dump it, but as I turn to go in, the wind carries their conversation to my ears.

"I can take her tomorrow."

"No, you *can't*, Shaw. He said Clark boys were due in *today*."

"But you gotta git rid of her."

"I know, I know. How 'bout the Tuxons over at Green Ridge?"

"Left their stake and bucked the tigelallereng a ding a....."

The wind has changed and taken the conversation away. I cock my head this way and that and strain with every muscle, hoping to hear more.

"We could get one of the boys to come out, but then..."

"Yea. Naw, I need every blasted one of 'em. I think we got to hold out."

"What if MacDonald comes lookin' for her?"

"We've got a few days yet. He's waitin' for her to come back from Denver."

"They think she took the coach?"

"Yeah."

More laughter.

I can't tell if the wind has shifted once more or the conversation has stopped.

Suddenly I hear, "Come on, Shaw. She's just a woman. What can one little slip of a gal do?"

And then I hear laughter again, but not from Shaw.

Silence, then suddenly I see Shaw's shadow heading back to his house. Quickly I make it back into the cabin and shut the door... just in time for the front door to shut, as well. Jones and I are staring at each other from across the room, and I can feel a blush slowly creeping up my neck.

With his mouth open in disgust, he folds his arms and shakes his head for a moment. I put down the bucket and nervously wipe my hands on my skirt. Then, instead of chastising me for listening to their conversation, his arms drop to his sides and he walks over to the fireplace, picks up the broom, and begins to sweep the ashes.

I take a breath and venture, "I'll do that."

"Already done." And he puts the broom aside.

"Mr. Jones, I know I'm trouble. I'm trying not to be, really."

"Try a shade harder then," he says evenly.

A question springs to my lips before I can stop myself. "If this is such an irritation, why do you bother yourself with the Good Gentleman?"

He leans against the wall and asks, "Do you read Scripture, Miss Hay?"

"Yes," I say, trying not to sound defensive.

He lays his arm across the mantel and scratches his ear with his other hand. His arm reaches more than halfway across the fireplace. "Well, I've read in Scripture," he says finally, "that 'the sword of authority was given by God to be His avenger... to bring wrath upon the one who practices evil.' I don't think God meant for Liam MacDonald to hold the sword." He pauses to watch for my reaction, but when I make none he continues, "So I think I might try to wield it some, and, God be with the project, I might succeed. God with us, and the proper authorities, that is," he adds with a smile that comes and goes like a shadow.

"I think that's a fine ideal."

"It ain't just an ideal to *me*." He removes his arm from the mantel with a jerk. "And I hope for *your* sake *your* ideals go a little deeper than words."

With that said he quickly leaves the house. I blink and think as calmly as I can, *I'll show him they do.*

Monday morning comes and I determine to work hard about this place. I am actually enthusiastic. In fact, I'm bursting with energy. I'll do as many extra things as I can think of this day: I start by making biscuits, then I mend his coat, bring in wood, clean the lamps and trim the wicks, clean my mother's curtains, scour the cooking pots, and dust to every nook and cranny. I even wash that disgusting blanket from the flatbed—any little thing that might draw his attention.

As I go about the place, I tell myself, "This is called heaping coals on the head of one's enemy!" And I sing as I do my chores and the time flies by.

In the early afternoon, I step outside to peer at the neighbor. Shaw is chopping wood, but he stops as soon as I open the door, so I just nod and make a quick retreat. A sharpshooter. In a strange way, this makes me feel protected. At least I know MacDonald will not be the one to get me.

Jonathan Jones returns from his clerking in midafternoon to do work on this farm. His job obviously gives him little time to do any real farming. From listening to his conversations with Shaw, I realize they must have an arrangement. I think he provides equipment and Shaw does the field work, or at least Shaw did until I came. They'd probably be hiring help right now for the planting if I weren't here, so I'm giving them more than just cause for a headache, I'm sure.

When Jones comes in today, I catch him looking twice at things like the lamp wicks. I watch him turn his coat sleeve over to notice the mended tear and then give me a sidelong glance. So after dinner, once the silent Mr. Shaw has left us, Mr. Jones settles himself by the fire with a book, and I come over and gingerly ask if he's noticed the extra work I've done.

"Yes." But he does not look up from his book.

"I'm glad. I..." I'm not sure how to proceed, and so I clasp my hands.

He looks up and then cocks his head. "Suppose you were gonna impress me with your good works? Think we'll let you go, then?" he says with half a smile.

Embarrassed, I reply, "Well, no... not put that way. I..."

"Miss Hay, I think I've said it's not up to me to decide what you are or are not." He resettles himself in his chair and goes back to his reading.

Now I'm angry. "Obviously that's not quite so, sir, or I wouldn't be here, would I?"

He brings his head up again and his voice rises a bit. "You are here, Miss Hay, because you work for MacDonald, and I would think you wouldn't try to argue the fact. I've got a thousand dollars says different."

"Please..." I shake my head with frustration. "I just mean to want to tell you how I got there at the hotel."

He stops and looks at me.

I take a deep breath and start again in a lower voice. "You're right. I wanted you to see my extra work as a gesture of my sincerity... that you might at least listen to my story."

With his voice still raised, but in an almost pitying tone, he replies, "Miss Hay, the law hardly cares whether you mend my coat."

There is dead silence and I bow my head. "All right. You've made it known you're a Christian man." I look up. "Do you claim to believe in his mercy?"

His smile is gone now and he simply stares.

"I ask for mercy to let me speak," I say quietly.

"Go on."

I pour out my story quickly, with fiery intensity. I give the bare bones of my childhood, how I came to Independence, and I end with how I allow myself to work for MacDonald until the authorities can get the man, how he sent me on an errand to Denver, and how I need to be back on Saturday or he'll come looking for me. Out of pride, I leave out the information about the ledgers, for I don't want him to know how I caused MacDonald to destroy his bank records. Besides, I reason, MacDonald's probably already destroyed the green ledger by now.

Jones keeps a poker face the whole time I tell my story, and as I speak by turns I stare at his face or at the candle on the table; the wick is about to falter and go out. For the life of me, I can't tell if he believes me.

But when I finish, I think I see the barest hint of sympathy in his eyes. Then he crosses his arms. "Allow me to add 'Fine Actress' to your many accomplishments," he says wearily, and he smiles like he has me figured, has it all worked out, and he's not about to let a woman worm her way into *his* sympathies. No, no, not for a second.

And I've lost. He's just like Shaw.

The little flame in the candle dies out with a halfhearted hiss, and all that remains of light in the room comes from the embers in the fireplace.

I glare back at him across the sudden darkness. "How could I have made that up?"

He pushes his chair back with a screech. "Well... you've had two days to make that up, and may I say I've been thoroughly entertained. But the curtain has fallen. I've heard a lot of presentations, but yours is rare, indeed."

My eyes smart with tears that will not hold themselves back. "That is the truth, Mr. Jones. And you wouldn't listen to it two days ago."

"Oh, come on, Miss Hay," he says with a laugh. "If you're gonna make something up, start by making it believable. How could anyone be so *dad-blamed naive* as to trust a prairie rat like Liam MacDonald?"

I could. I could! I think and I stamp my foot.

"And tears? Not many actresses can bring those on command. Well, I am duly impressed," he says, drawing his hand to his chest in mock reverence.

"Why won't you believe me?" I ask in a whisper.

"Well, gol-lee, I don't know," he says snidely. "Let's see. Let's just try and recall..." He twiddles his thumbs as he recounts, "Miss Marilla Hay takes the money I gave her for this farm—a fair sum as I recall—then she goes and... with all that money and with all the employers she might choose in this territory, she takes a job with... who? Liam MacDonald... and she up and *gives* him her money! Not only that, but she's been taking his money to Denver for him so it can get washed up and prettified..." He looks up at the ceiling and then back to me. "Nope, nothing else comes to mind, but I'd say those'll put you right up there with a snake, Miss Hay. You got to be in on the profits from MacDonald and the Clark boys."

This is too much. It is so easy to insult me. "Oh, yes, it's obvious I'm just dripping with money. I just dress up like the help and pretend to work at the hotel to throw people off."

He shakes his head and laughs.

It's doing no good. So now I will match fire with fire. "You know, you should tell more people how you like to kill dogs, Mr. Jones. Not many think you're man enough to do such a thing."

He just leans back in his chair and laughs some more. "That's right! That's right, and I better hope they don't!" I want to push the chair right over with him in it. I even take a step forward and raise my hand, but he stops mid-laugh and mid-lean to look at me with narrowing eyes, and all my courage shrinks away. One hand on the table, muddy work boots dangling above the floor. If he were the sliver of a man I thought he was, the teller I knew as Jonathan Jones, I could push him right over... but he is not. I don't know what he is, exactly, and it's the *not knowing* that holds me back.

So I turn from him and run out the front door, fling it shut behind me, and fall to the cold ground with a sob. Through the door I can hear him laughing still.

I grab the nearest object, a piece of kindling, and throw it at the door with a frustrated scream, and then I look back down to the ground and notice the crocus patch. All their little heads are nodding sadly at me in the light, night breeze. And he's still chuckling. I am a sad lot. It strikes me that these flowers are my only friends in the world.

What a silly thing to think, Marilla, shake yourself out of your self-pity; get hold of yourself! I remember the day we planted these. Aunt Betty back east sent them. We'd get a package from her about once a year, and it was always Christmas the day it arrived. She sent ribbons and cloth and other goods we couldn't always buy in Independence. She always sent along new bulbs of amaryllis, Mama's favorite flower and my namesake. And Aunt Betty is the one who sent Mama the beautiful bottle of rose hip perfume. She helped us to feel civilized in this hard new land. I stand up and decide that I will rise to meet this challenge.

After a sleepless night I rouse myself, and then decide that baking a cake will make me feel better. Today is wash day, but I don't dare touch Mr. Jones' things unless he asks, and my clothes are fine for another day. Yes, today would be a good day to bake a cake.

I look about the kitchen. "Let's see, Mama kept the sugar loaf locked in the trunk by the door. But the key is gone from over the lintel. Ah!" I bless Mary's head as I realize I can pick the lock. I stoop in front of the trunk and am busy with a hairpin at the task of picking when Jonathan Jones reenters the front door.

"Woman, what do you think you're doing?" he asks sharply.

"Sugar. I am looking for the sugar." I sit on the floor in disgust.

Jones leans on the door frame. "Yes, and 'a good woman knows how to pick a lock,' eh, Miss Hay?" He brings a finger to his lips in thoughtful repose. "You know, in the list of virtues to look for in a woman, my mother failed to mention that particular gift. Why, your talents are just gettin' too numerous for me to count! But allow me to save you the trouble of looking: there's no guns, poison, or knives in there."

Now he steps in completely and I see he's carrying a large basket.

"And this... this here's my laundry."

"So it is," I say through tightened lips.

"And by the by, our conversation of last night put something in my mind I realize I haven't stated clearly," he says, his voice growing cold.

I look up quickly.

"You may consider our unusual arrangement as *house arrest*. And another thing..." he says with mild irritation, "I told you to keep this door handle IN."

He turns to take his hat from the hook. I'm feeling a mess of things as I watch him go, and they're all tangled up in me and I can't get them out. I want to argue with him. I want to restate my case, my innocence, vow my trustworthiness. Tell him I hate Liam MacDonald as much as he does... no, *more!* I want, for heaven's sake... I want a sharp knife to cut potatoes! But instead of saying anything of importance as he leaves, only the last thought comes to my lips. "Mr. Jones, you know more than once a bear has come down off that mountain to knock on our door, and it takes a sight more than a shut door to keep him out. Just how am I supposed to protect myself?"

He wags his head. "You forget. Shaw's out there and he'd have ole Bruin down before he reached the back fence."

"And if he doesn't?"

"If he doesn't..." He smiles again. "I'd say you'll have to use your best talent."

"My talent?"

"Acting, Miss Hay! I suggest you simply act like a *bigger* bear." He snickers at his own humor as he shuts the door behind him.

Oh, so clever.

Well then, as far as he's concerned, I'm already under arrest and it's obvious he won't listen to anything I have to say. I shake my head back and forth and whistle. "Can you make things any worse, Marilla?" I give a little sniff and shake off a tear. "I will not see it this way! I will not! I'll be all right." I nod a violent nod, rise up, and draw the thong back through the door latch. Then I bend down again to try to finish picking the lock. But suddenly I can't see the lock through my tears, and so I give in to their comforting wetness.

Finally, with drier eyes, I finish the task and open the old lid with a creak. I see the sugar box set to the right, just as I remembered it, and Father's guitar lying to the left. "Ah, the Spanish guitar! *This* should lighten my burden considerably!"

I take it out and pluck at the old strings with awe. Out of tune but so pretty to my ears. In town, I was forced to borrow a guitar from one of "the girls" if I wanted to play. They would make me stay and play for them, but then they'd make fun of my songs. At first I really thought they hated me and my music, but after a while, I think we all knew better.

Well, today I can play and sing for myself with no one to laugh at me. As I sit and tune it and then play, my head becomes clearer, and somehow the hurt stops hurting so deeply.

When I'm done with every song I can remember, I put the

guitar back and whistle the tunes while I do chores. I even do Jones' wash.

By late afternoon, it's become a fairly warm day, so I open the casement window and take in the view. The fruit trees are just turning out their tender leaves, and the lower mountains are shaded in pastel greens. It's been so long since I've seen it in anything but my dreams, it doesn't quite look real. Higher up, there's still a lot of snow on the peaks, and I have to blink for a moment from the brightness. Father told us the first trappers out here called these the Shining Mountains, so that's what we always called them between ourselves. I suppose it was some travelers, sour on their trip, renamed them "The Rockies," but I can see only the beauty my father treasured and shared with us by his choice of this land.

My eyes slide down the snow and trees until I notice Mr. Jones. He's back from town and standing stock still right out by the back fence, but he's looking away from me over the stream into the back field. I stand on tiptoe to look past him and now I see the reason for his stillness. A ways off, a spotted doe and her fawn are nibbling at the ground at the edge of the field. The fawn is nuzzling its mother in such a sweet way: the little tail is fluttering in circles of delight as it leans against her.

I look back to the fence. He has left his rifle leaning there, but he isn't moving for it.

In another second something snaps in the woods and the mother and child dart forward and then bound away in graceful arcs. What a pleasure it is to watch them run.

Now Jones turns back to his work, but even from this distance I can see the smile on his face. Puppy-killer, indeed. I'll bet I was right all along.

I watch him as he scrapes rust from a wheel band and then bends the metal back on to the spoke for nailing. My father had to have help to do the same task—and he was a strong man! Jones wipes his forehead with his sleeve and then removes his shirt. I cock my head to see Jones has hidden his muscles well— no one would guess the stooped figure behind the teller's bars is this same fellow. I smile and try to imagine the width of his arm from this distance. But as I stare at his limb, I notice he has stopped work.

He is looking straight at me.

My heart jumps and I quickly put my head down and blindly shut the window all at once. It comes to with a horribly loud thump.

An hour later, Jones walks in for supper, and I turn from the pot on the fire to carefully nod to him, hoping he's forgotten by now.

He hasn't.

He is not wearing his shirt. Holding out to me the balled up shirt, one brow rises as he says with obvious delight, "If the pot outside is still on the boil, this is for the wash."

I whirl back around to the fireplace and feel my face flaming red with embarrassment.

Keeping my eyes to the fire, I say tersely, "Thank you, Mr. Jones. Please place it in the basket to your left." I will not turn around. A few more moments pass.

"Miss Hay, I'm decent now. You can turn about." He laughs and I hear him step toward me.

I am so angry I still cannot look at him. Tears have brimmed to my eyes. Now they roll down my cheeks, but I will not give him the pleasure of seeing me wipe them away. "No... no." I laugh roughly. "I think you are anything but *decent*, Mr. Jones."

"Pardon me?"

I turn about with the ladle raised and he steps back in surprise. "I said, 'NO, you are not a decent man, Mr. Jones!'" I take a deep breath and quickly turn back to the fire, sputtering, "I know as much about men as six months in Independence can teach a girl, and I've been insulted in possibly every form a woman may imagine, but I have never, *never* had a man do to me what you just did.... Standing there... bold as a peacock, as if I were a... a... I have had *enough* of this!"

"*You've* had enough. *You've* had enough! You ain't had NOTHIN'!" He takes a deep breath before he continues. "Were you or were you not watchin' me work a little while ago, or would you like to act the innocent?"

"Yes! *Yes!* YES, I was watching you. Is there a law against it?" I wave my hand into the fireplace, throw the ladle into the pot with a clatter, and cross my arms. "And does the fact that I have eyes give you the right to... to..." Clenching my teeth I say, "I was simply watching you put a rim on a wheel. If that is a crime in the Territory punishable by insulting behavior, I didn't know." I turn my back on him again, watching the fire. "But apparently... apparently I've been crossin' the law again. It appears I am either the most law-crossin' piece of female criminality Colorado Territory has ever seen... or perhaps I am just the most completely stupid piece of work my parents created."

"Oh, I never said you were stupid, Miss Hay," he says with that knowing tone that makes me want to kick him in the shin.

More evenly I continue, "I was only watching. In fact—and *please* don't take this as a compliment—I was thinking what a good ruse you've played in town making people believe you're a spineless little bank teller."

He gave a crooked smile. "And you'd be the one to recognize a good ruse, now, wouldn't you, Miss Hay?"

"Oh, you! You twist everything I say!" Despite my resolve, the tears roll down my cheeks once more and I sweep my sleeve across my eyes.

"Now, look here," he says angrily, suddenly stepping behind me and whirling me about.

"Don't you DARE touch me!"

He holds up his hands and dips his chin. "Sorry. I'm... I'm sorry," he says, backing up.

I am full ready to grab a ladle of stew and throw it in his face if he does it again. My lower lip comes forward and I step back toward the fireplace. I'm ready.

He looks down at me. "Don't... don't get your dander up. I... Look, I'm not used to somebody..." I blink and gulp as he tries to collect himself. "I've seen a lot myself, Miss Hay. Folks who get so good at lying they believe themselves. Makes it hard to get at the truth, sometimes. But I've always... I've always made it a point to get at the truth," he says a bit unsteadily.

"And are you never wrong?" I hiss.

His shoulders fall. "Most times I don't get the chance to find out."

The flatness in his tone is bone-chilling.

"Anyway, I've apologized. So even if you're..." He hesitates. "Well, I've apologized... and you can take it or leave it."

"Take it or leave it." I laugh. "Take it or leave it! I left this house once, thinking to be gone a day. Two, at the most. I'd do anything to be able to take it back."

He presses his lips together and turns to go, but his step slows as he reaches the door. Turning to me he says, "By the by, your words remind me, Miss Hay. I imagine you might want to look in the trunk in the loft."

"What?" Oh. I look back up and over to the small loft. Mama's trunk. I had forgotten. I soften at the thought, but then I'm angry again as I turn back to the fire. Many times I'd wished for our things these last six months. They obviously mean nothing to him. I begin to stir the pot again. "Yes, indeed, I would," I say tersely. The door is creaking closed behind him when I add, "And wouldn't it have been nice if you'd offered my mother's and my things to me six months ago? You know I would have bought them from you."

The door has not shut. He seems to be thinking on it. "Well... I don't believe you ever asked me."

His response startles me. But as I think about it, I realize that he's right. I was in such a muddle then. I suppose MacDonald wanted maximum profit and I wanted the minimum in pain, so after the house sold I never even asked after our things.

I heave a great sigh. Jones' reply has taken all the vinegar out of my questions. "Yes. Yes, that's true. Well, do I buy them from you now or are you offering them? After all, there's probably only a bit of time."

"Take 'em!" And he slams shut the door.

I'm glad he won't be here to hear me cry, for I can't seem to hold the tears back anymore.

After dinner that evening, I am given the rare treat of their peculiar form of "companionship." Jones and Shaw prop their feet up by the fire and begin to tell stories to each other. I've gone through the trunk and taken the work clothes out that I can use, so I sit back away from the men and do some mending by the large oil lamp. But I listen to every word and, despite my wanting to hold on to the anger of the afternoon, eventually I begin to smile and laugh silently at their tales.

Of course, Jones does most of the talking. Jones can be charming when he wishes to be. A little vain, perhaps, and utterly wrong about me, of course, but I'm glad the low firelight hides my cheeks as I think back on this afternoon. I believe I saw some scars on one arm, and I wonder how they got there. They looked like bullet scars to me—like the one Father had on his leg from the hunting accident. Perhaps he's played the Good Gentleman before in other towns. It makes me wonder.

Now I listen to Shaw and Jones tell tales, and they bring back the memory of all my father's stories, and I can imagine my father pushing back in his chair to listen in. Jones is propped back, his feet touching the floor now and then. During the conversation, one of his boots will rise to the side of the mantel and in time he'll switch it. He's restless, very restless, I note. Shaw, on the other hand, sits as still as a rock the whole while. He stays in one place with his feet propped on a low chair, puffing at a pipe. Shaw's arm, with the pipe firmly attached to his hand, is the only thing that moves—lighting, puffing, tapping, filling—as the stories come out one by one.

The room is silent for a time and so I know another tale is coming.

Slowly Jones begins to speak. "Heard about a judge."

"Yep."

"Judge Pokum."

"Pokum?"

"Yeah. Judge Pokum had an awful duty to perform," says Jones.

"Mm."

"Held a man's life in his hands… Well, in his pocket, anyway."

"In his pocket, you say?"

"Had a statement in his pocket that would condemn a man to die—an *eyewitness* account of a murder. Yes, sir. All he had to do was take this paper to court and the man was certain to be hanged."

"I see. So what's the trouble?"

"Court was a far piece. Court was over the mountain and across a flooded river."

"Well, he was a judge, weren't he?"

"'Zactly." Jones waits as Shaw refills his pipe.

"Please go on, Mr. Jones."

"My pleasure, Mr. Shaw." I am the audience. It makes me smile. Jones shifts his footing. "Well, Judge Pokum had a horse. More specifically… a nag, but she got him over the mountain."

"Good horse."

"But she wouldn't swim the river."

"Shoot the dang horse."

"Din't have to."

Silence.

"Pokum had to swim the rest of the river by himself. Got to the other side and found an empty cabin."

"Nice luck."

"Firewood in the fireplace."

"Mm."

"But nothin' to light it with."

"Too bad!"

"Just one sheaf of papers on him."

"No!"

"Yes, sir." All is silent, and I hold my needle still as I wait for the ending. Suddenly Jones says, "Judge Pokum came to court. He stood before the jury and right away said the man was free to go."

"No kiddin'."

"'Lack of evidence!' Judge says."

"Ain't it the truth."

"'An' furthermore,' says he, 'no ladies was hurt in the fracas, so I don't see as any real harm was done.'"

"Mm."

"They let him go."

Lord, I wish my father could hear this. I laugh quietly and can't quit laughing no matter how hard I try and soon I can't suppress the sound.

Jones says, "Do you think she's laughing with us or at us, Shaw?"

"Must be at us. We didn't ask her to join in."

"Oh, no," I pipe up with some irritation. "If you don't wish me to laugh, don't speak of him again."

Jones smiles but Shaw is reserved. Now he looks at Jones and pushes out his lower lip until Jones clears his throat and settles back into his chair once more. A few more stories follow, but I try harder to concentrate on my sewing. Well, actually, it isn't the sewing at all that keeps me busy. It's my family that has settled in my mind once more.

As the two let the fire die out, I begin to actually ache with the memory, and I think to my lonely self, *This must be what it feels like to have a broken heart.* These little fits of melancholia seem to strike hardest in the late evening. I determine to go to bed quickly and lose these thoughts in dreaming.

FOUR

The next morning, I reckon it's not such a bad world after all. *At least my situation is forcing me to appreciate my days,* I think with dry humor. So, I'm glad some little good is coming out of this.

It's a warm day again for March, so I open the casement window and realize that we're going to have an early spring. From between the high clouds, the sun is drawing a wide curtain of light over the pale green mountains, and the bubbling stream behind the house, touched here and there with sunlight, dances with diamond light all down the hill. *Like a string of lanterns at the foot of a bright stage,* I think with a sigh. *That's how I saw it as a child, anyway.* I smile to know that, whether these mountains are seen through a little girl's naive vision or a woman's more critical view, the curtain still rises on the Shining Mountains and they are always ready to perform.

How can such a glorious morning be anything but welcomed? On a day like this, the words "house arrest" just make me laugh. I begin to work with renewed energy.

And all through the day, when one chore is done and before another is begun, I stop and play the guitar and sing. And in that way the day moves more quickly than any I've had here so far.

At supper, when Mr. Jones looks at Shaw and nods toward the guitar leaning against the mantel, I realize with a slight blush I forgot to put the instrument away.

"You play, Miss Hay?" he asks.

"Yes. My father taught me on that guitar." I will not apologize for playing the guitar my father intended me to have.

He just stares at me awhile.

Perhaps he sees the way my jaw is set and is suddenly tired of butting heads with me, for he asks, "Would you play something for us?"

I think of refusing as I look back and forth at the men. Jones looks quite sincere. Shaw... well, no expression is his usual expression. I waver another moment and then decide that for *my own* pleasure I will, and if it helps them see me in a better light, that's fine. I nod my head once and walk to the guitar.

They say not a word as I tune the instrument. I clear my throat and sing to them without looking up.

First I sing them a sad ballad, and when I'm done Mr. Jones says thank you but straightway asks for a certain minstrel tune. I happen to know it so I play it for him, and his enthusiasm for the song, keeping time with a boot and a slap to the knee, loosens my mood a bit, and so the next one I sing is one I know even Mr. Shaw might appreciate: "The Lane County Bachelor." Set to a rolling, rustic melody the song begins:

Hurrah for Lane County—the land of the free,
The home of the grasshopper, bed-bug, and flea;
I'll sing of her praises and boast of her fame
'A starvin' to death on my government claim.

And ends with...

As for all you claimholders who are bound for to stay,
You may chew on your hardtack 'til toothless and gray,
But I'm traveling on; I'll no longer remain,
To starve like a dog on my government claim!

Mr. Jones smiles and nods approval. Even Shaw is smiling. I suppose I wasn't really sure he could.

"You have a fine voice," Jones says. "Will you play after supper from now on?"

"If you insist," I reply with a mild blush. Now I feel a little like David asked to play the harp to calm King Saul. Perhaps then he'll trust me; at least I can give my own soul over to some pleasure in the meantime.

As I place the guitar back in the box, Shaw takes his leave but Jones stays. I sense he has something to tell me and so I turn to face him, folding my hands before me and hoping for the best.

He sniffs. "I want t'apologize."

My eyes grow quite wide.

"I mean to say…" He pauses for emphasis. "I shouldn't have *insulted* you the way I did the other day."

"I believe you apologized then, Mr Jones," I answer quietly. "Although I don't believe I had time to thank you. I accept your apology."

Jones cocks his head. "You're a puzzle, Miss Hay. A confounded puzzle." And then he stands up, says good-night, and leaves— rather quickly, I think.

I look around the cabin in amazement. *I'm glad I have finally made him wonder about me,* I think, *and there's some hope to be found in that, I suppose.*

Early in the morning the next day, I am scrubbing the hearth when I hear chaos coming from the chicken coop. *Stray animal,* I tell myself. *Well, I know how to handle that.*

Sweeping up the bucket of wash water from the floor, I fly out the back door. "HEYA!" I yell, and a black, mangy dog drops his paws from the chicken fence and begins to high-tail it toward the front of the house. I chase after it as it gallops around to the front yard. Just as it squares the west corner of the house, I gain enough ground between us to throw the bucket and hit him smack-square on the haunches. Must be used to this treatment, for the cur doesn't even yelp.

And so I continue to chase after him across the front yard and suddenly see myself as a little girl: *just as plain as day, I'm running barefoot across this yard because I hear Papa's wagon coming. He's been to town, and he's brought me something*—I run to the fence with abandon and am about to make a jump and step on to the bottom board when I careen to a stop, falling forward slightly and grabbing hold of the top board.

In one split second I have forced myself into the present, and a fine sweat has sprung to my brow as I've remembered just in time.

Matthias Shaw.

My head begins to throb as ever so slowly I turn my head to look back over my shoulder.

There stands Mr. Shaw, his Whitworth rifle, telescope attached, aimed dead upon my back. *Oh, Lord.* I pull my hands together and begin to wring them over and over. "Don't tell Mr. Jones," I whisper. "Don't tell Mr. Jones." I begin to yell, "Oh, please, Mr. Shaw, don't tell Mr. Jones!" I run back to the house, and as I run I realize how close I have come to death.

He told Mr. Jones that night. I should have let him shoot me.

While Mr. Shaw expounds on the particulars of the afternoon, Jonathan Jones stares at the floor, listening. *I have to have a chance to explain myself; I have to make them understand.* I turn to Shaw. "I was chasing a dog, Mr. Shaw. Didn't you see the dog? Didn't you hear me whoop?"

Jones looks at Shaw and Shaw shakes his head "no." I look back and forth at the men. *Lord, help me; I can't believe this.* I fold my arms and then squeeze them in exasperation. "Why would I just run like that knowing Shaw could be there? Wouldn't I have seen him first and stopped? Why would I want to endanger myself?"

"Yea," says Jones. "You tell us why. Was there somebody over that fence?"

"No! I was chasing that dog, that's all, and then I was remembering..." I blush and halt. "And then I didn't remember Shaw 'til the last second..." I gulp.

Jones looks down again and shakes his head. Finally he stands up with his back to the fire and spreads his hands to warm them. His form casts a great shadow over me as he explains steadily that I will work Shaw's garden tomorrow, as it's been neglected by needing to watch me. That way I'll be easier for him to watch and can stay out of trouble. When Jones is finished, he sits at the kitchen table. Shaw sits. I find that I'm shaking with a sudden cold chill.

As I lay out the meal, everyone is quiet until I whisper, "I am obviously a terrible trouble to you both. Why haven't you just taken me to Denver by now?"

Jonathan says evenly, "As I've said before, if it were possible, we would have done it. *Believe* me, we would have, but it won't be long, now."

Shaw shoots him a glance like he's said too much.

I sniff, shake my head, and smile. "Fine. So now I will work Mr. Shaw's garden."

"Fine," Mr. Jones repeats. Then we all sit at table for a silent and, by now, very cold supper.

That night I think back again to my parents and what they would think of my predicament. Almost a year of my childhood was spent traveling with them to this place. In '58, Father headed us for Oregon, gold country. As we traveled, he found out this territory had gold of its own, and he determined to mine in Colorado instead. The trip seemed like fun to Henry and me. No school. Hardly ever a bath. Playing freely and running wild as the wagon rolled along; we did have fun, my brother and I.

But one day when we'd reached and crossed the North Platte River, Henry was riding on the wagon tongue like all the boys liked to do now and then, and our wagon hit a rock. Before you could blink an eye, he had tumbled under the wheels. He was killed instantly.

My father blamed himself, his gold fever, for his boy's death and swore he'd never mine. We broke off from the train to come this way and settle as soon as possible. Mama just couldn't bring herself to bury Henry on the trail. So Henry had a lot to do with our choice of property, set as it is between the trail and the mining camps. But it had to be farmable land.

The trick was that the western slope was Ute territory, and Father certainly didn't want trouble from them. He found this odd place in a hollow between the ridges. It's not quite western slope, but it's better farming than anything east; from the way they sit, the mountains seem to have trapped soil into this place. My father knew it was right the moment he saw it from the ridge, and so we buried Henry on the mountain, under a pile of rocks, and then we came down and became squatters on the plot of land along this stream.

Two other children died while we were in that train, but it hadn't affected the families the same way at all. Most had come from worse than poor and couldn't blame themselves for trying for something better. They all went on—some to California, some to Oregon.

And so I grew up with hard work and farming in my blood, bound and determined I would help my father. I think I was trying to replace my brother, but Father wouldn't really let me. Nevertheless, by my twenty-second year, our family had averted a series of disasters together: drought, fire, and crop-eating insects. We did well during drought, since we had first rights to the stream, thanks to "the doctrine of prior appropriation" and the fact Liam MacDonald hadn't come to our part of the territory yet. The year of the mountain fire, it only killed half our crops since it couldn't leap the stream. And we'd only seen grasshoppers once. All in all, our farm was quite a success. The only things we hadn't known were Indian attacks and disease.

But by the time I was twenty-two, it looked to my parents that I would be a spinster, for all I had in mind was to keep the farm going.

Then the fever took them both so quickly, leaving me the last of my little family. Even Aunt Betty has passed on, the last of our family back east. It occurs to me I could have ended the whole line of us this afternoon chasing that dog.

The next night, I cry silently as I prepare supper, because my hands ache with fresh blisters from hoeing the garden behind Shaw's cabin. I had never seen it before today. It stretches out in a narrow field and is larger than any kitchen garden we ever had.

Most of the plot first needed hoeing, as the ground was hard as rock from the cold.

But it isn't sorrow or self-pity that makes me cry right now —I haven't even gotten that far in my thinking—it's the raw wounds themselves, the pure pain of them. Well, I did like being out there in the sunshine for a while, but it's been a long time since I've had good, callused hands, and my arms became too tired too quickly. *Maid work has made me soft*, I think with disgust.

Oh, Lord, I feel utterly beaten down and rotten tired. I begin to chop some jarred potatoes and suddenly notice Jones is standing next to me. "I'll do that," he says. "Don't expect you'll want to cook tonight." And he just takes over and begins to make the stew. I walk to the fireplace, not quite realizing what he means, but when I touch the broom he says, "Miss Hay, *sit down...* please." And so I clean my hands and sit at the table, silent as can be, but I don't have the energy, let alone the charity, to thank him for his trouble.

Today is Friday: I've been here seven days. And now there's no time to get to Denver with the money. I am filled with self-pity, half-wondering why God has abandoned me and half angry thinking I know the answer. He must hate me. I don't want to eat my supper, but I look at Jones and he at me as he lays the stew before me, and so I quickly take a bite of each thing and then retreat to my bedroom corner. I work and work at holding my tears as I wait for them to leave.

When they finally do, I cry aloud to God for a long while. "Lord, I still don't know if you're listening, but I'm going to say this anyway. If I don't show tomorrow, they'll come looking, and that'll put Jones and Shaw in danger... and me." I wipe away the tears with the backs of my hands and try to think of something to be thankful for. "I'm thankful my parents loved me, that I'm in my childhood home. That I could enjoy the sunshine this morning and that I am well." This is the way Mama taught me to hold back my tears. But I look down at my hands, and I feel like a bird with broken wings. My hands hurt so I can't even play my music to soothe my soul.

Just then I hear a knock on the door. "Miss Hay?"

"Yes?"

"It's Jones. I need some things…" I reluctantly come out from the corner and unlatch the door.

"Come in." As he enters, I ask if I can do anything for him and push at my hair with the back of my hand to wipe a tear away.

"Have you tended to your hands?" he asks.

"No." I try to shoot him a withering glance, but instead my eyes tear from the stinging pain, for my hands hurt again from pulling up the latch.

"I'll get the balm." He takes it down from the cupboard and tells me to sit down. He rubs the balm in as gently as he can, but his rough hands make mine smart all over again. He sees me wince and says with irritation, "Well, it's your own blasted fault! Nobody asked you to work so hard!" I bow my head and begin to weep. "I'm sorry, I'm sorry," he says suddenly in a low voice. "Hush, now. I'm sorry." I bite my lip to keep myself from crying more. I look up at him, wondering at the gentleness in his voice. He keeps his head down. I am still staring at him when he is done. Without looking at me, he turns my palms up and studies my hands in his. "And I'm sorry you can't play, now," he says quietly.

I am swayed by his concern, but I don't want to feel anything at all. I pull my hands away and quickly thank him for his trouble. "What did you need?"

He looks back up at me and grins sheepishly. "Well, I came for some of your cake. I'll get it myself." He goes and gets the cake from under the bowl and cuts a piece. He sits for a little while eating. Not wanting to stare at him, I get up and warm my poor hands by the embers in the fireplace.

When I glance back at him, it's his turn to look uncomfortable. He's been watching me, and now his face becomes flushed and I look down and carefully wipe my hands on my apron.

"I made a mistake," he says suddenly.

My heart leaps with joy, and I sit up straight. "Yes, yes, you have, Mr. Jones, but it's…"

He interrupts with, "Making you work Shaw's garden. I apologize."

I make no response, but my heart has sunk to my toes.

"I didn't think you'd work yourself like a mule," he adds under his breath.

My head shoots up. "Guess you were wrong about me after all, then," I say bitterly.

"I don't know…. Some people work hard to try and make up for things they've done."

Narrowing my eyes I say, "But as you've pointed out before, it's not up to you to decide what I am or am not."

He seems to come to himself at that, and gets up and walks quickly to the door, but he pauses to add, "Well, whatever you are you don't have to go to the field tomorrow."

I look down again and nod. "You'd do a sight better to send me back to town, Mr. Jones. If Mr. MacDonald doesn't see me tomorrow, he'll…"

The door has come shut. He's gone.

I don't want to feel anything, I repeat to myself, *I just want someone to listen to me!*

That night I sit on the edge of my bed and stare mindlessly at the whitewashed wall, unbutton my muslin shirtwaist, and then pluck at the sleeves with my raw fingers to try to take it from my shoulders.

Then I see an odd thing.

Candlelight reveals a tiny crack in the chinking between the logs. It appears to be manmade. There is another crack to its left. The space between the two cracks is about the size of a brick. I reach out to tug at the thing. It is a brick and comes out easily when I pull. There behind it lies a little black leather book.

"Mama's diary!" I had forgotten it existed. I sit down on the bed again and my hands shake as they open the cover. There is my mother's beautiful handwriting in her light brown ink. I become lost in its pages as I read her entries from the early days of our homesteading: there's the very day we planted crocuses! What a love for this place she had… and for us.

As I near the harder years, a thought occurs to me. Maybe she mentions the document!

I quickly flip to the last days of entry, and the truth slowly comes clear.

It reads, *"Mr. Prue died last night and now Papa tells me he feels unwell. I told him it's the burying, but he went on about how we cannot care for the farm alone if he should die, Lord forbid. At supper he says today he went to town and has made an agreement with the hotel's owner, Liam MacDonald. Upon his death, the sale of our farm will go toward a partnership for Marilla and myself in the hotel. As God wills. We can own half interest in the inn and will be well settled then, he says. I will not tell Marilla of this, for I don't want her to be frightened for her father."*

Within a day of this last entry, Mama contracted the fever, too.

The book falls to my lap and I cry aloud for joy and then laugh a good, strong laugh. I can't stop myself laughing and crying.

Mr. Jones raps loudly at the door. "Miss Hay? You all right? What's going on in there?" he says roughly. "Open this door!"

I throw my shawl about me and bring the diary with me to the door. As I let him in, I say, smiling, "I'm quite all right. Very much all right."

He looks confused.

"My mother's diary!" I hand it to him, opened to the last entries. He reads and his eyes grow wide. He sits down on a chair with a thump and reads the last page, taking it in.

Taking in the truth.

When he is done, he looks up at me and his eyes are rimmed with tears. Quickly he looks away toward the fireplace, into the embers of the fire. "Well..." He plucks at one corner of his mustache as he stares. "Well, well..." His voice drops. "I was dead wrong about you, wasn't I?"

Now my eyes fill, too. "Mr. Jones..." I sit down in the chair next to him. "I told you once before, I am a good woman. I was... stupid to trust MacDonald, I know, but I think you can see I came by it honestly."

He looks down for a moment, nods, and then looks at me

hard, as if to say, "I had to do this, you know."

"Yes, I know you had to do this," I say confidently, and I see a corner of his mustache quiver briefly.

"And, so, I have to add 'good woman' to your... many... accomplishments?"

FIVE

ove took up the harp of life,
And smote on all the chords with might.

Old Saying

With that awkward beginning, Mr. Jones stands up and walks to the table. He seems to want to apologize again, turning back to me once, then twice, reminding me of the cat dance he did in my room at the hotel a week ago. I can think of nothing to say to ease the awkwardness, but I finally think of the one thing we can both agree on: Liam MacDonald belongs in jail.

Talking about how to best lay a trap for MacDonald and the Clark gang, Jones is visibly relieved to move to a subject he's comfortable with. Although MacDonald destroyed the bank records, Mr. Jones kept his own personal list of MacDonald's subscribers. Now for the first time, I am able to tell him about Sheriff Potter and MacDonald's ledger.

"I KNEW it!" Mr. Jones says with agitation. "I *knew* he had a safe. I figured he must hold records on his investors, and that'll back up my ledger. Man like that likes to keep something on his people. Why didn't you tell me about the ledger before?"

"I... I was embarrassed he'd thought to ruin the bank records because of my stupid attempt."

"Wasn't stupid. Dangerous maybe, but not stupid. You mighta done all right if Potter hadn't been such a skunk. Trouble is, you trust folks too much. Me? I don't trust 'em more than I can throw 'em."

"And look where it gets you, Mr. Jones," I say with irritation. "If you'd have trusted me I could have stayed in town to help you!"

99

He looks at me, looks away, and then looks at me again and smiles. "Guess you're right about that. Even if you woulda told me about the ledger and the safe, I would have figured it for a setup."

"But what did you mean when you said this thing would be over soon?"

"Oh, Denver says the Clark gang are in the territory again. They'll probably be coming around Independence anytime."

Denver. That reminds me. "Mr. Jones, I need to go to Denver for McDonald. If I don't deliver that envelope for him he'll be suspicious. He might come looking for me."

"The thousand dollars. I almost forgot. Now why would a man give you a thousand dollars to deliver when you'd just tried to get him arrested?"

"I figure it's because I'm the only one working for him who wouldn't steal it."

"Or..." His brows rise.

"Or?"

"Or, he figures you'd run off with it," he says thoughtfully.

"That's... I don't think he... I think he knows me well enough to know I wouldn't. And, remember? I told you I asked for my money back before and he just laughed at me... just laughed."

With no answer to the puzzle, we ramble into other conversation—how I came to Independence, my family, and this house. I begin a little monologue about the house, and in it I say, "You know, the black-and-white rooster's name is Rudolph, and the yellow hen is Peg..." He smiles as I add, "And I've been calling the little runt pig Jonathan Jones."

"So much to learn." His lip curls.

"I'm fibbing."

"Well, I'm bein' more than half truthful. Tell me about this place. For instance, for the last six months I've been wondering how in heaven's name you people got so many chairs? You have prayer meetings here or something?"

I smile and sigh a little, happy to be asked. "No prayer meetings." I look at him and his face tells me he really does want to know. So we begin to walk around the place, and with growing animation I tell him every little thing I can remember since we left the wagon train and built this homestead.

Jones points to the table. "And what were those handles on the sides of this table?"

"Handles... Oh. You took them off, didn't you? That was one of mother's ideas. Mama hated to do wash, so she liked everyone to use the same dinner cloth for a couple of days before she had to clean them. If they got mixed up on the table, she'd have to wash them sooner, so she asked Father to put handles at each place to hang the cloths. He thought it was a wonderful idea, because then he could move the table around more easily, and..." I catch Mr. Jones' amused look and I stop. "It sounds silly, doesn't it?"

"No-o-o. Well, yes... but useful, very useful. Think I'll put 'em back on." He grins.

I laugh a little. "My parents were an unusual pair. Mother used to say Father's specialties were husbandry and husbanding. Father used to call her 'little chick.' They were... sweet on each other." I'm embarrassed I've said so much, so I stand still for a moment, smiling at my memories. He points to something else and asks a question, and we go on.

Every once in a while, he says, "I thought so," or "Amazing," or something complimentary to Mother and Father and me. I can hardly contain myself talking about it all. It gives me the greatest sense of peace to share these things with someone.

But he doesn't want to speak much about his own past, except to say he likes what he does for a living.

"Farming or clerking?" I ask with a smile.

"Those are my only choices? I'll take farming any day."

Then we talk about the future of this town and the territories. Talk of anything and everything. At times I feel guilty to be enjoying a conversation with him—as if the seriousness of MacDonald and the problems of Independence should keep me from laughter. As if I didn't deserve to enjoy someone's company. And so now and then I sort of pinch myself to make sure it's real.

"Miss Hay?" he asks, startling me from one of those quiet moments. "Miss Hay, if you're pinching yourself to keep yourself awake, I think it must be time to retire."

I'm sure I've never turned more bright red in my life, and thank heaven there's little firelight to reveal me. "Oh, no, I... Yes, I suppose I am tired, but, no, I don't want to. I guess I should go to bed. But if you'd like to stay up..."

"Well, I would, but I can't stand to think how many pinches it'll take."

I shut my eyes firmly, trying not to give away my laughter or my embarrassment.

"Good-night, then," I say with a smile, and when I open my eyes he has the smallest smile on his face through that lovely thick mustache, and his head has bent toward me and it makes me wonder.

"Good-night." He lets out half a laugh, yawns, and stretches back in his chair. Soon he has gone and I fall back into the bed. In a twinkling it's morning.

As we greet each other over breakfast, I see that his discomfort from the night before has been replaced with a firm sense of friendship and trust. And I realize how much I've felt the burden of not being trusted and not trusting in return. Six months and more, but the burden is lifting. I want to dance around the room. But then I remember the errand to Denver. "Oh. What about my errand to Denver? What will I tell Mr. MacDonald?"

He pulls his chair forward with a screech. "You're not going to tell him anything. You're not going back."

"But, Mr. Jones, I need to see MacDonald today."

"No, you don't," he says edgily. "Don't you see it? The deputies will be here soon and we'll get MacDonald, Potter, and the whole bunch in no time."

"Yes, but if I don't show, Mr. Jones, he'll get suspicious."

"Yea... yes." He leans back in his chair. "All right," he says unhappily. "I don't like it. Shoot, no, I don't like it, but you're going to have to go back. And then you're going to have to tell MacDonald something." He thinks for a while. "Well, we can have Shaw deliver the envelope in Denver," he says finally. "It's just to a post box, and he's got to go to Denver anyway."

"Yes. That would be good." But my heart's not in my reply because I'm thinking about what the days might bring.

He is silent for a little while, as well, but then up and says, "Well, if you're going back, I'll have to check on you now and then."

I feel my cheeks grow hot at his words, but I'm forced to reply, "No, no. You know I've never had gentleman callers—good, bad, or indifferent, Mr. Jones. That would truly make him suspicious."

"Well, then I'll have to ask the Good Gentleman to check on you."

"Don't you dare! You'll scare me to death—you and your costume hat." I laugh, but then I look down and add, "Really, I'll be all right. The Lord seems to be looking after me, Mr. Jones, although I'm not certain why," I mumble.

"Please call me Jonathan."

My face feels hot once more. Mama always said first names were for lady friends and lovers. Although I know that's not as true today, I look back up at him, and his eyes, his beautiful green eyes, are looking at me with... *Don't be silly, Marilla. He hardly knows you.* I shift in my seat. "Well, somehow I need to come to town by coach, don't I... Jonathan?"

"Right. By coach." He looks down and away and clears his throat. "And I need to see Shaw." He then excuses himself to go next door.

I watch him leave and a feeling of joy and fear interwoven wells up in me. I fold my hands on the table and then clutch them together nervously. I will get to know Jones better; I know I will. I feel the bond between us and am glad for it.

He must have explained my status to Mr. Shaw as they walked back. Mr. Shaw, as quiet as ever, draws out half a smile for me as he enters. Then he pulls off his hat and holds it to his chest. "I'm sorry, ma'am," he says. With an even greater effort he adds, "Sorry... for the... rough time we gave you. I... want to thank you for your work."

I don't know quite what to say, so out comes, "You are welcome," rather flatly. But I think, *And how sorry would you be if you'd shot me?*

Even as the thought occurs to me, Shaw says, "And I'm sorry 'bout leveling my gun at you... but I got to tell you... it weren't ever loaded." Both men look at me carefully, not quite sure how I'll take the news.

The anger I've begun to entertain falls away as I trip over his words. "Not loaded!" I sputter and then say with a grin, "Well, hey, just what kind of vigilantes are you boys anyway?"

Jones begins to smile and they look at each other. "The gentle vigilantes, of course," Jones says in a sweet high-pitched voice, and Shaw whacks him in the side.

I look at Jonathan. "And I suppose you don't kill little pets as a side interest?"

"No." And he straightens up to add, "I happen to like puppies." He pulls on his nose for a stray second, then, "Suppose we three need to keep things honest between us from here on out, 'cause we've made a proper ship of fools so far."

Shaw and I nod and I smile.

With things finally straightened out, we then work out a plan for me to get back to town. We decide I'll catch the Denver coach at Nichol's Fork about an hour's ride from here. Shaw will ride me to the fork on his way to Denver with the diary. They figure the diary will be proof to bring local charges against MacDonald, as well.

A ride to Denver takes about eight hours by horseback, and, this being Saturday, Shaw won't make it back until Sunday. Jonathan will go to work as usual. Then he points out that we have to wait for the Clark gang to show, so the deputies will need to hide out here at the cabin until Jonathan can tell them the gang has arrived.

"I can tell you when the Clark boys come," I pipe up.

"NO!" comes out of Jonathan faster than a blink.

"But... but I could tell you secretly!" I begin. "I could..." I hesitate as I think of a way. "Here, I could drape my shawl... this shawl... in my window." And I pull the paisley shawl from the back of the chair.

"Well," Jonathan says grudgingly, "that'd be harmless enough, I guess." Shaw reluctantly agrees. Then Jonathan adds, "Just you stay low after you've given the sign, all right?"

"Oh, yes." I laugh. "I know how to stay low."

The joke isn't lost on him and he grins and shakes his head.

Mr. Shaw suddenly glances up at Jones. "Jones, what'll become of Lillian?"

My eyes widen at the oddity of the question.

"Well... she's not an investor, but she'll be needed as a witness."

Shaw gathers his eyebrows in a dark cloud and goes into a long silence.

"Mr. Shaw, do you mean Lillian Wirsching?" I ask innocently. He continues to stare at the table. "May I ask why you..."

He quickly stands up, makes fists with his hands, and then lets out a sigh. "Tell her if you want, Jones. I ain't gonna bother with it." And he walks out.

I stare at Jonathan as Shaw leaves, full ready for an explanation.

Jonathan turns to me. "What's your *honest* opinion of Lillian?"

"Honest? Well, she's... she's a cold sort. All bitterness. All lemon juice and fish scales, and I always imagined it was MacDonald's fault she was that way... and that I'd be like her in a few years." I think for a moment. "No, wait, but she's not all bitter. Just the other day when she told me to see MacDonald, she told me to be careful. I thought that odd coming from her."

"No, Miss Hay, she's not all bitterness, at least she wasn't. Fact is, she and Shaw know each other... came in on the same wagon train. Coming separate as they did, and Shaw knowing he needed a helpmate, they hooked up with each other and decided to marry when they arrived."

"Marry?" I try to imagine Shaw and Lillian together. I can, but it's not a pretty picture.

"Yea, but something happened. She got sick on the trip. Day before they got to Independence, rumor had it she was with child."

I was beginning to understand the bitter root.

"He took off right after that, and never spoke to her again."

"But does he love her?"

He shrugs. "You tell me, Miss Hay."

I think back at the hurt in Shaw's eyes as he asked after her. "Ah. Yes, he does. But, Lillian… she doesn't have a child."

"Guess a man's pride does funny things sometimes."

I think on that story later as Shaw and I ride together to Nichol's Fork. Try as I may to broach the subject, I know it can't be done. And I'll probably never be able to speak to Miss Wirsching on it either. When we finally arrive at the Fork, I dismount and smile brightly at Mr. Shaw and thank him.

He cocks his head and lets out a half grin.

"Your father ever teach you how to use a gun?"

"Not Father—Mama did, though."

"Well, good, 'cause Jones thought you might need this." And he pulls out a hefty Colt. "It's a single action… called a Peacemaker," he says by explanation, as if I know what he is talking about.

"But I know how to use a rifle, not this Peacemaker."

"Well, it's got a similar kick, small as it is."

"Funny name," I say quietly. It doesn't look so very small to me. I just stare at it as he holds it out for me to take.

He sees my hesitation. "Well you don't have to use it. I've found pointing a gun is just as effective at times."

"That's true." I stare at the barrel and wipe my hands on my skirts. Guns make me nervous.

I reach out for it delicately, and he hands me the heavy gun and a soft leather bag of cartridges. "Know how to load it?" he asks. I shake my head, and he deftly demonstrates the technique and then holds the bag and gun out once more.

"Oh, Mr. Shaw. Really I don't think I should take it. What if, what if…" All sorts of horrible accidents are forming in my mind's eye.

"Just self-defense, Miss Hay. You really should have had one a long time ago, living where you do." His horse steps side to side impatiently there in the heat.

I give in and take it from him.

Then he tips his hat and rides off.

I timidly wrap the gun and bullets up in my things and place them in my bag, hoping I'll never have to use them.

The coach comes in a few hours and the driver, a slightly dusty man by the name of Hale, gives me a strange look as I reach up for the door handle.

"Good thing we come along, eh, Miss Hay?" he questions.

"Yes, sir, Mr. Hale. Thank you, but I didn't wait long." I step up and in and keep my eyes to myself as I sit down.

The coach starts off and soon settles into its rickety, bumpy sway, and when I finally do look up, the gentleman straight ahead is staring at me. A shock goes through me as I recognize Noonan, one of MacDonald's own, and my blood runs cold. "Good afternoon, Mr. Noonan," I say as calmly as I can.

He looks at me a while longer. "Af-ter-noon," he drawls like he's thinking on it. Noonan is skinny in the arms, fat around the belt, and squinty-eyed, with sharp points of unwashed hair stuck on top of his head, just as I imagine a rat might look if he ran to six feet tall.

I quickly glance at the other passengers. Sitting to Noonan's right is a rather handsome fellow with dark hair, dark eyes, and a plain black suit. A pleasant smile greets me from his well-formed lips and I quickly look away. A lady sits at my right. *The fellow's wife*, I decide. A plump little sausage in pale blue with a kind look. We nod a greeting toward each other.

The fellow dressed in black begins to speak to me. "Miss, you know this fellow?" He grins and nods toward Noonan.

Noonan flashes him an evil look.

"Yes, sir." I gulp and look again at the man. Striking eyes, large and brown, thick wavy hair combed back and lying on his collar. Quite pleasant to look at but must not be too clever, for he's picked a poor fellow to joke with.

Crossing his arms, the stranger says in a jolly tone, "Well, he was just telling me a while back he'd shoot me if I spoke any further on the gospel, the good news of our Lord Jesus Christ." Noonan is looking angrier and angrier as the man continues. "Madam, do you think this gentleman capable of shooting me for such a reason?"

Noonan isn't laughing. He is, however, interested in my reply and watches me intently, his hands planted on his bony knees.

I glance at the now frightened look of the woman next to me and then look back to the new fellow. "Yes, sir. He's quite capable of shooting you for such a reason." I lower my voice to add, "Reason will have little to do with it."

The preacher is still smiling, but as I finish, he clears his throat. "Thank you," he says briskly from lips that seem a shade paler.

Then Noonan smiles, lets a good spit out the window, and pulls his hat over his eyes in satisfaction as the preacher begins to stare out his own window.

And we bump along uncomfortably like this all the way to Independence. I begin to perspire thinking about what Noonan will tell MacDonald. When we finally arrive, my clothes are wet with perspiration, for I can think of no reason to let go of my worries. My final concern is for what I will say to MacDonald if he asks me any questions.

My worst fears are realized when I see Noonan head straight for MacDonald's office door in the lobby, giving me a backward glance with those little black eyes. I groan, but then I shake myself. *Well, of course, he always checks in with MacDonald. Don't make too much of this, girl.* I walk into the hotel and wait by the same door for Noonan to be done.

I can hear Noonan and MacDonald discussing somebody being shot here the other night. I stand away a little. I don't want to know.

As I wait, the handsome fellow from the coach comes up to

our reception desk, but where's his wife? I look to the front window and see the little woman being greeted by friends. She begins to walk with them to their open wagon.

So, he's not married, I think to myself absentmindedly, but then I hear MacDonald's voice.

"Marilla's back?"

He sounds surprised, and I think briefly maybe Jonathan was right. "Mr. MacDonald?" I say, meaning to announce myself.

"Yeah?" I open the door with a trembling hand, and he shakes his head in unbelief. "So... you deliver it?"

"Yes, sir." *Lord, give me the words to speak.*

He scratches his beard. "Know what it was?" he asks nonchalantly.

I tense. "Yes, sir."

He looks at me with wide eyes. "Well, you're just a good little girl, ain'tcha?" And he lets out a laugh.

I nod blandly.

"So, what were you doin' at Nichol's Fork?"

"I rode with a couple from Denver and helped the woman care for her sick child, but they went off west there." It sounds fairly believable as I spill it out; please, let him believe me.

"Then you tell me why nobody saw you get on the 7 A.M. to Denver last week."

The words shock me so, I stare past MacDonald to the animal skins on the wall. I'm sure my face has gone deathly pale as I struggle to think up an answer. Animal skins. I focus my eyes back to MacDonald. "I'm sorry, Mr. MacDonald. I'm so tired. What did you just ask me, sir?"

"I asked how in blazes you got to Denver, since my horse and wagon are still at the livery..."

"Well..." I try to smile. "It was the horse, actually, that made me miss the coach in front of the hotel. I went down to check on him before I left and then I caught the stage at the end of town."

He smiled his thinnest smile. "You better watch where you're stepping. I've got my eye on you, Marilla."

I nod uncertainly.

"Well, go on then!" And he waves his hand for me to go and shakes his head as I back quickly out.

I close the door with a trembling hand, and relief begins to flow out of every limb in my weary body. I head for my room up the main stairs, but as I make my way up, Mary Baylor is coming down, and she pulls me aside. "Welcome home, honey," she says with a sad smile.

Her perfume almost wakes me up, but still I suppress a yawn. "Thank you, sweet Mary."

She pulls my arm closer in and her smile fades. "I heard what you tried to do. Everybody has, an' you're lucky you weren't killed tryin' it. The next time you do something like that, ask my advice, would you? I could have told you all about Potter."

Potter! I want to laugh and then cry at her words, but in light of how tired I am, I can only yawn again.

"Hey, now..." Her voice grows hushed. "You look as if you haven't slept for a week." Her quick assessment makes me blush all over, and she pulls my arm closer. "Good for you, honey, you needed some fun. I hope it was fun."

"Oh, Mary." I can't explain a thing now and tiredness is creeping all over me. "I have to go to sleep."

"By all means!" She smiles widely as I turn to climb the stairs.

She'll understand sometime soon, I console myself. When I reach the top landing, I go into my little room and collapse on the bed, too tired to think, too tired to...

"MISS HAY!" I awake with a start as the sharp voice pierces my door.

"Yes, Miss Wirsching."

"Get up, girl, it's past six. Don't laze about."

"Yes, ma'am."

I roll out of bed and stare out the window before I can really believe it's morning! I've slept all afternoon and night? Good heavens.

I quickly look at myself in the mirror, then throw off my things and put on my work clothes. I couldn't even bring back the work clothes I used at the cabin. Horrible. To be there so long and still not bring something with me.

As I dress, I think back on those seven days. It's not true. I did bring something with me. *What strange and wonderful, hard days they were, Jonathan Jones.* My hands are still sore as I wrestle with my buttons, but I smile anyway. I open the door and walk out to find Miss Wirsching standing two doors down.

Again it's hard to look her in the eye, but today it's for a different reason. I know someone loves her—a carriage ride away can be found a man that loves this woman— and so I see her differently now. The edge in my voice is gone as I speak to her.

By the end of the day, she asks if something is wrong, just as she did eight days ago.

If I lie, she'll know it. "Yes," I admit.

She looks at me awhile and I hold my breath. "Well, I knew it," she simply says and walks away.

What a strange reply. But on reflection I think it isn't so strange. It's just what you'd say if, *what?* If you're defeated and beaten down. She doesn't care about anything anymore. *I wish he'd give her another chance.*

When my work is done, I go to the kitchen for dinner and find Mary.

I smile at her over the stove, but she gives me a cold look and draws me aside. "See here, girl, I've been thinking on it. What do you mean giving yourself away like a... *You* always told me you were gonna hold out for *true love.*" Her eyes are flashing, and at first I'm a little stunned by the change in her attitude.

Mrs. Philipus Reed is trying hard to overhear. The ample woman with the smooth, reddish face loves to gather gossip and then fling it far and wide like seed. I believe she enjoys this more than her chosen profession, possibly more than the obvious pleasure she derives from yelling at the help.

I draw Mary to the table as a little righteous anger rises up in me at her words. *There's no harm in telling her what happened,* I think, *as long as I leave out the details!* "Look here, Mary," I whisper. "I haven't been with a gentleman the way you think. We spent time together, and we stayed up talking the last evening. That's all."

We stare each other down for a while, and then her voice is soft as she says, "Leave it to you to find a man who'd just want to talk all night, Marilla." And she smiles.

"Is that a veiled insult, Mary?"

She continues to smile. "I'll tell you after I've seen the man," she answers cattily, and I can feel my face grow red. At that, we sit down to eat. "So tell me all about it, eh?" she immediately asks.

I'm afraid to begin—afraid I'll say too much. "It's done—over with. I don't want to talk about it." Besides, Mrs. Reed keeps finding reasons to come stand over us, getting things from the wall shelf, undeniably leaning in to try and listen.

But Mary waits patiently. Mrs. Reed works at the shelf slowly. I almost laugh as she finally lets out a little sigh and waddles back to the stove.

"You stayed up talking all night with a man and then tell me it's over? Marilla, you're a liar."

I feel myself blush once more and I drop my head. "It wasn't all night." More silence.

"All right, tell me when you can," Mary says. "I'll wait." And she winks at me.

I smile back at her. "Thank you." In a bit, I ask her how she knew about my taking the ledger.

"Anybody who wants to know knows it by now. Was all the talk the first couple of days you were gone, 'cause MacDonald was so proud of himself."

Anybody? That'll be everybody. The next few days will be harder than I thought.

That night I retire to my room to think over the last few days and sort things out. There's so much ahead.

I lie awake, my mind running at full tilt through the horrible possibilities the days may bring. I begin to dream in fitful starts: gunshots, running, MacDonald's beady little eyes staring me down, but then my parents' cabin, the fireplace. Then an even sweeter dream: Mr. Jones and I sitting on a cozy porch, and he's telling me to listen to him, and he's drawing me near and I can't hear him and I want things to be quiet so that Jonathan can tell me, and I am being drawn awake to realize there is a tapping on my side window. I throw my face forward and begin to shake. Someone's on the porch roof tapping at my window.

It must be Jonathan.

I drag a blanket about me as I pull myself up, then I toss my braid over my shoulder, brush the stray hair from my face, and walk over and push up the side window.

But no one is there.

I poke my head out to look around the roof, but I don't see a thing. "Oh," I say in a disappointed tone. I wanted it to be Jonathan so badly I've imagined it all.

A rattle to my left makes me jump such that my head hits the window sash. "Miss Hay?" someone whispers.

"Ow. Yes?" I rub my head and feel fresh humiliation along with a familiar pain. Apparently, Jonathan was almost gone but must have heard me finally open the window. He walks in a crouch back toward my window in his long coat and dark hat.

"Hurt as much as last time?" He smiles.

"I told you you'd frighten me to death."

He coughs into his fist. "Shaw's back from Denver," he whispers. "Bad news is they could only spare two men. I'll have to drum up some more help from town and that'll take some time."

A vision of the hanging pole at Cherry Creek sails into view. Oh. Oh, no. "You... you wouldn't start a vigilante committee, would you?"

He looks at me and wags his head. "No. I told you before. We're all just going by the book. The Denver men are deputies, for heaven's sake."

"So?"

"Look, I can't explain now, but it's not like that anymore." He looks around. "I hope the gang gets here soon. I don't like this waiting. And I'll keep looking for your shawl in the window. Got to go." He wheels around on one boot and then wheels back. "And if you think there's anything to worry about, you come to the bank and nod to me two times—once if everything's all right, but twice if something's up?"

"A good idea. Yes, I will. Mr. Jones... Jonathan... you be careful, now won't you?"

"Aw, we *gentle* vigilantes are oh so careful, Miss Hay. Wouldn't want to hurt ourselves," he says in a playful whine.

"Please, I'm quite serious."

He is quiet for a moment then whispers, "Well, all I can tell you is it would be a shame if I died now... a real shame." He is looking at me again through the darkness and smiling as his voice trails away, and I am looking at him in quiet empathy and smiling back. He says a quick, "So long, now." And just as quickly he is gone.

SIX

The way we got them out was to go along the
gulches and tell the people in their cabins and
saloons where the preaching would be at night, and
then, just before the time, to step to the door where
they were at cards and say, "My friends, can't you
close your game in ten minutes, and come and hear
preaching?"

From the book *Snow-Shoe Itinerant,*
by John L. Dyer, Methodist Circuit
Preacher of the Colorado Territory

Early the next morning I am performing my usual duty of
waiting for Lillian Wirsching in the lobby. I am reading the
usual copy of *The Rocky Mountain News* that has been lying here
for two months, once more looking over the article on crop-rota-
tion, which I can by now quote verbatim.

I hear a cough. I look up to see before me the face of Billy
Snead, the reception desk man. He's a wiry fellow in his forties
whose glasses are always set at a precarious rest on the tip of his
sharp nose, lending him the air of a scholar. I am never fooled.

"Miss Hay?"

"Mr. Snead?" I say carefully. Somehow I always expect him to
reply, *Gesundheit.*

"Did you really take the ledger to Potter?"

I am surprised at the question, but I realize I have nothing to
fear from him. "Yes, Mr. Snead, I did."

"Really." I am now expecting to hear, "Good show," or "Too
bad it didn't work," but he surprises me with, "Thought you
mighta had better sense." And he walks back to his desk.

I see. That's probably the way everyone sees it. *And why should it surprise me?* It is this very attitude that makes people like Liam MacDonald possible, and suddenly I'm incredibly angry.

As I sit there and fume, I also realize not a little of my pride has been hurt by the remark, as well. I suppose I expected someone to think I was a hero, to thank me for risking my life. Instead, I've taken my reputation all the way from "naive" to "plain stupid."

No. Truly stupid is to care what Billy Snead thinks of me, and so I will stop worrying about *that* right now.

As I stare at the wall trying to think better thoughts, I catch bits of a conversation that force me to prick up my ears and listen: two fellows out on the porch are laughing about the fact that there's a preacher here who wants to hold a meeting in town tonight.

Lillian comes soon and gives me my list. When she's done, I scurry over to the kitchen to ask Mrs. Reed for information about the preacher, assuming it's the fellow I saw on the stagecoach. Mrs. Reed always knows what's going on in town.

She tells me his name is Matthew Post, and he's tacked handwritten signs up and down the street about his meeting tonight at Swan's Boarding House.

I ask if he is the fellow staying at our hotel.

"Well, guess he *was*," she replies. "MacDonald told him to get out when he found out he was a preacher. Noonan threw his bags right out in the street."

Mrs. Reed's assistant, Emma, her gaunt face cracking open with a wide smile, says with a cackle, "He oughter be used to that kind of treatment out here."

Mrs. Reed decides to agree with her—just for the novelty of it, I suppose. "Yeah. Can't remember when we last had a preacher."

"Sometime when I was a child, I think." I stare at my shoes absentmindedly.

Emma agrees. "I 'member. That was that feller who up and quit and struck out for gold." I look up at her. I hadn't remembered that... more likely I was never told. "Decided he was gonna store up them treasures on earth." She laughs a strong laugh. I draw my eyes away from her large, toothless grin to excuse myself.

But as I turn away, Mrs. Reed points her butcher knife toward me. "You better watch yourself, Missy," she says, "or MacDonald's gonna turn you out like that preacher man." Immediately Emma joins in the heckling. I don't want to hear the rest, and so I step out quickly, wishing I hadn't asked.

As I head back to clean the last of the hotel rooms, I think, *Too bad the Reverend can't wait a few more days; his job will be a lot easier when they have MacDonald and his men in jail.* And I let out a slight whistle.

I want to lie low and not involve myself in anything, but I also want to go to the meeting. The fellow was so cheerful. He's probably a good speaker. I certainly need cheering, but I'm afraid to go alone.

And so that night, over supper, I up and ask Mary to come with me.

She balks at the question. "Have you lost your mind, Marilla? I wouldn't be caught dead there."

I try to think of something that could convince her. "You sure would shock some people, Mary," I say slyly.

She smiles a half smile and then shakes her head. "No, I don't need that. No preacher's gonna tell me how to live. I've heard it all before. They don't know nothin' about what I've been through in this life."

"But you haven't given him a chance, Mary. He could be different."

"Well, you let me know."

The last resort presents itself to my mind. "Mary, hands down, he is the handsomest man I've ever seen!"

Mary lets her mouth fall open and begins to lazily scratch her lip. "You mean... he's got all his teeth?"

We both let out a chuckle.

"Tall, dark, and handsome. You know I never lie to you, sweet Mary."

Almost to herself, she says, "I'd put on a good show for the ladies, wouldn't I?" She smiles impishly. "Besides... chances are I'll see him sooner or later."

I feel myself blush at the implication and shake my head. "I don't think so, Mary."

"Oh, as if you know anything about men."

"Mary," I say slowly as I lower my eyes. "Truth is, I'm afraid to go by myself."

She bats her eyes at me once or twice in thought. "Oh, all right," she says finally.

So now I am walking to the meeting with Mary Baylor. I smile and shake my head as we walk along.

Never one to err on the side of subtlety, she is wearing her best (and lowest-cut) visiting gown: the one of blue velvet. Her black hair holds a bright white plume, and held loosely at her shoulders is a shawl begging to be stared at: row after row of downy white ostrich feathers have been sewn upon it. They sway and flutter with her slightest motion.

It has rained all day, and the lamp lights from the open establishments send shimmers of light into the little pools along the street, such that even the clapboard buildings seem to sparkle. The town looks rather dreamlike at this moment, and I am enjoying its temporal beauty as I step slowly and carefully along the way. Mary, long used to this streetscape, practically floats along the road and yet does not appear to gather one drop of mud on her expensive hem.

The Swan is just a little ways down Liberty.

As we pass one saloon, a man steps out on unsteady feet, and Mary and I instinctively make our way to the other side of the road. My blood freezes as I realize it's Sheriff Potter. He looks our way, and I hold my breath as we move quickly along, but I soon realize that, inebriated as he is, he barely grasps the knowledge that we are, in fact, women, let alone ones he might wish to bother.

I can't believe I once trusted Potter, and I can't believe I tried such a stupid thing with the ledger without speaking more to

Mary. The more I think about it, the more irritated I am with myself.

As we enter the lobby, we see about ten people—mostly women—gathered at the wide front desk, and they are looking a little lost. No one knows quite what to expect, least of all me. Mary has her reward for her efforts as some let out a gasp as she enters. But soon Reverend Post appears and ushers the little crowd into a dining hall. He smiles broadly and nods as I pass him at the door.

It is honestly hard not to stare at him. I look back at Mary to see she is enjoying her view.

Some take chairs, but a few remain standing, ready to bolt out the door if necessary.

Post seems to notice the apprehension on everyone's face, so he quickly introduces himself and immediately states his credentials. He says he had just been graduated from an eastern seminary when he felt a calling to come west to preach the gospel. Reverend Sheldon Jackson sent him out personally. He would like to establish a Presbyterian church here and in a couple of towns nearby to which he could circulate during the week. He then asks if we think Independence would like a church.

I and three or four others nod, some more vigorously than others.

He smiles broadly. "The Scripture says that where two or more of you are gathered, He is there in your midst, so I suppose we make a heavenly quorum."

I smile and Mary smiles, but no one else seems to appreciate his humor.

"Unless you're planning to take us for a ride, like that fella in Sedalia," comes a coarse voice from the back of the room. Mary looks at me in question and I whisper, "Circuit preacher—took the church building money and ran." She snickers and turns back.

Reverend Post answers the question by briskly stating the boarding house dining hall is fine with him and that a church is not built with hands, but hearts.

"Good," another fellow in the back calls out. "We work hard enough as is." A couple of fellows laugh.

"Yeah," another one agrees. "How strong's yer heart, Rev?" A few more laughs drift forward.

But the Reverend laughs good-naturedly, and to everyone's surprise he straightway works his reply into a message. He begins to speak of the life of Jesus and its similarity to the rough life we live in the territory. No one interrupts him after he gets going.

At first I have trouble concentrating on the sermon. Watching his face is like staring into the light of a beautiful gemstone, a diamond perhaps, and as his head moves with the animation of his speech, it is as though the stone is being turned before my eyes. His beauty is mesmerizing.

I finally make myself look away so I can keep my mind on the subject matter.

I hear him begin a story to illustrate a point.

Two boys trying to find something to do on a summer's afternoon came across a tall stone mill that had been only half-burned out during the war. The boys, twelve and eight, decided to climb way high up to the fourth floor and walk across the blackened ridge pole to test their skills.

Halfway across the timber, the pole gave way. The older boy fell first and grabbed hold of the younger boy's feet as they made their descent. The younger grabbed what was left of the fallen ridge pole and almost lost his grip as his brother's weight pulled at his feet.

And there they hung way high above the cold, hard ground. Blackened timbers and loose stones waited fifty feet below. Swinging. Swinging.

The younger boy was just strong enough to hold on for dear life to what was left of the beam, but he was not strong enough to pull himself up with the older brother hanging below him.

They struggled this way a few moments when the older boy asked his brother in a cheerful voice, "Hey, Ezra, bet you couldn't make it back up even if I weren't hangin' on."

Without thinking, his brother replied, "Why, sure I could."

"Then, God bless you, Ez," the older brother said. "Good-bye." And he let go of his brother's feet. He did not survive the fall.

Here Reverend Post pauses, and around the whole room not one sound is heard.

In a moment he continues, "My friends, this is a true story. I rode through that town a year later and called on folks to be saved, and young Ezra Book presented himself immediately. He stood up and told the congregation the story of his brother and added he didn't need to hear more about how Christ came to die for him. His brother had provided a perfect example of that story, and he was ready to give himself to God."

And then Matthew Post goes on like a wave overtaking the shore, speaking of Jesus as if he's seen him, touched him, as if he walks with him, as if he *knows* him. "I don't believe any man here would disagree that that little boy who died for the sake of his brother was as brave as any full-grown man facing a band of hired guns..." He pauses again. "And if you can see that, you can understand how much courage it took for Jesus Christ to die for us, that it takes more courage to love another human being than to do anything else under the sun. *Anything.* Do you see it? And it's also true that it takes more courage to walk down the street with Jesus Christ as your master than to face a row of hired guns." All is quiet as he lets the words sink in. Then he leans toward us. "Difference is," he whispers, "He'll be with you. He will make you strong."

As he speaks, a longing wells up in me to want to be like that: knowing He's always with me.

Then Post straightens up. "If you'll confess your sin to God and ask Christ to enter your heart, to live in you and change you into His image, He will come to you. And don't think to impress Him with your sins." A few men chuckle. "Because He's heard it all, brothers and sisters. He just wants to give you the courage to walk away from what you've known is wrong." I like the sound of it, the simplicity of it, and the words go straight to my heart.

But suddenly I don't want to pray.

I think on it more and realize I've been enjoying my sin, this strong burning wish for revenge on Liam MacDonald, a feeling so strong I can taste the salt and vinegar of it.

I can't love my neighbor. I work too hard at hating him with my very being.

I begin to fiddle with the fringe of my cloak.

I don't want to sit here anymore.

I look over at Mary and am struck by her rapt attention to his speech. *Probably admiring his face, as I was a moment ago,* I think sarcastically.

No, I can't bring Christ into my heart. Post can start a church here if he likes. It will be good for the town, a good influence, but I can take care of myself.

I look at Mary's face to try to get her attention to tell her I'm going, but suddenly a worry comes to me. Mary plays such a dangerous game. She's going to get caught someday. If the Clark boys ever find out she takes their money, they'll kill her.

I'm suddenly struck with a desire to pray for her. No, I don't need God, but she certainly does. I look back at the preacher and grate my teeth along my lower lip. As Post continues, I shut my eyes and begin. First I pray for Mary—for her safety—and then for Jonathan, and then... I feel a tingle in my body that begins in my toes and wells up within me as I realize with a shock that I am not speaking to the air.

I am addressing the Lord God, the Creator, my Creator, and He is... *listening.* This sense—no, not a sense—a *knowledge* of the reality of Him, a God who would listen to the forlorn prayer of a Marilla Hay, overwhelms me.

I place my back firmly against the seat, for I fear I'll fall if I don't steady myself. Tears are beginning to stream down my cheeks, and I pray earnestly—so earnestly—that I would come to know Him and be willing to do all that He asks of me. To know that He is, that His Son came to die for me, makes the bitterness in my heart just melt away. The anger I've felt over my parents' death, the rage I've felt toward Liam MacDonald—slip from me like leaves rushing down a fast stream. They are gone.

And then a great peace washes over me, and I am filled with the knowledge of God's love for me. I am not alone.

As Post's talk ends, he encourages anyone who would stay and pray with him. I quickly wipe my eyes and sniff. Although I am happy for the newness I am feeling, somehow I can't really stay. I squeeze Mary's hand and slip out.

As I return to the hotel and observe the glowing lights of Independence and the bustle and hubbub of the street, I see that physically it is the same, but I am seeing it differently. I am completely different. I know God loves me. He forgives me. I am new. And I am not afraid.

Like the wonder the first explorers must have felt when they discovered the earth was not flat but round, I have grasped a new view of my world. I am amazed by it. In my joy, I find myself praying again: now for Shaw, for Lillian Wirsching, even Liam MacDonald! I pray the men from Denver can do their job well and do it soon!

I go to sleep smiling and I wake up the next morning smiling because I finally know I can face whatever comes. No need to walk this world alone.

Late in the afternoon, Liam MacDonald asks me to make a deposit for him at the bank. I can see Jonathan! I hide my eagerness as best I can and then make my way to First Independence.

A light snow is falling as I maneuver down the road toward the bank. Just enough cold in the snow to make the sandy mud a little thicker, but even as I plod along and almost despair of making it across the street, still I can't help feeling elated. I don't care what the weather does. I'm going to see Jonathan. I think how I will nod and smile at him—only once—to let him know I'm all right.

I enter the bank's warm lobby and head to my left. He is there behind the bars, and I come stand behind a short fellow and stare at Jonathan over the man's shoulder. He doesn't see me, but I'm glad, for I'm looking at his face, the twitch of his mustache, his eyes. He is not a diamond, but then I've never wanted a diamond. I smile as I finally slip up to the bars. His head is still down.

"Good afternoon, Mr. Jones," I say timidly, and as he lifts his eyes I nod and smile—once—and he fairly beams.

"Miss Hay. In for a deposit?" he says in a whining voice that gives me a start and makes me look again. Ah, yes, it's the timid Mr. Jones.

"Yes, sir." I wish I could just speak with him.

"Did you enjoy Reverend Post's talk the other night?" he asks. I look at him quizzically. "I was there at the back, but you slipped out at the end, didn't you?"

"Yes." Others are standing around us, so I simply say, "It will be so nice to have a church here." And he agrees. I want to ask him what he thought and tell him its effect on me. I want to speak freely like the last night at the farm! But now is not the time, and I have to go.

As I take my leave, he admonishes me to double-check my deposit slip to make sure it is correct. This is in character with the slightly patronizing Mr. Jones the town knows, but not with the fellow I've begun to know, and I look at the slip while leaving. A note is written on the back.

I rush back to my room to read the message. "Need a shawl," it says simply, and my heart thumps to think the time is coming.

I realize his information is correct when, after supper, I see a gang member head upstairs. I go quietly to my room, place my standing lamp nearer my window, and dress it with the proper signal: my paisley shawl.

And then I pray, and I wait. For the first time, I do both with utter confidence.

SEVEN

How happy am I when I crawl into bed,
With a rattlesnake rattlin' just under my head,
And a gay little centipede, without any fear,
Crawls over my pillow and into my ear.

From the song,
Lane County Bachelor

The next morning I am busy with my duties again, but with the unknown weighing heavily on my mind I've determined to high-tail it to my room at the first sign of trouble.

Early afternoon creeps on but still nothing. I don't see Liam MacDonald anywhere. I decide not to ask anyone for fear of raising suspicion. I figure he can't have been taken by the deputies because the gang is still here. In fact, they are making a horrible caterwaul in the bar; you can't miss them. *You can't miss them, Mr. Jones, Mr. Shaw. Where are you?* I think anxiously as I clean each room. I continue to pray, but my earlier confidence is being sorely tested.

I've left for last the rooms the gang usually stay in. I'm afraid to go in them. I'm afraid one of them will come along, and I'm not sure I can feign calmness. My hands are already shaking and there isn't even anyone up here.

I make myself go into the first room, number 13, and I clean it up in record time. I've heard them joke about taking the unlucky room number. "Anybody'd be unlucky to run into us," I heard Tucker Clark say once. *Thank heaven I'm done here*, I think as I step out. "And one to go," I whisper and plunge into the work in number 14.

I'm almost done here, too, when the door suddenly swings opens. My stomach lurches as I whirl around.

It's Lillian. I breathe a sigh of relief and she stares at me oddly. "What can I do for you?" I ask as I catch my breath.

"Just checking the rooms," she says coolly, continuing to observe me.

"Of course. Well, I'm all done."

She crosses her arms, leans up against the door frame and her eyes burn into mine. "Tucker told me the other day he thinks somebody's been at their money bags."

I go pale and my back stiffens.

"You've been acting very odd, Marilla."

She wouldn't do this to me, would she? "Lillian, it isn't me. I swear it isn't."

She stares at me with her cold eyes. "If people want to die, there's a lot a ways to go. Lotsa ways—and easier ways—to go than this."

I nod and gulp hard, but I tell myself quickly if ever there was a time in my life to put on a good act, this is it. I fumble and say, "I may be ignorant, Miss Wirsching, but I'm not so stupid as to take their money. No." My face is surely bright red now, and with a thoroughly unconvincing laugh I say, "It's more likely Tucker just doesn't know how to count."

"Marilla, I just want you to stop." She turns and walks out.

I can't believe what I'm hearing. Beyond the humiliation of the moment I see that perhaps, just perhaps, the woman does have a soul. I thought she was going to turn me in for stealing, but that wasn't the way of it at all! She's actually trying to protect me. *Thank you, Lord.*

I walk back to my room slowly, and I sit on my bed for a long while wondering if I could have been so wrong about Lillian. Have I ever been right about anyone? I suppose if I think on it long enough it's true even Liam MacDonald could repent and be saved. He could. The bitter wishes I once held for revenge on the man become pitifully meaningless when I think of God's mercy— all encompassing, all loving. Beyond my understanding.

Although those thoughts consume me for a time, I realize it is now late afternoon and still I've heard nothing from Jonathan. A host of anxieties begin to play havoc with my senses. What if they've been found out? The gang is here and it's not working. Why haven't I heard anything? I get the deep impression something is wrong and I can't shake the feeling even when I pray.

By four o'clock, I've reached my limit. I decide to risk telling Mary everything; she's the only one I can trust and, coincidentally, the only one who might actually be able to help.

I come down the back stair, step lightly down the hall, and poke my head in the bar door. She's at the other end of the aisle, so I walk nonchalantly toward her. "Mary!" I whisper.

She sees me, but just then I'm being turned around in place by a strong hand.

"Where you been hiding, sugar pie?" the fellow asks, his bloodshot eyes taking in my form.

Quick as a flash, Mary brusquely pushes me back toward the door and starts talking at the fellow. "If you're not a good boy, I'm gonna show you where I hide my gun, Sam. Now go set yourself down over there and let Alice get you a drink. That girl don't work here." He blinks at her once or twice while she's talking, obviously trying to decide whether to get angry or give in, so Mary adds, "Tell you what, the drink's on me. That all right?" He smiles at that and moves to the table.

I am peeking at this from the door. "Thank you!" I say as she comes around to the back.

"What's the matter, honey?"

"I've got to tell you something." I look around to see if anyone is in the back hall. It's empty. "Mary, oh, Mary, please come to my room and let me explain." I'm shaking again.

"All right. Let me tell Alice to take the bar."

Soon we are in my room. I take her hand and drag her over to sit on the bed. "Do you know where MacDonald is?" I ask her outright.

"Oh," she answers. "I don't know, he's having some of his usual. You serious?"

I nod vigorously.

"Well, him and the boys started picking fights earlier, so I

guess they're still out busting up the town." She thinks on it
some more for a moment. "No, maybe not, 'cause we haven't
heard anything, have we?" She laughs and shakes her head. "That
poor excuse for a fella couldn't even throw a punch. They had
him down in no time."

I flinch. "Who?"

"That weasel of a bank teller, you know, Jones." I pinch her
hand hard. Her eyes widen. "Ouch!" And she pulls her hand
away. "What's wrong?"

I'm sure I've gone deathly pale. "Jonathan Jones?"

"Yes, but you know MacDonald, he... Marilla? Marilla... is
Jones..? He *isn't* the fellow you were with. No, not him, Marilla,
please not him. Oh, honey, I know you're soft, but he's a *pitiful*
thing, he's..."

"What did they do with him?"

"Well, you know MacDonald." She shrugs. "They beat 'im up
bad, but they always leave 'em alive, but Marilla... *Jones?* Lordee,
if I was gonna pick a man to die in one punch I'd pick Jones."
She smiles. "Trust you to pick a *gentle* fool, anyway." My spine
prickles at the word, but I wait expectantly for an answer to my
question. She shakes her head and looks away. "Well, now that I
think on it, I didn't see the weas... Jones after that. In fact, I
haven't seen any of them since." She looks back to me. "You
want me to ask around?"

"NO!" I fairly shout.

"*Marilla!?*" Mary cries with surprise.

"Mary, oh, Mary. Jonathan... You have to know. You have to.
Jonathan Jones is the Good Gentleman, he's the *Good
Gentleman.*

"You wouldn't believe it. No, you wouldn't believe how different he is. The bank teller is all an act. He's out to get
MacDonald and the Clark boys."

Not many things in life surprise Mary, but my last statement
has. Her mouth pops open briefly, then clamps shut. Mary and I
are silent for a moment. "So much for my retirement money,
eh?" she finally says. "Well, I got enough by now anyway."

I smile and shake my head. *Will you never cease surprising me, Mary Baylor?* Now quickly I tell her as much of the story as I can. The first thing she asks when I'm done is whether I told Jonathan about the money she's been taking. She's relieved when I let her know I haven't.

Then she says coyly, "So, *Marilla*, you've had an *adventure!*"

"You see, I've got to find him. I have to tell Shaw."

"Calm yourself down. I can help."

I nod. "I was hoping."

After talking a little, we decide that I will ride for Shaw's while she asks around and looks for MacDonald and Jonathan. We come out of my room to see Lillian at the top of the stairs.

"Baylor and Hay, what are you two doing up here?" she asks pointedly.

I look at Lillian and then at Mary's back. "Mary had a tear in her dress," I say quickly. "All fixed."

Lillian stares at us and Mary suddenly adjusts her dress as if she just put it on. Then she stares right back at Lillian and says, "Tough crowd, Lillian." She smiles as she sways past her. "But I told him if they didn't calm down, you'd come give 'em all a good-night kiss. That seemed to do the trick."

Lillian presses her lips together and draws her hands into fists.

Suddenly I think of a way to get myself out of here. "Mr. MacDonald told me to go for Mrs. Reed's vegetables tonight." It's a job Lillian hates to do and one MacDonald makes her do just because she hates it.

"Very well," she says, and I am out the door as fast as I can fly.

I walk to the livery and ask for the horse and wagon, and Peter Sams, the assistant, fits me out quickly. How glad I am he doesn't talk much.

I go out along the back streets, and as soon as the town is behind me, I run the horse as fast as he'll go. As we fly along my hair begins to unknot, and as the wheels jump the rocks, I realize I have only the barest bit of control over my speed-worthy horse. The ride has my blood pumping, though, and I think with a happy grin, *I should be riding with Wild Bill Hickok.*

I am out of breath as we pull up to Shaw's, and Shaw himself runs out of the house to greet me. Two fellows in suits run out behind him.

But no Jonathan.

I swallow and catch my breath. "Where's Mr. Jones?"

Shaw raises his eyebrows above his glasses to reply, "He's right inside. Whatsa matter, Miss Hay?"

He's all right. He's all right! I suddenly want to cry, but I close my eyes and swallow instead. "Mary Baylor saw MacDonald beat him, and I thought... I thought they had him. I was afraid..."

"Yea, they got him. He's here to rest up before we go in and get them. You want to see him?"

"Oh, yes, is he all right?" I quickly jump from the wagon.

"I've seen worse," says Shaw.

I walk past him and the two rather surprised-looking gentlemen to knock at the cabin door. I must look a sight. I scrape at the hair around my face to push it back.

"Come in," I hear from inside. I prepare myself for the worst and slowly open the door.

He is sitting at the table, but he slowly moves his head in my direction. "Miss Hay? What's wrong? Why are you here?" His face is marred with scratches and his right cheek is black and blue. He wears a bandage on his right arm, and I notice he can't turn his head toward me entirely.

Oh, I want to run to him and tell him how glad I am he is alive, but instead I look down, stretch my neck awkwardly, and say, "Mr. Jones, I thought MacDonald had... found you out." I swallow my pride and continue, "So I rode here to tell Shaw."

As the words leave my lips, I notice with a pang of embarrassment there are others in the room. Thank heaven I didn't go with my first impulse.

Jonathan laughs a little. "Yeah. I done turned the other cheek. Got a might more respect for the Quakers, now, these last few months." He stops when he sees my blushing face and smiles gently. "Thank you for your concern... Marilla." To hear him speak my name brings a pull, such a strong pull in me. I suppose

I've made it obvious that I care for him very much. But I would like to sink into the ground as I look at all the faces around us.

Jonathan asks the men to step forward and he introduces them to me one by one. There are three in the cabin, two I don't know named Dunwood and Moore, both miners, and then there's Jacob Stone, the carpenter. The two men with Shaw have come inside, too. They are the deputies from Denver.

I am introduced to Deputy U.S. Marshals Newton and Wood, who've been trying to catch the Clark boys for more than a year. Apparently the Clarks stole federal monies at some point, and since Liam MacDonald is their cover and financier, there's a federal warrant for him, as well.

Newton's face is thin and stern, not particularly well-suited for the muttonchop sideburns he wears. He looks more like an accountant than a deputy, but his holster is well-worn and he fingers the handle of his gun now and then like he's reassuring an old friend. Looks can be deceiving—how well I know.

Wood has a large frame, and he's blond and solid, and after he speaks, I realize, decidedly Scandinavian. He is in good humor. I'm sure they are glad to see an end to their quest. The fellows begin to speak among themselves, and Jonathan waves me to the table to sit down.

I hesitate uncomfortably but finally sit next to him. "Does MacDonald know who you are?" I ask.

"No." He chuckles. "MacDonald, he just up and decided he didn't like my face today." Then he says more seriously, "We're here trying to decide a plan, and I was just gonna ask Shaw if we shouldn't take a cue from Colonel Mosby's methods."

Shaw steps forward, looks uncertain for a moment, and then says, "You mean a night raid in the enemy camp?"

I remember my father mentioning Colonel Mosby, "the Gray Ghost." He'd walk right in on top-level Federals in the middle of the night, in the middle of their camp, and take them prisoner.

"Seeing Marilla here—she works at the hotel—she might know what rooms they're in. Right?"

"Well, yes, I do. That's right."

"We'll give 'em a rude awakening," says Shaw.

I nod. "But how will you get in their rooms?"

"We'll bust in the door," Newton says excitedly.

"But they hold two rooms," I say.

Wood laughs. "Ve'll bust 'em *bote* in." And the men chuckle.

I'm not laughing. "But then there's Liam MacDonald's room, too." The room gets a little quieter and I add, "What if I could get you the master key? You could do it all more quietly then, couldn't you?"

"For all the rooms? Can you get the key? Who has it, MacDonald?"

"Yes." I glance at Shaw. "But Lillian has a key, too. And beyond that, you know, I can pick a lock. Mary Baylor taught me—she's even faster at it than I am." I look back at Jonathan.

The Denver men begin to snicker, but Jonathan rebukes them. "She's right, boys. This is a woman of rare talents." If it had been anyone else saying it, I might have taken offense. Instead, I feel myself blush.

"Who's Mary Baylor?" Newton asks.

From the shadows, Jacob Stone replies, "She's a pretty gal from the lineup…"

"*Mary Baylor is my good friend,*" I interrupt, and everyone grows silent.

Jonathan rolls his eyes and then smiles at me, but I don't see the humor.

"Sorry," Stone says begrudgingly, and there are a few more snickers.

Jonathan looks at me and shakes his head. "There is no way on this earth we're gonna let you or Baylor be in on the raid."

"Well, then," I reply, trying to stay calm, "let one of us at least get a master key for you."

After some lively discussion, they finally decide to let us try to get the key. Shaw and the Denver men will go to the hotel bar and entertain themselves until we can slip the key to one of them. With that decision made, I then draw a map of the rooms for them. As I finish, Jonathan says I may as well draw one of the first floor, too, since the deputies have never been there.

When I finish that, they begin to look the drawings over. "An artist, too?" Jonathan asks.

"I'm no artist," I reply with a smirk.

He pulls the drawing up, marks an "x" in my room, and looks at me. "And stay in there..."

I glower at him and his look immediately softens.

"Stay in there, *please*?" he says with a slight smile.

We do seem to understand each other. I nod back evenly.

They study the drawings a while longer, and then they decide they'll go for the gang first, then MacDonald. Next, there's Potter. He doesn't hang around the hotel at all but generally sleeps in a room off the jail. If they have MacDonald and Potter, Noonan, Stubs, and Iverson will fall into their lap. Those men stay in a boarding house down the street and are unlikely to try to rescue MacDonald or Potter. Newton and Wood agree the gang is a priority, then Potter, then the "little guns," as they put it.

Then Jonathan says to me, "Why go back? Why don't you just stay here where it's safe? Mary can handle herself."

"Not on your life!" I say with fervor. "I've left Mary Baylor back there trying to find you or MacDonald." I flash Jacob Stone a look. "She's risking her neck for me. You don't do that to a friend."

They nod between themselves and Jonathan sees I'm not going to change my mind, so it is settled. He's clearly unhappy with the decision, but again, I believe he understands me.

Four of us head back to town.

Then, just before the last ridge, Shaw slows my horse and pulls in close to my wagon seat. "Miss Hay..." He flashes a little grin. "I'd fix that wild hair of yours before someone notices you."

I blush and make a quick knot of hair at my neck.

EIGHT

et six jolly cowboys to carry my coffin;
Get six pretty maidens to bear up my pall.
Put bunches of roses all over my coffin,
Put roses to deaden the clods as they fall.

From the song *The Cowboy's Lament*

here's an odd quiet in the town. I feel it as I ride down the
main road and circle around the back of Liberty Avenue to
return the horse and wagon. As I walk back to the hotel, I ask the
Lord to settle my nerves. Then I ask him to forgive my unbelief,
and finally I pray that Mary is already in the saloon. When I come
around to the rear of the hotel and step lightly to the side door to
peek into the crowded room, my heart sinks as I see she is not
there. A tap falls on my shoulder and I jump and whirl about like
a frightened rabbit.

"Looking for me?" Mary asks, grinning.

"Oh, Mary, you gave me a start."

She lowers her voice. "Was he there?"

I knew she'd find out somehow. I nod. "But where's Mac-
Donald?"

"Back in his office, drunk as a skunk."

I then pull her aside and explain the situation: The men need a
key to get into the rooms tonight.

"Well," Mary quickly decides, "I'll work on MacDonald for
the key. You work on Lillian for hers."

"Mary, you'll be careful?"

She winks, wheels around, and heads for MacDonald's office
with a lazy, chorus-girl walk. I can't help but smile at the way she
prepares herself for her work. As I turn back for my room, I try to
think how I'll get the key from Lillian. I've thought about it all

the way here, but there are too many options to choose—

"Marilla Hay!" It is Lillian Wirsching, calling to me from the lobby.

Keep your voice calm, Marilla. You can do this, I tell myself as I walk toward her. "Yes, ma'am?"

"Did you get Miz Reed's vegetables for supper?"

The vegetables! My heart jumps to my throat, but Miss Wirsching is suddenly looking away from me. She is staring at the door.

I turn and see Shaw walking in the front door with two of the gentlemen I've just met. Shaw has not seen her, and the men head for the bar through the dining room to our right.

Lillian is standing rigid, staring at the door even though they are gone. There is silence, and I notice with no small amount of fascination that her lower lip is trembling.

So. She loves him still.

She gropes to find her voice again. "I... I don't feel at all well." Her chin drops and she stares at each of her hands. They shake as she raises them. "Manage..." she raises her voice. "*Manage* for me for a while."

And then she pulls the master key from her corset and hands the thing to me. The key. A gift.

"Yes, ma'am." I almost let out an audible gasp as I take the key from her hand. I can hardly believe I've so soon an answer to my prayer. Now waving it, I tell her I'll do a good job, but she's not listening; she's already halfway up the stairs. And I realize she probably hadn't seen Shaw in all that time. *Lord, work it out.* Somehow I feel sure he will.

I turn to MacDonald's door and knock delicately. When Mary opens it, I smile and nod. "Alice wants you at the bar."

She sways her head toward MacDonald. "See you in a bit, honey. Alice needs me."

"Aw, Maree... I need you," he says in a drunken whine.

"I'll be right back, darlin'," she says sweetly and walks quickly out into the hall. I turn to her with victory in my eyes and hold up Lillian's key, but she mimics the motion to show me

MacDonald's key! Her eyes sparkle as she says, "Bravo. Keep it!" Then she turns and walks to the bar.

So now Shaw and the others will have gotten the key from Mary. That means there's nothing left for me to do but wait.

I go to my room, but as I close the door I remember the promise I made Lillian to watch over things. I need to do something or I'm sure to go crazy with the waiting. Jonathan plans to meet the men late tonight, and they said they'll begin their raid at three in the morning. I decide to go downstairs and help with dinner. Chopping meat, I nearly chop off one finger. I keep telling myself to relax, but it doesn't seem to do any good. Finally I begin to pray and, after a time, I get some peace.

At eleven o'clock, the kitchen is clean and I finally decide to retire. I return to my room and realize that, like it or not, it is time to wait. I am thinking out every detail of the plan when a horrid thought strikes me: *When MacDonald's really drunk, he sleeps in his office. The master key doesn't work on his office door.*

It's all right, Mary will certainly remember that, and she'll make sure MacDonald goes up to his room. This thought relaxes me a little. Besides, he'd be too drunk to think to lock his office door. But, then again, did he lock it after Mary left? I wouldn't know. And now there's no way to check on it. Oh, I wish I'd thought of this sooner. I could have warned Jonathan. Maybe I can catch him during the raid? Yes. I'll keep my ear out for them; I wasn't going to sleep tonight anyway.

So, tonight will decide everything.

With the likelihood of violence looming unwanted in my thoughts, my mind strays to the Colt in my drawer. With much fear and trepidation, I remove the thing from its hiding place and load it with bullets.

I don't like guns. People get shot in Independence all the time, and I've been lucky—no, blessed—not to take a bullet accidentally. I pray quietly that I won't need to use this to defend myself. Then I look at it carefully. The steel barrel is long (for better accuracy—that much I know), and I notice for the first time that the wooden handle is well worn. Jonathan's gun is well worn. What did Jonathan do before he came here? He never said.

But, then, this gun could well be secondhand.

I place it carefully in my vanity drawer and try to put it out of my mind.

I think the plan through again at midnight and decide that since the men have been drinking all day, they're likely to go to their respective rooms, and they're probably too drunk to take their women with them. Mary will probably make MacDonald go to his room. But if they find MacDonald is not in his room, I can tell them where to find him. Right. *It will work, it will work,* I tell myself over and over.

It is one o'clock.

It is one-thirty.

I am staring at my clock and the hand is making me think of a large snail—a large, stubborn, irritating snail. Slower and slower. A dying snail.

It is two o'clock.

Two-fifteen, two...

This is unbearable. I've not moved a muscle, but I am drenched with perspiration.

Two-forty-five and I am straining to hear something at the door.

Three o'clock... nothing, but the chime from the clock in the lobby seems unsaintly loud. The wick is gone on the lamp in my room and I have to light another.

At three-ten I hear something. I run to the door and crack it open to peer out. The full moon casts a strong light from the hall window down the way.

I can tell from the way he moves it is Jonathan coming up the back stairs. I watch as Newton comes up behind him, then Shaw, then the other man, Wood, then Stone, Dunwood, and Moore, all with their guns drawn. Shaw has his Whitworth rifle. Their movements are strained and unnatural, and I realize they are all tense as coiled springs. They move along the balcony hall to the first door. Now they all raise their guns and for a moment remain frozen there. Newton is at the lock, and slowly Jonathan places his back to the wall left of the door and turns to look my way. He sees me and snaps the handle of the gun toward my door to say get inside. I quickly shut the door.

This is doubly unbearable, and I force myself to pray.

Several minutes pass, and I peer out again to see the second door close shut. *One down, one to go,* and I smile shakily. Wood is outside on guard. He sees my light from the doorway and he nods. I nod back. Then Shaw is at the door motioning Wood to come in.

Soon Shaw and Jonathan step back out into the hall. They are successful again—their movements are relaxed now—but soon they'll see if MacDonald is in his room. I shut my door for a moment, then open it again. MacDonald's door is slightly open. They are coming back out, shaking their heads. No good.

Quickly I step out toward the back hall and wave them to me. They start at seeing me but come quickly, and though Jonathan looks as though he might kill me, with all my might I pull him by his sleeve to the top of the back stairs. As I turn to look up at him, I am shocked to see the blackness of the bruise on his right cheek from this afternoon. I gulp. "MacDonald must be down in his office," I whisper. "That key won't work his lock, but I can pick it for you."

"No," says Jonathan.

Shaw jabs his side. "Jones." The meaning is clear. They've come too far.

When Jonathan looks back at me and nods, it is with a look that freezes me cold. I shiver.

He cocks his head toward the stair. "Open it, then get back up here."

I nod but he doesn't look back at me.

They leave Wood and Dunwood upstairs to watch the gang. The rest of us quietly go to MacDonald's back door where I hold up two fingers and point around the corner. Jonathan gives a curt nod and sends Moore around to the other door, the one in the lobby. Then Jonathan tries the knob—it's open! He waves me back and I retreat... but only to the bottom of the stairs.

I am scared, but there will be just too much pleasure in seeing MacDonald arrested. Jonathan enters slowly, then Shaw and Moore, and I come out into the hall a little. I can barely see that MacDonald is slumped, snoring in the chair behind his desk. I'm looking over Newton's shoulder, since he's posted out here, and I'm making him uncomfortable, so I back away toward the reception desk.

Suddenly, MacDonald is awake and making horrible grunting sounds, and then from his fat lips come various slurred invectives. Jonathan tells him to shut up and asks the others for handcuffs, then begins to fill MacDonald in on his situation.

Ah, this is the second time I've seen MacDonald scared. I smile to think of this righteous judgment now visited upon him. The hand of the Lord. Newton turns and steps in to hand them some cuffs.

Just then, my eye catches a form to my left. I turn toward it and freeze.

Five feet from me is young Iverson, a dark and dour fellow, standing with his legs spread and his ear cocked toward the door. He knows exactly what's going on. He is holding a whiskey bottle in his left hand. As I stand staring, he removes his gun with his right hand and points it at me; he waves me toward the door, but I can't move. In a flash I've decided I won't go in; I'll warn them. The guard is moving to come out.

"Iverson!" I say with a shriek, and I twist and throw myself toward the lobby as a cannon crack sounds in my right ear.

I am lying on the floor of the lobby and my ears are ringing. Slowly I realize I've not been shot, but I can't hear a thing. And in the chaos of the moment, I am thinking the most preposterous thing: the lobby rug needs sweeping. Iverson could be preparing to get a better shot at my backside at this very moment, and all I can think is that the rug needs sweeping.

So now I know what people think about before they die.

In this strange state, I hear Iverson struggling with the men, and see before me something my mind is at first unable to take in: MacDonald is in the lobby, running for the front doors. I cannot imagine he escaped and so I cannot think why he is there, but—my mouth drops open—Lillian Wirsching is standing directly in his path.

Without hesitation, MacDonald turns and pulls her with one meaty arm in front to shield him as armor, then he deftly removes the hunting knife at his ankle and brings it to her throat.

Now he is saying something toward his office to my left, but I can't make it out. I wish the ringing in my ears would stop. I look to see Jonathan and Newton come out of his office, then Moore, picking himself up from the floor. I move toward Jonathan.

Everyone's attentions are on MacDonald. And Lillian has begun to struggle.

Suddenly Lillian yells, loud enough that I can hear, "But I don't want to live, you fools!"

Instead of being players in this game, all of us in the room are suddenly just watching as the scene unfolds before us. Lillian doesn't care if MacDonald kills her.

I see Shaw coming out from the office hauling Iverson. He yanks Iverson's arms around the nearest column and cuffs him, almost in passing. Shaw's eyes are riveted on MacDonald and Lillian.

The only struggle now is between MacDonald and Lillian, and they continue their tug-of-war toward the hotel doors. We cautiously follow them. The people from the bar crowd around the archway of the dining room door to my right, and I glance back to see the night clerk peering from behind his desk.

MacDonald calls out for his men, Noonan and Stubs.

But they don't come. Jonathan says something quietly to MacDonald, but I can't hear much of it.

The ringing in my ears has softened to a dull hum.

I see Lillian wrench away from him and throw herself toward us.

In a split second MacDonald raises the knife and pulls it down into her shoulder. The horror of it hits me like a punch. But MacDonald calmly pulls her limp body back to him and wrenches the knife out in one movement. I think I'm going to be sick, and

I take a deep breath and cover my mouth.

Lillian begins to struggle again, but now she is no match for him as they reach the doors.

MacDonald smiles his yellowed smile and I can hear him now as he says, "I'll just be moving on here. I think Lillian's gonna need some fresh air." And he pulls her through and out... to the horses.

I look at Jonathan and his face is pale.

I look back at MacDonald, who seems relaxed and cool as ice. Save for a crescent of blood creeping onto his shirt from Lillian's shoulder, there's no evidence that any violence has occurred. All are deathly quiet.

And we follow them out, Jonathan leading.

The full moon lights the night and a stiff breeze is blowing down Liberty Avenue. In the road, huge shadows jump and sway over the muddy ruts as MacDonald tugs with hard yanks at the reins of a horse out front. Lillian holds her shoulder.

Someone behind me says in a dying whisper, "Hey, that's... my horse."

MacDonald finally pulls the horse loose and walks backward with Lillian into a darker portion of the street. The horse side-steps nervously. The crowd that has gathered is fairly quiet. MacDonald can't seem to figure a way to get on the horse with Lillian. It seems as though he's decided to back all the way down the road this way. MacDonald yells to the crowd to stay where they are, and then he continues the retreat, with Lillian grabbing at her shoulder and then weakly trying to twist away.

Suddenly Lillian raises her voice in the wind. "Kill us! Come on and kill us. I don't mind to die. KILL US BOTH!"

One moment MacDonald is there with Lillian and the horse, casting a great slumping shadow on the road, and the next second the horse has torn away from them and the shadow is gone. It occurs to me my ears are ringing once more.

Someone has gotten off a shot.

Jonathan rushes out to the street and looks back up at the roof. I run forward, too. A man is crouched on the roof by my window. My eyes focus in the darkness and I see that it is Shaw, his rifle in hand. The crowd rushes to MacDonald and Lillian, and four men gather Lillian and quickly carry her off to Dr. Gilpin's house.

Someone beside me chuckles and says, "Jes' git a hearse there fer Mr. MacDonald."

Someone else points to Shaw. "Know who that is? That's Matthias Shaw. Crack shot. You know, he was with Mosby's Rangers."

"No kiddin'?" a fellow replies.

"Told you he was a sharpshooter," Jonathan says to me, and we smile grimly at each other. I am shaking like a leaf.

"Jones!" Shaw yells down in a quavering voice. "What's wrong with Lillian?"

My gosh, he wasn't there to see it.

"MacDonald put a knife in her right shoulder," Jonathan answers calmly.

Shaw snaps his head down as if he'd taken the wound himself. To see his concern for her makes my eyes well up with tears.

But in a moment he raises his head to Jones. "Where's Noonan and Stubs?"

What a cool sort, I think as I blink back my tears.

Jonathan glances around quickly, and the crowd answers with mutters about not seeing them. Then a couple fellows say they thought they saw the men headed for the jail when the trouble started. Jonathan looks back to Shaw and mouths the word "Potter," and they both look toward the jail.

Three men carry MacDonald past me; a blanket covers his face and chest.

As they pass, one bearer nods to Jonathan and says, "He's gone." And I shiver.

"Poor man," I say quietly as I watch them walk awkwardly through the doors of the hotel with their lifeless burden. It did not feel good to see him die. And I was so certain it would.

Jonathan turns to me. "Should have gotten Potter first." I nod mindlessly at that.

Just then Mary walks up and taps Jonathan on the shoulder.

"Mr. Jones, I've always wanted to know what a GOOD GEN-TLEMAN looked like." She says this for the crowd's enjoyment.

There is a hesitation while folks put meaning to her words, and then a few pull forward to Jonathan and shake his hand or pat him on the back. Some of the more politically minded begin to chirp that they knew it all along, and didn't they tell so-and-so a few days back that Jones was the man.

Jonathan removes his hat and bows to Mary and then to the crowd. "I enjoyed the ruse, folks, and I must say it was awful nice of the sharp ones here to play along so effectively." Laughter erupts, and someone loudly suggests they all have a toast to Jonathan and Shaw.

The words are hardly finished when, like milk spilling from a pail, the crowd disperses from the street with enthusiasm toward the various drinking establishments. But I see Jonathan methodically pick a few men out of the crowd and hold them back as the rest vanish. Those few he asks for help to get Potter and the others, now presumably down at the jail.

I look at the crowd of men. Eight of them. Good. The men Jonathan picked to help him are the sort that work hard and play hard. They are not necessarily strong or particularly agile; "reliable" is the word that comes to mind.

I stare at the uncommon face of Jonathan Jones, speaking with excitement and a light in his eyes, reminding me of the night we stayed up talking. He's filling the new men in on things and I can hear him giving instructions, but his words are a world away from the pleasant chatter he and I shared.

"Ever shot a man, Tyler?" he says. "Well, aim to the navel. That'll paralyze the brain and arms and then the fight's over, see, and they don't always die. You know, we want to get 'em alive if we can. You two get your rifles and set yourselves across the street behind the cart at the dry goods, you behind the... see that barrel down there... behind there."

How can he be so calm? He's talking about how to kill! But it's as though he were laying out the rules of poker... He's... Why, he's enjoying this! Part of me admires the courage and the daring, while another thinks, *This is like children playing a game, and this is not a game,* and I am disgusted by the conversation. I have come to a wall I cannot get through and I cannot get over—I cannot understand.

"And when they give up their guns, make 'em throw 'em down. Don't fall for the spin. I've seen Stubs use it."

"What's that?" a fellow asks.

"Road Agent's Spin—he'll offer you the gun with the butt forward, like this, but his finger will be on the trigger guard, like this," he says holding forward his Colt. "Then he can spin it around and have a shot off in a second." He deftly twirls the gun into place and pretends to shoot. "Yer dead." The man jumps back and gives a nervous laugh.

Lord, he's done this a lot.

The conversation resumes.

I've never heard raw talk like this, and I tell myself for the umpteenth time this year, *Marilla, you know so little about people.*

As another man joins the group, Newton turns to introduce Jonathan Jones to him. He says to the man loudly and with quite obvious pride, "Slim, meet *U.S. Marshal Jones.*"

Zing! The words go through me like a bullet and I step back for balance.

"Marshal Jones. *U.S. Marshal* Jones?" I whisper.

NINE

He made me some presents, among them a ring,
The return that I made him was a far better thing.
'Twas a young maiden's heart; I'd have you all know
He'd won it by riding his bucking bronco

From the song
The Bucking Bronco

The truth dawns on me as Jones keeps talking to the men.

But why didn't I see it before? He's been telling them what to do, giving them directions all night. He's their boss, for heaven's sake! I have watched him direct deputy U.S. marshals all evening, do all the planning for them yesterday, and it never even occurred to me.

This means he works for the government, which means he came here just to get MacDonald and the Clark boys.

Means he… he doesn't want my parents' farm, he doesn't want to farm at all. It means he's one of the finest actors I've ever seen and his job will be over soon, and…

Then he'll go away.

Oh.

Tears sting my eyes and I pull back up into the shadows of the hotel porch while the men disperse and head off to surround the jail. Jonathan looks back at me and motions for me to get inside. A little tear trickles down my left cheek, and I am glad he can't see it. I nod to him, then turn and walk into the lobby.

I am numb.

They've laid MacDonald's body out on the settee. A few men stand around the body. Someone has removed the blanket to look at the wound. I glance at MacDonald for a split second, and my stomach does a flip and a cold sweat washes my brow. I fumble backward toward the stairs, and Iverson, still shackled to the column, laughs at me.

MacDonald lies there with a neat hole centered in his forehead—it could not have been more perfectly centered—and then there is Lillian's blood covering most of one shoulder. *You are a sharpshooter, indeed, Mr. Shaw.* People mill about to stare at the body or join the revelers in the bar as if nothing unusual has occurred. How crude it all is, but then I think of how people come out for a hanging. *Nothing should surprise you in this territory, Marilla,* I tell myself. And the words come to me again, "U.S. Marshal Jones."

I turn to the stairs and I hear Iverson say with a drawl, "Well, sweet Marilla Hay, this is a nasty turn." I look at him for a moment and he smacks his lips. "You was the one s'posed to die tonight." And he laughs again.

"Yes, aren't I lucky the first shots you took tonight were whiskey?" I say in a half-whisper.

"Ho, that's ain't what I mean at'tall, darlin'. No, that ain't what I mean." His self-assurance riles me. "N-a-a-w-w. You see, you was s'posed to take that Denver money and run with it. Then MacDonald was looking forward to finding you and stringing you up for a little thief." He grins and waits for my reaction.

"MacDonald was going to..." I stand frozen by the coldness of his words.

"He was gonna hunt you down, sugar, but then you came back and spoiled the fun." He chuckles. "Oh, that's a good one... a little Christian 'jerked to Jesus,' oh-oh..." He leers at me again and laughs, and I turn away and stumble a little on the step, which makes him laugh all the more.

"An' he woulda got you too. Jes' one more day and he woulda had you for stealing Clark money. Fair and square."

As I make my way quickly up the stairs, I think hard. MacDonald thought I would take the money. When I didn't, he was ready to say I'd stolen Clark money. Either way he would've been done with me. Unbelievable.

At the landing, I slump a little toward the rail to rest and realize afresh how little I knew about MacDonald's ways. I sure didn't see that coming. I sure didn't. *Thank you, Lord.*

My thoughts turn to Lillian and I decide to check on her at Dr. Gilpin's. Lillian. I remember the day she asked if she could take the money for me. She knew then and she was willing to go in my place. *I was so wrong about her, Lord.* I stand there for a moment more, and then slowly make my way to my room. I'll need my cloak.

I am surprised to see Newton still standing guard outside the Clarks' rooms. He asks me what's going on, and I tell him as much as I know, then I ask, "So, Mr. Jones is a... a marshal?"

Newton grins. "Best marshal we got. Good actor, too, eh?"

I nod in full agreement. Things are happening much too fast. I pass on to my room and sit on my bed for a moment to quiet my nerves. I can see the jail from here, so I move to kneel at the side window and try to see what's going on. The moon is hidden behind the mountains now, but half the town is up with lights since the shooting. No lights are on at the jail, though, and there is no movement.

I pray for the men, then I get up, grab my cloak, and move out and down the back stairs, determined to avoid Iverson. At the bottom of the stairs, I head for the back door when around from the lobby comes the Reverend Matthew Post. We almost run into each other.

"Miss Hay?" He gently grasps my arm.

"Reverend Post?" Being so close to him suddenly makes me nervous. His hair is uncombed and his face unshaven, but darned if he isn't even all the more good-looking.

"What could you be rushing to?" he asks, smiling.

"I'm going to see about Lillian Wirsching, you know, uh, Lillian... uh, Lillian..." I can't think clearly while I'm looking into those eyes.

He looks puzzled and then his face clears. "Oh. Was she the woman who MacDonald..."

I nod.

"A good idea," he says. "May I join you?"

I nod and we walk quickly out the back door.

As we walk along, he tells me all about what he's been doing here. I am half listening to his words, as my thoughts are still scattered and my ears still ring a bit. Suddenly he's looking at me expectantly, and I'm all too aware that I missed his question. He notices, and to my embarrassment raises the question a second time.

"I presume," he asks, "that you are a Christian?"

"Yes," I nod and smile, but we are then at Dr. Gilpin's house, and I have no time to thank him for his part in my answer. I knock at the front door. The white door has a carved double arch crowned by a beautiful brass door knocker. Dr. Gilpin's home is one of the only fine buildings in Independence. Of course he's done well. He has an established business—where he knows he's always needed.

His petite wife opens the door and ushers us to the right-hand parlor: his office. Elegant, so elegant, with its wallpaper and moulding, etched glass lamps and potted palms. One hardly notices the medical clutter on the huge table plunked in the middle of the room. To the side of the table stands Dr. Gilpin, and he looks glad to see us. Lillian sits next to him, holding a compress to her shoulder.

The doctor peers at us over odd little blue spectacles. "I've cleaned the wound. We'll just have to wait and see now."

Lillian looks up at me. "Oh, you don't have to be here," she says curtly.

A strained silence ensues, but the doctor breaks the spell. "Nicked the bone. Good thing we could clean it. Ten years ago, there would have been no hope."

"Oh yes," Reverend Post says cheerfully, "we lost more boys in the war from infection and disease than from death on the battlefield, didn't we?" Dr. Gilpin agrees.

Lillian smirks. "Who is this idiot?"

I cringe slightly.

"A fool for God, ma'am. Reverend Matthew Post." He steps toward her and bows smoothly.

She looks a little surprised. "I ain't dyin' yet, you know," she mutters and then looks at Dr. Gilpin. "May I go?" she asks.

He says yes but tells her he'll bring her fresh bandages. He turns to me and begins to explain how to look for infection.

"I don't need a nurse," Lillian interjects. "I look after myself." She gets up and heads for the door. In stunned silence we watch her go. She slams the door shut behind her.

"That woman... that woman..." Dr. Gilpin shakes his head and looks at Post. "You should talk to her, Reverend. She wants to die, and with that wound she may come right close to getting her wish." Without waiting for a reply he turns to me. "And was it MacDonald's hunting knife, do you know?"

I nod, sadly.

"No, that's good. He kept it sharp and clean. Miz Wirsching says he was killed by a shot between the eyes. That so?" Dr. Gilpin is never one to put a thing too gently.

"Yes, sir."

"Well, I'll head down there, I reckon."

Just then there is a faint knocking and Mrs. Gilpin quickly opens it.

There is an awkward moment as we all recognize a woman from one of the three "houses" in town, looking wide-eyed back at us. She is plump and blonde, and her bare arms and low neck-line glow a vivid white against her purple cloak. She is quicker than any of us to regain her composure and right away asks after Lillian. Mrs. Gilpin is speechless and turns to her husband.

He kindly replies that Lillian may do well despite the wound and that she's just a little ways down the road, walking back to the hotel.

He then turns to us and says good-bye. We nod and leave, seeing he wants to say something else to the woman.

As the Reverend and I walk away, Dr. Gilpin begins to speak to her again, but now he speaks in a hushed whisper. All I can hear clearly are his first three words, "Now, Jane, don't..."

Reverend Post and I walk in the dark silence. I didn't know Lillian had a "friend." *Well,* I think to myself, *after all, Mary is my friend.* But Lillian doesn't have friends of any sort. I want to unravel the mystery, and I want to look back to see if Jane and Dr. Gilpin are following us, but I dare not.

I trudge back to the hotel in silence, barely hearing Reverend Post's energetic monologue. My mind is in the jailhouse at the other end of town. Seeing Lillian has made my thoughts drift to morbid paths. I wonder why God allows bad things to happen to people, even when you pray they won't. *What if something were to happen to Jonathan now?* In my prayers, I've confidently assumed God would make everything all right for Christians, but it's clear from the Scriptures that "all right" may mean many things, even unpleasant things, like the trials of Job.

The questions make me brave enough to interrupt Reverend Post. "Why does God wish us to pray?"

"Well, for fellowship with him, of course," he answers quickly.

"Well, why... if I may go further... if I pray for God's protection for someone and then the person gets hurt anyway, has God heard my prayer or not?"

He thinks on it a while as we plod back. "He always answers us. But he may well be saying the person would have come to a worse end if you hadn't prayed at all."

"I hadn't thought of it that way."

We are almost at the hotel. "Of this I'm sure, Miss Hay, he always hears us, for it's our purpose—fellowship with him—so I'm not surprised when he gives us what a businessman might call *a strong incentive.* He wants us to pray, and so he teaches us to pray according to his will... so that we'll get results and come to him again."

At the hotel doors, I turn and say with a contented smile, "Thank you, then, and good-night, Reverend."

"Am I left to hope my conversation was a help to you, then?"

"Yes, very much."

He smiles and nods, then, "Miss Hay, may I count on your help... to build a church here?"

I can think of no reason not to. "Of course."

"Ah, thanks."

He is pretty to look at, but my thoughts are on Jonathan. I

glance toward the jail. Jonathan is walking toward us with a couple of men. His distinctive saunter makes me blush as my feelings for him bubble to the surface.

Thank the Lord he's in one piece! *But he's a marshal, Marilla,* I tell myself, and all the nice feelings die away.

Tipping his hat to Post, he then removes it and turns to me. "It's all right, now. They were in there dead drunk, sittin' curled up like kittens in a basket. So... the jailor and his help are jailed."

"Really?" Post says. "The sheriff was in on this?"

Jonathan winks his unbruised eye. "Yeah, can you believe it? An actual, real live sheriff breakin' the law." He turns to me, pointing his hat toward the jail. "The gang is over there, too, so you can rest well tonight." He turns back to Post and grins. "You still want a church in this Godforsaken place?"

"Well, now that you've gathered all the sinners up for me, I have a captive audience, don't I?" They laugh as I politely smile.

But my smile turns into a yawn and I'm reminded I haven't slept in a day.

"Time for a rest," says Jonathan.

I didn't realize he'd been watching me. I blush and nod in agreement, then turn to head into the hotel. What can I say to him?

"I'll be by later today, Miss Hay," Jonathan calls after me.

I turn back around. "Are you speaking to me, *Marshal Jones?*" I reply in a high tone.

He doesn't miss a beat. "Speaking to you, Miss Hay," he replies with a grin.

As I pull my cloak around me I notice the inquisitive look of Reverend Post and gather my wits. "Would that be regarding the disposition of the hotel?" I say to Jonathan.

He smiles. "Perhaps." He rolls his hat in his hands once, rakishly, flirtatiously. No denying it.

Now I feel uncomfortable. I take in his stance and demeanor and something awful occurs to me. *You know what that man is, Marilla?* I say to myself as I survey his cocksure pose and handsome grin. *He's just an out-and-out flirt. That's all. And he's going to make a fool of you in front of Reverend Post and anyone within earshot, standing there acting like he's familiar with you. And what if Reverend Post finds out you stayed in this man's cabin for seven days?*

A little flame of pride rears up in me. "You needn't trouble yourself then, Marshal Jones, I'm sure the courts will handle the details." And I turn away quickly and walk inside, slamming the door behind me. I feel absolutely humiliated by his casual remarks. Reverend Post must think something terrible, the way he looked at me.

As I pass through the lobby, I notice, with relief, they must have taken MacDonald's body to Haskell's funeral parlor, but I feel a burning in my cheeks from Jones' conversation. I go back over it in my mind as I walk upstairs and enter my room. *That's right, he's just a flirt, a marshal and a flirt,* I think bitterly, and I repeat the phrase again to myself, but this time with sadness.

But then I yawn again. *I will sleep the day away!* And that is my last thought.

In the late afternoon I awake and decide to check on Lillian.

She doesn't answer the door when I knock, and that frightens me. The door is open and so I enter.

She is lying fully dressed on her bed, and her face looks pale and moist... feverish, but she picks her head up and looks over at me. "What do you want?"

"Like it or not, I'm here to check on you. What can I get you?"

She throws her head back on the pillow. "Water."

When I come back with a pitcher and a cup, many strained minutes pass before she speaks again.

"Marilla... I'm rememberin'... is MacDonald dead?"

"Yes."

"Well, there's one good thing." More quiet moments go by. "What cursed fool got him and missed me?" she asks finally.

I hesitate and draw in my breath. "Mr. Shaw."

"Oh, Lord."

She turns away and to my surprise she begins to weep.

A short time later I realize she has cried herself to sleep. I cool her forehead with a wet towel, then sit back and begin to watch and wait. I look around the room. It's a bleak little place. Bed of black iron. Stuffing coming out the edges of the armchair. A vanity like mine, but no wallpaper to hide the plaster cracks, and no personal "things" about the room. It looks like all the other hotel rooms, in fact, like she's only staying here a little while.

One thing in the room finally draws my eye: a beautiful hand-tatted antimacassar lies over the back of the chair, with matching ones resting on the arms. The linen is bright white, and the work around its edging is an incredible three inches of intricate lace. I know how long that took because I once tried to learn tatting from Mama. Ever after I've always hated to see lace things lying on armchairs. They should be in frames. I wonder if Lillian tatted them herself. I stand up, stretch, and walk over to the chair. I notice the vanity has one too, a linen cloth with two inches of the same tatting in scalloped edging. I'll just bet she did them. Or maybe her mother. It's hard to think of Lillian having a mother. She? A little baby sleeping in her mother's arms? Hard, hard to imagine.

An hour or so later, Dr. Gilpin knocks at the door. I answer it and tell him she's asleep. He gives me fresh bandages and camphor and instructs me on rewrapping her bandages.

"Nothing to do for her fever but what you're doing," he says. "And a little prayer wouldn't hurt."

I nod and he leaves quietly.

I sit and arrange the bandages on the table. Then I rearrange them and stare into the camphor bottle. I think awhile about my future. What will happen now? I wonder. Who will run the hotel? How soon will the trial be?

And what will I do? What do I want to do? The thought leaves me empty. I haven't asked myself that in years. Once, I wanted to help manage a farm. I still love to work hard all day and stand back to see what I've done—to look at something I helped build, or plant, or mend.

Kitchen work has short reward and I do enjoy it, but a farm's labor is enduring, if you protect it well. And it takes everything you have to protect it. You need to be creative and shrewd to know when to plant, what to plant, and how to irrigate the land and care for the soil so it gives back to you each year. That's the way Father was, and I smile to think of how much he loved farming. But I must put away pleasant thoughts like these, unless... but then, that's not going to happen.

Jones already has a profession. One I respect him for, I think; I wouldn't have met him if he wasn't doing his job. Well, *there's* a great irony.

Now, Marilla, you're not in love with someone you've known only two weeks! It's just too, too romantic for words. I laugh at myself—at my hopelessness—and whisper, "You've lived without a man twenty-three years, little spinster, you can 'bide a wee' longer."

But even as I say it, an old, tender longing springs up in me: I never wanted to farm alone. I've always wanted someone to give to and share with. It's the strongest feeling I've ever known, an actual physical yearning to give my heart, soul, and body to a partner in life, to build a place, a marriage, and a family. It is something I would work at with all my strength, if God would just point him out, point out my other half. How will I know when the right one comes?

My thoughts are interrupted by a moan from Lillian as she begins to toss her head back and forth. Another half hour passes and her restlessness increases. I try not to be alarmed, but I step out and call for Mary and ask her to get Dr. Gilpin. He said he couldn't do anything for her, but I have to do something!

The memory of my parents' illness comes back to me as I watch her fight the fever. Dr. Gilpin couldn't do anything for them, either, and I don't want to go through this again! I can't do this again! I begin praying earnestly, *Lord, give me strength to handle whatever comes, but, please, please, don't let her die.*

I'm deeply grateful when Mary comes in, sits beside me, and holds my hand.

Dr. Gilpin finally arrives and changes her bandages. We have to hold her so he can manage the task. When he's done he cools her forehead and tells us to keep praying! "It just ain't in my hands anymore," he says finally, and Mary and I nod. "Let me know if it breaks." And he leaves.

Mary stays with me and I tell her in a whisper how Lillian wanted to go in my place with MacDonald's money, that she must have known how he wanted to kill me. I bow my head, and in the intensity of the moment, I suddenly pray aloud for Lillian, and before I know it Mary and I are praying together. When we say, "Amen," we open our eyes and smile at each other. Mary surprises me again when she gives me a bear hug as she leaves.

The hours of watching and praying ache past, and I memorize Lillian's walls, and the features of her face. I try not to think about my parents, but I look for a sign of spasms, anyway. So far, they have not come. In a few more long hours, just when I think things might be getting worse and I'm not sure I can take much more, she falls off into a deep sleep.

This is good, I think and thank God aloud.

Mary comes in a little while later and tells me to go get some rest. I thankfully let her take over, but step downstairs to have the clerk send someone to Dr. Gilpin's to let him know the fever broke.

Now I can sleep.

Back in my room, I see on the clock by candlelight that it is midnight. I puff out the flame, and as my head touches my pillow, I fall into a deep slumber.

In the next second my clock rings six A.M. I feel as though I've been run over by a team of eight, but I make myself get up, stretch, and dash cold water on my face. I dress and step carefully to Lillian's door, hoping all is well. Mary is stretched across Lillian's old chair fast asleep, her feet propped up on the end of the bed. The oil lamp holds a bare flicker and I blow it out.

Lillian looks peaceful, although her face is still pale. I shake Mary to wake her up and tell her to go get some sleep at home. She obeys.

At around eleven, Lillian stirs, opens her eyes, and looks at me a little bleary-eyed.

"You made it," I say with a half-smile.

"Well, hallelujah."

We stare at each other and then she looks away. "I'm hungry," she says.

"Coming." And I go downstairs and make her the best meal I can find.

When I bring the tray up, she eats it in silence. Every once in a while, I catch myself staring at her, and every once in a while she catches me doing so and gives me a sharp look each time.

Finally she says tiredly, "What are you looking at? You feeling sorry for me?"

I blush and look down.

"Oh, Marilla. You're such a child. If you knew anything about me, you wouldn't stand to be in the same room."

That makes me think about her association with Jane and I blush all the more. I look up at her with eyes set wide and I open my mouth to speak, but I don't know what to say, so I clamp it shut quickly. I wonder how well Shaw knows her.

She sees my hesitation and her eyes narrow. "What?"

"It's just… It's just I found out from Iverson how MacDonald wanted to… hunt me down, and I remember how you wanted to go in my place. I want to thank you for offering. I didn't understand it then."

She gulps, and for a moment I think she's about to let the wall come down between us. But then she says, "Yeah, well, you still don't understand. I would have taken the money and gotten out of there."

"And he would have gotten you instead of me."

"I didn't care. Don't think for a moment I did it for you."

Oh, but I don't believe her. Her voice cracked in the telling. "All right," I say just to ease the conversation.

I only wish she knew how much Shaw cares for her. I can't tell her about how Shaw still feels. I can't. So I change the subject and tell her the only thing I can think of. "The deputies…" I hesitate. "The marshal… is probably going to subpoena you as witness at… I guess it would be Fort Smith, you know, Arkansas."

I can see the possibility had not occurred to her. She becomes lost in thought then and seems to be weighing her options. "Yes, I guess I will enjoy to see the Clark boys hang, if the Indians don't get me on the way there."

Well, at least she isn't talking about suicide.

In a while, Lillian asks if anyone is running the hotel.

"That is a fine question. I haven't the slightest idea."

"Well, go find out, or are you my keeper?" she says sarcastically.

"No, Lillian." I sigh. "I'm not your keeper." So I walk out the door to see Mr. Shaw coming up the stairs, slowly removing his hat. I'm shocked but glad to see him.

"Good afternoon," he says. "And how is she?"

"The fever's broken now. You want to go in?"

"If she'll let me."

I turn back around and knock at the door. "Lillian, can you see Mr. Shaw?"

There is dead silence, and so I poke my head in. She is turned to the window. "Yes," she finally says in a tired voice.

He walks in past me and right away asks how she feels. I notice, as I shut the door, she keeps her eyes down when she speaks to him. I hear her reply that she's fine, that he needn't bother to worry about her.

I walk toward the stairs, but I can hear Shaw say, "I'm glad you made it." I pray that she'll respond in kind.

But Mr. Shaw is already coming back out the door. I admit defeat. Shaw catches my eye on his way toward me, gives me an angry glance, and then clips past me down the stairs.

Well, Lillian can't be made of ice, can she? After all, ice cannot *will* itself to remain frozen forever—there comes a day when it begins to melt. *Lord, help her to melt.*

TEN

They say I drink whiskey, but my money's my own,
And them that don't like me can leave me alone.
I'll eat when I'm hungry, I'll drink when I'm dry,
And when I get thirsty, I'll lay down and cry.

From the folksong
Jack O' Diamonds

As I descend the stairs, I see by the lobby clock that it is a little after noon. The place is eerily silent; I look around at the cracked plaster and the dirty rug. Ugly and empty. Perhaps it was always meant to be this way.

I walk through the dining room to look for Mary in the bar. The bar is empty of customers, too, but Mary sits at one table alone and waves me over as I enter.

"So, where is everyone?" I ask.

"Well, I guess they're all waiting to see what's going to happen. We've still got a few overnights, but they're out at the other bars. You know, Clyde came in here and took the Faro tables—even took the cards—saying MacDonald owed him." She adds with a sneer, "Cheese in a rat hole."

"I've never seen this room empty." I notice for the very first time the heavy paneling and ball chandeliers. "It looks all right in here, you know?"

Mary's eye scans the place, but she ignores my comment. "So, what's going to happen?"

"I don't know. I feel as lost as the day I came here. Should we try to run the place?"

She thinks on it. "I got no other appointments," she answers crisply.

So we spend the next hour or so talking about managing things and who is still here to work.

"Miz Reed and Emma had a 'falling out,'" she tells me. "You should have seen it. Miz Reed almost got her throat cut, but now she's merry enough down in the kitchen wrapped around her bottle of plum brandy."

"But where's Emma?"

"She flew out of here like a witch on a flaming broom. Then comes Miz Reed, huffing and puffing from the kitchen, swinging her meat cleaver. As you might expect, she didn't catch Emma."

"Let's hold off on supper," I say wanly.

We stay silent for a few minutes, then I fold my arms and say more brightly, "Mary, you know much more than I do about this place. Why don't you run it?"

I've sparked something in her, but the light dies as she says, "I don't know. I don't really know so much. No."

She was talking herself right out of it, so I laid into it the best I could. "Look, this place is all we've got right now, and you know it, Mary. It's certain I can't run the thing. And if you fail, you can just go to some other town and start again. Come on, now, what are you afraid of?"

"Marilla, I have enough for both of us to go somewhere else."

My jaw pulls forward at the thought. There is something I have to say and I am loathe to say it. I take a deep breath and let it out in one fell swoop. "Mary, I can't use that money."

Her head snaps up and she glares at me just as I thought she would. "My money ain't good enough for you?" She folds her arms and pushes back her chair.

"It isn't your money." For once in my life I have strength enough to look her in the eye and speak my mind. The Lord has truly changed me and I know this can only be His power. As we stare each other down, her eyes begin to soften, and when I think it will do the most good, I carefully say, "Besides, I don't know if they will, but they may ask us to take part in the trial, so we may have to stick around. Both of us. And they may ask us to take care of things here."

"Jones... You want to stay for Jones." Her eyes roll in her head.

My lower lip trembles. "N-o-o. That's not it at all. *It's not*," I say with more emotion than I wish. "No, it's just... Well, Mary, after all the bragging you've done about how you could make this a better place, I thought you'd jump at the chance to run things. Come on, if... if you had this place, what would you do with it? Tell me." I am hoping beyond hope for a kind reply.

She does not look at me, but ever so slowly a smile comes to her lips. "You're going to think I've gone around the bend, but what do I care what you think, eh? All right, then, I'll tell you. I'll tell you what I'd do. First off I'd take down the wall between the dining room and the bar and I'd make... "

She lets me wait a long time for this.

"... a *real* eating establishment."

"A meal house?"

"No. An eating establishment—*fine* food. Yeah. That all right with you? It's just an idea, and I can't do it 'cause we don't own the place, right?"

"Oh. I wish you could. That'd be real nice." I tally in my mind that there are only two other restaurants in town, and from what I've heard, even stray animals won't eat their leftovers.

But Mary is saying, "See, my family owned a place in Virginia when I was a girl. I learned it young. That was instead of schooling."

"Uh-huh."

"And that's what I want—a restaurant and hotel—bigger than they ever had." She is looking off toward the street.

A long silence elapses. "You've got something to prove, haven't you?" I say finally.

She nods without looking at me. "Yea, I've got something to prove."

I can empathize. I wanted to show my parents I could run a farm, once....

"Actually, I was thinking of clearing out," Mary says, "buying something in another town and starting over."

I can't hide my displeasure.

She looks in my eyes and pats my hand. "But I won't do that 'til you're settled, all right, little sister? Don't look at me like that, honey. I said I'd stay."

"Thank you," is all I can say. I feel rather stupid and helpless.

"But, hey now, where's the Good Gentleman?"

I look away. "You mean, the good marshal."

"A marshal? Well, surprise, surprise. Not so good and not such a gentleman, eh?"

"Maybe. Maybe, but I don't know, Mary. He once tried to tell me they were doing things differently."

"Lord, I hope so." She's looking at me now and taking in the situation. "But he's a marshal, then? Not a farmer."

"No, he's not a farmer."

"Guess I'll be here longer than I thought," she says facetiously. And we both sit silently for a long, long time.

Our quiet moment is interrupted by the selfsame Mr. Jones, and I blush just to think on what we'd been saying not so long ago.

"Miss Hay, Miss Baylor." He walks over to the table without a smile.

I can't quite look him in the eye. "Yes, sir?"

"I need to let you all know what's going to happen now."

"That is a going concern," Mary says. "So why don't you have a seat and tell us, *Marshal*." I feel myself blush beet red.

He stands a moment, obviously sensing her disdain, then pulls off his hat, runs his hand through his thick, red hair, and takes a seat next to me.

I want to shift away, but I sit still. I want to look at him, but I'm afraid of what my look will say. I glance quickly and see his bruises are still dark, but his eye is less puffy. No bandage on his arm now. I go back to studying the knife marks in the table.

He tells us they've arrested all of MacDonald's partners with little trouble, and then he turns to me. "You know, Miss Hay, the partners all knew MacDonald destroyed the bank records, so they felt like they couldn't be touched. You can't believe how surprised they were when we came and arrested them."

I smile into the table.

He says there will be a wagon caravan of prisoners and a few subpoenaed witnesses leaving for Fort Smith in a couple of days, as soon as the wagons can be refitted. They won't need either of us as witnesses.

My heart sinks and I'm immediately wallowing in self-pity.

"And, Miss Hay, we had the Denver authorities look over your mother's diary, and they feel that a court session will give you ownership of the hotel. Miss Hay... Miss Hay?"

"You're... you're kidding!" I finally blurt out.

Mary puts her chin in her hands. "I work myself to death getting enough together to buy something, and the courts just give you a hotel," she teases.

"Mary, you know I don't..." I pause. I don't want Jonathan to know how little the idea of ownership pleases me. "I don't want to run this hotel alone. We'll work something out."

"Well, the judge should let you know in a week or two. They told me it's a pretty clear case, and all you'll have to do is go to court in Denver for a day or so."

During this entire conversation, Jones and I have not looked each other in the eye more than once; we are obviously uncomfortable with each other. But now I force myself to turn my face to him.

"Mr.... Marshal Jones, what will the government do with my farm?"

He looks at me oddly and then leans his head toward me. "*My* farm, Miss Hay. It is *my* farm." The blood rushes to my cheeks. "Government isn't generally known to buy land for marshals," he adds with a touch of anger.

"That's right," Mary cuts in. "Marshals usually just take what they want."

"What do you know about it?" he shoots back.

She crosses her arms. "I know a sight..."

"*You* purchased the farm?" I say as my back straightens.

"Yes," he says more quietly, "and that's another thing I need-

ed to speak with you about…" He looks at Mary. "Alone…
please."

"With pleasure." And Mary stands and glides away from the
table.

As she leaves I ask, "Mary, will you look in on Lillian?"

"Yea," she calls over her shoulder.

I turn back to Jones and my face is burning. I clasp my hands
together under the table and rub them nervously.

"I…" he begins but falters. He looks away and that seems to
ease his tongue. "I want to tell you how I wound up with the
farm."

"All right."

"I became a marshal at the request of a Judge Parker. Time I
met him he was a senator from Missouri my family knew in
Washington. Someone in the government suggested him for an
appointment as Justice at Fort Smith, and he had the nerve to
take the job." He smiles and continues. "I started bounty hunting several years ago. I was good at it, my parents, uh… spoke
highly of me to Judge Parker, and so when he took the job last
year, he asked me to join his band. He's straightening up the out-
fit."

I know enough to know a U.S. marshal is appointed by the
President and approved by Congress and has a score of deputies
beneath him. I know, too, he is awfully young to be a marshal.
Senator Parker must have liked him a lot, no matter what his parents said.

"Fines 'em if they beat up prisoners or take a witness without
subpoena," he says with defiance in his voice and a sharp glance.
"Heck, he even makes you pay for burial if you kill a man and no
one comes for him. Anyway, I agree with the judge on most
everything. He's fair. He'll hang you if you kill a white man, or a
Negro, or an Indian, doesn't matter to him, and I call that justice."

I surmise he's had this argument with folks before. But I nod
my head in wholehearted agreement. "I've never heard of anyone
like that out here."

"Yea, I know," he says more quietly. "We'll be the first real law out this way, that much is certain." He looks away, again. "Anyway, I saved up some money over the years when I was bounty hunting, getting ready to buy some land and settle down to farming. Then this job came along, but I didn't know if I wanted it, told the judge I'd farm awhile and think on it, so I bought the land. I really did come to farm, but, well... you know it turns out it was just right for this game. I don't usually stay in one place so long. I'm kind of a chickaree that way... too many nests..."

His meaning is becoming all too clear; he likes his job, and so he's decided not to keep the farm.

"So, uh, I wanted to ask if you'd be kind enough to take care of things while I go on," he adds.

"You mean sell the place for you? No, sir, I'll not..."

"No!" he says in consternation, and I jump in my seat. "I mean *look after it*. I still ain't decided what I want."

"Oh." We look at each other for a moment and a little flicker of hope rises up in me. Will what he wants include me?

He looks down. "Shaw'll manage the farm, but the house needs looking after now and again—y'know, keep the cobwebs out—if you can spare the time from this place. Shaw will take care of the animals for me. You'd just..."

"Yes!" So much for hiding my enthusiasm.

He takes a deep breath and looks at me with a strange eye. "Look, Marilla, you're... you're..." He shakes his head and lets out a grunt as he shifts in his chair. "I could have been put six feet under several times in just the last two days. You'd think that would stress a man, but it just makes me want to keep on doing it."

He wouldn't be trying to explain this to me if he didn't care for me. *Please, Lord, let that be true.* "I'll sure look after the place until... whatever." My eyes drop away, and I study the pattern on the worn rug.

"You were angry that I didn't tell you, weren't you? That I'm a marshal? I'm sorry, Marilla, but there was never a right time, and after a while, I kind of thought you knew." He taps his fingers on the table and looks away.

"Well, I hate being played for a fool, but I do it so well, don't I?" I am trying to lighten the conversation, but it's not working.

"You know, marshals aren't known to die of old age," he continues solemnly, "and... although they say it's bad luck to mention a will, I want you to know the farm will go back to you."

I've got tears in my eyes, and if I say a word I'll lose control. I can't tell him what I want. I can't say anything, so I quickly place my chin in my palms. I hate to think of the danger he draws to himself, and that reminds me of what Iverson told me. "By the way, speaking of dying, you were almost right about MacDonald." I repeat Iverson's words, how MacDonald was wanting to string me up. I end my narration, saying, "As I think on it, I suppose I made the mistake of thinking money was more important to MacDonald than power."

He nods and then quickly shakes his head. "I can't believe I let you come back here." He rolls his eyes. "I should have seen that coming."

I spread my hands. "I'm obviously all right. God was looking out for me." I'm pleased I can say the words with confidence today.

"And I thank Him." His smile drops as another thought occurs to him. "Oh, and Lillian. Now she's got to come to Fort Smith when she's able—whenever Dr. Gilpin says it's all right. I've got a summons, here. Would this be a good time to tell her?"

"I already warned her she might be called."

"Yea. Bad luck for her, but she probably knows more about this operation than anyone besides MacDonald himself."

"Probably."

"Anyway, they'll keep everyone over there 'til she comes. Two months or three, it don't matter. Dangerous trip, though. I'll be safer with my gang of thieves than anyone in a lone wagon."

I nod, then a thought occurs to me, and I smile like a kitty in catnip. "Do you think Mr. Shaw would take her there?"

He smiles. "Oh, now, Marilla... Think she'd go with him?"

"You tell her she has to!" I sputter.

"Well, I will," he says with a grin.

My mind wanders to another question. "I've been wanting to ask you," I say gingerly. "I don't know much about marshals, but how come you all didn't just come in and take MacDonald right off... six months ago?"

"Well," he rubs his chin, "at first there were only warrants out for the gang. They'd stolen federal monies off of trains, that kind of thing. I came... well, I honestly came to make a go at a homestead, but on my way out here—in Denver—I got a tip from somebody about Potter and the Clark boys. Then when I got to town, I decided to kill two birds with one stone, so I contacted Mr. MacDonald about purchasing a farm. Yeah, I liked the idea of a farm, but I already knew too much to let MacDonald go. All I had to do was hang out for an evening, real quiet like, and pretty soon I knew all about how Potter and MacDonald protected the gang and backed 'em and how there were folks in town who were in on the deal. Of course, by the end of the night I also knew the going price of gold hour by hour, the cost of land, who shot who, and how some poor bank teller got it at a Faro table the night before."

I nod as I remember the very fellow.

"I also... had a farm. Anyway, I decided the next day to present myself as a bank teller, 'cause I wanted to find a way to get them all at once, and the bank needed a new teller, so Jonathan Jones fit the bill. I got the job, then I wrote Parker for federal warrants for MacDonald and Potter and sent the letter by coach the next day. Marshals don't usually sit still like this for so long, and neither do thieves, but Parker figured since it was my first time out, he'd give the plan a chance."

"Did he approve the concept for the Good Gentleman, too?"

He blushes to his collar. "No. I sort of picked that up myself. See, I found out about MacDonald's ledger, the one you took, and I had to think of a way to get it from him. I'm more of a bang-the-door-down-type, not so much a see-the-door-and-pick-the-lock-type." He winks at me. "The men I warned off first were just to set the stage, so to speak, so's I could raid MacDonald. Besides, those poor fools were only backing the gang out of fear of MacDonald. I figured I'd just scare 'em more than he did. Sometimes it worked."

"Well, you certainly gave the town something to talk about, Mr. Jones."

"Jonathan Beauregard Jones," he pulls his hands to his vest and puffs out his chest, "the Third."

"And a fine actor," I say in true admiration.

"Actually, I come by that honestly, as they say." And he settles back in his chair.

"Oh?"

"My family... my parents are both actors, my grandparents, my sisters, too."

"Really!?"

"Yeah. I started bounty hunting by accident while we were traveling around. One of the fellows who signed on with us turned out to have a reward on him."

"Convenient. And I suppose the troupe is where you picked up your hat." He hesitates. "Your Gentleman Jones hat," I say with half a smile.

"Oh, yeah." He leans back in his chair, and one foot comes up to the table's edge. "The hat. Indian name of Black Whirlwind — pretty name, ain't it? He gave it to me a long time ago. Uh, he cut his hair once for some stupid purpose I can't recall, but he didn't want his woman to see he'd done it. So he took his hair and sewed it into his hat. Wore the thing until his hair grew back... all day and all night... fer months." He laughs. "Being in an acting troupe, you meet some *strange* folks. Mother likes to call her people 'on the fringe.' I'd say, 'Mama, why does Lucy wear her clothes inside out?' and she'd say, 'Oh, that's just because Lucy's *on the fringe*, dear,' and I would nod and wonder where in the world *the fringe* was. One day I got up my courage to ask her what it meant that all these folks were on the fringe, and she told me with a perfectly straight face, 'Why, I mean the lovely fringe on the silk shawl of *regular* society, dear,' and I nodded and walked away thinking I really knew something." I laugh and begin to easily imagine where his odd sense of humor comes from. But he quiets down as he says, "Kind of a dreamlike way to grow up, though, on the boards. You know that trunk in the barn loft? It's filled with costumes, pictures of the troupe and stuff. Wish I had some time to tell you about it all. I think you might appreciate it."

My eyes twinkle at the thought.

"Guess I'll just have to come back here," he says.

"I guess so."

"And tell you more..."

"And tell me more..." We look at each other awhile, and the way he is looking at me makes me tremble.

"I want to tell you how I got your property," he says then, breaking the spell.

"Please do." I pull forward in my chair to listen.

"The first week I was here, I put out the word I was looking for land. MacDonald being the land baron he... was, came to me right off and made it clear anything good would have to be bought through him. The next day, the fellow from the land office called me over and sold me your property." He shakes his head. "That very afternoon I deposited your money, the money I paid you for the farm, into MacDonald's account and wrote you off as a partner. I heard folks in town call you an innocent, but I figured they just didn't know what I knew." He pushes his chair back, looks at his shoes, and smiles. "But, then, people like to surprise me."

Jonathan's gaze roams to the walls of the room, the ceiling, and then move back to my face. "You gonna fix this place up, then?"

I smile but shake my head. "I don't think there'll be money for renovation..." I am thinking of Mary's funds, and I gulp as I wonder whether I should tell him what I know, betray Mary's confidence.

But the tension of the moment is abruptly ended by the odd statement I've heard from Jonathan.

"Wha-what did you say?" I ask, not able to keep my jaw from falling open.

"I say, I think the two-thousand dollar reward for assisting in the Clark gang's capture will go a long way—even in these parts." He is grinning at my look of amazement and obviously thoroughly enjoying himself.

"A reward? There was a reward?" I whisper.

"You wouldn't have seen the advertisement," he chuckled. "Can't imagine why, but Potter failed to put that one up on the board."

"Two th... two thousand dollars?" My head is spinning.

He arches one brow and says, "Worth every penny, don't you think?" And then he stands up and gives a slight bow. I spread my hands on the table, shaking my head in wonder. "Well, I'll leave you to your thoughts, then," he says gently, and walks slowly out the hotel doors.

"Two *thousand* dollars," I repeat. I could help Mary renovate, we could move to another town, I could... oh, my goodness, I could buy the farm back from Jonathan. A world of possibilities and no one to turn to for advice. My eyelids close as I murmur, "Lord, give me the wisdom of Solomon, quick. Oh, please be quick."

The next week passes slowly but pleasantly as Mary and I reorganize the hotel in the day. I didn't tell Mary about the reward, and I didn't tell Jonathan what I'd like to buy from him. I decided to wait and pray. I spent my evenings with Jonathan. We'd start with dinner at the hotel and then we'd talk. I keep going over those talks in my mind, recalling his stories, his humor, his sense of things. I've never met anyone like him, not anyone.

On two of his visits, it was warm enough to take walks out of doors, and we'd always head away from the noise on the road toward the cabin. There is a bend in the road just outside of town that winds itself around a huge stone; the noises from town disappear like magic as you come around that rock. We walked quickly to the rock the first night, and then slowed our pace when all became quiet.

When we did the same thing the next night, we looked at each other and laughed out loud, knowing each other's thoughts. That's a pleasant feeling. That night we named the place "Quiet Rock," and decided it belonged to us.

The hours would fly by and it would suddenly be one or two o'clock in the morning. Jonathan would know from watching the sky. He'd guess the time and then pull out his watch to see how close he was to being right. Then he'd hold out his arm for me, and without another word, we would walk back.

When I think about those long visits, I realize we never talked about us. Of course that could be why the evenings seemed so restful. He never tried to kiss me or hold me, and I suppose that made it more peaceful, too, although... there were times I wished he had. I feel two ways about it: I was grateful for his respect; after what we'd been through, I needed that from him. The other side of it is, I've never wanted so badly for anyone to just up and kiss me, but he never would! And that made me wonder how he felt about me.

Yesterday morning, Jonathan left with the caravan, and I found myself wishing we'd talked about us. Then it occurred to me I hadn't told him about my desire to farm. An awful feeling rose up in me that I should have been more open and honest with him, but what can I do now?

The day he left, the hotel staff packed his wagon with the food we'd made. Mary and I had worked around the new kitchen help, cooking hard-tack biscuits and curing meat that could last most of the trip, all to be shared by Jonathan, the deputies, and their prisoners.

Potter, Iverson, Stubs, and the Clarks sat in makeshift cages set in two wagons. I couldn't look at them.

I was on the hotel porch when Jonathan came up to say goodbye. We stood a few feet from each other. Though I had tried to prepare myself, I couldn't get my thoughts in order.

I did manage one thing. I held out to him one of Father's red bandannas. I told him it was one of my father's—that I thought he should wear it to remember homesteading and because I was sure my father would have been proud to know him. He stood there, weight on one foot, looking at it as I held it out to him. Then he took it and thanked me and he actually blushed. I know he did.

He shifted weight to the other foot and asked, "Hey now, this didn't come from my cabin, did it?"

A flush of irritation lent itself to my cheeks. "No, indeed it did not! I had it with me from before."

"Too bad," he said with a grin. "I could have had you arrested for stealing, and then I'd of brought you along."

I laughed but didn't know what to say—well, that was all right because he had more to tell me. He told me plainly he couldn't use the mail except for official business when he was out on a job, so it would be a while before I heard from him. He would be stationed at Two Fork, below Fort Smith in Oklahoma, and he would come back when he could.

All I could do was nod like a dumb sheep. There was a lump in my throat, but I held it down. I knew there was something there for us and that we both felt the pull. I knew it without a doubt.

He cocked his head to the side and looked me up and down in a sort of "take it in, for you won't be seeing this for a while" gaze that made me tingle from head to toe. But he bowed his head when he said, "I've got something for you, too."

My heart began to pound like thunder wondering what it might be. I took a step toward him, my hope just flapping in the air like laundry in the breeze. He dug into his vest pocket and pulled out an envelope.

"Matthias brought this in from Denver yesterday—reward money."

"Reward money," I said, with *reward* coming out flat and *money* coming out in an odd squeak, so as not to make my disappointment so painfully obvious.

His brows pulled together for a moment, but then he smiled. I stepped down the stairs and took the blasted money. I looked into his eyes and held up the envelope for a moment. Would there be anything else he needed to tell me?

"Marilla, uh, I don't do... g'byes—s'pose I hate to see the show over so soon."

So. The show was over. That was that. I took a deep breath, and with the iron will mother trained me to raise within myself when locusts eat six months of work in the space of five minutes, I kept my tears back. Utterly. I gave him a curtsy and said, "Good-byes are not so troublesome to me, Mr. Jones. I wish for you the very best on your journey; may God be with you and keep you safe all your days."

"Marilla," he said sadly, "I'm saying I'll be back. I won't say good-bye, because I'll be back."

I smiled then, "I'm sorry. I'm sorry for being peevish, Jonathan."

"It's all right. I understand."

My eyes widened. "You do?"

"Yeah. Sometimes marshals don't come back," he said quietly. "Easier to distance yourself. I know."

His answer bowled me over. I hadn't even been thinking about the risk, or had I? I grasped my hands together in a little knot as Jonathan tipped his hat to go.

It began to rain, then, and I just turned and walked through the hotel doors, thinking, *I can't keep him from doing what he loves, and he'll probably die doing it, and there will be an end to it... and an end to me, as well.* Still, I came around to a lobby window to watch him through the wavy glass as they trundled off, and a sad thought occurred to me: if he died, I wouldn't know his kiss.

I went upstairs, sat down at the vanity, and opened my drawer for a hair pin only to find the Colt lying there. I stared at it and finally allowed myself to cry.

ELEVEN

Women ought every morning to put on:
The slippers of humility,
The shift of decorum,
The corset of charity,
The garters of steadfastness,
The pins of patience

Anonymous author
A Little Book of Happy Thoughts

Today, on this clear and sunny Friday, I will head for the Denver courthouse to hear the judge's decision and perhaps sign papers to become the owner of a hotel. Mary will tend to things here while I'm away. Lillian has been up from her bed some, but she stays in her room, and I worry at her thoughts.

I get on the stagecoach bright and early Friday morning, wave good-bye to Mary, and promise her I'll see a show in her honor! On the long trip, I think about where I am and where I'm going and marvel at God's hand in all this. So many unimaginable things have happened, but then I know the Scripture says He answers our prayers beyond what we ask or think. I guess, by all rights, constant surprise should be the natural state of a Christian, then.

A new sheriff came from Denver yesterday, and his first major task is to preside over the trial of MacDonald's partners. Since we have no "town hall," court will be held right in the hotel dining room. I understand I won't be called as a witness for this trial either; with MacDonald dead and the gang in custody, no one fears to testify and so there is no shortage of available witnesses.

As we bump along toward Denver, I pray for everyone, mainly Jonathan, and I think on his last words, that he would come back when he could, that he'll write when he can. It will take at least a month for them to reach Fort Smith. I pray hard for the patience to let God work His will. But in the back of my mind I am wondering how I can encourage Jonathan to choose farming. I'll make the cabin a showcase for him. Should I use the reward money on his farm? Perhaps I could plant something unusual or turn a profit for him and impress him with my ability to farm. I'll... I'll... *Oh, Marilla, just pray, for heaven's sake.*

With prayer, my thoughts do begin to clear. Visions take hold of me, and decisions that I could not make before suddenly come easily. I begin to feel peaceful, and I know the Lord is guiding me with His Spirit. Although the journey takes half a day, by the time we reach Denver, instead of feeling tired and worn I feel refreshed. And I know where the money will go.

Rather than rest before my appointment at the courthouse, I decide to take in the town of Denver. The city has grown mightily since I was last here. I half expected the streets to be narrow and cramped from all the new business, but most have been left wide open, and so the air is kept clean and the view of the wide blue sky is unhindered.

As I stroll along one of the main roads, looking into the store windows, I find myself thinking of Jonathan constantly. *He would find that interesting,* or, *I wonder if he would like that?* Sometimes I whisper as I look, as if he were there beside me still.

I stare into the window of one particularly fine-looking clothing store. The display includes three of the most beautiful gowns I've ever laid eyes on. And a strange thought occurs to me: for the first time in my life I think how much I would like to have such a dress. In fact, I am suddenly burning to have such a dress. *Good gracious, Marilla,* I tell myself, *where's the Scottish thrift your father was so proud of? These dresses must cost a small fortune!*

Fully intending to further chastise myself for such frivolous thoughts, I turn my eyes upon my reflection in the glass, and the sight fills me with horrible dismay.

My dress is more gray than black from heavy work and washing, and the collar's frayed edge lies against my pale throat looking every inch as if someone had tried to yank the thing off. Pulling my hand to my throat self-consciously I think, *No wonder Jonathan would rather be a marshal. Who would take me as I am?* I've never cared much for fashion, but suddenly I'm beginning to see a point to it. I'm beginning to understand this odd desire welling up in me.

Looking back into the window I whisper, "Perhaps if I dressed like this, Jonathan would have wanted to stay with me. Would it have made a difference?" I imagine Jonathan's face when he returns to visit me—how I will descend the hotel stair to present myself to his eyes in all my earthly glory.

Yes, I see it. Why, his face is in rapture! Glorious! He's... he's down on one knee right there in the hotel lobby!

My hand falls to my purse and I make my decision.

I have never purchased a store-bought dress in my life, but by George, I will buy one today. I'll wear it to the court and I'll wear it to the theatre whether I'm a hotel owner by then or no. It will be a "Sunday Best" dress, the finest black silk I can afford. And when Jonathan comes back to me, I'll see that it was worth every penny.

I grasp the great brass handle and swing open the door.

But once within the store I am accosted by rude looks and whispers from the clientele as if I've no business being there. Pursing my lips, I stand my ground and, with narrowing eyes, look about me for help. A lady assistant soon comes, and when she sees that I'm in earnest and intend to pay, she gently guides me into the intricacies of the day's fashion.

An hour and a half later, I leave the shop wearing a group of newfangled underthings, the order and construction of which are so complex I wonder if I will ever get them on me again: there's a corset that already makes my ribs hurt, three new petticoats, a chemise, and the latest bustle ("A fancy word and fancy price for a pillow on a string," the shop lady said). But most importantly, I now wear a beautiful black silk. I chose a gown in the newest style, and I find a reflection of myself in a barber shop window just to admire the thing again: intricate jet black bead work on the bodice, gathered skirts hanging from the dropped waist, and wide pleats falling to the floor, with a lovely gathering of Brussels lace at the neck. On my head is a new little hat to match, with baby rosebuds of silk crimson and black velvet braid trim all around.

I have to laugh as I catch my silhouette in the window again: that bustle. *Fashion is so ridiculous. However do we stand it?* I think as I try in vain to adjust the corset with a healthy stretch.

But still I smile as I walk away: I see the apples in my cheeks are making a bold return.

I make my way to the new courthouse, and although my fashionable skirt has a ruffled sweeper attached to the underside of the trailing skirt, I try to keep from crossing the muddy streets unless absolutely necessary. Ah, I remember the last time I was in Denver, my father proudly pointed to the territory offices... in a log building! My, how things have changed.

Statehood for Colorado this centennial year is the goal, says everyone, and this certainly looks like a state capitol to me. Good things are happening. Even Independence has a church of sorts now, so perhaps we can attract a teacher soon. The mining fever is starting to cool, but people are staying anyway. There's gold to be made yet in beef and sheep, not to mention farming. I smile to myself.

And so a great feeling of optimism pervades my senses as I walk up the steps of the courthouse.

In a few hours, the judge makes a quick decision toward my ownership. Papers are signed and I walk away... the proud new owner of a hotel!

Outside, standing on the courthouse steps in my new black silk, I look again at Denver. *So, let's see,* I muse... *I love farming and hate town living, but I sold the farm and now own a hotel. Bought a dress for a man I don't know if I'll ever see again. Life is odd.*

Then I head for the office of *The Rocky Mountain News.* The gentleman at the front desk asks if he may assist me. I tell him I would like a year's worth of back copies, if possible. He says "Of course," and heads for the back room.

Well, that was easy enough, I think. The old copies at the hotel were mostly scraps by the time I saw them. I need a good shot of confidence and this could do it for me, and it's the only way I'm going to learn recent farming techniques.

As I wait, William Byers himself walks through the doors. I know this only because the famous editor is quickly surrounded by his staff as he makes his way back to his office. Now there is someone I would like to congratulate, truly a man of vision. But he's obviously busy, so I will admire him from a distance.

Soon enough, the fellow returns with my load of back issues. With my heavy parcels, I have to hire a town coach to take me back to the hotel—my first ride in one! I'm feeling quite elegant and refined.

I attend the theatre that evening to see the comedic farce Mary suggested. Beautifully appointed, with giltwork and frescoes and walls painted chocolate and cream, the place is so crowded, I needn't have worried about coming here alone. In fact, I think if I died in the lobby, they wouldn't find me until the show was over and the place was empty.

The show is marvelous to my eyes. The actors and actresses, dressed in brilliant costumes, exaggerate all their movements and voices and make the crowd cry with laughter. Many of the jokes and nuances are lost on me, however, being that I'm a girl from the country. But I'm sure of one thing: Jonathan is a better actor than any I see here.

I go back to my hotel by town coach for the second time in my life and go to my room to dream happily of the future.

In the morning, I catch the coach for Independence. For once in my life, I look forward to going there.

When I arrive back in town and I see the hotel lit with night lamps over its broad double porch, I feel a great sense of anticipation. As I come in, Mary greets me and right away begins to circle around me and look me over and up and down.

Then she lets out a whistle. "You're looking rather smart."

I thank her profusely and say I enjoyed the theatre, but

thought she would make a prettier leading lady and Jonathan could do better than the sour-looking leading man.

Then Mary tells me what's been going on. "Reverend Post has been here, planning his church," she says, amused. "Since you weren't here, I took the liberty of standing in for you."

"Mary," I say mockingly, "I didn't know you were interested in church planning."

Did I see that? Did I see her blush?

"I haven't really talked about it, Marilla, but you know, you're not the only one who... who..." She looks away. "Marilla, I never told you, but I stayed at the meeting we went to, and made a... a... commitment that night."

"You goose! Why didn't you say so before?" I drop my bags and grab her in a hug.

She laughs uneasily. "I didn't think you'd take it serious. In fact," she whispers, "I had to find out if *I* took me serious. After all, I had a lot to answer for. But I'm sure now, and Marilla, *I've even bought a buggy.*"

Ah, the symbol of town respectability! I hug her more tightly. It's her way of telling the men in town to treat her differently, that she's unavailable. "Oh, that's nice. I'm so glad you... you have a *buggy*!" And we both laugh at the word and I shake my head.

But I look into her eyes and smile and blink. "Isn't it incredible? The forgiveness, I mean.... Isn't it incredible?"

She has tears in her eyes and she nods. "Yes, it is but don't make me cry right out in front of everyone. I'd never hear the end." And we hug again.

"Mary, we have to talk. Let me get out of these things." I untie my bonnet and grab up my bags again. "I'll be down in a minute."

As I move up the stairs, Mary calls out, "So, d'you own this hotel or not?"

I smile broadly. "Yes. Isn't it ridiculous? I own this hotel!"

"Unbelievable."

I drop my things in my room, wash my face, and go to check

on Lillian. She is sitting up but staring out the window. I extend a greeting, but she looks away again.

"Food was so bad I had to go and fix it myself," she says in her usual manner. At least her wits are still sharp as pins.

"Can I get you anything?"

"Yes. A gun and a bottle of whiskey." But she says it with the barest hint of a smile. "Or how about a decent meal?"

In short order, Mary and I fix a supper for her in the kitchen, and Mary takes it up to her. When Mary returns, we begin to fix plates for ourselves, and I hatch my plan.

"Mary, I want you to manage this hotel."

She puts down the bread knife, stands back, and crosses her arms.

"The reward money is enough to start a homestead west of Jones."

"You're really going to farm!"

"I can't explain it, Mary, but the Lord told me to do this. He just did, and I'm not going to argue."

"You're backing out of the hotel, then."

"Well... " I hedge. "I suppose you could look at it that way, but, then, Mary," I lean in to catch her gaze, "you know I'm a farmer—I'm no city mouse."

Her jaw pulls forward slightly; she nods once.

"But there's something I haven't told you. Clear as the Lord has called me to farm is the message that I'm supposed to share half the reward money with you."

Now she's really irritated. "Aw, beg off, Marilla, that's ridiculous."

"Mary, don't be bullheaded. You know we both took risks to help catch them."

"And they couldn't have done it without you..."

"Well, I couldn't have done it without you and you know it!"

She stares me down, but my back straightens as I stare right back. "Look here, Mary. I'm looking you right in the eye and I'm telling you..." I dig into the front fold of my skirt, pull out a leather envelope, and throw it down on the counter. "...I'm not keeping this money, and that's final. Now, what you do with it is up to you, but it's yours, now. Burn it, for all I care!"

Mary glances at the envelope and back to me.

"Burn it... or do something constructive with it."

Her brows arch.

"Since you're my best friend, I'm going to let you in on a secret. Tomorrow morning I'm posting a for sale sign on this hotel, Mary. The terms of this agreement are that you will be manager of this establishment."

Mary's eyes widen for only a split second before she purses her lips together. Tapping her toe, she crosses her arms and says, "How much?"

"You know I won't take the Clark money, Mary."

"How much?" she snaps.

"One thousand, no more, no less." I manage to keep the smile from my face as I cross my arms and stare her down.

"Marilla, is this your weak idea of a joke?"

"I'm not near as humorous as all that," I reply.

She glances at the packet. "You're going to sell me the hotel by taking the money you just gave me not a minute ago?"

"It's a thought."

"And I'll own the hotel."

"You'll own the hotel, fair and square."

She smiles ever so slightly and wags her head as she stares back at the envelope. "Fastest money I ever saw. Amaryllis Hay, you've got yourself a deal." She holds out her hand.

"Deal." And I wipe my hands so we can shake, but then we move to hug one another. I think I hear her whisper, "Thank you," but I'll never quite be certain. As we pull away, Mary's face grows somber. "May I ask you something, Marilla?"

"Sure."

"I told you I made a commitment."

"Yes," I say cheerfully as I remove my apron.

"Well, I've got a problem. One reason I'm not sure about this is... there's the money, of course, and then there's... the times I've seen men murdered. The last time, you remember, it was one of the girls who shot, you know... just 'cause he didn't pay, but I can't turn in a friend."

"Yea, I remember that." I think on it a while. Life is never as simple as it seems. "I don't know, Mary. Maybe you ought to ask Reverend Post."

"Right," she says, unswayed.

"Oh, come on. I was right the first time I said to give him a chance, wasn't I?"

She stares at me, her eyes half shut. Finally she blurts, "Oh, why not. All right, then."

We eat supper, and I go up to get the tray from Lillian's room.

"Lillian," I say boldly as I pick up the tray, "by the way, the court decided in my favor."

"Congratulations," she says rather sarcastically.

"Thank you. Now, would you like to stay on here as head of staff?"

"You mean if I make it back from Fort Smith alive?"

"Yes."

"All right."

"You should know, too, I've sold the hotel to Mary."

"No, sir. *No.* I'm not going to manage any house of ill repute." She sniffs.

"She's... she's no longer in that line of work, Lillian."

"Oh, *really?*" Her eyes grow cold.

"Mary just wants to run a hotel and restaurant. She's had training. Honestly. You can see for yourself."

She finally waves her hand. "Six of Marilla, half dozen of Mary. I don't think this place will succeed under either of you, but I suppose I'll stay put for now."

She must have some confidence in us, I think wryly, or she wouldn't stay at all. But I'm not finished. "Good. Now there's something else I came to say, if you'll let me."

Her eyebrows rise for an instant.

I am suddenly unnerved. I don't know how to begin. So I sit down and fidget with the lace on my sleeve.

"WHAT?" she finally says.

The sound gives me a start and right away I say, "You and Shaw have feelings for each other still, Lillian. It... it's wrong to waste them!"

She just stares at me and her eyes narrow. Now with her mouth rigid with anger she says slowly, "You don't know anything, Marilla Hay."

"I know about Shaw."

"Bosh. Shaw doesn't even know me."

"Well, he's going to *get* to know you all over again," I say with vehemence, "all the way to Fort Smith. You're going to have to talk sometime."

"IF I told him anything, he would more like as not leave me to the Indians," she says in a deadpan voice.

"Oh, have it your own way." I stand up. "But I don't know any mules more suited for a double harness than you two." I walk to the door, slamming the tray on the door jamb for emphasis as I leave.

I let out a little frustrated scream as I run down the main stairs. But I blink when I reach the bottom and look around the empty lobby again.

For a brief moment in my life I truly owned a hotel and suddenly the whole thing strikes me as funny. I let myself laugh out loud for a full minute and then I return to the kitchen with... *Mary's* tray.

TWELVE

"Mining is only a lottery,
and only a few draw a prize."

From "A Gold-Miner's Story,"
***Our Young Folks*, 1873**

In the morning two days later, I lay out my beautiful new dress and look it over carefully with loving eyes. *Is it wrong to love a thing so much, Lord? I'll try to appreciate the beauty of it and not let it go to my head. Lord, help me to look at it this way.*

But I get silly looking at myself in the mirror when I'm finally dressed. I stare at my face and frown. "Now, who's a peacock, Marilla?" I think of Jonathan again and smile.

It's time for business, though. I've helped Mary with the hotel in the daytime, and I've stayed up late nights reading enough of *The Rocky Mountain News* to make my head ache with statistics and information. I suppose I'm as ready as I'll ever be for this.

This is a fine dress for a business meeting.

I step down the stairs with careful determination and head for the land office across town. The sorry little building is at the beginning of Liberty Avenue, one of the first things built here, and I tread toward it with my thoughts wrapped around business deals, land values, water rights. I hardly watch where I am going, except to see the porches and dirt road crossings pass beneath my feet, and I realize that I am halfway there.

"Lady? Ma'am?" I hear a fellow say in reverential tones.

As I turn my head to look, I think, *Oh, no, not again. Please, not now.*

I look to see a tired, dirty face on a thin body. A miner. He draws his hat off and holds it carefully on the tips of his fingers as he asks me to join him in the blissful state of matrimony.

Every time these fellows approach me, I'm at a loss for words. But it occurs to me that today I have a wonderful way to discourage him without killing his pride. "Sir, I'm sorry, but I help manage the Independence Hotel, and I'm afraid I'm far too busy to make a home." It sounds like a wonderful excuse, and it makes me feel quite heady to say it aloud.

He changes track in an instant. "Then, lady, could you give me money to make it back home? I'm give out, here. I want to go home."

"Oh." What? Good heavens. "Uh, yes, well, uh, you just go to the hotel, and I... I'll speak to you about it a little later. I have business." What in glory am I going to say to him later?

That satisfies him, though. "All right. My name is Ferrin Kolb. Ferrin Kolb will be by later." And he strides away with a little smile on his face.

I pray about it all the way to the land office. *Lord, let your will be done,* but I'm also of a mind to pray he doesn't tell his friends.

Finally, I step up the stairs of the land office and I can't help but notice the windows are so dirty I can't even see inside. I open the creaking door of the office and am greeted with the smell of thick dust and tobacco.

I look ahead of me at the new land agent behind the desk. MacDonald's man is long gone. I've never met this fellow before; he looks to be a very little man behind a big fat desk. The first thing he does when he sees me is to spit in the direction of the pot to his right.

The first thing I do is shudder, thinking, *What a slimy little creature...*

"May we help her?" he says doubtfully.

"And who might I be addressing?"

"We're Hopkins."

"Well, Mr. Hopkins," I say glancing about and wondering why in the world he said, "We're." "My name is Amaryllis Hay, and I'm here to take out papers on a claim..." He looks skeptical. "Un-under the Homestead Act."

"She's here to stake a claim of the Homestead Act."

With an edge to my voice, I say, "Sir, I know it's unusual to find a woman at your desk, but I am qualified."

"She's *qual*ified." He laughs in a high pitch.

"Yes, and I would like to put a claim on the 160 acres set next to this plot here." I show him the plot on a map tacked to the back wall. Jones to the east, Shaw farther east.

He stares at the map awhile, then looks back to me, and his eyes go over my fancy dress. "*She thinks she's* gonna squat?" And he spits again.

"Yes."

"You a widow?"

"No."

"You a man?"

I purse my lips at the impudence of the question.

"Right, then. And *no* to her, too. She can show herself out."

I grit my teeth. "What are the written requirements of the Act?"

"If it's a she, she's a widow. If it's a he, he's head of the household."

"Well, I'm head of my own household."

"But that ain't the intent..."

"But it doesn't *say* it has to be a *man* to be the head of the household."

"Don't need to."

Tears burn my eyes, but I refuse to let this worm see me cry. I'd rather die. I slam the door as loudly as I can when I leave, and I'm satisfied to hear at least one of the panes of glass break in the dirty windows of the land office.

Mary finds me in my room an hour later, and I can hardly speak.

"Wouldn't let you have it, would he?"

I shake my head.

"Aw, you're a sorry case. I should have told you not to get your hopes up."

"He said... said I had to be a man... or a widow." I sniff dramatically.

"Did he, now."

The odd way she draws out the words makes me turn to her. She's smiling and the smile catches me off guard.

"You know, there's a way for you to…"

I blush a fiery red. "Ask Jonathan to marry me?"

"Heavens, no. I'm serious."

"Dress up like a man? I don't think I cou…"

"Just… stop it. Hold on there. Simmer down and hear me out." She straightens up. "It's just that… it's just that *I'm* a widow." In the barest whisper she says, "Mary Baylor… is my married name."

My jaw falls open.

"Yea, I know. But it's true. There's… there's a lot about me you don't know, and a lot you ain't ever gonna know. That's right. But I am a bonafide widow, and… if you could wipe that look off your face… Look, I didn't kill him, if that's what you're thinking."

"Of course not." I blush and gulp. "But…" I don't know what to say, so I clamp my mouth shut.

"His name was Thomas Baylor. He died. Killed, actually… on the way out here. We were only married a little while, but he was so kind to me—took and married me when no one else would have me and stole me out of a cold life. I'm afraid I've dragged his name through the mud and beer and you know what all else until recently." Her shoulders slump slightly as she continues. "But anyway, I told you, and I told you for a reason. I've got my marriage license and I've got the certificate of his death, and I'll lay a claim on that property for you, and you'll prove it up, and then in five years I'll… I'll sell it to you."

"But that wouldn't be legal."

Her eyes grow to slits. "Which?"

"You'd… you'd have to prove it *with* me. You have to live there."

"Now, wait a minute. I know a little of land law myself. Improvements have to be made on it. The owner has to 'prove up,' but I don't have to live there. Doesn't say the owner has to do the improvements himself—or herself."

"But the intent of the law…"

"… is to keep single women from owning property. Well, how 'bout whenever you need me to come play 'owner,' I'll come over."

I am so desperate this is beginning to sound reasonable to me. "You'd do that?"

"Yes, I'd do that, but if you don't wipe that smarmy look off your face, Amaryllis, I'll take back my offer."

* * *

"Well, we'll have to do a survey."

Mary glances at me. I nod.

"I knew that," Mary says nonchalantly.

"Then there's a claim fee."

"Yeah."

"Yes, sir," I say, trying to help the atmosphere. Mr. Hopkins of the land office is trying to irritate us, but we can't let ourselves be baited. These claim fees were never President Lincoln's intention when he created the Homestead Act, but they pass for law out here.

"Gonna run her round twelve hundred dollars."

I press my lips together. That's four hundred dollars more than a man pays for the same, and he knows it! I look over at Mary. She's mad as a hornet, but I shake my head to get her to understand. I shake my head again and raise my brows in supplication, *Please, Mary, don't make a scene.* I know if we exasperate this man, we'll get absolutely nothing.

But suddenly Mary's attitude completely changes. I've seen it many times before, yet it never ceases to amaze me how quickly she can change her mood. Her head falls leisurely to one side and she steps up to the table and twirls her finger on the map. "But, Mr. Hopkins," she says, sweet as honey. "You must be mistaken. My good friend Marshal Jones told us that wasn't the case."

"Who there? Gentleman Jones?"

"Yes." She points to the map. "He told us the fair price was eight hundred dollars... so, *you must be mistaken.*"

I look at Mary wide-eyed. Mr. Hopkins is staring hard at her, but she's staring right back. I forgot how often she's played poker in the past.

"Eight hundred dollars, she sez." He leans forward and cocks his head. "Oh, it is. Whadya think I said?"

"Why, eight hundred dollars. You said eight hundred dollars." Her voice is cold.

She glances at me just as he does, and I gulp and nod in agreement.

"Yes, indeed, and so she'll buy it for eight hundred dollars," says Mr. Hopkins.

I smile. "Yes, she will." We have all come to an understanding.

All the huffiness and posturing is gone from the little man as he begins to draw out various papers from his desk. Although Hopkins still speaks as if we're in the next room, he gets down to business and we talk about the water rights, options, and how long this will take. Mary makes an appointment to settle a week from now.

As we walk out the door, I hear him say happily, "Well, she's gone!"

I shake my head at Mary and we laugh as we head for the hotel. "Feel better now?" Mary asks.

"I don't know whether to laugh or cry."

"That sounds about right."

As we pass through the hotel doors, I notice business has picked up. It's been better for the last two days, in fact. Mary has advertised for a "real cook," as she says, and she meanwhile makes herself useful in all the chores of running the hotel. Things have never looked better.

While the town was leaving us alone a week ago, Mary had the lobby replastered. She even found a man to clean the rugs, although it didn't do much good, and now she's ordered new rugs for the lobby and future dining room. She even found a limner in the mining camp to remarbleize the lobby columns. They look mighty fine, now. In fact, they are so pretty, it's not so you'd even notice the rug.

Mary moves silently to the lobby desk, and I watch as she folds herself back into business as usual, gently giving orders and smiling at the customers. She looks as happy as a fox in a henhouse. And she looks every bit a businesswoman. I walk to the reception desk and smile.

"Things are picking up, Marilla."

"I see that!"

She smiles with satisfaction and nods toward the dining room. "I'll have the men come Thursday to tear the wall down."

"Good heavens, Mary. You're quick."

She looks down and moves her shoulders up and down with a sigh. "Well, I keep thinking something bad is going to happen, so I want it all done now."

"Nothing's going to happen." I put one hand on her shoulder. "What could happen?"

"Oh, I don't know. It's just that something always does, for me. Something always happens... to ruin things."

"But you're not alone anymore, Mary. No matter what happens, that's not going to change." I give her shoulder a firm squeeze.

She rolls her eyes and laughs. "I'm having the worst time believing God will let me do the thing I've always wanted." She whispers, "Really, Marilla, I feel I don't deserve this!"

"Well... if you feel that way, you're going to have a rotten time in heaven!"

She laughs. "By the way, Reverend Post came by while you were out. He wants us to come to a meeting right after service this Sunday. I think he wants to start a Sunday School or something."

Mary must have worked out her "confession" with him, but I decide not to ask about it. "Good. I'll be there. Who would have thought two months ago we'd be doing this—reorganizing the hotel, planning a church? Strange isn't it?"

Mary nods and smiles. "Marilla, I've been meaning to ask you something. You know how you went and got the newspapers in Denver. I... I like the way you just decided to read everything on farming to educate yourself the best way you can."

"Yes?"

She takes a moment, then, "Well, I want to do the same thing."

"You mean... for the hotel business?"

"No, not for the hotel. I *know* the hotel business. I mean I want to be able to talk with people about *things*... anything. Like you. Where'd you learn the rest?"

"Well... I guess you mean the books my ma and pa raised me with."

"Yea. Those, I guess. Could you give me a list maybe?"

"Well, the books are still at the cabin, and I'm sure Jones wouldn't mind. They're a little worn, but..."

"How many?"

"Twenty or so."

"That many?"

"Yes, that many," I answer smiling. "On our way here by wagon—when they unloaded furniture to lighten the load up the mountain—Ma always said the books would be the last things to go. She said, 'You can't make a book from a piece of furniture, but you can make a piece of furniture if you have the right book.'" Mary smiles. "Books kept me sane in the winter, too, especially that first winter when I'd lost my little brother and didn't have anyone to play with. Ma would say, 'You see what I mean? You couldn't curl up in bed like that with Grandma's sideboard and get near the comfort from it." Mary laughs at that. "But between you and me, she mentioned the loss of Grandma's sideboard a bit too often. Anyway, you want me to bring you some of the books?"

She looks relieved. "Yes. I mean to stay up nights and read just like you do."

"Fine."

Just then, the clerk comes up to her with a question, and I start to head back up to my room. But then I remember something. "Mary? Has a miner been by here asking for me?" She blinks. "I think his name is Terrence or Ference... something."

She shakes her head, and I must admit I am glad for it. He must have changed his mind... again. I won't have much money to spare to do what I need to establish the claim. *Thank you, Lord.*

When I get back up to my room, I draw out the blue ledger I will use for the farm. I couldn't bring myself to buy a green one. Looking at it, I sigh with satisfaction. So I'm going to farm again. It's really going to happen. I open to the first page to read the quotation I've written there, taken direct from an editorial in *The Rocky Mountain News.* Colorado's future will be in "farming, manufacturing, scenery, and climate—not gold." Farming first. I heard my father say the same thing so often, it tickled me when I found it in the newspaper. It was a quote from none other than William Byers, Editor.

A great sense of peace pervades me as I sit here in my little room, and when I finally stand, I thank God for his good gifts. Now I'm ready to go about my chores.

In the late afternoon, Mary and I are at the desk in the lobby when Dr. Gilpin comes by to inform us Lillian can leave in two weeks for Fort Smith. He then passes us to walk upstairs and let her know.

At dinner, Lillian hardly speaks a word to anyone, and I wonder what she is thinking. She has a way of putting on the poker face of a hardened gambler, as if emotions never run through her at all. At times I wonder if it isn't so.

This week, I'm busy working in the hotel and planning my move. Sunday arrives, and we hurry down to Swan's Dining Hall in the cool of a mid-April morning, and then Mary and I stay after service for our "meeting."

Reverend Post is even more animated than usual in his conversation. We can hardly get a word in as he lays out the plans he's worked and prayed over for so long.

Finally, Mary raises her voice a touch. "Reverend!"

"Yes?" He actually stops for a breath.

"I've been thinking we're getting too big for this room."

He and I nod in agreement, but Post replies, "Yes, but I don't believe it's time just yet to build a church."

"Right. SO…" She raises her voice again and smiles. "Just wait until we've renovated the hotel dining room. It won't be but two weeks or so, and it will be twice the size of this room."

"Really?" Post says, purely pleased. "That's wonderful. What are you making there? A restaurant?"

Mary turns red. "Well, yes, as a matter of fact I am."

"That's fine. Real fine. You can hire me to say the blessing before meals."

That gets us all to laughing.

Then he turns to me with those warm eyes. "And, Miss Hay, where will you teach the children's Sunday School at the hotel?"

I gulp. "Sunday School? But, Reverend, I've never even had schooling myself."

"You have enthusiasm and that counts for everything out here. I've seen how you treat the children in our group, and I think you'd be mighty fine as a teacher."

I blush to think he's been noticing me at all. "You're awfully hard to say no to, Reverend Post." I feel myself blush again, hoping I haven't sounded too familiar. "I mean, the way you put things… you make it sound all right."

"Well, I count on people responding well to encouragement, and they usually do, that's all."

"Well, all right. I won't say no, but you'd better give me a few weeks of preparation while… while I'm preparing my fields for crops."

"Ah, to sow the seed of the Word?" And he smiles.

"No, I mean literally sowing seed." I look around me, wishing there were some place to hide.

"I don't quite understand."

Mary comes to my aid, placing her hand on mine. "Marilla has put a homestead claim on a property near to her parents' place, Reverend. I'll be managing the hotel."

He looks toward me briefly, then to Mary, and back to me.

"Oh, I guess I heard something about that..." he says with a blank look. He gives a quick smile then, as if he just put something out of his mind. "And Miss Baylor will be proprietor of the hotel? Excellent. Congratulations... to both of you." But he speaks with a noted lack of enthusiasm.

I can barely look at him. I'm afraid of what he thinks of me. I can hear his thoughts, *Running a farm is no business for a single woman.* I want to run out of the room, but I just smile. "Thank you." I realize, sadly, how very much I want to impress Reverend Post, and that he may be just now regretting his request for a Sunday School teacher. I'm painfully remembering the look he gave me the night Jonathan spoke to me on the hotel porch.

But he goes on to summarize the plans we've made for the church, and finally Mary and I leave.

"What a lovely afternoon," Mary says on our way back.

I can't appreciate it in quite the same way, so I just nod. Mary doesn't seem to understand my mood, so we walk back in silence. As we reach the hotel, I think tiredly, *Lord, I leave it in your hands, and if you think I can teach, please show me the way.*

The next morning, it is time to return for the claim. But at the Land Office, Hopkins tells us the total comes to $810.00.

"And ten dollars?" asks Mary.

"Administratement fee," he announces.

Holding my breath I turn and look at Mary and she to me. Everybody in this town wants to line their pockets! Will we let him get away with this?

I tell myself, *You have to draw the line at important things or you'll never get anything done, Marilla!* Before Mary can speak, I lay the money down and tell him, "Well, if you're looking for a place to spend the ten dollar admini*strate*ment fee, Mr. Hopkins, try the restaurant at the Independence Hotel. Gentleman Jones will be stopping by when he's in town."

That gives him a start. Mary gives a lopsided smile. He looks at us sharply and then says, "Try the restaurant, sez she."

"Yes, sir, she does. Good-bye, sir."

I step lightly down the stairs. Mary comes behind me, shakes my hand, and saunters toward the hotel. I want to jump up and shout! I look around me. It's the same tired faces, the same loud voices and rolling wheels and horses and dust, but at the moment I am insanely happy because *I don't have to live here anymore*! Yahoo! I almost skip down Liberty Avenue toward the hotel, trying to catch up with Mary.

"Ma'am?"

Oh, please, not now, I think and look to my left. Why, it's a towheaded boy not more than sixteen or seventeen! He approaches with hat in hand. "This is really too much," I say without thinking. "You are too young to be…"

"Ma'am?"

This gives me pause, and I stop and start again with slight repentance, "I'm sorry. May I help you?"

"My name is Liggon Tyler, miss, and I saw you come out of the land office, and I thought maybe you knew where I could find some work, 'less you think I'm too young? I'm strong for my age, though, and I can learn just about anything," he says hopefully.

"No, not too young for work." I break out in a wide smile and then look him over. Could use a meal or two, but he looks fairly strong and he's certainly eager. His hair is a little whiter than mine, and he has a short but well-formed nose and roundish blue eyes set in an oval face. Right out of a Currier and Ives print.

"You want to farm?"

"Sure. Yes, ma'am. It beats digging."

"Know how to use a plow? A gun?"

He nods to both. "Yes, ma'am. I grew up on a farm in Ohio."

"Do you have kin?"

"They're still in Ohio. My father brought me here to mine, but he was put down two weeks ago, and I've run out of money."

How pathetic. He speaks of his father's death as though a horse had died. "I'm sorry. Don't you want to go back to Ohio?"

"No…" He hesitates. "Least ways, not until I can bring some money with me. We were here to get money for credibers."

"Creditors?" I ask gently and step closer. My goodness, he even has freckles.

"Yeah. Them things."

"All right, Mr. Liggon Tyler, let's talk business." I raise my arm to his for escort and we walk back to the hotel.

Thank you, again, Lord.

As Liggon and I walk and talk, my mind runs on to the plans I have: It will take a week to gather the things I'll need to begin farming. Thankfully, it's not too late to clear some land for a late summer crop. And this summer I can live at my parents' homestead, and Liggon can sleep in the barn. After all, Jones did ask me to look after the place, and by about August we will have built another log cabin on my own property.

But I wonder what Shaw will do when he has to go to Fort Smith? They probably won't be back for at least two months, if they don't have any trouble. I'll need to speak to him—about that and other things.

The next day it seems the whole town knows I've made a claim, and several creative fellows have thought up some rather cheap jokes at my expense.

They don't believe I can manage.

The next day, I realize it is time to visit Mr. Shaw and make arrangements. I doubt he's been to town to hear about my new claim. I'm certain he'll think I've lost my mind. I tromp over to the livery and Peter Sams fits me out with my horse and wagon. "You must have a lot of courage, Miss Hay, to try a claim out there," he says shyly.

"Courage? I don't know, Mr. Sams. I've had some experience, though, and the property is almost home to me, you know?" I wonder if he's heard the nasty things people are saying.

"Uh-huh. Well, I always thought you was brave trying to put Mr. MacDonald away, and, well, we'll all be watchin' to see how it turns out for you."

My horse wants to be out the doors, so I hold up on the reins just briefly to add, "I'm sure you all will. And I hope I surprise every one of you."

He smiles and out I go.

On the way out I think on Peter's words. Bravery and courage are odd virtues. I don't think I'm brave at all. If I am brave, it's a virtue I certainly can't feel. Not like humility or kindness or such. It's a strange thing that brings strange thoughts to mind, and I determine to look up "courage" in the Scriptures at the first opportunity.

Arriving at Shaw's cabin around noon, I think he must be having supper. I didn't realize it was so late. Oh, well.

I draw up the wagon, jump down, and breathe the air in. *I'll be back here so soon, I can taste it*, I think. A deep peace comes over me at the thought. I walk up to Shaw's door and knock.

Shaw answers the door. "Miss Hay? Come in, come in." He pulls the door back, and I realize I am looking into his eyes. I think it's the first time I've seen him without his little glasses. His eyes are a nice, soft brown, and I surmise from the shape of his face under his beard, he's probably not too far from handsome.

I step in carefully. The last time I was here, Jonathan was sitting at Shaw's table, battered and bandaged. I didn't even look around then, so now I take a quick look as I walk in.

Neat as a pin. I always figured him for a perfectionist. When I catch a glimpse of home-canned goods on the shelves, I realize that perhaps Mother and I took for granted a man doesn't do that sort of thing. Come to think of it now, knowing Shaw, I wouldn't doubt he took our gifts of food as an insult.

I draw up a chair and rest my hands on the table.

Mr. Shaw sits down across from me with a plate of food. "What brings you out here? Come to check on Jones' cabin?"

"Yes, I will, but that's not the only reason I came today. I need to discuss some business with you."

"Business?" He raises his plate of cheese and bread. "Care for some?"

"Thank you. Yes." He gets a bowl for me, and I smile and take portions gratefully.

We eat in silence. As we eat, I try to prepare my mind for my presentation. But I'm nervous and can't quite seem to get all my thoughts in order, and so I decide I may as well come right out with it. After all, this is one man who'll want to hear everything up front. "Well, Mr. Shaw," I boldly state, "I've put a claim on the acreage west of Jonathan Jones."

If I'd told him his house was on fire, I don't think he would have been more surprised. After a shocked moment of silence, he says, "Why?"

"I want to farm. It's what I've always wanted to do."

"Well, wantin' and havin' are two different things." He wags his head.

I'm hoping to find a bit of humor in his words, but there's not a trace. "No. I've researched farming techniques, and I've worked on a farm all my life. I know what I want to do."

"You think a little studyin's gonna help you clear and plant fifty acres or ward off a slew of grasshoppers or keep back a wild fire?" His eyes are wide. He shakes his head again and pushes himself back from the table.

I raise my voice a little. "Mr. Shaw. I don't think you know me well enough to know how I'll handle such things. I've already got help." His look makes me change my tack. "Look, I came here because you're going to be... because you are my neighbor, again!" I lower my voice even more and look down. "I know you have or have had an agreement with Mr. Jones, and I'd like to have a mutually beneficial arrangement with you, also." He crosses his arms but he doesn't interrupt me. "I'll do anything you find you don't feel like doing, laundry or whatever we agree upon, if I can count on you to help at times, like... right now, when I need to borrow equipment to clear the fields. And I do have help—a boy of sixteen—who will help me establish the place. I was planning to live at Jones' until we can build another cabin on my place. Jones did ask me to look after the cabin, after all."

I look up to see his mouth wide open and his eyes staring at me in wonder. Then he snaps his jaws shut. "Well, I suppose you have thought it out some."

"You'll probably need some time to think about it."

"Nope."

"You mean you don't need time?"

"Nope. I mean nope. I don't need help. Already have two fellas." His eyes come to slits and he is looking me over.

I know my face is becoming bright red with fury as I realize he's not the least interested in helping me. Well, I should have known better. He doesn't need help, and he has a right to that. I can't expect something from him, yet I suppose I thought we had some sort of friendship.

"And don't think I don't see what you're trying to pull," he says slowly.

I tilt my head and stare at him. His tone is like it was a few weeks ago, like he thinks I'm... "Mr. Shaw, what do you mean?"

"Yer just doing this so Jonathan will want to marry you—then you can get your place back. You're as obvious as an angry skunk."

I jump up, but my voice is steady as I eye him. "Mr. Shaw, that has to be one of the most mean-spirited things I've ever heard. I'm sorry you don't know me better. And you must think very little of Mr. Jones to believe he'd be tricked into something he wouldn't want. He's never said *anything* to me about marriage. He hasn't even decided if he wants to farm! You're right to think I love my parents' homestead, and the idea of seeing it, even from a distance, every day, would give me pleasure. But the reason I purchased the property is because it's something my father always wanted to do but never could, and this ground is the only kind I know how to farm. I could give you a hundred more honest reasons for my buying the property next door, but I wouldn't, I wouldn't..."

I stop, because there is a nasty creeping sensation crawling up my spine. The truth is I do want the property to make Jonathan think... think about me. Just like the silly dress. It hits me full force, and I throw my face in my hands and turn away as tears spring to my eyes.

How could Jonathan possibly see it as anything less than a ploy to interest him? It's what Shaw sees. What the town sees. As if

I'm bribing him with more land. I could think of so many other reasons to do it, I had put this one reason out of my mind. Shaw thinks I want my parents' farm back. Only Mary knows how I really feel.

"Oh, Mr. Shaw, I would never want Jonathan to think that way, but that's just what he'll think, isn't it?" I turn my head toward him and steady myself by holding the back of a chair. "Of course it is," I say while watching him.

Shaw stands and comes toward me, nodding.

I lower my eyes, sniff, and wipe the tears away with both hands. "You're right, mostly right, Mr. Shaw. I could want him to marry me, but this much you don't know... I could be as good a marshal's wife as a farmer's and *just* as willing." I whack the back of the chair with my fingers for emphasis, but then I grab my aching hand. "Oh, *DAMSON PLUMS!*" I cry out, wanting to hurl the chair across the room for hurting me.

The room is silent for a moment, and then much to my surprise, Shaw begins to laugh in a low rolling chuckle. "If you want to farm, you're gonna have to learn something about cussing, Miss Hay." I give him a frail smile, and then in his most gentle voice he says, "Don't cry now, don't cry. I should have seen it, and I'm an idiot to say what I did, Miss Hay. Just 'cause a woman had the good sense to cheat me don't mean you're all that way."

I nod. "I have to tell you, I'm not even sure you're right about her." And I laugh a little.

He waves his hand. "Psh," he says, as if the whole thing doesn't matter to him now, anyway.

I make a decision. "Well, then, there's only one thing I can do," I say matter-of-factly. "I just can't tell him I've bought the place. I'll build the cabin on the other side of the acreage, and he won't know I'm there, until... I don't know what." I look straight into Shaw's eyes. "You know, I don't want to lose his respect now, Mr. Shaw. It took so much to gain it."

He nods soberly. "Well, I believe I've just now changed my mind about some things, too. Truth is," he peers around his cabin, "I like to cook, but I hate doing the danged laundry."

He says it so seriously it makes me chuckle. "Well, if I'm going to do your laundry, I think you can start calling me Marilla."

He nods. "Matthias." And he holds out his hand to shake on the new arrangement.

I ask if I can watch the place for him when Lillian and he travel to Fort Smith, and he gratefully accepts my offer. He's hired two men to help him work the fields and they'll appreciate a woman's hand because, as he says with a laugh, these fellows can't tell a cooking pot from a chamber pot. I smile and then, after a slight hesitation, I say, "Mr. Shaw, that trip will be hard for both of you, I know, but if you keep an open mind it might turn out well."

He shakes his head. "What's past is past and it don't matter to me." I watch him and hold back a smile. He could say those words all day to whomever he pleased, and he still couldn't put any heart into them.

I leave his place feeling grateful that Mr. Shaw—Matthias—started the conversation about Jonathan, painful as it was. But I'm a little concerned as to how I'll respond to a letter from Jonathan when now I'll have very little to tell him about myself. I walk across the field toward the cabin, leading my horse and wagon.

I realize I'll have to build my own home as soon as possible. I couldn't have Jonathan come and find me here. I'll have to hire more than one helper. *Well, I'll cross that bridge...* and I walk into the cabin and begin cleaning it top to bottom.

I get back to the hotel late that night, tired but deliriously happy.

THIRTEEN

Where the Rio Grande is flowing and starry skies are bright,
She walks along the river in the quiet summer night.
She thinks if I remember we parted long ago;
I promised to come back again and never let her go.

From the song
The Yellow Rose of Texas

The next morning, I set about making lists of things to do, supplies to purchase, errands to run, and such. Liggon will help me gather things this afternoon, and we can start making trips to the property. Mary interrupts my list-making with a knock on my door and a cheerful, "GOOD morning, Marilla." I let her in and she waves a letter in my face.

"How much will you give me for it?" she asks coyly.

I let out a half-laugh. "Mary!" I try to snatch it, but she's too quick. "If that's a letter from Jonathan, I'm going to give you a knock on the head if you don't hand it over!" And I lunge for her.

We fall in giggles to the floor, and she gives it up. As we finally stand, she brings her elbow to my shoulder as if she plans to read it with me.

"See you later." And I push her gently toward the door.

"Fine. Read me the good portions later, then." She winks and closes the door.

"WAIT! Wait!"

Mary opens the door again.

"I almost forgot. Here are the books for you. They're pretty hefty. There's at least half a college degree here, just by weight." I giggle. "Here... Gibbon's *Rise and Fall of the Roman Empire*, Bunyan's *Pilgrim's Progress*, and selected poems by Keats. Oh, how I love Keats. And don't lose this little fellow, full of William Shakespeare's sonnets. There are more where they came from, but that should get you started."

"Well, at least I've heard of each of them. That must count for something."

"I'll give you one college credit for that. Just a hundred or more to go. Now go!"

She leaves and I'm alone with my letter. My hands are shaking as I turn it over. Jonathan has a fine hand, and I smile to see it. I tear the envelope open and sit all at once and then breathe deeply as I begin to read.

"Dear Marilla..."

First, he speaks about his trip. He's already passed through most of southeastern Colorado and is heading for Oklahoma Territory. He likes the travel, but he'd trade in most of his travel companions for one kind and obedient dog. He says he's listened to some of the men's stories over the campfire, and he knows he's been on the road too long because now and then they begin to sound human. They've noticed him reading the Bible and try to rile him about it, but one fellow asked about it in earnest while the others were asleep. I read the name and I can't believe my eyes: Stubs.

Stubs curious about the Lord? Stubs, with a face red and wrinkled by the sun, eyes slit like a rancher, and a nose—well, a nose true to his name. It must have been broken a dozen times. Face forward, his nose curves side to side like a snake in action. It's a comical thing to see, really, although I can't think of anyone brave enough to laugh out loud when they see it.

I laugh aloud, though, as I catch Jonathan's next paragraph. When he asked Stubs how he wound up with MacDonald, Stubs just laughed and said, *Guess I've always follered my nose.* Now I can't tell if Jonathan has made this story up or if it really happened, but then he says he went on to explain the gospel to him and that Stubs seemed mighty interested. "People like to surprise me," Jonathan once said. How very true.

In his next paragraph, he speaks about his job, how he'll probably be sent to track someone as soon as he gets to Fort Smith, but he'll have to be back there for the trial. He says he's been thinking a lot about his future, and I involuntarily gulp, and my cheeks and forehead begin to tingle as I read the next line, "I am going to ask for reassignment to Colorado Territory, Marilla. I think nothing suits me better than Colorado. I've only been gone a week and already wish I were heading back. I miss the homestead and I miss Quiet Rock and I find I miss you. Yours sincerely, Jonathan." I stand up and am surprised that I'm not flying to the ceiling. No, but I do begin to pirouette right there in my little room.

But I can't be limited to time and space; they are suddenly just so much unimportant detail. There is really only Jonathan and me, and I know now that I was not imagining anything. "THANK you, Lord." I'm so happy, I think I'll burst.

"I've got to go tell Mary!" And I run out and down the stairs to find her. She's at the front desk and takes the news with a great smile.

I can't help but get teary. "You know, reading this makes me know I can wait for him. It's going to make me patient."

"Would you really want to be the wife of a marshal?" she says with unusual seriousness.

The question makes me look past her and sigh. "I wouldn't want to. Who would? On the other hand, all you have to do is look at someone sideways to get shot these days, so what's the difference?" I grin halfheartedly, but Mary shakes her head.

"No. I wouldn't want the not knowing," she says matter-of-factly.

"I can really only see it one way," I say suddenly. "I want to be the wife of Jonathan Jones." And I color as the words come rushing out.

She looks at me. "I don't like what love does to people," she says seriously.

"Mary, you don't mean that."

She looks down and straightens the lace at her collar. "I meant it when I said it. Sometimes I don't like being a Christian, Marilla."

I gulp to hear it. "What?"

"It... it makes you feel responsible for things. It gets you all jumbled up inside. It... it hurts, sometimes." She looks up. "You know?"

"Yes, I know. Did I make the mistake of telling you being a Christian would be easy?"

She smiles and shakes her head as she sees my worried look. "Don't worry about me, Marilla. Once I make a decision, I never go back on my word."

"Good, Mary, that's good," I say with unbridled irritation. "Now would you simply believe as much of God?"

"But, Marilla, it's so much easier for you. You got no past. Everything here reminds me of what I was."

"But look at the good you've done... giving the girls in town something to work at besides the lineup..."

"For which I might get shot."

"Helping the church get established."

"Anyone could do that..."

"Then why haven't you left?"

"Why haven't I?" she says flatly. "If I hear one more old customer joke with me about the *good old days*, I'll..." she raises tight fists to the air.

"Mary, I don't know what it's like for you. I can't pretend to know. I only know for certain God's seen it all before."

She stops and smiles slowly. "Like Mary Magdalene?"

I hadn't thought of it before but smile slightly in agreement. "Guess so. Guess she knew."

She gazes around the room and back to me. "Come to think of it, she didn't leave town, did she?" Sniffing, she throws back her head. "That gal must have had some spunk." Her head shakes back and forth as she smiles cynically, "But I ain't that brave." Now the look on her face grows cold, "Somedays, I just plain *hate* this place."

I gulp. "Maybe it wasn't bravery made her stay—maybe she was waitin' to see what God would do. After all she'd been through," I whisper, "she got to see the resurrection."

Mary swallows and puts her head down. I watch her think on it as she pulls her hand to her chin. Her eyes glint up at me as her hand falls away. "Guess it might be worth the wait... just in case."

I take a deep breath to keep from crying, but then I grab Mary's hand and squeeze it hard.

Finally I clear my throat. "I'm taking things out to the cabin with Liggon this afternoon, so I won't be much help around here. I figure it will take us until Sunday to get everything out there."

Mary is rolling her fingertip in slow circles on the desk and seems to not hear me. "Shaw and Lillian are supposed to leave Monday," she says finally.

"Oh? And so will I."

Mary just looks at me, and neither of us can speak. "I'm going to miss you, Mary Baylor," I say quietly.

"And I you." She comes from behind the desk to give me a big hug.

Back up in my room, I realize I have to write Jonathan. He won't get the letter for a long time, perhaps another month. I draw a piece of stationery from my desk and stare at it. And I wonder and wonder what to write. I begin, but the words come haltingly, in spurts. I tell him I miss him, also, and how much our talks have meant. When I look back over the letter, I realize nothing is untrue, but it doesn't sound right either, because I can't be completely honest. But I sign it, "Waiting at Quiet Rock, Marilla Hay."

That afternoon, we begin hauling supplies: equipment first, food to be held for last. By Saturday night, I am aching but happy as I return to the hotel. All this time, my letter to Jonathan has rested on my vanity, unsealed and very unmailed. But I have something to add to the envelope now that makes me smile.

That morning Mary let me take a couple of chairs to my cabin from the old bar—those considered unworthy of the new hotel furnishings. Since they were broken up anyway, I saw off the spoke backs to make kitchen stools.

One chair had a one inch split up the leg as well, so I saw it off and then proceed to "correct" the other three legs. Some time later, I am still making sawdust with the chair legs when I finally discover the real trouble: the floor isn't flat! I laugh aloud. "Of course. It's like everything else. I'm busy whittling at chairs, when it's the floor that needs planing." I stare at the mess a good long while, letting a little self-pity creep into my bones, but finally shake it loose. "No, that's not fair, Marilla. Jones hasn't decided. He hasn't decided anything." But I say it with half a heart.

When Liggon comes in, I say with a laugh, "Look at this, Liggon. I shouldn't have started this when I was so tired!" He comes over to see my work and starts chuckling.

"You've made a batch of wooden nickels, Miss Hay! And a footstool, too."

I stare at the squat little stool and then at the scattered wooden circles, and I shake my head. *If he could see this, Jonathan Jones wouldn't pick me for a maid, let alone a wife.* But that gives me an idea. Straightway I borrow Liggon's whittling knife, picked up a likely looking circle, and started carving.

I carve out a little plow on one side and a saber, "the sword of the Lord," on the other. Then I slip it into my apron pocket with a contented smile, and decide it is time to return to town.

Now that I'm back at the hotel, I look at the lonely little letter on my vanity and I sit down, slip the "coin" into the envelope, and add a postscript to my letter.

"Jonathan, when you finally come to deciding your fate, remember how the Lord has used the casting of lots to determine the way His people should go. You can toss this coin with prayer to decide between professions, or you can just keep it as a token of friendship and hope."

Now I can rest.

Monday morning, and it is time for Matthias and Lillian to head to Fort Smith. Matthias comes over from the livery with four new horses on his rig. The rig has been fitted for prairie schooning, with a canvas tarpaulin over a frame, but it looks a bit more like a peddler's cart than a wagon. We spend quite a while packing their things into the flatbed. Memories of my family's trip come to me as we find a place for everything, snug as we can.

Lillian was silent and unsmiling all morning and now simply nods to Shaw as he finally escorts her up into the wagon.

Shaw gives me final instructions for his farm and tells me to use his boys if I want to put up a cabin while he's gone. I thank him profusely for the offer, and he thanks me for helping out, and then his eyes grow big as he turns away from us to face the wagon seat. He mounts up and looks back at me. The seriousness of the trip makes me swallow hard, and I'm so glad, because Shaw's lost look makes me want to burst out laughing.

As he starts the team up, Mary turns and nudges me. "He looks as happy as a caged raccoon, doesn't he?" And we shake our heads and laugh as we walk back into the hotel.

That afternoon, Liggon and I pack up the last wagon load, and Mary and I have a final hug.

"Well, you'll see me every Sunday, at least!" I say happily.

"At the hotel!"

"Next week?"

She nods.

"Mary, have I mentioned how impressed I am with what you've done here?"

"Several times. You trying to swell my head about it?"

I nod.

"Well, keep it up, 'cause my knees still shake every night we open for dinner."

Her openness still surprises me. I smile and then look over her shoulder to the front of the hotel, and a thought occurs to me. "Mary, there's something terribly wrong here."

Mary whirls around to face the building and looks over the facade. "What? The porch?" She points. "I just have to replace these two front columns..."

"No. More serious than that."

"The roof? It only leaks in the kitchen by the side window, and..."

"No. More important."

She looks at me worriedly.

"Mary, the sign's all wrong. It needs to say, 'Baylor's Hotel.'"

She goes a bit pale and drops her head. "Yes. I suppose so."

* * *

The first week at the farm is full of work; we begin clearing a spot for the cabin, just Liggon and me. Shaw's boys are planting, and I don't want to take them from it. I reread Jonathan's letter at night before I go to sleep, and I sleep on the floor just as Jonathan does; there's no time to manage fleas.

By the end of the week, my hands are raw despite the home-made woolen gloves I wear. On the first Sunday, I invite Liggon to the hotel for services. He respectfully declines, so I head into town on my own.

I don't remember the service; I think I fell asleep.

The second week, I work in a mind-numbing state: I concentrate on digging bushes and shrubs, hauling scrub, piling it for burning—I get so tired, I can't think past the object in front of my eyes.

The second Sunday, I try to get up and go to church, but I push the bell off on my clock and that's all I remember until loud knocking on the door awakens me. I pull myself up and ask who it is.

"Miss Hay? It's Reverend Post and Miss Baylor. Are you well?"

Oh my goodness.

"Yes, yes, I'm fine. I'll be to the door in a moment." I stand up quickly only to find I ache from my bare toes to my sleepy head. I am one tall bruise.

I slowly pull my calico wrapper about me, smooth my hair, and then braid it the best I can. I wish I could hurry but my bones will not permit it.

Reverend Post and Mary's concerned faces greet me as I open the door. "Please come in. I'm sorry to worry you all. My bell went off and I went right back to sleep! I'm so tired these days."

Mary brushes past him to look me over. "Okay, honey. I thought all sorts of horrible things."

I rub my eyes and feel myself blush as I see Reverend Post looking me up and down. I offer them Sunday supper and we sit and eat a little. Later, I walk them around the area we've cleared, and they tell me it's a beautiful spot. I know they think it's just dry dirt, but they don't know what it looks like in my mind's eye. As we walk back to the cabin, we pass Liggon at the barn and I introduce them all.

"Town's giving a May Ball next Saturday night, Marilla," Mary suddenly says. "Why don't you all come?"

"At the hotel?"

"No, there's a new business going up. They've just laid the floor, so somebody decided it was a good time for a dance."

"It's always a good time to dance," Reverend Post adds with a wink to me.

I feel light-headed all of a sudden. I turn to Liggon, and he's looking uncomfortable. "Have you ever been to a dance, Liggon?"

"No, ma'am. What do you have to do for one?"

There's a slight twitching of adult mouths, but I compose myself. "It's just for fun, Liggon. Pure fun. If you like, I'll teach you how to dance this week, and then you may escort me."

His freckles disappear into deep crimson, and he stammers, "Well, I would, uh, but I... I got, uph, a lot to do this week."

"Yes, you do, but I'm the boss, and I say dancing will be on the roster, too."

He looks as though he's eaten a green-gill oyster, but I won't be dissuaded.

So on Monday we lay the foundation logs and floorboards for the new cabin, and throughout the week, within a rising rectangle of hewn logs, I teach dancing to Liggon Tyler. He's a fast study, as I might have guessed—he's caught on to any new task here in no time—and so by Friday night I feel certain he can handle a reel, a waltz, and a fine imitation of anything else the musicians may throw at us.

Late Saturday afternoon, after putting on my black silk, I unfold a surprise for Liggon I'd been thinking on all week. I call Liggon into the cabin, and when he steps in, his eyes catch the clothing laid out for him on the kitchen table: my father's dress clothes.

"Miss Hay?"

"Liggon, these are my father's clothes. I want you to wear them this evening."

"Begging your pardon, ma'am, but, don't they sort of... belong to Mr. Jones now? Won't Mr. Jones mind?"

I know I'm blushing, but I try to keep the edge from my voice as I reply, "These are a little small for Mr. Jones, Liggon, and if he'd intended to sell them, he would have done so by now. I believe we're going to find they fit you like a tailored suit. Try 'em on and see. And if you're still wanting to feel odd about it, just remember you're only borrowing them for a night."

The white shirt buttoned up, the dove gray vest, coat and pants—they fit him beautifully. I suppose I should be sad to see my father's things out, but on the contrary, it feels good to see them being used. Very good. "Liggon, you do those clothes proud."

"Thanks, Miss Hay." But he looks doubtful. He's tried to catch a view in the mirror by the dry sink, but it's too small to do any good.

"Aw, this little thing does no good. Go do what I used to do to see my whole self. Go to the river to the standing pool by the willow, hold on to the lowest left branch, and then hang out over the water 'til you can see most of yourself. You'll see."

As he walks away, I'm reminded of Jonathan's trunk in the loft... filled with costumes and pictures, he said. I'd give anything to look through those things, but he has to be with me. Unless, of course, he dies out there. I bring my hand to my neck and gulp back the sorrow; I miss him so.

When Liggon finally returns from the river, he doesn't speak, but I notice he walks a little straighter and it makes me smile with pride.

On the way into town, we talk about what to expect, and I confess I haven't been to a dance since my teenage years. "The farmers used to have dances out here all the time, but I think my family kind of left ourselves out of the circle after a time."

"Miss Hay, I have a 'fession to make, too. I been to a dance before."

"You have?"

"But it didn't turn out so good, and if you wouldn't mind, I'd just rather dance with you, tonight."

"That wouldn't be much of a dance, Liggon. We could do that at the cabin! So, what didn't turn out so good?"

He's quiet for a time, but finally lets out, "Well, nobody would dance with me for one."

"Nobody... would... Well, did you know how to dance back then?"

"No. And I was shorter than all of them and fatter than most."

I have to laugh.

"It wasn't funny, Miss Hay, it was awful."

"Liggon, I'm not laughing at that. You just don't know you've grown up, do you? You're pretty near a man, now, with a man's height, and a man's kind manners, and... heavens, you've even got on a man's suit! I wouldn't let you touch it if I thought you wouldn't fill it! There may not be many girls to go around out here, but I don't believe any of 'em are gonna say 'no' to Liggon Tyler tonight. You know I was once a girl myself, so I think I may say so with a certainty."

But I may have said too much, because he suddenly seems lost in thought. I hold my tongue when I catch the look from the corner of my eye, and we ride quietly the rest of the way.

Downtown Independence by nightfall is as jammed and noisy as I remember, but it doesn't overwhelm me the way it used to. I wonder why, then it comes to me: there's a peace in knowing I'm free to turn right around and leave if I like. There's the stark difference. A marvelous difference. And Liam MacDonald doesn't own anything right now but a little plot of ground.

The dance commences promptly at seven o'clock and is destined to go until dawn, and Liggon and I start the dancing with vigorous steps. Before too long, the musicians have switched to a waltz, and I'm finally given the opportunity to peruse the ladies' corner to see if any young ladies have noticed Mr. Tyler.

I needn't have worried.

For three songs in a row I see bright little eyes watching us whenever they think they are getting away with it. I smile and smile as we dance, some for the music and some for the twirling, yes, but not a little bit for the knowing the wonderful and terrifying world Mr. Liggon Tyler is about to step into tonight. I only pray he's ready.

After we have danced the first set, I tell him I have to stop and catch my breath. With utter truth I tell the boy I can no longer keep up with him, and that it is time to change partners.

So with great hesitation and a grave look on his pale face, he nods and then walks to the first available young lady to request a dance. Melissa Pruett, nervously holding her two thick braids before her when Liggon approaches, practically melts at the question, crosses her braids with delight and nods, and from all the way across the hall I can see Liggon's face turn red as strawberry pie, but I don't get a chance to watch them after that. A fellow asks me to dance and I oblige. I don't have another rest for an hour, and I have to watch Liggon's progress from a distance, but I am pleased to see the girls—really only four old enough to dance with him—set themselves close by him as each song ends so he'll ask them next.

As for my own partners, some are quick and some are slow, some lead and some beg to be led, but except for an occasional foot stomping, I am having a very good time.

This fine evening I've also noticed Reverend Post carefully ask each of the ladies from the church to dance with him, and that has satisfied everyone so well they don't even seem to mind when he dances with Mary Baylor. Now I see Reverend Post making his way toward me, and I feel my heart rising to my throat. Inwardly I groan at my nervousness and wish he weren't so good-looking, but he's smiling his most reassuring smile as he holds out his hand.

And so we begin to twirl to a lively two-step, and I soon realize he is by far the best dance of the evening. His timing is perfect, his smile genuine. With a slightly firm touch at my waist and a warm, smooth hand gently holding my own, he imperceptibly gives direction to our dance, but then I think how rough my hand must feel in his.

But the song is energetic and I am twirling under softly swaying lamplight with the most handsome fellow in the room, and I feel absolutely wonderful. All too soon, the music stops, and Reverend Post bows gracefully and moves to the next lady. I realize he's done no more and no less for me than for any other woman he's danced with tonight, which is to say we are each feeling very much like queens.

I pull back to the wall for a moment, and without my bidding a vision of Jonathan comes to mind. I wonder how he dances. I wonder if he dances at all. I almost feel guilty for enjoying myself with Reverend Post. My daydream is interrupted by a request to dance and I shake my head pleasantly, and so the fellow decides to strike up a conversation. He's chubby and red-cheeked, with a full beard and a pointy nose. He tells me he's a miner who has just gotten here and he wants to know a woman's view of this town.

Now that's an unusual request, so I turn and smile. "Why ever would you want to have a woman's view?"

"Got a wife in Arkansas a' beggin' me to send her out." His eyes tell me he's in dire earnest. "Ya think I should?"

"Well... how used to rough living is she?"

"Growed up on a farm with thirteen."

"She like washing and cooking?"

"Hates 'em."

I nod sympathetically and give a half-smile. "Does she like you?"

"Loves me, dang it all. 'At's why she wants to come." He kicks at a nail in the floorboard and chuckles.

"Then I don't think you should stand in the way of love."

He looks at me steadily and says with a wink, "Well, that settles it, then. Thank you, miss. Now, you want to dance?"

I grin. "If you don't think your wife would mind."

"I'll give her the next dance, miss. I'll give her the very next dance."

True to his word, he leaves the floor right after our dance, and I go to find Liggon, because I want to go home, too, all of a sudden. *Besides,* I tell myself, *I have to teach my very first lesson in Sunday School tomorrow, and what kind of impression will I give my students if they see I've been up dancing all night?!*

I find Liggon at the punch table with the wide-eyed young ladies around him and a bevy of young boys around their inner circle. From the looks and glances some of the young men are giving each other, I am taking him out of here none too soon.

As we ride out of town, I sigh deeply as we pass by Quiet Rock. "So, what do you think of dances now, Liggon?"

"I don't know, Miss Hay, I think farming's a lot simpler. I mean, I couldn't keep the dances straight. I thought I was taking turns, but one girl would say no, it was her turn again and the other'd disagree. I'd know I was right, but then they'd look so sad and pretty, I'd figure I was wrong and..." He shakes his head. "I tell you, I'm all wore out trying to be polite." I hold back my laughter and look up at the sky. On a clear night like this, the sky looks on fire with stars. The sweet smell of mountain flowers rises up unexpectedly and brings a gathering of good thoughts.

I sleep well that night and dream of waltzing in the clouds with Marshal Jones.

The next day, I begin my first Sunday School lesson in the kitchen of the hotel. There are five children in attendance, including Melissa Pruett, who is very attentive.

I teach about Jesus calling the children to come unto him and then talk with them about why he would do that. Julian Sanders, age ten, says brightly, "I only come when Mom really lets a yell." Anne Foster asks with concern, "Would Jesus yell?" These and other issues are addressed in the coming hour.

I ask them if they would invite others who might want to learn about Jesus, and we decide to write "invitations" to Sunday School for their friends.

At the end of the hour, I realize two things: I have a lot to learn about children, and I have a lot to learn about teaching. I determine to put in a different effort in the coming months. Before leaving, Melissa Pruett, with her brown eyes large and fearful, shyly presses her invitation into my hand, then rushes out, her dark pigtails flying behind her. I look at it and it says, "For LIGGEN TIGER" on the outside, and so I can't help but burst out in a giggle.

I run into Mary in the lobby before the service starts, and immediately she says, "Marilla, I have something for you. Don't hate me, but I forgot to give it to you last night." She holds out a letter.

My heart begins to thump-a-thump as I see it's another letter from Jonathan! "Thank you, thank you, Mary! I don't care if it's a day late, it's here. Oh, and look at this. Melissa Pruett gave it to me for Liggon. An invitation to Sunday School!"

She laughs with the sound of a string of bells as she sees the address. "Oh, that's sweet."

We go into church together, and I realize with dismay that I will have to wait until the ride home before I can read Jonathan's missive. I do my best to concentrate on the sermon, but it isn't much use. As church lets out, I quickly hug Mary good-bye and rush to the livery to get my wagon. I ride in a trot out as far as Quiet Rock so I can read it.

It's three pages long, and begins again with "Dear Marilla..." He says by the time I get this, he should be in Fort Smith.

Maybe he's gotten my letter by now. I wish I knew.

He says he hasn't had much trouble with the men, and Stubs continues his "Bible studies" with him. Last week he was grateful to know the big fellow so well, as Stubs found a knife on one of his fellow prisoners. Jonathan adds, "He even took it upon himself to mete out a judgment on the man. But it put me in a spot to know whether to thank him, seeing as the man's more dead than alive right now. But anyway, I'll be letting the judge know what Stubs did for me, and since he's not in for murder (assuming this fellow pulls through), maybe Parker'll go easier on him."

Then he describes the bright Oklahoma sunsets and says how he loves the road, but adds he'd still rather be in Colorado 'cause the wind never quite stops blowing in Oklahoma, and it's beginning to get on his nerves. He says the wind is so bad all the corn plants grow in one direction and that the stalks look sort of foolish leaning that way—although, he admits, it would probably taste just like upright corn. I don't know if I should believe him or not, but it's charming anyway.

The nicest part of all is when he talks about our visits, and says how he's never spoken so easily to anyone before, that he sees we have the same ideals, if not the same goals.

Oh, I wish he hadn't said that.

He wonders how I wound up with so many talents, and wishes he'd known my parents so the thing could be explained. I wish he'd known them, too.

Then he says he hopes the hotel is working well for me and figures I'll forget all about farming in all that comfort.

Ooh, that hurts.

But he signs off, "Thinking of you. God grant us time for each other again one day. Jonathan Beauregard Jones III."

And I cry soft, slow sort of tears all the way home.

When I arrive at the cabin, I dry my eyes, seek out Liggon, and give him Melissa's note with a smile. His face turns a bright pink as he walks slowly away, unfolding the little note as he goes. He turns back and smiles a bit, but he looks a little concerned, too. I just have to say it. "I'll have lunch ready in no time... TIger."

"Oooh, no," he wails and walks toward the barn.

When he comes in for lunch, I can tell he's still embarrassed. "Melissa is sweet, isn't she?"

He thinks on it. "Yep."

"Pretty."

"Yep."

I let it go, but I'm glad when he breaks the silence himself. "I like her name. It's nice, like your Christian name, Miss Hay."

"Thank you, Liggon. It's about time you addressed me as Marilla."

He thinks on, like he's tasting the idea, then he shakes his head. "No. No, I couldn't.... But I've been meaning to ask you.... You any relation to the President?"

I have to laugh at the thought. "Rutherford B.? Oh no, Liggon, I'm a singular Hay."

"Well, I knew you wasn't married to him," he replies with irritation.

I bite my lip. "That's right." Under my breath I add, "I'm not related to him at all, *Tiger*."

FOURTEEN

The western fields give thousands wealth,
Ho! Westward Ho!
And yield to all a glowing health,
Ho! Westward Ho!
For all inclined to honest toil,
Ho! Westward Ho!
Secure their fortunes from the soil,
Ho! Westward Ho!

From the song *Ho! Westward Ho!*

The next week, I borrow Shaw's help and we get the cabin completely up by Friday. We chink between the logs on Saturday, and Sunday comes all too quickly. Liggon surprises me by deciding to go with me to Sunday School. But he grumbles all the way about always having to be polite.

He can't hide his satisfaction, however, when Melissa Pruett bestows upon him a lovely smile as he walks in the room. I teach Sunday School, attend church, and go home with a whistling driver at my side. Upon arriving home I fall fast asleep.

Within the next week, we clear more acreage, working on the cabin when we can. Thankfully, Shaw's fellows know of another young man needing work, so I now have two hired hands. Samuel Trent is a year older than Liggon, with sandy hair, dark eyes, and a large rounded face. He's a bit thicker in the middle than Liggon, but has the same grit and determination as "Tiger" when it comes to work. Sam's father works in town as a cobbler's assistant, but the father's boss told Sam he had no room for him there, and so Sam had to look elsewhere. Thankfully, he gets along well with Liggon, and by the end of two weeks, they are fast friends.

I let the nickname "Tiger" slip once, and Samuel picked it up, so now we both call him Tiger. Poor Liggon.

Our work is simple and tedious, draining both the mind and body, but we can walk off ten acres of cleared land when we finally decide to take a couple days off, and walking off those acres feels about as good as anything I've ever done in my life. That I can watch a gangly bunch of scrub become a rolling field ready for planting gives sweet promise to my dreams. The heavy gurgling stream runs through it, blessing the ground with moisture, just like my parents' land.

When we are done marking off the acreage, the five of us head back to the cabin, and I provide the best feast I can render in thanks for their hard work. A fat stew, simmering with spring vegetables and fresh sausages from a kind neighbor, with some of Shaw's canned goods thrown in for good measure. Soda bread (for still I have no time to wait for bread to rise), a molasses cake, and best of all, a strawberry fool, with fresh cream from Millie and new strawberries from Jones' place. I believe the boys feel properly thanked.

On the last day of May, I figure the trial of the gang has begun, and I travel into town to scan the papers for news of it. Nothing yet.

I move my things to the new cabin when the fireplace is completed. When I'm done resettling, I step out and walk down the path, turn, and look at the thing. The place has two halves, like a city house, each side with a front door and a window. The shake shingles look a little haphazard, but it was my first try at roofing. The place is so little, wrapped around by these woods, it reminds me of a babe in arms. And I have to laugh. "Well, if this is a child, it's a mighty homely one—guess that makes it a home child." That makes me laugh again and roll my eyes at my own foolishness.

Tiger and Sam can stay comfortably on the right side with a wood stove, while my new cook stove and I reside on the left. The hotel spoiled me for fireplace cooking, so I had to give in and take the hotel's stove when Mary purchased a fancier one.

Tiger and Sam and I continue to clear fields in the day. Shaw's men have gone back to work his fields. In the evening, the boys and I sing or mend or whittle or tell stories. They're both pleasant fellows, and I find great blessing in the fact Sam plays guitar, too. He brought his old guitar with him, and so we trade songs back and forth during the evenings. Tiger plays harmonica. It's warm enough now to leave the doors and windows open at night, and we've probably scared a few grizzlies off with our homespun melodies, but we don't care who hears as long as it makes us smile.

I told them all about Jonathan Jones but had to tone down some of the things they'd heard around town about him. Besides, I think the truth itself is pretty spectacular, and they grudgingly agreed. I suppose it's obvious how I feel about Jonathan. I think they caught on after I spilled hot soup on Tiger's lap when he asked, "You care for him, Miss Hay?"

Sam snickered and said, "Dangerous question!"

On the seventh of June I go into town for supplies and finally see word of the trial in a newspaper. Lillian is mentioned, so I know they made it. Marshal Jones' part in it is hailed gloriously. I take in every word and reread it several times, hardly caring what the prisoners' sentences are... except Stubs. I want to know about Stubs. Only five years hard labor for helping MacDonald, it says. The story about Stubs stopping the fellow with the knife had a positive effect on Judge Parker. *Thank you, Lord.*

I return to the cabin with a light heart, hoping Jonathan is already on his way back, and enjoying the fact that, even if he isn't, he wants to be.

By mid-June we have cleared another five acres and begin planting for a late summer crop. That week, I notice I've finally quit thinking of Jonathan in every little thing I do. After all, the planting projects are unusual, and I do have a good time working out the details. But the thought bubbles up to the surface now and then that all along I'm doing this work... for us.

I go into town Saturday for yet another wagon of supplies, and I stop in at the hotel to visit Mary. The restaurant and business have been in full swing for more than a month now, and there's a definite look of prosperity about the place.

When I find her in her office—MacDonald's old office, with the walls as full of art, calendars, and notes as they once were of hides—she grins at me and says, "Another letter for Marilla Hay!"

"Ah. Give it over!"

"Only if you'll read it here."

"Fine. But not if it gets too personal." And I wink. I take it from her and open the letter.

Something's not right. It's short and it begins, "Dear Miss Hay." *Dear Miss Hay?* I look at the outer envelope and the signature. Yes, it's Jonathan.

My brows come together as I look down the page. Mary sees the look and asks, "What's wrong? Is he all right?"

"I don't know, Mary. It doesn't even sound like him. He says... he received my letter. He's gotten the transfer to Denver, took a job there as Deputy U.S. Marshal. *Denver, Mary!* Will start first week of July. Probably be too busy to visit the property any-time soon." I look up at Mary. "Too busy? I don't understand." But I go back to the letter. "He's... he's thinking of buying a place near Denver and... selling this one."

"Selling," says Mary.

"Yes. Here he says... he... heard I might be interested in re-acquiring it. Oh, Mary." My head begins to ache as I reread the words. "Mary, somebody told him about my purchase, and he took it... he took it the wrong way. Oh, no." I bring my other hand to my mouth and let out a little sob.

Mary comes around and holds me in a strong hug while I cry on the shoulder of her new blue silk.

After a minute or two, I pull my head away and shake it. I look at the letter once more and notice a postscript. "Thanks for the wooden nickel." That makes me smile despite my tears. "Ooh, what's the point? Why did I do it? Why couldn't I have waited for him to decide?" And I stomp my foot.

Mary surprises me with a quick reply. "Look, Marilla, a woman shouldn't wait her whole life for a man to tell her what to do next. It'd be a waste of the life God gave you. He meant for you to farm, honey!"

"But, Mary, I don't even know if I'm good at it, yet. I always seem to be whittling when it's the floor that needs planing...."

"Try that on me again?"

I'm too hurt to explain the sad joke of it, so I say quietly, "I could have waited for him... I should have."

"Waited? Waited for what? 'Til he got tired of marshaling? Waited until he was dead? What if it were years, Marilla? There you'd be, running a hotel which you *hate*. Remember when you used to work at the hotel? You used to be so afraid you'd get like Lillian from working there. No, honey, you did the right thing."

"Lillian..."

Mary takes it in and her eyes grow cold. "Yes, by go... golly, Lillian. She must have told him."

We nod together. "Guess she didn't enjoy the trip," I add slowly, with a slight smile. Mary's eyes are flashing, and I know exactly what she's not saying. "Come on. It's not Lillian's fault. 'Cause I agree with what you first said. I am doing what I wanted to do. I'm just going back to my first love."

That makes her come out from the storm. She looks up and lets out a sigh. "Isn't that in Scripture?"

"Yes, I'm sorry. Yes, spiritually, the Lord is our first love."

"I've always liked that one."

I shake my head slowly and place my hands on her shoulders. "Mary Baylor, you're just what I need right now." And we fall into a hug again.

After a quiet dinner at the hotel with Mary, I sit somberly at the table. The plush surroundings give me no pleasure. I look up briefly to notice Mary staring sadly at me.

"I'm sorry I'm no good company, Mary."

She brushes that aside. "I've been thinking you ought to write Jonathan and tell him how you feel. Put all the cards on the table."

I shake my head. "Mary, when he thought he liked me, he

didn't want to leave marshaling, so what difference could it make now?"

"I don't know. I just think somehow he'd understand."

"Understand if he marries me he can double his property? No, thank you."

"Why does it always have to be black and white with you, Marilla?" she says testily. "What's wrong with marrying you for that or any other reason he can come up with? He'd be gettin' a good deal." She pounds her fist on the table for emphasis.

I give her half a smile. "And why do you see things in gray? A marriage can't start off on a bad footing like that and have anything good come of it. He has to marry me for love. I wouldn't have it... him... otherwise. That's all. It's that simple, because... it's that simple!" I wave my hand in the air for emphasis and then cross my arms.

She trills her tongue. "So, now what? You're saying you have to sell the farm until he makes up his mind?"

"The thought had occurred to me," I say somberly. "But I let it pass. Besides, he's made up his mind, hasn't he?" I smile weakly.

She smiles, too. "You're not giving him a fair deal, Marilla. Lillian didn't give him the truth to choose from."

"Oh, the sweetness of the pain!" I say poignantly. This time Mary doesn't bother to even ask me to explain. I smile. "Keats. *A Song of Opposites*. Have you read Keats yet?"

Mary shakes her head. "Can't understand his fancy talk."

"Oh, yes, you can, Mary Baylor." I grow serious and pull my chair forward. "You just didn't have my mother to walk you through it. The trick to poetry is to forget trying to understand each word. Let it give you its meaning as you read along. You'll get it. Keats' poetry is half a century old by now, so of *course* you're not gonna catch every word of it."

"You mean, you don't understand all of it?"

"No. And sometimes I memorize it even when it doesn't quite make perfect sense just yet, then somehow when I need it, it comes to me, same as Scripture. I'll be working out in the field and a passage will come to me. Sometimes a poem or a song."

"'Nother words you don't give up on it. If it's good, you don't give up trying to understand."

Starting with enthusiasm, I say, "Exactly! You don't give..." But then I catch the look in her eyes and see the thin smile grow across her face. "Oh, Mary." I bow my head quickly. She caught me and caught me good. You don't give up on a thing when it's good. Do I love farming more than I love him? Will I take him on his terms? The answer doesn't come quickly—wrapped as it is in my parents' expectations, the things I think would have pleased them if they'd had the ability to see things clearly—and so I have to pray and remove all that before I can finally feel the truth. But when it comes it comes as clear as daylight. "All right, Mary, I'll write to him tonight."

"Good girl."

Back at the cabin that night, I try to form the letter in my mind. With pen in hand I try to write something, but I am attempting to state rationally feelings in me that have essentially no reason or logic, and therefore no words to express them come to mind.

More than once I let out a cry of frustration and throw a crumpled paper into the fire. Finally, I try to put Jonathan's face in my mind and think what I would say to him. I try to imagine him sitting across from me, and I realize starkly I can't imagine his face just now. How strange.

Oh, Lord, let me remember: green eyes, a long mustache, a rectangular face, I think, a rounded dimpled chin, red hair. Why can't I put them together in my mind?

Imagination doesn't work. I stare at the paper some more, thinking I should give up. But I said I would do this. And I shouldn't let Lillian get away with what she's done. Ah. "Jonathan. I think Lillian has taken liberties with informa..." No. Too formal. "Jonathan, I need to speak plainly. Lillian has lied to you about me. I bought the homestead next to yours because I wasn't sure how long it would take for you to decide your future and I thought I should go ahead and farm..." No, too much.

Let's be totally honest, Marilla. All right. Let's try total honesty, since all else has failed. With that, I suddenly feel him sitting across the table, like the first long night's conversation, and the words suddenly flow from my pen:

"Dear Jonathan, If you asked me to be yours, I would. Nothing else matters to me, for I know that I love you. Marilla." With that I put down my pen and watch the flames embrace the last of the firewood.

I mail the short note the next day, sending it to Denver care of the marshal's office. He should be there to meet it soon.

We have planted the summer crop now, and as the weather gets hotter and drier, we realize we'll lose them if we don't get water out to the fields. We've planted some unique vegetables and grains that will be difficult to manage, but they are special order for Mary's hotel. If we succeed, Mary will probably make a name for herself by providing the most unusual fare in the territory. But it won't be easy: the asparagus patch alone won't come for four years. Who knows where I'll be in four years? In any case, they'll die before that without water. I haul out all of my copies of *The Rocky Mountain News* and have Tiger and Sam help me research every irrigation technique we can find. After many tired hours, the rubbing of eyes and the yawning of yawns, we decide on the method: dig ditches like fanned fingers away from the stream, let them run parallel to the stream through the fields, and then bring them back into the stream at the property line.

That night, I dream of efficient Egyptian water levers, powerful English water mills, and ingenious American canals, but in the morning I face the nasty reality of an old shovel in packed mud.

We dig the shallow ditches, but still we find the days are suddenly longer.

As I dig a trench for irrigation toward a five-acre parcel, I realize this coming Tuesday will be our Fourth of July celebration. I stop and rest on the handle of my shovel and ruminate on the festivities, smiling to think how Colorado will be going crazy with it. From all accounts, we're going to receive official statehood on that very day. The town of Independence will throw a party, as will the rest of the territory... state, that is, so I'm going to the hotel for dinner and dancing that evening.

I stand up straight and force my back into an arch with my hands at my waist, and I groan and press and rub. "Perhaps I'll just sit by the dance floor and shuffle my feet," I say aloud through gritted teeth. Though the boys are working near me, neither says a word. They're used to me mumbling to myself now and then. I go back to the shovel with a snicker.

No. I need a good break. I will dance. By golly, I will. I groan at the thought, then tell myself, "I'll dance my boots off if it kills me."

Tuesday comes quickly, and Tiger, Sam, and I head for town. On the way, we pass the time chatting about what each of us will make of this new state of Colorado.

The boys say they will become rich and have a high time until they settle down and marry beautiful girls. "I'll marry when I'm forty," Tiger says cheerfully as he pops the reins into fluid motion in front of him.

Not if Melissa Pruett has her way, I think merrily. Then they come down from the clouds long enough to ask me what I want out of life. "I want the farm to do well enough to keep me, Lord willing," I answer honestly. They both shake their heads in sorrow at my utter lack of ambition.

Just then we pass under a high canopy of cottonwoods. "You know the clump of aspens down at the river? Well, when I was a little girl on a day in autumn ever as bright as this one, I lay down under that clump and looked up. The wind was about like today, and just as I looked up, right then and there, every one of those pale little leaves began to shake and shiver, and it looked to me for all the world like a mass of shiny coins right over my head. I wondered why in the world men would hole up in caves to mine, when all the gold they could ever want was up there for the viewing."

There are a few moments of quiet as we watch the wind in the trees above us, and I think with not a little hope they have caught my point.

But the spell is broken when Tiger says slowly, "But, Miss Hay, you know... the leaves on a quakie... just ain't the same as legal tender."

I shake my head and laugh. "Oh, you've got yourselves gold fever. I can see it. Go on, then. There's no talking to you two!" And they laugh with me as we move along. Still, when Sam thinks I'm not paying attention, he turns back to look at our mountain and I smile to myself.

FIFTEEN

Buffalo gals, won't you come out tonight?
Come out tonight? Come out tonight?
Buffalo gals, won't you come out tonight
And dance by the light of the moon?

From the folksong *Buffalo Gals*

When we arrive in town, Mary meets me in the lobby and takes me aside. "You know what you need, Marilla? You need a beautiful new dress to show yourself off."

"Mary, what's gotten into you? This is new."

"Black won't do for this dance. Just so happens I have two beautiful new dresses for the party tonight, and I can only wear one at a time."

"No, Mary, I couldn't."

She nods. "Yes, you could. You're too young to wear black all the time, Marilla. Live a little!"

"Well, I wrote that letter. I've done enough living to hold me for a while, I should think."

She cocks her head and smiles. "All right," she says reluctantly, and we walk to join the gathering in the dining room.

Here Mary has organized a sumptuous feast for the friends of the church and a few miners, to boot. A lively titter begins as we catch up on things, but as our five-course meal progresses, the conversation becomes more quiet.

Reverend Post holds his own, placed between the silent Mrs. Morton and the jolly Mr. Card. Post's stories are charming, his humor is contagious, and in time even the solemn Mrs. Morton succumbs to his optimistic wit.

By the end of dessert, the room has the type of pleasant atmosphere that only a well-managed meal, good humor, and good friends can create. I'm embarrassed when Reverend Post toasts the Sunday School teacher, and the table says, "Hear, hear!" Then we all join in a toast to Mary's health in thanks for an excellent meal.

When we are finished, Mary asks me to help her dress for the dance, so I follow her up to her room. Below us the dining room tables are being taken away, and musicians are setting themselves up for the dance.

I help Mary into her new dress and can't help but ogle at the finery.

The gown is a green silk, with a low square neckline edged with delicate white lace. The short puff sleeves, in a pale leaf green, are edged with more of the fine lace, while the waist is a deep forest green. The skirt is hung with panel overlays of the dark and light greens and spreads to the floor with ruffles and pleats. But the back of the dress is most amazing: a dramatic gathering of green silk and ruffles and lace, graced by a three-foot train.

"Is it from France, Mary?"

"Heavens, no. I had a dressmaker in Denver make it from a fashion plate."

"The color is beautiful on you. It looks, I don't know, like... something from the Renaissance."

"Really." Mary colors and I realize she doesn't know what I mean.

"Kings and queens," I say quickly, "chivalry and all that."

"Oh." She winks. "You haven't brought me anything about kings and queens."

"Oh, then you should read the story of King Arthur in Camelot, but we don't have it at the cabin. Ma just told it to me." I circle her to look again at the dress.

Her hair is piled high and studded with three pale pink silk roses. She critiques herself in the full-length mirror and then asks, "Marilla, do you think this is cut too low?"

"Too low for whom?" I joke.

She smiles and roughs the lace up around the neckline, but her shoulders drop. "It's too low."

"Never have I heard such a complaint from you," I chide. "But here." I pluck a rose from her hair and hold it to the middle of her bodice.

She laughs. "Yes," she says and pins it on.

As she finishes, she looks me over head to toe. "At least let me do something with your hair."

I glance quickly in the mirror and see I've pulled it back rather too severely. "Please," I whimper.

In no time at all, she has it pinned into graceful curls behind my head and has softened the front by letting it come back in loose waves.

"Now I have a hair comb for you." She shows me a large tortoise shell comb, inlaid with mother-of-pearl in the most intricate pattern I've ever seen: a trellis, rose, and ribbon pattern in pale shades of pink and blue and white mother-of-pearl.

"I've never seen anything like it, Mary."

"It's yours, Marilla. My thanks to you for selling me this place. You probably saved my life."

I think she's joking until I look into her eyes. "Thank you, Mary."

As she places it firmly in above my curls, I draw my arms out and curtsy. "Now I know what it is to be crowned!"

The dance is a mixture of business owners, churchgoers, and miners of all shape and demeanor. Folks have gone to a lot of trouble to clean themselves up, I see, and for some it's undoubtedly the first bath they've had in a year. The tables and chairs are piled to the side. Mary turns her new gaslights to a low setting, and so the foot stomping begins. And by that softly reverberating blue gaslight even the grizzly old miners look charming.

Reverend Post makes his rounds, as is his habit, and again my insides lurch when he holds out his hand to me, and as we begin to twirl, I am conscious of an uncomfortable closeness to him. He seems to be holding me in to him. Or is it my imagination? I look up with a smile, and he looks at my hair and says, "Miss Hay, you look like a princess."

I feel myself blush. "Thank you, Reverend."

"I've never seen a lovelier comb."

"Mary gave it to me. It's the prettiest thing I've ever seen."

"I agree." Now he does pull me closer to him in the dance. Then, with his warm hand over mine, and the scent of his cologne, and his very closeness, a feeling comes over me like a drug and I close my eyes. In my sudden daze, I trip on the next step and he twirls me out of the circle smoothly as if it were part of the dance.

"Would you like to catch your breath?" he asks with a winsome smile.

"Yes. Perhaps some punch..." I want to send him far, far away, because I know I'm not going to catch my breath until he leaves.

But the fact of the matter is, it isn't Reverend Post going around in my head like a potion just now, it's Jonathan. I'm wishing with every fibre of my being it had been Jonathan dancing with me. When my head clears a moment, it occurs to me they wear the same scent! For heaven's sake, I hadn't even remembered Jonathan wore cologne, but I know it now. He wore it each time we walked to Quiet Rock. The memory makes me ache, but at least my head has cleared. By the time Matthew Post returns with a punch cup, I've gathered my wits, and we chat about Sunday School until the song ends.

At midnight, everyone pours into the street to watch and applaud the fireworks, and after the grand finale, folks begin a hooting and hollering contest that lasts at least an hour. I decide Colorado State is bound to do well, judging from the enthusiasm of its new citizens. The dinner guests are soon invited back inside for ice cream and cake, and at about two in the morning, the boys and I decide to go home. We all agree it's been the best festival we've ever had the pleasure to attend.

On the road back, I can't quit thinking of Jonathan. He's probably in Denver by now. Any day I should receive his reply, and the thought momentarily terrifies me. I've put my heart on the line, and I'm soon to find out if he wants it; the finality of it makes me shiver.

A few days later, in the early hours of the morning, I find

myself half-awake and wondering why as I lie under covers on the floor. Through my window I can hear the low snorting of a horse.

Wait.

A horse? It makes no sense. Our horses are all the way over in Jonathan's barn.

I draw myself up and rub my eyes. Either a horse has gotten out of the paddock or somebody's coming up my road. I stand up and go look out my front window to see what it might be. The sun has just risen, but there is a mist in the air so thick the morning light is only barely able to penetrate the folds. I have to squint to make anything out, and the knots of trees keep me from seeing the whole road, but I can glimpse a figure on horseback coming this way.

Whoever it is, it's too early in the morning for a natural visit, and so I go and collect the Colt from atop the kitchen cupboard and load it as best I can. Stiff from yesterday's labors, my fingers aren't working too well, and it takes a long time to load as I fumble with the pouch and bullets. I hate guns anyway, so fiddling with the thing is making me twice as nervous. When I finally come back to the window, I stand away from it for fear the person is already at the door. As I peer around carefully, I see a fellow about fifty feet out on a tall, graceful horse. The horse is pulled sideways, and the rider seems to be looking the cabin over. It makes both my head and heart pound. The horse's nostrils throw little puffs into the air as they stand there silently, and the animal—an Appaloosa—shifts its weight once or twice.

The man is sitting straight and tall, with one hand resting on his hip; he's wearing a suit but the hat of a cowboy. Then, just as I am realizing it's Jonathan Jones, he turns the animal away from the house, bends forward, and hits the horse's flanks rather hard. I am trying to decide what I should do, when the horse is already carrying its rider away.

My head throbs as I try to understand. I don't know exactly what just happened, but it didn't feel right and it didn't feel good. I look down and hold the Colt sideways. I stare at it awhile, and for the second time now—once at the hotel the night they got MacDonald, and once this morning—the sight of it makes me cry.

As day breaks through the fog, I pace the floor of my cabin, trying to decide what to do. What did Jonathan's visit mean? Did he think to come and speak to me and then decide not to? Should I see if he is at his cabin? And what will I say to him? I don't think I could bear it if he sent me away.

Ah, but it's love, and there's no sense in waiting, anymore. I have to go and I have to explain. I make a hasty breakfast for the fellows and dress myself for the walk.

We located this cabin a quarter of a mile from Jonathan's. I suppose I didn't want to be obvious. I walk the quarter of a mile with that early morning picture of Jonathan fresh in my mind. How could I have forgotten what he looked like? The way he held himself? Maybe I don't know him as I thought I did. *Lord, prepare me for whatever you have for me,* I say as I plod along. As I begin to see the cabin through the trees, I observe no evidence of a tenant and my shoulders drop. I walk to the door and force myself to knock. No answer.

I step inside slowly and give a little start as I see a note on the kitchen table. I hold my breath and walk over to it and read:

Miss Hay,
   Stopped by for a look. Thank you for taking care of the place. If I decide to sell, you'll be the first to know.

                                                                        JBJ

I pick it up and something makes me glance at the table again. Under the note is a crisp twenty-dollar bill.

"Payment for services rendered, Mr. Jones? Thank you for the insult." I scoop up the bill and want to tear it to pieces right then. "No, I didn't know you! I didn't." I want to cry, but I won't, I won't! He's trying to humiliate me, and if I tear this up and leave it he will have succeeded. As I breathe deeply in and out and try to pray, a better idea comes to mind. I'll donate it to the church.

After church service the next day, I pull Mary back to the lobby, bend her ear with the story, and ask her what she thinks.

"Honestly? I don't believe he got your letter, Marilla. Don't you think he would have responded a little more *directly*?"

"Well, yes. Yes, I guess I do." I gulp.

"Then you have to write him again."

"Again?" I cross my arms and squeeze them in dismay. "Oh, that would be awful. What if he *did* get the first one... If I send a second... Mary, I can't."

"Marilla, he didn't get the letter. You know he didn't get it." She looks at me a moment and then shrugs. "Do what you must."

"You're right. You're right. He would have said *some*thing. I'm going to have to write to him again." But I turn crimson at the thought.

"And send it by special messenger this time."

"Yes, yes, that's good. All right."

That night, I write yet another short letter to Jonathan Jones and begin it with another line from Keats.

Jonathan,
    "But now of all the world I love thee best." I found Keats to say it for me, for my own heart is too full of fear to speak. Please give me more than silence as reply.
                                                            Marilla

SIXTEEN

"Western farmers were blessed by crop
yields richer than those of the Vale of
Kashmir or the Holy Land."

William Gilpin
First Governor of Colorado

Time moves slowly for me through July. Although the messenger said he took it straight to the marshal's office, Jones wasn't there to receive it himself, which makes the waiting worse.

There is hard work on the farm to keep my mind off him if I would only let it, but the rewards of planting won't come until August, and the drudgery of ditch digging continues. Lillian and Shaw return from Fort Smith in mid-July, both retreating eagerly to their corners. I give up on them utterly. It seems impossible, but I believe they never did speak to each other the whole trip. Mary tells me Lillian is as sullen as ever and never speaks of the journey.

Shaw, of course, tells me nothing of the trip. He says he saw Jonathan once, shortly, and I try to be casual as I ask how he seemed.

"Seemed fine," is all he would say.

I tell him what Jonathan wrote me about becoming Deputy U.S. Marshal and possibly selling the homestead and the note he left recently, and Shaw is very surprised by it all.

"He didn't tell me nothin' about selling, but I guess I'll find out when he does." He eyes me. "What you gonna do?"

"I wrote him, but he hasn't replied."

"Well, he will. If there's anything Jonathan loves, it's a chance to jaw."

I nod and proceed to tell him how we've planted Jonathan's fields and his together with hay and alfalfa. I feel his respect for me grow as I proceed.

"Well, then, there's only one thing left to do," he says finally.

"What's that?"

"Sell it and make the profit, girl, that's all." And he gives me a well-rounded smile, which shocks me even more than his words. A smile and nod, and suddenly I have become uncomfortable. Since there is apparently nothing left to say, we walk back out to our respective fields, but I feel good despite finding out nothing about Jonathan's.

As time goes on, I try hard to give myself wholly to the tasks at hand, but my heart just isn't in it. Tiger and Sam try to cheer me up, but I'm afraid I'm "uncheerable." The very next week, we work to harvest Jonathan's fields. Shaw, his boys, and ours all work together. Shaw and I go to town to sell, but then Shaw steps back and lets me negotiate. I couldn't be more proud than if my father stood there. We get an excellent price for the grain, if I do say so myself, and I promptly walk to the bank and put it in Jonathan's account. I feel wonderful then, but in the next week, to temper my joy, there is still no rain. A true drought has begun, and so we begin again to work hard at irrigation. Our plants survive the drought through our efforts, and we thank the Lord.

Good heavy rains pour down on our thirsty fields in the first week of August. We have won! After the rains, the boys and I have a celebration dinner at the hotel with Mary for the rain and the status of OFFICIAL statehood, which was granted to the fine, new State of Colorado on the first of August.

By mid-August, signs of our work push their little green heads up from the soil, and in the mornings, I make it a habit to walk over every field and marvel at creation. The diversity of the crops is fascinating, and every fifth day I take meticulous notes on the results of irrigation and rains.

Things are going well, and yet fits of melancholy strike me now and then. One morning, while in one of my more sullen moods, I stare at the rising plants and think aloud, "Just as things begin to grow, I feel as though I'm dying." I tell myself I hardly knew him, but it's a lie. I knew him as if I'd been his childhood friend. I knew him forever the moment I met him, and I can't explain the thing, but there it is. I tell myself for the thousandth time he hasn't gotten those honest notes I have written. But then it does seem strange that *both* would fall by the wayside. "But I do know him. I *do*. Somehow it will be all right."

August passes and then September comes. We've been harvesting since late August, and September is busy for us, as well. At first harvest, Tiger took himself to town and ran the horse up and down the street, yelling, "Fresh vegetables. Fine vegetables. Mary's hotel!" Business has been even more brisk for her ever since.

But still no reply from Jonathan. My only comfort is that he hasn't tried to sell the farm. I used to get uncomfortable thinking he would just show up one day, but as time goes on, the whole thing seems more like a strange dream, occasionally bordering on a cold nightmare.

With all the hard work, time flies for us, and it is soon the first week of October. We are hard at work harvesting Jones' grain, and we share this burden with Shaw and his men, according to our previous arrangement, so the work goes relatively quickly. After this we'll build a barn for our own store of crops and dig in for the winter.

Through all this Mary continues to be a great comfort. After I mentioned King Arthur, she took herself to a bookstore in Denver to find a book on Camelot. Now she goes about once a month to the city to buy anything the clerk there suggests, and she gives them to me to read when she's done. I've never seen so many books in my life. Mary's capacity for learning is incredible, and I joke with her that she's gone on to become a college professor, while I'm still back at the one-room schoolhouse. She's the one to quote things to me now, while I'm the one too tired to remember the lines.

The very first time she traveled to Denver, she asked if I'd mind if she visited Jonathan. I told her yes, I would mind, and she's never asked again.

By the middle of October, when the chill in the air holds the sweet scent of fallen leaves and everything seems more crisp and bright and alive, I am feeling a fresh sense of expectation. Surrounded by bright autumn leaves, the cabin is more beautiful to look at now. It has taken on the cast of a dark little jewel in a setting of brilliant gold.

The harvest is almost complete and, thankfully, our crops have already brought in more at market than we had ever hoped. Very few farmers are providing for Independence the way we are. Most had been using farms eastward, toward the plains, and the farms there had been getting some trouble from Indians, or, even more often, from ranchers who want open fields for their traveling herds. The eastern farmers' sad loss is our gain, as the stores and restaurants have turned to us. We're fairly high in the valley away from the ranges, in a good spot to grow hay for the dairy cattle, and so the ranchers simply ignore us. More than once I have blessed the choice of land my father made, and now that the ranchers seem determined to use violence to get what they want, I am grateful once more that we are far away from such troubles.

On one promising, impossibly blue-skied, mid-October morning, Tiger and I are mending the fence around the chicken coop when Sam strolls over from taking care of Jonathan's animals.

"Need any help?" he asks quietly.

"Yes, please, Sam, hand me those wires while Tiger holds that in place."

Sam hands me the wires and then digs his hands into his pockets. "Uh, Miss Hay? There's a fella... up at Jones' place."

My face goes pale and my heart stops. I'm afraid to ask what he means. I make myself keep working. "Someone to sell it?" I finally ask in a none-too-certain voice.

"Don't know. He says he's Jones."

I finish with the wire and rub my palms down my apron. "I suppose I should go over."

The boys just look at me.

"We'll come along?" Tiger asks.

"Thank you, Tiger, but no." I give an unsteady smile. "Guess

I'd better get cleaned up right away. After all, he might come over here."

As I turn to go in, Sam adds, "Miss Hay?"

"Hmm?"

He looks down, shakes his head, and says reluctantly, "Thought I should tell you, too... there's... there's a woman with him."

I laugh a little nervously. "Well, what sort of woman, Sam?"

"Well... a pretty woman. Pretty dress."

"Oh." I rub my hands on my apron again as I walk to the cabin. "Oh, my. I'd better dress real nice, then, eh?" Sam nods blankly, and they look at each other as I turn away.

This I hadn't thought of. I shake my head and step into the cabin. "A woman, a woman," I mutter. "Well, that's a reply of sorts, isn't it? From the Lord and Jonathan all at once. I didn't expect such a sudden answer to prayer. No, come on now, maybe it's a relative. He has sisters. Maybe a sister. Maybe..." But I don't believe a word I'm saying. And I cry out to the Lord as I dress, "You've got to help me, here. Lord, please." I hop to get on the other Sunday boot. "This surely looks like one of the worst moments of my life coming up on me. I don't want to go, but there's no getting around it either. Suppose I'd rather go there than find out what's going on from someone else." As I tie on my petticoats, my gaze falls to the trunk that holds my "pillow on a string." "Yes, I'm going to wear that dress. Bustle and all— I'm going to be the most elegant farmer he's ever seen."

I look at myself in the mirror, pin my hair up quick but neatly, and press my lips together in prayerful acceptance. Then I put on the bustle and my black silk, and try in vain to wash all the dirt from my hands and nails. I go over all the details of my attire once more and then again. I am deathly afraid I've left something undone, and then I slowly realize I'm just trying to avoid the reality of thinking that thought... that awful hideous thought: *Jonathan... with someone else. She could be his wife.*

On the short walk there, I pray and pray hard. And as the house comes into view, I look at my hands once more for dirt only to find they're shaking. I decide to clasp them together for the duration of my visit.

As I walk up to the cabin, I hear a high-pitched laugh to my left. The trill sends a strange tingling through me. "Not his sister," I mumble. They must be at the fruit trees in the back, I decide, and so I step around to the left.

The fruit trees are curled and yellowed but still hold a few of their sweet desserts. On any other day I might stop to enjoy one, but now I am gravely concentrating on the path under my feet. I clear my throat as I approach, look up and find a dark-suited Jonathan Jones pulling a crab apple down for a lovely young thing in a gorgeous pale pink, blue trimmed traveling dress. They both look toward me as I come, and I try to smile firmly. Jonathan looks stunned, but the tight little smile on the woman never wavers.

"Mr. Jones."

"Miss Hay," he says, almost in question.

"Enjoying the last fruits of summer?" I say with feigned spirit, hoping he'll catch my meaning while I valiantly work to hold back my tears.

"Yes." He waits a moment, looks down, then looks back up, and he has turned as red as the apple he holds in his hand. He finally gains composure and clears his throat to say, "Allow me to introduce to you Miss Aventine Hill of Denver. Miss Amaryllis Hay of… a… neighbor hereabouts."

"How do you do?" she says sweetly, ever so slightly smiling, as she takes the apple from his hand with a neat flick of her wrist and a mild giggle. Her eyes are deep blue, her hair a thick, dark brown. Her lips are full and her cheeks dimpled. She's as pretty as a porcelain doll and it's hard to keep from staring.

"Very well, thank you."

There is an awkward pause, but Miss Hill fills it right up. "Jonathan was just showing me this lovely fruit garden, Miss Hay. I'm very impressed. I understand your parents had a little something to do with this place?" Long lashes bat against her delicate, rosy cheeks.

"Yes, indeed they did," I finally manage. "They planted this fru... the orchard."

She laughs. "Oh, I understood they did more than plant the trees."

I look to Jonathan and his face is still quite red.

"Yes, they built this place, Aventine," he quickly says. "I told you that, didn't I?"

I don't think I can take much more of this. I make sure my hands have a firm grip on each other.

She turns to him and, sweet as you please, says, "Oh, yes, I'm sorry. And what a beautiful, *quaint* little place it is." Her body sways a little as she speaks, and I cannot hide a wince as she says "quaint."

He smiles back at her, and she lowers her gaze to me again and the grin returns. She is marking her territory before my eyes, the little... Well, she needn't worry.

"I'm so glad you like it, Miss Hill. I just thought I'd pay a call, since Mr. Jones hasn't visited here for quite some time."

"Yes, yes," Jonathan says uncomfortably. "How goes the farm?"

"Well, I must say I've enjoyed taking care of the *charming* little place in your absence." I can hardly help myself. I have begun to babble. "If you haven't had a moment to peruse your bank account, allow me to tell you that your hay on the north and northeast fields of twenty-four acres brought in $352.45 and the alfalfa on the west twelve acres brought $215.31—we were able to raise the prices because of trouble with the supplies from the plains and a flux of new wealth from gold strikes here-abouts—for a total of $568.76, deposited to your account on the day of sale to an independent grain dealer, Lyle Tanner, of Petertown, who supplies stores in Independence and Petertown, as you probably know. Your two fields remaining of ten acres each were left fallow this summer sowed with clover.

"We've been using your stable, so the boys have cleaned it reg-ularly, built a milking stall for Millie..." I smile at Miss Aventine and say, "the cow," then turn back to him. "They put in a new hay rack since the old one was failing, and they had to put on a new roof. No cost to you. Mary Baylor's cook jarred fifty jars of fruit from the trees which sold at five cents each at Pruett's, and the money went to building the new school, and then we gave another twenty jars to the church for needy miners. I left thirty more jars in the hutch for your use—I hope you don't mind our using it, because the fruit would have otherwise gone to waste."

He is blushing to an even deeper red now, almost a purple, and I'm all too glad for it. "I made the church contribution you left on the table a while back. I believe Reverend Post sent it to a missionary couple, the Berrymans, in the Kickapoo Nation." I smile and cock my head and wait.

Mr. Jones' mouth has dropped open, as well it should.

Aventine Hill lets out a stunned little half-laugh. "Well, you are a *real, live* farmer aren't you, my dear? And *no* mistake!"

But Jonathan ignores the girl's rudeness and smiles at me. "That was kind of you, Miss Hay. An excellent update. And how *is* the Reverend Post?"

"He's holding church at Mary's hotel now. The place is filled to capacity every Sunday."

"*Really?*" He seems a little too surprised.

And Miss Hill, who had kept such a beautifully calm exterior all during my visit, has become a little flustered now. "We were just going in for some tea, Miss Hay," she says quickly. "Would you care to join us?" But her pretty mouth is turned up in a sour smile.

"No, no, thank you. We're still in harvest. I must get back."

In fact, I'm thinking how I want to go back and bathe myself in lye to clean off the greasiness I'm feeling from having this conversation.

She's smiling again since my polite refusal. "Well, it's been such a pleasure meeting you," she drips.

"And you. Good-bye now, Miss Hill, Mr. Jones."

She squeezes Jonathan's arm and giggles as she looks me up and down. "I'm sure you meant to address him as U.S. Marshal Jones."

"Aventine, I'm sure you meant to say, *Deputy* Marshal Jones."

"Pardon me, but I've said all that I've meant to say." I turn on my heels and walk as steadily as I can out of the backyard.

I can hear her saying, and I'm sure it's as much for my benefit as his, "Imagine! A girl farmer! Why, Jonathan, you never even told me about her." And she laughs her trilling little laugh as they stroll arm in arm toward the front door.

He must be laughing with her right now. And I can imagine his reply, "*Well, I didn't think she was worth mentioning, Aventine.*"

I feel very much like screaming, but I wouldn't want to give her... them... the pleasure of hearing me.

"Miss Hay!" Jonathan suddenly calls out, and although I want to run away, I try to turn nonchalantly around to face him as he trots up from the door. Miss Hill waits impatiently behind. "Miss Hay, how the devil am I going to repay you for all you've done?"

I'm not ready for this. "I, uh... it's been of mutual benefit, Mr. Jones, a business arrangement—that's all." I hope my voice sounds calm.

"A business arrangement..." he says flatly. "Well, that usually requires payment, and it seems to me you wouldn't take my money."

I look down quickly as Aventine approaches.

"Miss Hay," Aventine Hill says, slipping her arm through Jonathan's, "has an amazing head for business, I think. You couldn't have left your place in better hands." She looks at my hands, and a look of horror has filled her pretty eyes. I have held my hands out to protest his offer of thanks: thin hands, gray and blistered—awful to see. She could not have chosen a better way in which to humiliate me at that moment.

I pull them quickly to my stomach and, with growing horror, find I can't stop myself from wiping them on my dress, my beautiful silk dress.

I look back at Jonathan. "Yes, exactly, no thanks needed. For all you've done for the town... for my parents' farm. It... it was a pleasure, really." And I turn and steel myself to walk away.

From behind me, Miss Hill says with touching sorrow, "Did you see those hands, Jonathan?"

As I clear the front yard and walk the road, I swing between sorrow and outrage. I come into our yard and say loudly, "How could he not see what she is? She's slippery as bear grease, but he's got his boots stuck in it anyway. She's a... a..." I throw my arms to either side as I speak and wag my head with emotion.

Tiger and Sam are staring at me as I walk toward them.

I stare back. "Well, I've had quite enough humiliation for one day," I yell in exasperation. "I *am* a farmer, and I'm GLAD to be a farmer, confound it! So let's get back to work!" I tromp into the cabin, but I walk to the bed and fall to my knees and weep until I've no tears left.

SEVENTEEN

... A woman may be a mystery to a man and
to herself, but never to another woman.

The Spinster Book
by Myrtle Reed

The next day, Wednesday, I seem to be in a state of shock: shock at seeing Jonathan and shock at meeting *that woman*.

The weather fits my mood by staying overcast and ugly, but we get in a good day of harvesting before it rains, so I tell myself I deserve a little rest. The truth of it is, I desperately need to speak to Mary, and I think if I don't, I will go out of my mind.

I tell the boys I probably won't be back until early tomorrow morning. I can't bear to go to Jones' to retrieve the animals for fear of running into him, and so I have Tiger go over to get my wagon. Likewise, I travel toward town, careful to avoid his place. I find myself more perplexed than angry as I make the journey to Independence, wondering at his choice of a companion, amazed that he could care for someone who has nothing in her. "As flighty as a bird, 'Whose song is sweet though its bones be hollow,'" as my father would say. Well, maybe Jonathan decided he's had enough of solid women. Maybe he just wants a songbird. Many men do, so I've been told.

Thankfully, the rain holds back until I reach town. When I arrive, I find Mary in her office and tell her everything in a description filled with disappointment and consternation.

When I'm done, she comes around the desk and hugs me. "I'm sorry I ever told you to write to him," she says quietly.

"It's all right. So much water under the bridge." I sniff.

Mary pats my shoulder. "You caught her name, didn't you?"

"Aventine Hill, a beautiful name for a beautiful face."

Mary lets out peals of laughter. "Well, it's an old name, anyway."

"What is so amusing?" I ask mildly.

"Marilla, Marilla…" She's starts to laugh, and then laughs so hard she can hardly get it out. "Aventine… is one of the seven HILLS of Rome…"

I let out a giggle. "Did you get that from Gibbons?"

She nods, with her eyes twinkling.

"Oh, that *is* funny."

"Yes, she's a solid girl," Mary says stoutly in a low voice. "A little hardheaded perhaps, but… we couldn't give her up—she's such good ballast for the carriage, you see…"

I begin laughing uncontrollably. "Stop, stop…"

"… *Rocky Mountain News* Exclusive: scientists find mountains *can* be moved; they simply require proper traveling attire…"

"STOP!" I'm laughing so hard my sides hurt.

"Mohammed's exact words were, 'Let's not try to cross that mountain, boys. Aventine'll come when I whistle.'"

We both collapse into sobs of laughter.

"OOh, oh, I hurt. Stop making me feel better than I should!" I punch her gently and laugh again.

Mary is looking me over and says through half-smiling lips, "What you need is a clean-up and a good supper. And I won't have you wearing that poor calico to my good restaurant."

"Oh, no, please, I thought we'd eat in the kitchen."

She jumps up. "No. No! NO! You are going to wear my green silk, or I'm not feeding you a thing."

"No, I couldn't. Mary, I couldn't…"

"Well, you're right. After all… it's just a shabby little restaurant. In fact, maybe I'd better go borrow something from Cook to wear. Come to think of it, we could both go in one of her dresses…"

That makes me smile, despite my sorrow. "You really think I could fit in your green silk?" I whisper.

"Well, I don't know as you've noticed," she says begrudgingly, "but we're shaped quite similarly." She winks and adds, "Colonel Brigand once had his eye on you, y'know. He sat me down at the bar and asked me all about you one day."

I am embarrassed to think he considered me for "employment."

Mary catches my eye. "But I'm sure he figured you'd feel too bad about taking men's money...."

"MARY!" I cry in mock outrage, and she escorts me out the door and upstairs, laughing and shaking her head.

As we enter her room, she says more seriously, "No, Marilla, he was serious. And the man gets so few original thoughts, he has a tendency to hang on to them like fever. But I told him if he didn't leave you alone I'd... well, let's just say, he understood a threat."

"You did that... for me? Thank you. 'Course, I would have told him 'no' myself."

Mary smiles a little sadly. "Of course you would have... but the Colonel doesn't take 'no' for an answer." The look in her eye gives me a sudden chill.

"Mary, what you've been through, what you know... it's hard to believe God could allow it..."

"It wasn't God who designed saloons, Marilla. And no one made me take part. Besides, He only gives us what we can handle, dearie." She bumps my shoulder playfully. "Now, you can wear this dress or you'll go without supper, and I believe you and the Colonel both know I never make idle threats!" And as I smile and nod, she turns me to the wardrobe and the matter at hand.

After squeezing into Mary's corset, I'm forced to borrow her underthings, too, for all but one of mine have sleeves.

But, oh, she was right about the dress. As we pull it over my head and she strings up the back, the dress fits me perfectly. One slight difference in the look of the dress is that I do not fill the top in quite the same way, but I'm slightly relieved to find it out, as I'm uncomfortable enough with my neck and arms showing.

As she fixes my hair, I have to tell her, "Mary, I'm cold."

She turns me around. "You know, Marilla, your coloring is just right for this. I believe you look prettier in it than I do."

"Mary... I'm *too* cold."

"Oh, *all right*," she says peevishly and grabs a shawl off the hook. "Now, shall we dine?"

As we enter the dining room, I am not quite prepared for my reception. Several people whisper and stare and some even point in my direction.

"Ignore it all, Marilla," Mary says curtly, "and enjoy the beauty God gave you."

"But, Mary, I don't want to offend anyone."

"You've got a shawl, haven't you?"

I'm uncomfortable a few seconds more, but the dress has brightened my spirits so much, I can't help but feel a little better. I take her arm as we walk. "Mary, I'll do my best. It does feel lovely—if a little snug. However do you breathe in this thing?"

She smiles. "You're not supposed to breathe, dear. In fact, I've read death gives one's skin that lovely look of china we all strive for..." I wish she wouldn't say things like that in public, for I can't help but giggle, which makes the people stare at us all the more.

We are seated at the table now, and so we take up our menu cards and begin to chat about farming. Mary tells me what's been happening in Independence, who got shot at the tables last week, and a horrible story about a fellow who killed his wife in the mining camp. Then we discuss the new governor, and I'm forgetting all about yesterday as we eat. But Mary's animated conversation suddenly stops mid-word. Slowly, she rests her chin in one hand and smiles.

I turn my head to the right ever so slightly to see Jonathan Jones and Aventine Hill coming in the doors. My next thought is to get out of the dining room as quickly as I can.

Jonathan nods to Mary and smiles and she nods back, but he ignores me, although my head is still turned a little his way.

"I want to get out of here," I whisper.

Mary looks hard into my eyes. *"Don't—you—dare."*

I sit back and stare at her. "But, Mary! This is impossible!"

"Fine time to become a coward."

My eyes widen as I take her words in, and I throw my napkin on my plate. "Well, I'm glad I've already eaten a little something, for I've just lost my appetite."

They have been seated for a while and are looking over the menu, when Jonathan looks back toward us. I have been unable to stop myself from staring at him now and then, and I'm telling myself once more to quit doing it, when he catches my eye. His look is blank at first, and then a little color comes to his cheeks and he looks back to Aventine.

I look down at my plate and study the situation, and with a sudden smile of triumph and the arching of one brow, I say, "Mary, I believe he didn't recognize me at first!"

"I shouldn't wonder!" she says coolly. "You're the freshest little peach in here, despite that little waxen thing he has with him. He last saw you playing the farmer's daughter."

"Or the little farmer." I look at my hands. At least they are clean tonight. Blistered but clean.

Now Mary stares at Aventine unmercifully. "She shouldn't bring her face too close to that candle..." I can't look back at them, but Mary proceeds to give me a running report: "He's speaking to Aventine and glancing our way again... Now Aventine is looking our way... Oh, she's unpleased... But look how she smiles back at him, now."

"Mary! You know I can't look, and for heaven's sake, stop watching them."

"All right, Marilla." She turns her face back to me.

"Thank you!"

"They're coming over here."

"I'll excuse myself now." But Mary grabs my hand under the table.

"Marshal Jones, won't you and your lady friend join us?" Mary says, slick as ice.

"We'd be pleased," Jones says. "Miss Baylor, it's been too long. And it's a pleasure seeing you once more, Miss Hay."

I look up briefly and smile, but my face is burning and I draw my shawl up around my shoulders self-consciously.

"Allow me to introduce Miss Aventine Hill. Aventine, this is Miss Mary Baylor, proprietress of this fine establishment."

Miss Hill nods and arches her neck by means of a reply, like a tomcat, and then she takes her sweet time adjusting her bustle to finally become situated in her chair. "Miss Baylor," she begins, "your *dear* little dining hall is lovely. I'm sure the food will be equal to the surroundings." The words drip readily from her tongue like new honey.

Mary eyes her with a steady gaze and replies with newfound polish, "I've worked hard to have the food and service surpass the surroundings. You might say it's been a philosophical challenge to me—just as the soul is more important than the outer garment."

Now she has just sent a bolt of lightning through Jonathan Jones, and I almost laugh as he looks at Mary in utter amazement.

"Now, do tell me... your name, *Aventine...*" Mary says innocently.

Oh, no, Mary, don't do this to me.

"... it's so very pretty and... un...*u*...sual." Mary twists the word like a knife.

"Yes." Aventine colors slightly. "My father chose it."

"Do your brothers and sisters have such beautiful names, too?" Mary asks coyly.

"Yes, they're all unusual, all..."

Jonathan, without knowing what he is unleashing, says, "Yes, Aventine comes from a family of seven daughters."

Mary digs her nails into my wrist so hard it hurts, and I can't breathe for trying to hold my laughter.

"We were one of the first families of Denver," she says haughtily.

"Oh, were they there when it was Cherry Creek?" I ask gently.

Her face is flushed, now. "My, no, we helped establish a *real* town there. My father is the U.S. Marshal of Denver."

U.S. Marshal Daniel Hill; yes, that should have occurred to me.

Jonathan looks extremely uncomfortable now, and I believe no one but Mary is enjoying the conversation.

Just then someone from a nearby table calls over for Gentleman Jones to come and speak with them, and he leaves the table so quickly he almost drags the tablecloth with him. Oh, I wish I could laugh.

Aventine begins to bubble on about Independence, and then Mary makes the mistake of complimenting her dress. Aventine proceeds to decorate the conversation for what seems like an hour about her dressmaker, where the fabric came from, how it looked when she first tried it on, and then, when I think I'll fall asleep or go insane, she blithely tells us, "But I think I'll have her make my wedding gown, anyway." I look up attentively as she blathers on. "Yes, we like Denver ever so very much. We'll probably marry at Garver Presbyterian on Main. Have you seen it? It's a grand building..."

But I'm not listening anymore.

I'm standing on the porch of the Independence Hotel, hardly caring how I got there, thinking about the night I heard someone first call him "U.S. Marshal Jones."

I'm not aware of much of anything until Mary stands beside me and hugs my shoulders. "I just told her you have fits like this now and then." We are quiet for a while. "Don't know as it'll help or hurt you now," Mary says, "but she said they're going back tomorrow." I continue to stare ahead of me into the darkness. "Marilla, it's cold out here. Let's go up to my room and talk." She roughs up my shoulders with her hands.

But I weave my head back and forth, and wipe my nose and sniff. "No. I need to take a walk, Mary. Alone. I'll be back soon. I... I'll be careful with the dress," I say in parting.

"Hang the blasted dress," Mary says behind me, and I hear the doors open and shut behind her.

I wander down the main street and away from town, and before I know it I am standing at Quiet Rock. There I think how dreams are not always meant to be, and how pain can make you appreciate life or make you hate every waking moment, and that it's your decision. God leaves it to you. But just now I don't want to make a decision at all.

I say aloud, "I can lean into You on this, Lord, or lean away."

I think on that. Then, with a resignation that comes from the depths of my sad soul, I finally whisper, "Well, I can't imagine living without You, so I have to choose to lean into You." And then the words are born away on the wind. I rest my head on Quiet Rock and cry silently, letting the chilly air pull at the shawl as I watch the cold stars sparkle in a silent sky. *I will lean into Him, and maybe someday the pain will go away.*

That night I fall asleep in a hotel room, making the pillow wet with my tears. The next morning I wake up to the awful memory of the night before. Mary brings breakfast to my room and we talk, and as I dress to leave, she says, "Marilla, you should come back over Saturday. There's a harvesters' ball at Norville's place." Norville is a new farmer south of Independence who's done quite well. I knew he was building a bigger barn because Tiger and Sam have gone over to help him, and now Norville wants to hold a dance there to celebrate before he starts using it. "It's to benefit the new church," Mary is saying. "The proceeds go for a new church building."

I groan. "Mary, you know I'm in no mood for it."

"I know, but only wait and see how you feel on it Saturday." She gives me a friendly nudge. "You know how dancing can cheer the soul."

"I will only promise to think on it."

"Listen to me, Marilla. Remember the talk we had? If you don't walk through this fire, you'll stand and burn in it. You understand me?"

"Mary, it's too soon. I can't take it in, and if you keep talking at me I'll just get angry."

"You love to farm, don't you?"

"Yes," I say begrudgingly.

"And everybody thinks you're crazy." It wasn't a question. "Well, when I was a child there came a time in my life when I had to make a choice. I could either go on living the way I was and die a slow death, or I could go through a painful door to see what was on the other side."

"But I don't like pain. I've felt it. I've gone through the door, too."

"Well, the thing is you have to keep getting through it. You have to keep right on living and think about the things you love, like farming and even Jones, to get to the other side."

She has made me angry, but she's also made me curious. "What was it made you get through?"

"Well..." She gets a little smile on her face. "There was a woman in our town. Everyone thought she was crazy because she used to hunt. *I* thought she was crazy until I met her. It sounds so downright sensible now... to hunt like she did. Everybody was nigh on to starving during the war. The men were gone, soldiers took everything there was to eat, and so she took up hunting."

"So a lady isn't supposed to hunt," I say tiredly. "And that makes her crazy, I suppose."

"Oh, no. She also thought she'd seen graves dug up." My eyes grow wide. "Well, there was a logical explanation for that, too, but that's not the point. The point is she kept right on doing what she loved to do no matter what anyone thought of her. She gave me the strength to leave that town. The Lord sent her to me. I see that now."

"Just as He sends you to me now."

"I wouldn't be so bold as to say that. Let's just say I'm here if you need a little push through the door."

"Well, thank you. You make me mad as an angry hornet, but you also make good sense."

We hug and she whispers in my ear, "So, come to the dance, all right?"

By Saturday morning, the boys and I are finishing another five acres, and I do try to think about the dance. In fact, I have thought on just about everything but Jonathan Jones, and I could use a rest from the effort. I know my fellow farmers will be there, some of whom have a little respect for me by now, and more than likely the lovely Reverend Post will be there to crown the women with his princely presence. It does sound like something I need. Besides, it benefits a church building. Oh, all right, I'll go.

The boys are happy to hear my decision; they were going to go anyway, and so we all stop early that afternoon to clean up.

We arrive in Independence later in the day, and I meet Mary in the lobby of the hotel. She tries to convince me to wear the green dress again this evening, and I protest but lose ground when Lillian comes to stand with us to arrange things with Mary for the evening before retiring. I look at the door as someone enters: Matthias Shaw. I jump as Mary's newly painted front doors slam to either wall and he comes toward us.

Mary and Lillian jump also, but I am looking at Shaw's eyes, and it's as though I've never seen them before. They are burning with energy and fire. He stops two steps from us and stares at Lillian, clenching and unclenching his fists. I take a step away from him.

He takes a deep breath and points a shaky finger at Lillian. "Lillian Wirsching, I'd know the devil to look at you." And he angrily wrenches his hand back down to his side.

She sets a glare in her eye and stares right back at him. "What do you mean?"

Mary and I both begin to back away, but he spits out, "You can hear it. Concerns Marilla, anyway." There is silence and everyone stays still as he continues. "Yesterday, I was a might surprised to find Jonathan Jones with a woman visitor, and I knew enough to ask him whatever happened to Marilla. And he told me what you said to him at Fort Smith, Lillian."

I want to intervene at this point to tell him we know all this, that it's all right, but Lillian shoots back, "I told him nothing but the truth." Her lip curls on the word "truth."

"You wouldn't know the truth if it bit your nose, woman. You told him..." He sways to hold himself back. "You told him, no offense, Miss Baylor, that Marilla had sold her hotel for a whore house... that she was living off Mary's land on a homestead next to his property, and that she'd like to marry Jonathan for to get the old homestead back, 'cause it was the only way she could get it."

My neck hairs bristle.

"I told him the truth," snaps Lillian. "She *is* livin' off Mary Baylor's homestead, and Marilla sold the hotel to her..."

"You knew what he'd take it for..."

"... and that Marilla wanted to marry him." She looks at me. "I doubt you'd deny that, you little chit." My face burns. "And that she'd like her farm back."

"Oh, you may have said it all, but you knew 'zactly how he'd take it. Well, you can ruin us with your lies, but you got no cause to go and ruin other people." One of his fists rises up.

"I never once lied to you, Matthias," she says in a whispering hiss. Her arms are crossed and her face defiant.

"LIAR!"

"I never did."

"You told me you were with child!"

People have gathered to watch the fight now, and she looks around her unsteadily. She immediately whirls to walk away, but he grabs her firmly by one arm and yanks her back. She cries out in pain; he's grabbed the arm with the shoulder wound.

"You're HURTING her," I yell and fall on his arm to get him to release his hold, but his grip on her is as firm as welded iron.

He grabs her face with his other hand. "YOU WERE NEVER WITH CHILD! *SAY IT!*" His voice echoes through the lobby.

"Yes, I was, you old fool." But the challenge in her voice is gone.

I'm sure everyone has heard her reply with perfect clarity, as her voice is the only sound in the place, and the room becomes as silent as a tomb and Shaw releases his grasp.

"You didn't want to marry me, so you *lied*..." he says in a raspy voice.

"I wanted to marry you, you stubborn, arrogant... But I wished to God I'd never wanted..." Suddenly she bows her head, a gesture so unlike her that my mouth drops open at the sight.

In another moment, she turns and walks up the stairs. The

folks who have come to listen stare at Shaw and then begin to talk among themselves and wander off.

"Lillian?" Shaw takes a step forward as if she were still there.

Mary and I look at each other, and a hot tear drops to my cheek.

He swallows hard and walks up the stairs behind her, calling her name as he goes.

"Well...there's a start," Mary says weakly. "Let's..." She stops and shakes her head. "The dance?"

Both of us look back up the stairs.

"Nothing we can do for them but pray," Mary says.

I check myself. "Yes. And I... I believe I still want to go to the dance. Isn't that strange?" Mary nods but just as quickly begins to shake her head, and we laugh and walk slowly up the rest of the stairs.

Thinking of Lillian as a woman in love stretches my imagination considerably—probably a good exercise, all told. In Mary's room we stop to pray for the two before we prepare for the dance. After our "Amens" we begin again to wonder at it all. "Maybe something good will come from my loss after all, Mary."

"Oh, don't try to be such a flaming martyr, Marilla."

I give her a sidelong glance but choose to ignore the remark. Then I remember to tell her about the visit Dr. Gilpin had from Jane the night MacDonald stabbed Lillian.

"Oh, yes, Jane Dunn. I know her. It was her friend Donna that shot that fellow two weeks ago for not paying up. I'll have to ask Jane how she knows Lillian—could be interesting."

I smile slightly at her cheerful delivery of such strange bits of information and silently thank the Lord for letting me live away from town.

But the conversation wanders back to the night's proceedings, and it doesn't take long for Mary to wheedle me into wearing her green silk again. When I protest it has a train that I will surely trip on, she counters that there is a hidden loop at the back to hitch up the train, that it was added just for dancing. Eventually I give in.

When we finish dressing, Mary steps outside her door to peer with curiosity down the hall to Lillian's room. "Can't hear anything," she says, and we look at each other and shrug.

"At least they've made a beginning," I reply, and Mary nods.

We talk more about Shaw and Lillian on the way to the dance. Tiger and Sam are driving the wagon oblivious to the female chatter, and Mary and I realize how little we know of Lillian or of Shaw for that matter, and eventually we pray again for them as we ride along.

Mary winks at me when I look back up. She mouths the words, "Love will conquer all."

I try to nod bravely and match her smile, but my heart isn't in it.

EIGHTEEN

here's velvet on the willow an' there's velvet
    on the horn—
There's new silk in the tree-top an' the
    tassel o' the corn.
The woods are trimmed for weddin's—
    an' we're all in Sunday cl'os,
An' the bark upon the ven'son-tree is
    redder than a rose.

**From the book *Silas Strong*,
by Irving Bacheller**

The dance is as busy as any dance I've ever seen, with a band twice as large as usual, and barely heard above all the stomping and yelling. At the door, we hand over coin to benefit the new church building. A few more dances like this, we reason loudly to each other, and we'll have a new church built in no time.

I'm wearing the beautiful hair comb Mary gave me, but, although I feel like a princess in this gown and "crown," it is Mary who truly looks the part. She wears her other "French" gown, a cream-colored silk with a graceful, curving neckline, set low but not too low. The curve at the neck is repeated in the trumpet sleeves of the jacket trimmed in lace. A cluster of pale pink silk roses is pinned at her waist, and the full bustle is gathered at the back with more of the delicate white lace.

Curls fall gently to either shoulder, while one braid of her blue-black hair provides a crown for her head; no other ornament is necessary. She looks every bit the Denver society lady, except for the smile. Mary's smile is genuine.

The faces of the musicians glow with the light from the fire in the large wood stove, while the strings of lanterns hung on either long wall light the whirling dancers as they fill the floor. The music makes me tap my feet before I even realize I'm following along—and soon the floor is jumping with the rhythmic thumping of the music, which makes me worry for poor Norville's future barn.

I have more requests to dance than ever before, and I realize Mary's green dress has worked a little magic, for every one of my partners feels compelled to comment on my good looks. If they could have only seen me threshing a few hours ago....

Halfway through the dance, around midnight, Reverend Post comes up and holds out his hand to me. Perhaps I'm convinced by now that I am Cinderella, because I am not nervous to think of dancing with him, and I step up to his hand with a confident smile.

We twirl to a lovely tune, and then Reverend Post, too, lends a compliment that makes me blush.

Then, as we dance, he asks slowly, "Marilla, I must ask you something."

I'm smiling and turning my head this way and that with the music. "Yes?" I say in passing.

"Do you think a woman... do you think a woman of property could leave her responsibilities to... to..." I've never heard him hesitate for wording, and a little shock goes through me as I smile and question him with my eyes. "...become the wife of a pastor?" He looks away from me as he speaks, but he smiles nervously and looks down at me as he finishes.

He's asking me to marry him? Me, the wife of a pastor? I've honestly never thought... much... about it. The room still spins around us, and the blood rushes to my face as I look away. "If a woman loved a man," I begin, "I suppose she could leave everything, but she would have to love him very much. Once a woman sees what she can do, it would be hard, very hard, I think... to go back."

We continue the twirl and all I can think is, *Please don't ask me, please don't ask me,* followed with, *I hope I don't trip.*

"I don't have anything to offer but my love…"

But how can I marry for anything but love? I like Matthew and admire his work, but his constant optimism is downright irritating at times; on the other hand, Jonathan is gone….

"Marilla, I have to ask you…"

No! No! NO!

"Do you think she could love me?"

"She?!"

"I'm afraid Mary'll turn me down if I ask her."

"Oh, Matthew, I… I don't know." I am relieved and startled; part of me wants to laugh. I try to adjust myself as quickly as I can to this new thing. I turn the thought over in my mind, to look at it, as it were, upside down to the way I'd been thinking. I realize I'd never thought he could care for her in that way… in light of her past. Strange that in my own love for her as a friend I excused her past in a twinkling, yet I couldn't imagine a man doing the same.

In sympathy with my thoughts, he whispers, "I keep thinkin'… she's got her own, now. Could be the hotel is all she's ever wanted, and that… she's had enough of men. I would understand that."

I bow my head and work to remember how Mary's spoken of him. It's quite possible she *does* care for him. I just don't know. How awful that Mary knows me so well, and I know so little of her. I've been too busy with my own troubles to be watching and listening.

I only wish I had an answer for him.

I realize my last words have made his shoulders slump, but he adds, "Just look at her. They don't give a plug nickel about her past, and neither do I. Do I shock you, Miss Hay?"

I shake my head but then nod ever so slightly. "I mean to say, a man is… sometimes a man is more…"

"Yes, well, that would assume a man had no past of his own," he said, smiling that handsome, melting smile.

Ah, now I understand.

"Yep. Every one of those bees around that buttercup would be willing to marry her tomorrow, and she could have anyone she wanted," he says, pensively looking into the corner of the room as we dance past.

I follow his eyes to see Mary speaking with animation to a group of people. She sparkles. I knew it before but never saw it so clearly. She looks like a star brought down from the firmament. She is beautiful, but it's more than that; it's the smoothness of motion and the light in her eyes that make her shine.

I look into Matthew's eyes with concern and try to give him encouragement. "You know, if I think on it long and hard, I'd say you have as good a chance as some, and more of a chance than many."

But he shakes his head.

"Oh, come now, don't tell me I'm to be responsible for your not asking her. You mustn't do that to me, Reverend Post," I say half joking. "You have to understand that Mary is… a very private person. She's never told me how she feels… about anyone."

He smiles tentatively. "I see. Let me think about it, then."

We finish out the dance with my head in a whirl. I'm so thankful I didn't say anything foolish when he first began to speak to me. I decide to sit out a few dances and retire to the side. A couple of miners ask for the next dance and the next, but I say 'no' politely.

Still, the last fellow plunks down beside me, like the lonely husband at the May Ball. This fellow has a large belly, a scruffy beard, little colored glasses, and a truly comical brown stovepipe hat perched on his head. The top has popped up, so it sits on him like an open tin can. At least he's had the decency to take a bath before the ball: he smells like mud instead of sweat. I smile politely and then look away.

"Wanna dansh, darlin'?" he says.

"No, thank you," I say politely, not looking his way.

"How come you won't dansh with me, sweet thing?"

The whiskey in his words wafts over the music and tickles my nose. I remain as polite as possible and carefully plan my escape.

"I'm just tired. I may need to go home soon."

"Well, I'll 'shcort you, then."

"No. No, my hands—the fellows who work my farm—will take me." I point to Sam and Tiger, who are hanging at the punch bowl.

"Unh," he says, unconvinced. He puts his hands on his knees and stays right where he is. I try to think how I can get away, but he asks, "That yer beau?" And he points toward the Reverend Post.

"No. I have no beau," I say with a touch of bitterness.

"Oh." His voice rises. "Then a fella has a chansh with ye."

I grimace.

He slumps back down and shakes his head. "Jez jestin', ma'am. My rotten luck. Gesh I'll try 'nother go at the fishpond." He bows to me unsteadily and saunters away.

My relief is palpable. I search for Tiger and Sam, for if this man's state is any indication, it's likely the party is going downhill quickly. I don't see the boys anywhere, though, and so I decide to step outside to get some fresh air.

The sounds from the dance disappear as I shut the side door behind me, like the sounds as they disappear around Quiet Rock. I gaze with wonder at the fall sky so bright with stars and right away see a falling star. I quickly make a wish as it falls away. I wish Mary would say yes to him. The more I think on her behavior, the more convinced I am Matthew has a chance with her. And now Shaw has his Lillian, and Jonathan has his Aventine, and I have...

"*Hullo* there, missh!"

Oh, no. I turn to make a start for the door, but he puts his arm around me as if to go for a walk. I look up at him with a mixture of disgust and horror, and I try to decide if I should turn and run.

"It is sush a night fer walkin'." He turns his face toward mine, and I am forced to breathe whiskey for a moment.

"Sir," I say shakily, "I want to go back in."

"What'sh yer hurry?"

"I have to find the boys."

"Can't shpare a lil' time for a fella down in his luck?"

He does not release his grasp and weaves with me away from the barn—away from safety.

"I warn you, I'll scream if you don't let me go."

He stops. "Oh, yeah?"

I gulp. Surely he can be reasoned with. "Look, now. You've just had a little too much to drink. All you need is a good nap, and I need to go home."

He takes a half-stumble but still holds me fast. "Well, thish is a shame, lady... I...jush want to tell somebody me troubles..." His eyes are actually filling with tears. If he would release his foul grip, I could run...

"I am going to scream now," I say calmly and look for his reaction.

He drops his arm immediately and steps back. We are fifty feet from the barn, and I feel fairly certain I could get away from him if he went for me now. I begin to step away from him toward the barn—slowly but deliberately.

"Well, by gash, I got rotten luck." He takes a step toward me. As I keep walking backward, he continues into the night air, "I got rid o' my claim, 'cause it looked like it weren't never gonna come..."

I stop a moment as he stoops forward and begins to hold his knees. I think at first he's going to be sick, but then he sounds like he's crying.

Suddenly he says, "SO'sh I take another, and it ain't got 'nuff in it to fetch a tooth..." He throws himself up and back and I think he's going to fall. "And I find out today..." He's crying freely now. "An' I find out today, my first claim's struck gold and gonna make a feller rich, and I been a fool." He falls to his knees in the wet grass and brings one arm across his brow.

I'm halfway to the barn when I hear him cry, "And then I see a pretty little thing like you, an' a pretty thing like you's jush got luck lining up to court ye, don't ye? *Course* you do. Why shoun't you..." And he begins to sob.

But I don't wish to pity the man. I am too busy pitying myself, and so a spark of anger flies up in me. "Do you call it luck to be courted by a drunk in the middle of the night? You do me no favors by your conversation. You've had enough whiskey and I've had enough of men's compliments. Good heavens! Goodnight!"

"Oh. Ow. Dishhappointment." He throws his head back and sets himself in a comical stance, and I pause to laugh at him, despite my mood.

"My disappointment or yours?" I ask sarcastically. "Or could you understand me at all right now, I wonder?"

He looks at me and struggles to get to his feet. I step backward toward the barn but remain.

"I'm not so bad in the mornin' lady," he whimpers. "You could do wors'in Ben Frrryyy..."

As he stands there, his tin-can hat silhouetted by the dark light of a velvet sky, a horrible sense of humiliation overwhelms me. I have continued to listen to this man because I am starved for any sort of male attention; I've been jilted by one, left unchosen by another, and there isn't a soul on the horizon who even comes close. At any other time in my life, I would have been back inside the barn two seconds after he released me, but I just stand here listening to his drunken caterwaul, knowing he won't even remember this in the morning... if I'm lucky.

I look up at the stars, ask the Lord to give me strength, and begin to cry.

"Aw," he says, "I've made jou cry. I din't mean it, wha'ever I shaid..."

He walks closer and I hold out my hand for him to stay where he is. "You haven't!" I say with a sob. "You didn't make me cry, and please stay there. I can't go in to the dance like this. Just give me a moment, please." And I stamp my foot in frustration.

At that he sits in the grass with a thump. I wipe my tears away and try to smooth my hair as he watches me. "Saw that jack-a-daw-dandy given you a twirl," he says. "He the one broke yer heart, lil' gal? A'll bust him fer it."

"No. No."

"Ye love him?"

"No! No."

"But he's a beaut, ain't he?"

I smile. Then I wipe my eyes upon my shawl. "Yes, sir, *he's a beaut*, as you say. But I prefer a... Well, I love a man who doesn't want me." There I've said it. Suddenly, I want to shout it.

"Oh. Le' me at him. Don't care if he *is* a preacher... I'll show him what a fool he ish." And he raises and circles his fists as he stumbles up and toward the barn.

I laugh harshly. "He's not in there. And I don't think you could beat him... drunk or sober. He's a deputy U.S. marshal."

"A marshal? Oh, thash terrible." He leans way forward. "Lady, I do feel shorry for you," he whispers.

I smile through my tears. "It doesn't matter now. He's in love with someone else."

"Naw."

I nod and wipe a tear away.

"She pretty az you?"

"Prettier," I say sadly, "but with a heart of... stone."

"How humiliatin'..."

"You have the picture." I cross my arms and look away. It felt good to say it out loud; it seems to have released the tightness of the bonds. "I'll be going in now," I say quietly.

"Wull..." He rubs his hands across his eyes, as if there were still tears there, and makes himself stand. "Lady, your sad shtory is makin' me feel better." And I have to smile.

We stand there for a moment, with him swaying in the breeze, and me wiping away more tears with Mary's good shawl.

"Wull then, I got shomethin' you need more'n I do." He draws the words out carefully, then digs in his pants pocket for a long, long time, and stumbles toward me. "There," he says finally. "You need... thish... fer luck." At first I shake my head. A miner's lucky gold piece means a lot to him. I wouldn't want to take advantage of his kindness, because I know he'll regret this in the morning. But he just keeps standing there acting as though he might fall over at any moment, and finally I am a little curious. Besides, I'll give it right back if it's valuable. I haven't seen gold in a long while, and so I hold out my palm, and therein he deposits his treasure.

I hold my hand up to the lamplight by the barn door; I am looking at the nickel I carved for Jonathan. I look back at the fellow who is now taking off his glasses, removing his hat, and pulling away a false beard, and all the while his eyes—lovely green eyes—are steadfastly looking into mine.

"Jonathan?" I say in wonder, but I am being kissed long and hard in the cool night air.

When we finally take a breath, he picks me up and twirls me in circles, and we laugh and laugh until we both plunk down side by side on the grass. I look again at the coin in my hand and cry with joy.

"What... what just happened?" I laugh. "Tell me what just happened?"

"Come sit on my lap," he says, "and I'll tell you. You'll ruin your dress if you don't."

"You're here... you're here."

"Yes, I'm here, gal. Now set down."

I feel myself blush as I slide my arms around his neck, pull my skirts onto his lap, and sit.

He draws the shawl up around me, looking at my arms and shoulders in such a way as to make me wish he'd kiss me again. He doesn't make me wait. He pulls my shoulders in closer, and he kisses me once more. "Shaw told me how you felt," he begins in a whisper, "and I... realized what a fool I'd been. I wish I'd kissed you before—didn't know what I was missing. I ran into Lillian when they got to Fort Smith, and I'd just spent six weeks with the criminal element, and for pure stupidity I took everything she said, you know, the wrong way. My land, girl, your lips are soft."

Kissing him feels like the most natural thing in the world, and I realize I'm not blushing anymore. "I'm glad. Go on."

"Anyway, pull away a little there, or I'll never finish. When I got to Denver, Aventine was waitin' for me... kind of in ambush, you might say. And I got pretty complimented by her attentions, but to heck with the story, kiss me again." And he pulls me in.

"Stop. Stop. I want to know more!"

"All right. I'm almost done, anyway." And he winks. "Anyway, she sort of wrapped me around her finger, and I guess I was ready to be wrapped, thinking all you wanted was the homestead and all. I looked at the nickel like you were taunting me to decide." He pauses. "In short, I'd gotten as bad as Shaw about things." He looks at me and holds my face and kisses each cheek.

"At Quiet Rock I often wished you'd just kiss me."

"Wish I'd known that." And we let the story wait for a while.

"Marilla," he says suddenly, "you must know I want to marry you."

"Is that by way of asking me, Mr. Jones?"

"That's by way of askin' you, Miss Hay."

I look into his eyes, as green and soft as new leaves, and then hug him. "Yes, yes, yes." And he laughs and falls backward with me into the thick grass. I roll away, with my head resting on his arm, and we study the stars in happy silence.

"Guess that answers the burning question."

I turn my head toward him. "The 'will I marry you,' question?"

"Naw, naw. You said yes before you knew whether you'd be a marshal's or a farmer's wife." And he grins pleasantly.

"Oh, my goodness, that's true. Not that I care, but which is it?"

"Uh, let's see then... I'll have to go on with the story to explain. When I first got back, I came out to see your place, because I sort of couldn't believe you'd done it—the cabin and all."

"I saw you."

"Foggy morning, wasn't it? Yeah. And I left without speaking to you or anybody. Your cabin looked snug and well-cared for, and I felt like a fool for worrying about you. Told myself you didn't need me—you needed the farm. So then and there I decided to sell my place, but when I come over to write the note,

I looked around again. I'd always wanted a place like that, and I knew right then I couldn't let it go. My competitive instincts, I guess."

"The farm grows on you, doesn't it?" I say with a tearful, happy smile.

"Yes, indeed. So I went back to Denver, and Aventine made herself useful by being in my office almost every day. She, uh, makes herself hard to ignore."

I nod generously.

"Time wore on, and I finally decided to visit the place again. Aventine insisted on coming with me."

"I could see she had you roped and tied into it."

"Not with so much rope, no, but she has a way of wheedling whatever she wants from folks—right now, I want another kiss."

And the story waits again.

"Well, the last day we were here, I stopped at Shaw's to let him know I wouldn't sell the place just yet, and he asks me about you. I tell him what Lillian says and he gets mighty angry, but he doesn't forget to mention you wrote me letters to tell me how you felt, and he asked why I never answered them. Well, I never got 'em, I says."

I pull myself up on one elbow and look at him. "You never got my letters? I sent them to your office, the second one by special messenger straight to your door."

"Nope..." And his eyes flash. "Aventine. She used to go through my mail... like it was hers."

"Oh, my."

"Ain't she a wonder?" He brings his arms up under his head and makes a clucking sound with his tongue as he laughs.

Just then the side door opens on the barn, and Mary comes out, the Reverend Post behind her. I turn to Jonathan. "Shhh," I quickly say and lower my head. They are twenty or so feet from us, but they haven't looked our way.

We can hear Matthew say, "And I've been wanting to speak to you privately, Mary. It's timely you needing a ride home right now."

I smile as they walk toward the wagons, and when they're out of earshot, I tell Jonathan about them.

When I'm done, he just laughs. "Well, he's why I had on this getup. I knew how I felt, but I wasn't sure just how you felt anymore, Marilla, 'cause your conversation with Shaw was, what, now, almost four months ago? I was afraid you might be forgetting me for someone else, like Reverend Post. I was on the edge of my seat watching you two dance tonight. I thought he looked like a man about to go over the edge."

I trace his nose with my finger and giggle. "He was, but it was another edge entirely. Oh, I'm glad I made you suffer a little after what you put me through."

"Well-l-l, you can just take it out on me forever, then." We kiss again and settle back to watch the stars once more.

A far way off, I think I hear a bird calling in the night. But the wind shifts, and I realize it's a woman yelling, screaming, far up the road.

We both bolt upright as I yell out, "THAT'S MARY!"

NINETEEN

Perhaps you have a mother, likewise a sister too,
Perhaps you have a sweetheart, to weep and
     mourn for you,
If this be your position, although you'd like to roam,
I'll tell you from experience, you'd better stay
     at home.

From the song *The Texas Rangers*

In a split second Jonathan is up, springing over the fence and pulling himself up on his Appaloosa. He turns the horse out from the fence, kicks fiercely at his flanks, and begins to fly up the road toward Mary's voice. I see him swing his carbine up as he rides away.

I begin to run frantically behind him. It's more than Mary's voice I hear. At least two men are up there, also yelling. I can hear her saying, "No-o-o-o," in a drawn-out wail. The pain of it almost stops me in my tracks, but I pray for strength and keep on running.

Jonathan is up there now. I hear shots and running horses, more than one horse. The scream of a man in pain. No more of Mary. I am lurching forward in the road as quickly as I can, wishing I weren't wearing this stupid dress and praying as hard as anything that everything's all right.

When I finally reach Post's wagon, Mary is sitting with Matthew's head cradled in her lap; his body is limp. *No, Lord. Not Matthew.* I move closer.

Mary looks up at me and says in a soft whine, "They've pistol-whipped him, Marilla." Matthew's face is as white as Mary's dress in the moonlight. I look at the right side of his face, and what I thought was a clump of his dark hair turns out to be an ugly black and bloody mass from his temple to his cheek.

"The doctor's at the dance, Mary," I say with surprising calm. "I'll get him." Then I turn and run like fury toward the barn, realizing as I fly that Jonathan is right now chasing the men who did this. "Lord, protect him. Please don't take him from me now." I pull up my thick skirts as best I can as I run.

I throw back the door of the barn with a slam and run in. The music halts and everyone stops dancing to look at me. "Dr. Gilpin," I say breathlessly. "IS DR. GILPIN STILL HERE?"

From the back, I hear a small voice. "Yes, I'm here. Who wants me?"

I sigh with thankfulness. "Reverend Post—pistol-whipped— up the road, come quick."

Dr. Gilpin grabs his bag—thank heaven he always has his bag—and we rush back out the door and up the road. The whole dance empties out behind us to come see.

I turn back to the crowd. "And Gentleman Jones is in pursuit up that road in case anyone wants to join him," I say loudly. Immediately at least two dozen men have sprinted to their horses and are heading up the road toward Independence. I'm so grateful to see them go.

When we get back to Mary and Matthew, I notice for the first time that Mary's dress and jacket are ripped at the shoulders. I don't wonder what was happening when Jonathan rode up.

"They took all the money for the church," Mary says and then she begins to rock him gently.

I come around and pull the shawl from my shoulders and put it around her bare ones. She rests her head against me while Dr. Gilpin bends to look at Matthew's wound.

Just then, a fellow above us says, "Hey, look. There's some-body lying up there in the road." I jump up, twirl around, and break into a cold sweat.

"Is it Jonathan Jones?" I force myself to ask.

"Naw. No, ma'am."

I feel light-headed with relief.

"And he's mighty dead, boys. Don't look, Miss Hay. It's to the head." I take his advice.

Three fellows lift the limp body, flop it into a farm cart thick with straw, and throw a tattered blanket over him.

In a few minutes someone pulls up with a low wagon, and four men slowly and carefully move Matthew to the empty flatbed. He groans as he's brought over and then passes out again. Dr. Gilpin carefully washes the wound by the light of five neighbors' oil lamps. There is very little talk as he works.

Little Charlie Norville runs up from over where the man had been shot and finds his father in the crowd. "Pa, Pa, can I keep it?!" He's got the gun the fellow threw out as he was shot.

His father beams. "I guess so," he says, "but ya better go ask Ma." And Charlie takes off running for the house.

In the northern distance, we clearly hear gunshots and that sparks chatter through the group. I pray for protection over the men and for Jonathan: *Please, Lord, not now that we've found each other again.*

The wound is cleaned and bandaged, and once more Mary pulls Matthew's head into her lap, ever so gently, and then carefully pulls his hair away from the bandage, almost one hair at a time. I watch her expression as she moves and I nod to myself.

The crowd has been talking in hushed circles for a time when the farm owner's wife steps toward us in the flatbed and clears her throat to say something.

Mary looks up. "Mrs. Norville?"

"Honey, we want you to know, you tell Reverend when he wakes up that if those boys got the money, there'll be plenty more where that come from." The crowd mumbles and shouts in agreement as she finishes.

"I'll tell him," Mary replies in a whisper, and she looks at me with a sad question in her eyes. I bow my head to pray again.

Dr. Gilpin tells us not to move Matthew until he can understand the damage, that he needs Matthew to wake up to decide. "Unless of course, he doesn't wake up." Dr. Gilpin is never one to mince words.

We sit there, just praying, and waiting and hoping, and time slips slowly past. Every once in a while we hear a faint gunshot, and the thrill it sends through me makes me think, *So this is what it's like to be wedded to a marshal. It will certainly make a prayer warrior of me… or a mad woman.*

Then I realize he never told me his decision, and I fall to thinking on his warm kisses and how he held me tonight, and a tear trickles down my cheek. It hits Matthew's thumb, and his whole hand gives a jerk. Immediately his eyes open and he tries to focus on the situation.

Mary and I both start to see it, and she quickly moves her head over his. "Matthew?" she says hoarsely. "Matthew?" I quickly hand a lamp to her, and she moves it over his pale face.

He looks up, obviously trying hard to concentrate. Then he squeezes his eyes shut, grimaces, and opens them again. Finally, he raises his hand to his bandage and gives Mary a weak smile. Dr. Gilpin comes close to scrutinize his features, but Matthew doesn't take his eyes from Mary.

"Well, I suppose he's well enough to move now," Dr. Gilpin says quietly.

The wagon trundles slowly toward the Norville's home. Mary whispers that she'd like me to stay awhile, if I would. I smile and pat her hand. Mary holds his head cradled on her lap with her left arm and keeps it from moving side to side as the wagon rumbles on. His face, by turns, holds either a grimace or a smile.

Soon we arrive at the house, and I look out and up the road and note I haven't heard gunshots in a while. They're either done or they've moved the battle on. I sigh and look back to Mary and Matthew.

Four men carry him gently into the house and lay him on the children's bed, while the three little Norvilles gather round the bed's foot to stare forlornly at him. I hope they wear their look of concern for the sake of Matthew's health, but I can't help thinking they're also concerned as to where they'll sleep tonight.

I come over to stand between Betty and Charles, the oldest children, and hug them. Charles smiles up at me. "Ma says I can keep the gun," he says proudly, and I don't know whether to smile or cry.

But Matthew is looking around again and calling for Mary. Mary bends near to him.

"Yes, Matthew?"

"Good." He tries to smile. He raises his hand up to her face and passes out again.

Mary looks startled, but Dr. Gilpin pats her hand. "It's all right, Mary. He's gonna fall in and out now and then, but he'll be all right in a few days. You'll see."

Eventually, it is just Mary and me in two chairs pulled up beside the bed sitting in vigil over Matthew. The clock on the mantel chimes three o'clock and Mary shakes her head.

"Marilla," she whispers.

"Hmm?"

"I have a little problem."

I look at her carefully by the yellow light of the oil lamp.

"I... I never had that... talk with Matthew about, y'know, my past."

"You'll have another chance," I say with certainty.

"But it's different now. I think... I think I care for him, Marilla. If he knew everything about me, I'm not sure..."

"Don't talk like Lillian, Mary, you know better. Matthew Post has heard or seen just about every sin in the book and he knows forgiveness. I don't guess you could surprise him any."

"I guess you're right, only, there are some things... Well, it ain't the Clark boys' money—I sent that back a while ago."

"I'm glad," I say with not a little relief.

"I was wondering if he could care for me... "

"I'm sure he could," I say, trying not to speak for Matthew more than I should.

"But if he could, what would happen to the hotel? Can a decent woman be married and run a hotel?"

"I'd say if the hotel were being used as the husband's church site, you might stand a chance of holding on to the property. But... it's not for me to say, Mary. I guess you ought to be prepared." I think back on Matthew's question to me while we twirled on the dance floor: something about a woman being willing to give up everything to be a pastor's wife. "I think you ought to be prepared," I repeat slowly.

After a brief hesitation, she blurts out, "But what if the money is doing good?"

"How do you mean?" I crook my head and lean closer to her.

"Do you remember a miner named Ferrin Kolb?"

"That sounds familiar."

"He came by the hotel looking for you months ago, saying you were gonna help him make it back home."

My eyes widen. "Yes, I remember now. I didn't know what I was going to do about him, what with starting the farm and all."

She winks. "I know. I knew you'd give him your money and that you couldn't spare any, whereas I was doing all right for myself."

"You helped him go home?"

"Yes."

"And you didn't tell me," I chide.

"You should have seen the look of relief on your face when I said he hadn't come by looking for you."

"Oh-h." I giggle. "You are a friend, indeed."

"I asked Ferrin to let me know, very privately, if there seemed to be anyone else in need of help."

"And then folks came out of the woodwork..."

"No, no, it's been working just fine, 'cause I don't hand out cash. I buy a ticket from the stagecoach driver or give them food, or send money to the train depot in Denver for a ticket. I know too much about people to just hand over money."

I smile. "I'd say you know just enough, Mary, not too much."

"But do you think that would make a difference to him?" she asks earnestly.

"I can just imagine it would."

She smiles faintly.

"Now, since we're bearing secrets, let me tell you how help came for you." Then I slowly explain Jonathan's return at the dance and how he jumped up to help.

Mary shakes her head in amazement. "Then it was Jones who shot the fellow who had hold of me. That fellow got on his horse right quick when he heard him coming, but Jones got him dead on as soon as he hit the saddle, and then Jones just kept flying up the road. I thought I'd seen a ghost."

"I believe he enjoys his work," I say with a little sadness.

"Well, I'm grateful he's good at it, anyway," Mary says matter-of-factly. "But, Marilla, there's something else you should know, 'cause... 'cause I've been made to think on it, and I want your opinion. I'd be real proud to name my hotel after my... dead husband, now... shouldn't I?" I nod, and she turns away to stare into the darkness of the windows.

She must sense Matthew's love for her—enough to want to tell him, enough to hope he'll understand. "Change the sign, Mary. Matthew will understand."

Her face fairly glows as she smiles and looks back to Matthew. "You're right. Somehow I know everything's going to turn out all right."

"Amen." Now, if I could only be as trusting, I might be able to settle my own stomach's butterflies for Jonathan's sake.

A few hours later, I stand at the kitchen window as the sunrise crawls over the ridge, hoping beyond hope to see Jonathan approaching any moment. In that first hour of light, while the rest of the household sleeps and the fields seem to float in mountain fog through the wavy glass windows, I pray for peace of mind, as I have prayed all night, and finally find myself able to accept whatever the day may bring.

The Norville family comes out for breakfast, and we begin to bustle around in the kitchen until the sweet smell of frying deer sausage and fresh eggs fills the house.

The scent works its magic on Matthew as well. To Mary's great delight, he comes out of his deep sleep, and so we give them privacy as Mary tends to him. She comes over for some water and quickly makes her way back to him. But when I bring a plate of food to them, Mary looks up with concern.

"He's not right in the head, Marilla. He asked if he's a pastor.

I said, 'Yes, you're a pastor,' and he shook his head."

I take a chair and look into Matthew's face. He gives me a half-grin and shakes his head. He looks frustrated, a little angry. His head falls back on the pillow then and he moans.

He grabs Mary's hand and she looks on him with concern as he tries again. "Could... you... marry a pastor?"

Now Mary just stares at him. She laughs once—a pathetic little gurgle—and right away begins to stare again.

I chuckle and nudge her. "Answer the man, would you? Unless, of course, you still think he's out of his mind."

With her brows still furrowed, she looks back at me and shakes her head as if to dismiss my words, but then she turns back to him. "Matthew, do you know what you're asking?"

"YES!" he says loud enough for the entire family to hear, and I begin to shake with mute laughter.

She looks at me and grows worried, and I know what she's worrying about. She turns back to him. "Then you don't know everything you should about me."

"Too... late, already love... you," he replies with effort, and Mary lets out half a laugh and then smothers her mouth with her hands.

She looks at me with hope in her eyes. "I shouldn't. I know I shouldn't, but I believe him." She looks back at Matthew, hesitates, and finally says quickly, "Well, then, let me think about it—yes."

He smiles broadly, though in another second he grits his teeth with pain, and Mary brings her hand to his forehead and strokes it. "Yes, yes, yes, so now try to quit smiling, for heaven's sake." And she gently pulls the strands of hair away from his bandage again.

I squeeze her shoulder as I stand up and walk back to the kitchen, while tears of joy ride down my cheeks.

TWENTY

Now all you young maidens, where'er you reside,
Beware of the cowboy that swings the rawhide,
He'll court you, and pet you, and leave you, and go,
In the spring up the trail on his bucking bronco.

From the song *The Bucking Bronco*

Later that morning, a wagon rattles up the drive, and as soon as I realize it's Tiger, I rush out the door to ask if he's heard anything. He says all he knows is the men chased the fellow through Independence down into the valley west of town, and he wants to know if I'd like to go back to the farm now.

Mary has come out behind me and she nods and says, "Go. Go! We're all right here." She releases me with a hug, and I jump up into the wagon, promising to bring her dress back soon. "Tell the truth, Marilla, I can't stand wearing it without that pretty comb I gave you, so just keep it."

Without thinking, my hand rises to touch the scalloped edge of my hair comb. "No, I couldn't, Mary."

"Oh, yes, you could. You think I want to be seen in that dress after the whole town's seen you in it twice over?"

"All right, Mary, guess I know you well enough to just say thank you. Thank you!"

"All right, then."

As we ride back toward the homestead, I try to concentrate on the matters at hand. "I wonder if anyone went to church," I say to Tiger.

"We can go by and find out," he replies and he picks up the pace toward Independence with a snap of the reins.

It looks as though church is meeting, but it's only everyone gathered to talk about last night and ask after Matthew. Many run up to our wagon when they see us, and I am quick to assure them Dr. Gilpin says Reverend Post will be fine, as to myself I think, *And I'll let him tell you about his new fiancée.*

As the congregation breaks up and they flow into the street, a man walks over from the jail. "Well, they got the money back," he yells out to anyone who cares to listen. Several folks walk up to find out the details, and soon he has a crowd around him. I want to ask after Jonathan, but I just stare down the road to the jail, half afraid to put the question to anyone.

"Marilla."

The sharpness of the sound causes me to jump as I turn my head. It's Lillian, looking paler than usual.

"Lillian? You all right?"

My tone seems to soften her features for a moment, but then she presses her thin lips together and tugs on my sleeve. "Please step over here with me."

I can't imagine what she needs to tell me, but I follow her to the side of a building.

"Now, I'm gonna say this only once. I don't usually waste my breath on apologies, but Mathias says... I must." My mouth drops open ever so slightly. "I am sorry for the trouble I caused you at Fort Smith. I did half believe myself when I told Jones what I thought, but Mathias was right," she gulps and looks away. "I was hoping it wouldn't go well for you. It was a time..." she lifts her head, "when I was jealous of anyone's happiness."

"I understand, but you were right, you know, about my wanting to marry Jonathan."

"Well, that ain't a sin." I can't believe it, but I think I see a slight smile.

"Any case, I've said my piece, 'cept for one thing. Mathias didn't ask me to tell you, but I don't want you to start any rumors, so I'm gonna..."

"Oh, I wouldn't."

"Just listen," she says sharply. I snap my mouth shut. "You heard me tell Matthias I was with child. I had to tell him the whole truth that night, and now I'm a'gonna tell you."

"But you needn't."

"O-o-o-h, yes, I do! Mary's already been pryin' the truth out of Jane little bit by little bit, so just stand by and you can tell Mary Baylor when you see her again. By the way, how's that Reverend?"

The last has taken me by complete surprise, and I stammer, "Oh, he-he's going to pull through, and he's asked..."

"Good." She shifts her shoulders and bows her head, "Now, hear me out. There was a man my father wanted me to marry. I didn't. The fellow got angry with me, and... he took what he thought was his. When I still refused to marry him, nor have nothin' to do with him, my father discovered what happened and threw me right out. That's when I joined up with the wagon train. When I started to get the morning sickness, I reckoned it was God's judgment on me for disobeying my father. Matthias took a liking to me, but I felt bound to tell him what happened. His manly pride was hurt. Then when I come here, I miscarried the child that first month. Jane cared for me. MacDonald took me in. By then, Shaw figured I'd told it all as a lie to keep us from marrying. Now, I've said it." One tear had begun to course down her cheek.

"Oh, Lillian," I say quietly.

She takes on her typical air and tosses back her head, "Don't cry for me, child. Don't you dare to cry for me. Today my life starts over again, and I'm in no mood for tears." I throw my arms around her and hug her with all my might and she stiffens like a washboard at my touch. But I won't let her go, and there comes a lump in my throat as I feel her soften and place her thin arms around my back. "I suppose this'll be all right," she whispers. And I laugh and hug her all the more.

She backs away. "There, now. Now I'll go."

"Please give my regards to Matthias."

With a fleeting smile, she turns and walks away.

As I stand watching her go, a fellow walks out the front door of the jail and turns his head to look up the street toward us.

It's Jonathan.

He turns his head back to the jail for a moment and then snaps his head back around, and I begin to smile. He's seen me.

Just then, Tiger comes up and asks if I would like to go home now, but I'm still smiling and staring at Jonathan as he approaches. I turn to Tiger. "No, thank you," I tell him. "Jonathan will bring me home later." Tiger looks over to see Jonathan, smiles, and thwacks his hat on his knee with pleasure as he walks away.

Like the day I came out of the land office with my new claim, I want to dance in the streets for joy that everything's all right, but all I can do is keep grinning like an old fool. Something about the way that man walks makes me... tingle, and so I smile all the more.

When he finally draws up to me, he looks down and pushes his shoulders back. "Miss Hay," he says, "may I have a word with you?"

"Yes, Mr. Jones, you may have as many words with me as you like."

"Shall we walk, then?"

I take his arm, and we walk together in silence through the town. I'm grateful for the stir over the money, because not a soul notices us as we walk by. We finally come around the stone, our Quiet Rock, and then the only sound we can hear is the approaching wind.

The mountain peaks are topped with gray clouds to the west, and an approaching storm has sent wind scouts ahead of the rainy troops. But a silvery sunshine still bathes the dusty road where we stand.

He turns to me and I slide into his hold, cupping my head into his shoulder with a gentle ease. He smooths my hair as we stand there and then he hugs me gently, and everything feels just about perfect in my world.

When he finally releases me, I look up at him and tell him boldly, "Well, I think I know a little of what it might take to be a marshal's wife now."

"Well, don't bother to get used to it," he says with a crooked smile.

"Ah-ha. I'm afraid that sounds mighty good to me, Jonathan Jones."

"Thought it might. The midnight hunt in the valley was tolerable, but… things are different now."

"How so?" I say with a smile.

"I don't know. Something about more to live for, maybe?" And he winks. "Besides, I'll have to warn you that around here, I don't think I'd ever be in complete retirement."

"That's the truth—the sad truth."

"Yea, well, I almost didn't make it last night."

The words send a lightning bolt through me and I look up at him.

"No, it wasn't that thief, it was town men…. Thought they were vigilantes."

"What!?"

"When I finally flushed that fella out of the woods, they were waiting for him down the hill and had him half strung up a tree before I got there. They'd apparently all had a bit to drink and were making some pretty poor decisions."

I shake my head in consternation.

"I had to hold Mr. Pruett at gunpoint to get him to release the rope," he says angrily, "and then stood there tryin' to convince 'em all this fellow would get what he deserved by the law. Must have stood there fifteen minutes, with the first five minutes spent with ten guns trained on ME." He slams his fist into stone at the last word, and I shake my head again, but he finally smiles. "Sometimes you can't tell the bad folks from the good… but most times *you just can't tell folks anything*."

"Did you have to arrest any of them?"

"No. They ought to be arrested, I s'pose. Ought to be, but I believe I'd be shot full of holes right now if I'd 'a tried."

I hug him. "On balance, though, I think you saved at least two lives last night, besides your own."

He nods gravely and stares at the rock awhile. "I had to kill the man who had a'hold of Mary. Couldn't have him getting up and hurting anybody while I went after the other." He pulls at his nose and sniffs, and then he stares off to the west, watching the storm clouds move our way.

I shiver at the accuracy of his words and how he can be so calm in their delivery. I want to know this man with all my heart, yet I don't believe I quite understand how he can do what he does. I remember the flight to his horse last night, the fierce and deliberate run toward danger, and I'm afraid I'll never understand. *There must be pleasure in saving someone's life, but does that help you forget that you have to kill? Does he take pleasure in the kill?* I'm afraid to ask. I suppose all I really know is I don't love him any less for it. *No, I don't love him any less.* I shake my head and slide my arms through his once more, and think how glad I am he's chosen another path. "So, I'm to be a farmer's wife?" I ask gently.

"Yea, that's what I want." He looks down at me and then kisses my forehead lightly.

"I told you in my letters all that matters is loving you. You really should ask Aventine for my letters. I don't think I like knowing they're in her hands."

"Yeah, I never finished my story, did I? How I sent her off?"

"No."

He releases me for a moment. "Let's see... Where'd we leave off? Uh, after Shaw told me how you felt—that was Friday afternoon—I was supposed to take Aventine back to Denver that day. I went back and apologized to her and said I'd like her to take the coach instead, 'cause I still had business."

I flinch. "But you did... you broke off your engagement, right?"

"Engagement?" he asks, bewildered.

"Aventine told us you two were to be married."

His eyes widen. "Well, if I'd gone on much longer, maybe that've been true, but I doubt that girl'd want to be a farmer's wife."

The image of that smug little porcelain doll digging ditches and burning shrubs in the heat of the summer suddenly makes me giggle. Jonathan watches me and the humor of it strikes him, too, and we chuckle over it together.

"Naw," he finally says. "She's out to get a marshal, like her daddy."

"So when did you decide about farming?"

"Well, you know all summer I couldn't bring myself to sell. Then after Friday at Shaw's, I was certain of what I had to do, so I headed back to the cabin with one of Shaw's men. I told Aventine I wanted her to take the coach and had Shaw's fellow drive her into town, then I sat down and pulled out this coin."

"Oh, I was afraid we lost it last night."

"No, first thing I did was slip it in my pocket as I ran." He laughs. "Anyway, see, I still had this idea that God wanted me to be a marshal, that I was gifted there and did some good. But I knew I wanted to retire, too.

"When I looked at the coin in the cabin after Aventine left, I was gonna pray over it and just flip the coin, like in biblical lots, like you meant for me to. So I took out my Bible to look up somethin' about doin' that, but when I opened it, right in front of me was the Scripture that told me what to do. Isaiah 2:4. Let me see if I can remember it, offhand." He looks up to the sky to concentrate. "'And... and he shall judge among the nations, and shall rebuke many people: and they shall beat their swords into plowshares, and their spears into pruninghooks: nation shall not lift up sword against nation, neither shall they learn war any more.'" He looks down at me and smiles. "I didn't need to flip the coin after that."

My eyes fill with tears as I catch his meaning. "And you just opened it right to there."

"That's right." He looks down and picks at the edge of his vest. "Now I know that Scripture wasn't written for Jonathan Jones, Deputy U.S. Marshal, but the fact that it came to me right then was like God telling me it was all right to go to farming, that it was time. I realized then maybe I could serve God in whatever I did, and then this kind of... I don't know, it was right." He looks at me. "Ever had that happen to you, Marilla?"

I nod and smile and feel a tear slide down one cheek. "As recent as last night."

At that, he grabs me up and twirls me around right there in the road. As he puts me down, he asks, "Lady, may I have this dance?"

I curtsy and hold out my hand, and we dance and kick dust in the road to Independence until it begins to rain on our duet, and it's the most charming dance I've ever had. *No offense, Reverend Post,* I think, smiling.

EPILOGUE

n a rare break from spring planting, when the snow has melted into memory from most of the mountains and the blanket flower has covered the lower fields with its yellow gold, Jonathan and I decide to have a picnic at our home, to which we have invited our closest friends. And so, on a Sunday afternoon in the beginning of May, Lillian and Matthias Shaw and Mary and Matthew Post arrive for a feast in our orchard.

It could be because of the quilt I'm working on so ardently these days, but as I walk out of our home laden with the last of the baskets and look up at the sky, the clouds look ever so much like little tufts of cotton on a bright blue quilt. *Sweet colors for a babe's quilt... blanket flowers,* I daydream and smile, but I keep such thoughts to myself.

As I set my basket down, I say aloud, "If an artist were to paint this sky, no one would believe it." Our guests heartily agree.

The leaves on the mountains are a tender yellow-green, and the trees above us are full of blossoms and young fruit. It is really the first fully warm, fully beautiful day of the year, and we have captured the sunshine all for ourselves; we lie like lazy felines on our quilts and blankets under the fruit trees.

Soon I am thinking back to the conversation Jonathan and I had not so long ago, how it takes courage to love people, but today there's no challenge in it at all. Tomorrow may be different, but today it comes easily, with the love fairly dripping from the trees, seeping up from the grass, and caught up in the bright conversation. I let it flow around and envelop me like the warmth of the sun on my face. All is as it should be.

When we are finally full from our repast, Mary raises her eyes to the mountain. "Do you two ever climb your mountain?"

I look up where the little cross stands. "Not since my parents..."

Mary shakes her head as if she's sorry she mentioned it.

"No, no, Mary, I like it up there. It has the most amazing view." I turn to Jonathan. "Have you gone up there?"

"Only the first month I was here. Wanted to see what the cross was for."

"Ah."

"Let's all go," he says with a quick grin.

With a few stray comments about leaving the day alone, most of us have rallied and decided it's the thing to do. The rest come along reluctantly. I anticipate the view and prepare myself for the climb as we walk across the river on the bridge Jonathan and Mathias recently built. I don't know how high the mountain is, exactly, but I know it takes at least two hours to get to the top.

As we climb, I think how much and how little has changed about my life, and I reflect on the blessings. I have to pause now and then, because the walk is making me dizzy. Halfway up, I have to stop to lean on Jonathan, and the others become a little concerned.

"It's all right. I just feel dizzy. It's been a long time since I've been up here."

"You haven't been well lately, have you?" Lillian asks.

Mary and Lillian suddenly give each other glances. "We all know how marriage can do strange things to a girl..." Mary chides.

Now the men give each other looks, and I feel myself blush. "All right. Perhaps it wasn't the best idea for me to climb up here."

Jonathan winks at the others and then looks down at his feet with a smile.

Matthew Post is the first one to say congratulations, but as I turn to Jonathan, I see he's not listening. He's still looking down, and his suddenly pale face sends a shock through me. "Jonathan, what is it?" I look down but I don't see anything.

"Sometimes I wish life could just be simple, you know?" Jonathan says slowly. "But I guess it just ain't meant to be."

With a tingle rising up my spine, I think, *But he danced around the cabin like a madman the night I told him about the baby! All those things he told me that night and since... He couldn't have changed his mind?* I look around at the others desperately and they look worried, too. I look back to Jonathan and clasp my hands before me.

But just then, he stoops down and picks up something, holding it out for us to see. It looks for all the world like a dull lump of...

By my soul, there's no mistake: it's a hunk of raw gold.